Cynthea Ash grew up and w
taught in comprehensive scho
before moving to France wit
managed a Bed and Breakfast during the holiday season
and compiled cookery books, in French, in the winter
months. Three were published and marketed in France. She
has long had a love affair with the Caribbean and has been
privileged enough to spend many winter months there. She
now resides in East Devon. 'A little Slice of Paradise' is her
first novel.

ISBN 978-1-913218-44-7

Printed and bound in England by Biddles Books Ltd, Kings Lynn.

A Little Slice of Paradise

Cynthea Ash

For all our Caribbean friends, and those whose dreams of a holiday home have turned into a nightmare.

Many thanks to my husband Mike without whose help and encouragement the book would not have been completed.

'You can fool some of the people some of the time - and that's enough to make a decent living.' W.C. Fields

'You can fool some of the people all of the time and those are the ones you want to concentrate on.' George Bush

1 Otherwise Things Just Stay the Same

Cassandra - Sainte Marie - 2009

A semi-circle of mottled turquoise backed by a pale beige ellipse of sand lay below them. Glittering, sparking water. A palette of continual changing patterns. The faint whooshing of the surf constantly unfolding onto a deserted beach. Palms growing at differing angles breaking up the ribbon of coastline. Perhaps a kilometre away, the opposite side of the bay rose up sharply. The slopes were painted a dozen shades of lush green tropical vegetation. Above the ridge, one could identify some of the steep hills which enclosed the adjacent cove. Her eyes took it all in. A very light breeze brushed her skin. The morning sun made Cassandra's bare, white arms glow. To her, it was all amazing.

It had been well worth the uncomfortable drive to the top of the rise to see it. They had certainly needed the 4X4 to reach the summit of the promontory. The car had lurched from side to side throwing its passengers into all angles, as the wheels sank into enormous pot holes and navigated many large stones and clumps of weeds.

It was all a world away from the busy town where she lived. Cassandra could tolerate seeing that vista as many times as you liked. But Mr Janes, the real estate agent, well, he was something else. She didn't think she could put up with too much of him. She'd met plenty of sales people in her time, but he took the biscuit. She could do without all his theatrics and posing. He was off again. He spread his arms towards the large curved bay below them.

'You can see that Fortune Bay is protected by a reef out there, making it inaccessible to boats, but also protecting swimmers from sharks, strong surf, and other dangers. Look at the beautiful natural pink sandy beach and the spectacular tropical vegetation behind it. All the beach front villas have incomparable views down the bay. You could have a luxurious property where you could both relax, mind, body and soul. The temperatures never go below 24 degrees, even in the winter. All that beauty at such a very reasonable price.'

Cassandra squeezed her husband's hand, turned her head towards him and discreetly raised her eyebrows. She was trying to pass on her opinion of Mr Janes. He was a real pain!

'You seem to have swallowed the promotional brochure,' commented Cassandra. She failed to say what she really thought.

He disregarded her comment and continued with his sales talk which he seemed to have learnt by rote.

'I think that this is my favourite bay on the island. There is a gentle breeze that blows from the sea most days, which stops the beach from becoming too hot, and also keeps the mosquitos down.' He paused, 'And that is where the beach restaurant will be built,' waving his arm in the general direction of further down the bay.

'Would you like to go and have a look? The site has been cleared and you can see the building work has been started.'

'That's what we are here for,' answered Mark, a man of few words.

Back to the 4X4. Once again they lurched along the bumpy, rocky track to join the road leading to the development site. Cassandra was enthralled by the views out to sea. As she rocked around in the back seat, Cassandra stared at the back of Janes' head and thought how she had taken an almost instant dislike to the man. He was far too much like her first husband, Grant. Both men were very self-opinionated. Her first husband had been a sales person of sorts too. Mr Janes really fancied himself as an ace salesman. Cassandra considered this was far from the truth. She had no time for people like that. On first meeting, Cassandra had been aware that Janes also thought he had got what it takes with the ladies. He was some sort of hunk. Just like Grant, he considered himself attractive to every female that moved. OK, he was slim and his face was put together in almost the right way. But in her opinion, he lacked an important quality. He had no class. He certainly did nothing for her.

'So, what part of Britain do you come from Mr. Janes?' Cassandra enquired, filling in a silence.

'Please call me Damien,' he smiled broadly. 'To the west of London, Fulham, in fact. I'm the biggest Fulham football supporter there is!'

'Figures,' thought Cassandra, who hated football and all the violence and hooliganism associated with it.

'Are you a football supporter Mark?' asked Mr Janes.

'No,' responded Mark, killing the conversation stone dead.

Janes stopped the car at a cleared piece of land. A steep tangle of tropical vegetation bordered it. Janes was immediately in selling mode. He trod a measure around the pegged-out areas. Like a dramatic actor on stage, he indicated where the swimming pools would be and the various types of villas. With more waving of his arms, he pointed out verbosely the situation of the health spa, the offices, the restaurant and so on. Then came a hard sell of the small beach-front villa he was proposing to them. Cassandra could no longer stand the prattling. She discretely left her husband with Janes studying the architect's plans.

She pushed her way through the undergrowth in the direction of the beach. Cassandra looked up and down the length of Fortune Bay. It was a natural beach with several logs lying along its length. Strands of ochre-coloured seaweed patterned the tide line. She walked into the centre of the sand. The surf rolled lazily onto the seashore.

Natural sounds rang from the curtain of rain forest bordering the mile long bay.

She loved it! What a paradise! What's more, she was the only person there. There wasn't another soul in sight. Dark sea birds circled above her. Cassandra was already captivated by the island's spectacular scenery. She was enchanted by its friendly, smiley people with their relaxed approach to life. They gave the impression that they felt that their cups were half full, rather than half empty. She found their attitude infectious. But, she also had sympathy with them. Life for many was tough. Wages were low. The cost of living was high. Despite all this, Cassandra wanted the island to be a part of her life. She hoped investing in a secondary home would help the island and help her. It would give a few some work and holiday rentals would supplement her miserable pension in the future.

She looked up and down the beach again. Bright sunlight reflected off the wet sand and glinted on the calm water of the bay. The odour of the sea and the seaweed filled her; the sounds of the shore enchanted her senses. How could there be a location more perfect for a holiday home? Reluctantly, Cassandra turned and headed back towards where the men were still talking, or rather Janes was still talking.

Later, back at their hotel, Cassandra and Mark sat outside their hotel room. They were very soon joined by local fauna. Mark lined up tiny morsels of bread on the small table. Within seconds, there were several small birds squabbling over the scraps. The fearless creatures fed from Mark's fingers. Tiny black finches scattered the crumbs carelessly. They bounced back and forth across the table, pecking as they moved. The crumbs soon vanished.

Feathers gone and recreation over, the pair got down to the business of the day. They both felt that Sainte Marie was the right island to invest in, and they should buy a slice of the action there. There were more tourists, more

4

international flights, and there was more construction work than on some of the other developing Caribbean islands. The island was on the up and up. They reflected on each of the properties that they had viewed. The ones that needed modernising. The ones near the facilities in Anse Argent. And finally, the off-plan one at Fortune Bay. Crunch time was looming.

Without warning, Mark prodded his wife's arm, 'Whilst I think about it, you could have made your dislike for Mr. Janes a little less obvious,' he slapped her playfully and laughed.

'I don't care. He's so self-opinionated! He's a pain in the arse! AND he reminds me too much of Grant. They came out of the same mould. Arrogant, conceited and dogmatic,' she said. 'I've been led to believe that sales people are supposed to make their customers feel important in order to clinch a deal. The only person Mr Janes tries to make feel important is Mr Janes. And he bombards you with far too many irrelevant facts. When buying something like this, one is guided very much by one's emotions. One gut-felt instinct is worth a dozen facts.'

'Possibly Cassie, but you made your dislike rather obvious! One positive thing Janes has got though,he has a good product to sell,' replied Mark.

'So, you liked the location! I just loved that beach!' enthused Cassandra.

'But listen, you have to hope that he can deliver the goods Cassie. You never know what might happen investing your money in a place so far from home. Some of these places don't have great reputations,' warned Mark. 'Another thing, with the furniture package, the purchase will be all your divorce money gone.'

'Yes, but are we agreed that we both prefer Fortune Bay? Yes, I understand that there'll be no divorce money left. But you know what people say, - "all the best things in

5

life happen because you say yes to something, otherwise, things just sort of stay the same,"' quoted Cassandra.

He accused her of being impetuous. She knew that she was. Mark, unlike her first husband, was fairly cautious. He had to reflect upon ideas for some time. He looked at them from every angle before coming to his calculated decision. One thing though, he was very supportive. And most importantly for Cassandra, didn't go running after every shapely pair of legs he fancied. She appreciated that perhaps simplicity and reliability were, for her, more desirable than excitement and glamour. She knew she could believe what he said. There were no hidden agendas with Mark. What you saw, was what you got.

Cassandra had told Mark that she really wanted some good to come out of the divorce settlement. It had brought so much pain and torment; streams of tears; blackness about her future. The purchase should be a positive thing; to aid themselves and others. To bring some happiness, pleasure and light into life.

Their decision almost thrashed out, their exchange eventually turned towards the following day. Since arriving on the island, there had been little time for sight-seeing. The visit had been more of a business trip than a holiday. As a sweetener, Mr Janes had suggested that he could take them to see Prosper, a small fishing port in the south. What's more he had said they would sail down in his own catamaran.

'Well, Prosper tomorrow! You know that I love it there! It'll be great to sail down there too. We'll be able to take photos of the coastline. Shame it's in the company of Janes! I could do without all his bullshit,' complained Cassandra whilst savouring her drink.

'Take note Cassie, that man's earning too much money from his villas if he can afford a catamaran,' stated Mark. 'Sailing boats don't come cheap!'

'Mmm, you're right. But we don't know, it could be one of these dilapidated heaps that we've seen in the marina,' laughed Cassandra.

'That I doubt.'

'If we find out tomorrow that it doesn't look seaworthy, I'll suddenly develop a severe migraine and we can make our excuses.'

'Can't see Janes as a sailor somehow,' Mark reflected.

'Why? Cos he doesn't have a beard or smoke a pipe.'

'No, 'cos he's too interested in himself and he doesn't seem as though he would be a good team player.'

'Anyway,' he raised his glass to his wife, 'Cheers my darling. Here's to the end of another day in paradise.'

2 Negotiating a Future

The Girls - Summer 2009

Angel and Laura Rose lay on Anse Argent beach under a large striped sunshade that they had brought with them.

It was Sunday afternoon and the beach was crowded. A lot of activity surrounded the girls. There were kids building channels and 'castles' in the damp sand with their legs splayed at different angles. Tourists lounged on hired deck chairs attempting to bronze up to display back home that they had been on holiday. Volley ball and football games were being played on the crowded beach and causing a nuisance to others. Local men and women carried trays of goods, pestering all, trying to scrape a living by selling their wares. Local conch shells, jewellery made from local volcanic stone, bottles of coconut water and soft drinks, were all for sale. Folks of all ages stood at the sea's edge chatting; a few jumping over the waves as they broke onto the shoreline.

The girls however were oblivious to all of it. They didn't care about the busy world that was revolving around them. They just wanted to flop, relax and do next to nothing. Their minds needed to slowly unwind; they needed to take time out for themselves and feel rejuvenated at the end of it. Life had been tough and intense for the last few months. They had both been very occupied with their respective final examinations. They wanted to empty their minds of Faucault's Analysis of Power Theory and Shapiro's Theory of Business Strategy. They fancied turning their thoughts to simple everyday tasks, like deciding what colour lipstick they should wear that day.

They had sent Merle to buy drinks for them all from the bar a little further along the beach. She seemed to have been gone a long time. Laura Rose sat up to see if she was on her way back.

'So, when you seeing this boyfriend again?' she asked.

'He's not really a boyfriend. He's certainly not a boy. I guess that he's quite a bit older than me,' muttered Angel who was feeling very lazy, lying on the warm, beige sand.

'So, how did you meet him?'

'Oh, he's a friend of a friend. I met him here on the beach a couple of weeks ago. I was introduced to him by a girl friend from the Business College. He has this spectacular car.'

'What do you mean by spectacular car?'

'A low, sporty, flashy Lambo. He told me that it's the only one on the island. It seems to be more important to him than anything else in his life.'

'So, why are you going out with him if he is more interested in his car than he is in you? Angel, you're the prettiest girl on the island. He must be some kinda jerk.'

'Laura Rose, don't be naïve, this dude has connections. He knows lots of influential people on the island. He has his own real estate business and sells high class villas. His parents own the distillery outside Prosper. He's not a boyfriend, he's a stepping stone.'

'Stepping stone! What do you mean bloody stepping stone? Do you like this guy or not?'

'Not a lot. He's not my type. Now my course is finished, he says he will give me a job at his real estate office helping to sell villas. It could be good. It could be one step nearer getting a job in Miami.'

'Oh Angel, you be careful. What have you got to do to get this job?'

'Look, God didn't give me my looks to waste them. I can use them a little to get what I want in life. It's not a serious relationship here; he's not taken me to meet his mommy and his daddy. We are just having a bit of fun.'

'But Angel, isn't that rather using him to get what you want from him?'

'And him, isn't he doing exactly the same godamn thing Laura Rose? Using me for his own pleasure and satisfaction. Ain't there two sides to this story? Hey look, I can see Merle. About time, I'm so thirsty I could drink every drop of the Caribbean Sea.'

'But Angel, I read somewhere about people are for loving and things are for using. And the world is in such a bloody mess, it's all turned upside down; and now things are loved and people are being used. Don't you think that's true?' Laura Rose took the can of cold drink from her sister and said, 'Oh, thanks Merle, you're a sweetie.'

'Merle, where has your sister been all this time?' asked Angel.

'At university,' Merle replied.

'I don't mean that sweetie. She's not living in the twenty first century. How many men has she been out with? I think you're the one that has got the problem Rosie. Merle, she thinks I'm using Wendell because I hope to get a job out of him. But, she can't see that perhaps he is using me as well. Neither of us wants a serious relationship, I am not in love with him.'

'But, if you not having a serious relationship, perhaps he shouldn't get serious relationship benefits,' Laura Rose voiced her opinion with a solemn look on her face. 'I won't give myself to someone I don't love.'

'Merle, what's wrong with your sister? She's been listening too much to your Mom and the preacher man. Listen Laura Rose; I just spent three years working myself silly to get qualifications to get a decent job. I'm just twenty-one. Why would I want to waste my three years at college by straight away tying myself down to some over-demanding man, who wants me to do all his smelly washing, feed his face every day, clean the house for him and satisfy his sexual needs whenever HE feels like it? And if I'm really unlucky, he'll leave me to go out to work, whilst he does as little as possible. It's not for me! I don't want a serious relationship at present.'

'But don't you want to get married Angel? 'Merle wanted to know.

'Perhaps, some day, but not to Wendell Thorner. It's just a fun relationship. He wants the same thing, I'm sure; to just have fun and not get serious. I need to find somebody that I really like and respect, but that could take time.'

'I've already started looking for Mr Right, but there are too many awful, selfish men out there! They are not really interested in me, they are more interested in what they can get from me for themselves,' sighed Laura Rose.

'My Mom calls them "Fun-Time Charlies",' replied Angel.

'Our mother isn't half as polite,' Merle giggled.

'Laura Rose, don't get bogged down with trying to find a husband. You know, too many girls are over anxious and let their hormones get the better of them. They confuse love with sex. Just look at the loads of teenage girls on island who've ended up with a baby they don't want, just because they thought they had found Mr Right. And how wrong they were! They get left with a baby to bring up all by themselves.'

'I ain't that bloody stupid Angel, or that desperate,' retorted Laura Rose.

'Honey, just focus on yourself and your own happiness. For the moment, concentrate on what YOU want out of life and don't go looking too hard for Mr Right. Your Prince Charming will come along one day. In the meantime, you can still have a good time with all the Mr Wrongs. You're the clever one; you should be able to work that one out for yourself.' Angel threw her arms around her friend's slim frame and hugged her. 'It's so good to see you again, my little school mistress. It seems like forever since I saw you last, and you Merle.'

'Have you got enough energy to go for a swim?' Merle asked as she got up.

'Shall we go and see what kind of fish we can catch in the sea today?' Angel sang out cheekily. 'What kind of fish are we going to find out there Merle, an elderly eel? Or perhaps an eight-handed octopus, and I've already met plenty of those. Or an old grouper, or do I mean groper? Do you think we got the right type of bait to catch anything?'

'You got the right bait Angel, but with my luck, I'll end up with some hump-backed whale!' shouted Merle as the three slim bikini-clad girls ran over the hot sand towards the sea. 'Look, there's one over there!' pointing in the direction of a rather rotund man standing at the waters' edge.

'Merle, shut up! Behave yourself!' threatened her sister.

'Yes, school mam.' Merle turned towards her sister and pulled a face, before throwing herself into the sea to cool off.

$$$

Wendell threw open the door and ushered Angel into the office. She was looking very pleased with herself. She had just succeeded in getting her first real job. She had just had a very informal interview in the reception area of the Tropical Island Villas building in Anse Argent. She was clad in her most business-like clothes. Her dark, fitted suit accentuated her tall, slim, but curvaceous form. Her long frizzy hair was braided at the sides, and held together at the back of her head with a ribbon, so it formed a halo of black hair around her face. She looked eye-catching in anyone's book.

'And this is where you will work Angel, in the main office. This is Adrian. He does the accounts for us and that's Laverna. Laverna does the secretarial work. Darius isn't here today, but I think that you have already met him. This will be your desk and PC. Mr Janes' office is that one, and mine is over there,' he pointed to the door at the far corner of the building. 'Angel will be joining us next week to help with the sale of the villas in Fortune Bay.' Wendell said to his two employees.

'Very nice to meet you,' Adrian greeted her warmly. 'I look forward to that.'

Laverna just smiled at Angel. She said nothing. Her mouth formed a smile, but her eyes did not sparkle with enthusiasm.

'Hi, great to meet you! I really look forward to working with you,' Angel replied confidently, looking around. 'I really like the reception area. It's very stylish isn't it? Mr Thorner has been showing me the plans for the different villas at Fortune Bay. They are very impressive. I'm sure they will be very popular, as the location is so prestigious.' She stopped, thinking that perhaps she was talking too much.

'That's what I like to hear,' Wendell replied encouragingly, 'A really motivated employee. You've got the right chat Angel.'

'I suppose I get it from my Mum. I've spent years listening to her convincing folks that they really want something that they don't need at all.'

Adrian and Wendell laughed; Laverna just looked blank. 'My mother works in Bourbon market,' explained Angel.

'Angel, let's introduce you to Mr Janes. Is he in his office Laverna?' enquired Wendell.

Laverna affirmed that he was. Wendell knocked on the door and opened it to show a white man of around forty, sat at a desk, speaking on the phone. From what Angel could see, he was slim with light coloured hair. He was wearing an in-vogue white and turquoise shirt which showed his tanned skin off to advantage. She noted his heavy gold watch.

'Give me two minutes,' he mouthed, putting his hand over the receiver.

'We can wait for him in my office.' Wendell led the way. 'I'll show you the plans from our last project. We still have some units there that need to be sold. I'm sure that Damien could get you to help him with that, as well as Fortune Bay.'

Wendell escorted Angel into his office, which one could see immediately was not as tidy as Mr Janes'. There were several sets of architects' plan attached to the wall, and he walked towards the plans of their Anse Argent project.

'Thank you for giving me a chance to work in your company Mr Thorner.' Angel was very aware that the office door was still open. 'I really look forward to starting next week. I have had a long-standing ambition to work in real estate, and at last I can start to mould my future.'

'I'm sure that you'll do well. You are eager, newly educated and bursting with good ideas. I like the rapport that you very quickly establish with people and I've noticed that they very soon have confidence in you. Let me show you the other site that we have developed. It's rather different from Fortune Bay.'

It was at this point that Damien Janes appeared in the open doorway. As Angel turned towards him, his face lit up.

'So, this is Angel. I've heard a great deal about you young lady. What a rare find Wendell; such a beautiful young lady.' Damien looked Angel up and down.

'She's got a good brain too. Angel has been telling me that she is very motivated in trying to help us sell more of our properties. She has got some good ideas that I think we could use.' Wendell smiled and put his arm around her shoulder.

Damien turned up his charm. 'Wow, a lethal combination. Dangerous - brains and beauty. Coming to work at the office will take on a total new meaning with such delectable distractions to entertain me. My day has just changed direction, from being a fairly lousy one to being one with lots of possibilities. You have some good ideas; I'm sure I'm going to love them. I've got plenty too.'

Angel was rather taken aback. 'What,' she thought. 'Is this a joke? Who behaves like that?' She stared at Mr Janes. After the fairly professional way Wendell had treated her in her interview, she hadn't expected such blatant comments from somebody she didn't know. Somebody she would be working with in the near future. 'No, he wasn't joking. Where did he get his attitude from?' He was exasperatingly over-confident. He exuded an air of entitlement. He made her feel uncomfortable. She wondered if he was like that because of his position in the company, or because of his obvious affluence, his male ego or perhaps because of his colour. Whatever, he immediately got her back up. She should have let it ride. But Angel, being Angel, retaliated.

'Am I invisible or what? Shall I disappear so that you can talk about me? Frankly, I don't consider myself to be a very good example of either brains or beauty. I'm not a doll to play with. I'm just myself. But I have enough about me to know that I don't think too highly of false, masculine flattery,' Angel stopped abruptly. She suddenly took on board that she had displayed too much of her irritation.

'Oh, but touchy too!' smarted Damien.

'I will be here to work Mr Janes. If we are to have a good working relationship, I propose that we start our conversation again, at zero,' Angel managed a smile, trying to rectify her over-reaction. She paused momentarily, held out her hand and said 'Good afternoon Mr Janes, it's a pleasure to meet you.'

Wendell smirked, looked at Damien and raised his eye brows and his shoulders simultaneously. 'Over to you bruv.'

'Right, OK,' Damien hesitated and then took Angel's outstretched hand. 'Good afternoon Angel. We'll see you again next week.' He returned to his office, openly displaying the fact that he had taken offence after being publically rebuked for what he had considered to be good humoured banter.

'We must get together on Monday morning to review some of the marketing ideas that Angel and I have been discussing, and plan how we can move forward with some of them. Make a note in your diary Damien,' Wendell called after him.

'Right,' muttered Damien, as he shut his office door. Wendell closed his door too.

'I'm sorry Wendell. I didn't start out too well did I? I was just taken aback. Isn't Damien a married man?'

'Sure, but when did that stop any man trying it on as soon as he walks out of his own front door.'

'If he wants to be promiscuous, why is he married?'

'Well,' Wendell paused, then smiled at Angel, 'I suppose marriage is like lobster dinner. The first time that you eat lobster dinner, you think, "Wow, it's great! I would like to eat this every day." So, every evening, you go to the same eatery, and you eat lobster dinner. Yummy! Then after a bit you get a little tired of it and want to try something else on the menu.'

Angel listened attentively to Wendell's analogy. She smiled in all the appropriate places, but didn't make the comments that she would have liked to have made about the situation. This time, she curbed herself, and kept the job she had just acquired uppermost in her mind. She regretted her spontaneous behaviour with Damien.

'You ever been married Wendell?' asked Angel.

'No, not me. I'd tire very quickly of lobster dinners every night. I like to try out all the tasty things on all the menus all over town.'

16

Angel laughed loudly, and pushed her fist into his chest, 'You're so funny!' Trying to make amends for her hasty conduct on meeting Damien she continued, 'Going back to Damien, I know some of the girls on the island have the reputation of being easy with any male that moves, but I'm not one of them. It was just his inference that I would be here just to amuse the men, mainly him, that made me rather t'd off. I found it rather insulting. '

'Don't worry about Damien; serves him right. He'll get over it. Now Angel, you here to amuse the men, that sounds like a very good idea,' he joked, running his hand down her back.

'Don't you start! I'll be here to work; that's what I'll be getting paid for. Anything else, I'll want a bonus for,' Angel teased.

'A bonus - well that can certainly be arranged.'

'We'll have to negotiate that some other time. I've got lots to do and I'll leave you to get on with your work. Are we still going liming tomorrow night at the street party at Doublon d'Or?'

'Yes, I'll see you in 'Splash' around eight.'

'Thanks again Wendell.' She kissed him lightly on the cheek. 'I'll be here bright and early on Monday. See you tomorrow.' Angel felt so excited, she wanted to exit doing cartwheels, but instead opened the office door and walked confidently towards the exit.

'Goodbye Laverna, Adrian. See you on Monday.'

'See you Angel.' There was a broad smile on Laverna's face and her eyes danced with amusement. After the conversation she had overheard between Angel and Damien, she felt that she was going to get on very well with her. She had decided that she already really liked Angel.

$$$

Angel left her future place of work feeling elated. The world seemed to be treating her real fine. She had met

Wendell by chance and now she had managed to get her first job because of him, a job that could offer lots of potential for her. Jobs were not easy to find on the island.

She walked to the nearest bus stop and stood in line waiting for a minibus to take her to Bourbon. The sun beat down and several of the other women waiting were using umbrellas as parasols. There was a hum of chatter in the queue; the women generally gossiping about their day and their families and friends, and the few males talking about their work. Angel, like most of her fellow West Indians, was open, smiley and very gregarious. The islanders viewed introversion as rather strange and odd-ball. So, even before the local bus arrived, Angel had struck up a conversation with the woman who was next to her. Angel initially admired her gold coloured sandals. The woman thanked her and told her one had to have some consolations in life. Angel then began to tell her all about her interview and obtaining her first job, whilst she listened to her new found friend's problems about her son being bullied at school. They communicated in Creole, as did the majority of the population. The arrival of their bus was signalled by a shrill claxon.

They sat together next to the open window of the mini-bus and continued their 'bavade' (chatter) as the vehicle advanced purposefully, swinging in and out of the constant line of traffic, stopping at the command of a passenger banging on the vehicle roof, or when people waiting at the side of the road signalled to the driver. Those standing inside the bus had to hang onto the hand rails for dear life. On this bus, the driver was obviously a reggae fan. He had the music turned up really loudly and sang along to the music as he drove. He shouted at the passengers as they mounted, trying to get them on board as fast as possible.

'Let's go, ya guys. I got a schedule to keep.' Each passenger paid their two dollar fare. The driver picked up

18

as many passengers as he could cram into the minibus going to the capital. 'Step it up now! Come on guys, we can get four more o' ya on. I got mouths to feed at home.' When one of his favourite tunes was played, he shouted, 'I loves it and I loves dem ladies too.' Obviously, he enjoyed his work.

Angel clutched her small handbag tightly on her lap and smiled at the driver's comments. She was also listening to Miss Golden Sandals' problems about her son, a child Angel was never likely to see. She made sympathetic suggestions about what she thought she would do in the same situation. They passed local landmarks without really observing the details of them, as they had both done the journey so frequently. They drove past stalls selling fruit, yams, coconuts and callaloo. Past cattle and goats tethered in green areas near the road side; and the cricket ground being inspected by cockerels and hens. Past new concrete homes, painted in vibrant colours, which were gradually replacing the wooden Creole cottages alongside the main roads. Past the duty free buildings, used by the cruise liner passengers and tourists. It was soon Angel's turn to bang on the roof of the bus with her fist as it approached the commercial area of Bourbon. She squeezed Miss Golden Sandals' arm and told her she hoped to see her again soon and stood up to leave the minibus.

She rushed towards the large covered market building which stood alongside the coast road that crossed through the capital. She had been visiting the premises since she was a little girl. Inside the market building the flash of bright colours hit her eyes. The perfume of local spices assailed her nostrils. Angel knew the path to her mother's stall by heart. She also recognised all the other stall-holders, most of whom had worked alongside her mother for at least 20 years. She greeted them all cheerfully.

Her mother sat by her stall making a hat from a banana leaf. 'Well, my Angel?' she asked her daughter. 'Mwen doudou (My darling), tell me what happen.'

'I've done it Mom,' cried Angel, jiggling up and down and clapping her hands over her head. 'I've done it, I've done it. I've just got my first job. I start on Monday.' Angel grabbed her Mom and danced her around the market stall.

'Thanks to the Lord my Angel. Who my clever girl den?' Her mother gave her daughter a hug. 'Ya Pa', he be real pleased.'

'Mr Thorner introduced me to all the other staff and showed me all the plans for the villas. He's going to take me around the site next week. He said he thought I was really motivated and good at persuading people; I told him I got it from you.'

'Ya always been good at selling things Angel. Ya remembers when ya was a little kid, ya sold all my eggs to the neighbour.'

'Oh, you were real mad! The hens had laid a load of eggs. You came home and wanted to make a cake for Christmas, and I'd sold them all. I remember I bought you a present with the money.'

'De neighbour, he real happy. But not me, 'specially when dere no eggs left in de stores when I goes to buy some. Yeah, selling runs in the family.' Her mother paused, 'And how's about de other folks dere?'

'I didn't start out too well with Mr Janes. He's the one that sells the villas. He seemed to be rather arrogant. He gave the impression that he thought I would be there for him to use as he pleased. He thinks he's a Johnny Depp. In fact, I got a bit cross. He didn't come over as being the ideal boss. I had just smiled at him and he came on a bit strong.'

'Ya needs give 'im a chance. Perhaps ya learns a lot from 'im.'

'From what I saw of him, I think he would love to try teaching me all he knows, but it wouldn't be anything about selling villas.'

'Problem is, my Angel, good boss or bad boss, he always de boss. If he a bad boss, it teach ya what not to do for when ya becomes a boss yaself.'

'That's one way of looking at it Mom. Hey, I think that you have a customer. I'll go home and phone Laura Rose and tell her about my job.'

Angel hurried away from the covered market, still sailing on a cloud of euphoria. She struggled up the hill in her high heeled shoes towards her home. From there, she rang her friend's mobile number in the hope that she would have finished work for the day in the school classroom.

'Hi Laura Rose, it's Angel. Are those kids behaving for you?'

'Hello sweetie. Oh yeah. They may be little kids, but some of them are real characters. There are some real cuties, but a few that are a handful. They already think that the world is theirs to change.'

'Well, I suppose it is in a way, but not quite yet. I hope that you let them know who is in charge!'

'Damn right I do! Mostly, it's a lot of fun, but you have to work your butt off as well.'

'I'm pleased it's not me in that classroom, with all these kids. But listen Laura Rose, I phoned to say that I'm no longer one of the many unemployed on the island.'

She excitedly repeated her story about her interview, all about the Tropical Villas building and the people that she had met, including the altercation she had had with Damien Janes. She then went on to inform her about something that she hadn't yet told her mother; that she was going to assist the two directors of the company, Misters Thorner and Janes, at a Vacation Home Fair in Miami. She eagerly told Laura Rose how she would be there to attract the customers, talk to them about the villas and the island of Sainte Marie, serve drinks and nibbles, and make sure that the potential clients were all happy. She had suggested to Mr Thorner that she should dress in Creole costume and serve local rum punch. He had liked that idea.

Laura Rose, true to form, instantly voiced her predictable opinion about Angel going to Miami with two men. She thought it would be very unwise. She considered that Angel could end up with serious problems which she might not be able to handle. She wanted to know if Angel would have her own room in the hotel or if she would have to share one with one of the men or both men. Angel wasn't really sure of the answer. Nevertheless, she reassured her that she was bound to have her own room. She was going there in a work capacity and not as a friend of Wendell Thorner. Privately, Angel thought that Laura Rose was far too prudent and her view of the world was too old-fashioned for her liking. Laura Rose seemed to think that both men could be wanting to use her without having met either of them.

Angel knew that she wanted to live her life. Live it with a capital L. She loved her Mom, but she didn't want to be like her Mom. She didn't want the same things day in, day out, for nearly thirty years. Her Mom knew what to expect from her day every time she got up in the morning. In Angel's eyes, life was too short and there were too many opportunities out there for her life to be as predictable as that. She wanted to breathe 'fresh air', have fresh ideas, and make new discoveries as often as she could. If Angel was to make changes to her life, she felt she would have to take chances. She knew that she could not be blind to 'the real world' risks, but would not let caution dominate her decisions. She had already met far too many people like that. She wanted to concentrate on the big picture. She wasn't going to be frightened off by things that only just might happen.

'Laura Rose, Miami has been my dream for many years now. I'm not going to let the 'what ifs' spoil it. I don't even have to pay my own fare.'

'You're right. It's great that you've got a job Angel! What are you going to spend your first wage on? A new phone or clothes?'

'Neither. I'm going to have a new image, a new me!'

'But, I like the old Angel.'

'But Rosie, you'll like the new Angel even better.'

3 Travel Opens the Eyes

JR - Late 2005

Some years ago, near my coming of age, I decided I was going to have what I really wanted. I was going to make life give it to me. I was not going to wait for the 'right moment' to try to achieve my goal, or waste my time any longer. I came to realise that this world is full of possibilities, and only a fool is not prepared to grab at some of those opportunities to change his life for the better. I was going to have to do just that. I was going to change my existence from the mundane to an adventure. I would make my place in the bigger world, rather than be an insignificant speck on a small Caribbean island. I would make something of myself and use to the full the talents that had been bestowed on me. People had made me see that I had to be the author of my own life. I had to write my own story and I should shoot for the moon.

So, what happened that made me change direction? What made me so determined that I was going to get something that an outside observer would have deemed unachievable?

Well initially, we received an invitation.

Just to put you in the picture, my aunt had moved away from Bourbon a couple of years before. She had escaped to another island. She, like my mother, worked in a hotel, but she worked as a receptionist. When her marriage came to an end, she decided she had nothing to lose by taking her chances in Martinique. She moved there with her two children and got herself a job in a busy hotel on the island. Lucky for her, she met a Martiniquais. She sent letters and phoned my Mom telling her in immense detail about her new friend. So, the invitation wasn't a complete surprise. We were both invited to her wedding. Our acceptance turned my world upside down.

My Mom's a worrier, perhaps even a pessimist. She fussed and was flustered by the invite. Like me, she had never left the island before, let alone flown in a plane. Her sister was going to pay for our flight tickets. Mom didn't know what she should do first. She asked so many questions; questions that I was totally clueless about.

'What's ya thinks JR, Martinique, it be like 'ere?' she queried. 'I knows dey French, but ya thinks dey like us? Ya thinks dey 'ave the same eats?' I told her I knew as much as she did.

'JR ya reckon we'z gonna like Bella's new man? He speak French, ya know.' I told her he would, as he came from Martinique.

'Oh Lordy, I'z must buys dem a gift for de marriage! What'z ya thinks I gotta buy? It not easy a buy smart stuff in Prosper,' she reflected, '......and oh my Lord, where de money come from?' I told her that perhaps I could try to sell some shells on the beach at the weekend to earn a bit of money.

'Ya a pain in de arse! I be paying for ya till de day I dies. Ya, ya finish wit' de work I gotten ya.' My mother had found me a job in the vacations on a water taxi. She was not best pleased when I chucked it all in.

Several minutes later she asked, 'And JR what we all wear to de weddin'? I got my church hat, but it black.' I told her that she looked just fine in her church hat. 'But it black JR! Not black for a weddin'. And ya JR! What I gonna do wit' ya? Sweet Jesus just look at ya!' I told her I didn't know what she was talking about, I looked real cool.

And so the questions went on. 'Where ya thinks we stay in Martinique?' I suggested that perhaps with Aunt Bella as I headed out the door. I dashed out to escape the tirade of questions and to catch up with my buddies. I didn't really understand what her problem was.

My Mom had it tough, though I didn't take that on board at the time. At home, there was just the two of us. I'd never known my father. For as long as I could remember, she'd worked in a hotel at the far end of Prosper Bay. She always left the house by six-thirty in the morning. The hotel now runs a bus for the staff, but in the past, when I was young, she had had to walk all the way there, around three miles and then back again in the evening, whatever the weather. She had to walk down to the town, through the streets of small, brightly coloured wooden houses and then down a long private drive, full of pot holes and cracks.

She needed to start cleaning the rooms whilst the hotel guests were at breakfast. She cleaned up after disorderly tourists, tidied up their smelly socks, dirty underwear and disarranged clothes. She changed their sheets. She made their beds; cleaned their mucky toilets and wash basins. She mopped their messy floors. Oh man, I couldn't do it, but my Mom didn't seem to mind it. She used to tell me about some of the emergencies that they had at the hotel and why she didn't get home until gone dark some days. She used to tell stories about what the hotel guests said and what the guests did. But that was exactly what they were to me; they were stories. I didn't appreciate how hard she had to work to get her puny wage or how difficult her life was.

$$$

Our flights to Martinique were arranged so that we arrived three days before the wedding. A friend of my mother drove us from Prosper to the airport. My mother was very nervous and chatted excitedly throughout the journey. We would spend two days in the company of her sister, and we would buy our clothes for the wedding, and the gift for the married couple, in Martinique. My aunt assured us that most things cost less there than in Sainte Marie, where everything had a heavy import duty. Aunt Bella had been able to negotiate a very reasonable rate for our stay, so we were staying in the hotel where she worked. Unfortunately though, my Mom and I were staying in the same room. Rats!

The wait for the plane was a real drag and very much longer than the flight itself. We checked in our luggage and hung around at the airport for what seemed like forever. We waited in the small departure lounge, my mother jumping nervously at each of the airport announcements. Our flight was inevitably late and my mother started to worry that it wouldn't arrive.

'Where our plane JR?' she asked anxiously, 'I wants to get to de weddin'.' I tried to reassure her that the wedding was still three days away.

'Ya go ask dat man over dere,' she instructed, pointing to the official at the departure gate. He informed me that it was delayed in Trinidad.

'Delayed in Trinidad, but why? Ya thinks it broke JR?' she worried. I tried to cheer her up by saying that I was sure that it would arrive soon. My mother was anxious and fidgeted. She kept looking at her watch.

Unfortunately, the plane was two hours late, so I had to contend with my mother's nervous twittering all that time. Eventually, we were herded to the plane by a slim, long-legged stewardess; we mounted the steps and then pushed and shoved to get to our allocated seats.

My mother crossed herself as the plane started moving. Her previous excitable chatter turned to stony silence. I felt much like a crated chicken going to market when I strapped myself into the seat; it was such a confined space and we were tossed around by the movement of the aircraft. Obviously, I had been acquainted with what the inside of a plane looked like by seeing it on movies and the television, but it all seemed much smaller and more cramped than I had imagined. Got to say though, I was actually excited by our flight, but I had no intention of telling my mother that. I found it all a great adventure; all my senses were alive; I felt I was doing a Superman zoom towards adulthood with all the new experiences I had to master in a flash. And at the same time, I was protecting my poor, old mother from the adversities of the twenty first century. I was fascinated by all the technology around me; marvelling at the ability of the plane to be able to rise, with such ease, to heights that mankind had only been able to dream about for centuries. I was enthralled by the view of my home from the same perspective as the angels and birds. I was getting a real buzz from everything. I'm sure that my Mom didn't share my sentiments.

My Aunt Bella came to the airport to meet us with her husband-to-be. He introduced himself as Louis. He and my aunt seemed to communicate mainly in French, though it turned out that he could speak good English. When we arrived at his car parked near the airport, I realised immediately that this man was not like her last husband. He had never even owned a car, but Louis' car was new, large and very shiny. This car was also very unlike the one we had been driven in to the airport in Sainte Marie; an old heap of a car with fairly bald tyres. My mother was delighted that her journey 'up with the angels' was over, but also as pleased as pie to see her sister again. So, both of them sat in the back of the car and jabbered away, whilst I was given the front seat next to Louis.

'Alors, je crois que c'est la première fois que vous avez volé par avion,' Louis asked me.

I said that I was sorry, but I didn't really speak French.

So fortunately, we continued in English. From my passenger seat, I noticed straightaway that Martinique was not at all like my home. Everything looked totally different. The roads were wider and in much better condition, there was far much more traffic and the sides of the roads were packed with smart commercial buildings. There were billboards on every corner. There were far fewer trees and other vegetation along the side of the carriageway. Everything was tidy, clean and spruced up just like an expensive hotel would be on Sainte Marie. But this seemed to be all over the island. I couldn't concentrate on what Louis was saying because I was blown away by what I saw. I hadn't imagined an island, so close to my home, could be so different. There were signs and notices all in a language I didn't really understand. My school French hadn't prepared me for all this. Even our capital, Bourbon, was nothing like this! I expressed my surprise to Louis.

'Mais, bien sûr, parce que la Martinique est une partie de la France. (Of course, it is because Martinique is part of France),' explained Louis. 'Sainte Marie is an independent island. You will see during your visit, that the islands are not far from one another, but they are very different in many ways.'

He then asked me about my school in Prosper and which subjects I was good at. I told him that I liked Maths and History, but I wasn't certain I was that good at History. He enquired what I intended to do when I left at the end of the school year. I mumbled quietly that I wasn't very sure, that I might try to get a job on a water taxi in Prosper. Louis looked at me, said nothing and then turned his head again to view the road in front of him. I knew my reply hadn't gone down too well. To try and make conversation, I asked what he did. He told me that he was basically an accountant, but he did other things as well, for example, he dealt with commercial liquidation. I was lost. I didn't have any idea what that meant.

The conversation had become more and more of a problem. I had started to feel rather uncomfortable. A little embarrassed. I was pleased that Louis' house wasn't too far away. It was basically a wooden structure. Well, our creole cottage Sainte Marie was made of wood. But, that was where the similarities ended. It was considerably larger. It was far more modern. It was top of the top. There were large areas of glass. There was metal along the balcony. It even had a large garage for TWO cars. I had seen similar houses in the north of Sainte Marie, in an area where only rich people lived. I was learning fast why it was that my Aunt Bella was so pleased to be marrying Louis.

The inside of his house was just as surprising, and was similar to houses I had seen in the movies. There was contemporary, chunky furniture. The place was decked out with fancy mirrors and abstract pictures. And the kitchen, well that was something else! Slick, matching cupboards and fitted appliances. All was neat and tidy. It was nothing like our old stove with only two gas rings that worked and the marked wooden table where my Mom prepared our meals. There was a terrace outside with some wicked cool, new garden furniture. At home, we only had a plain small back yard, no garden furniture. Outside, we met Louis' son, Yannick, who looked as if he was much my age. I smiled at him and said 'Hi'. He looked at me, checking me over, and replied to me in French. His welcome was cold; and for me, it seemed that he was displaying a total lack of interest in my mother and me.

Louis offered us all a drink around the glass-topped garden table. The drinks arrived balanced on a gleaming metal tray; all in choice, matching glasses, decorated with bits of fruit. We all sat around the table, chatting on in a mixture of French and English about our flight, the island and the forthcoming wedding. Everybody, except for me, that is. Me, I sat in virtual silence, sipping my Coke through a straw, as quietly as I possibly could. After Louis' reaction to my comments in the car, Yannick's attitude towards me, and my inability to understand a word of their French, I was feeling like a complete air head. All of my previous great feelings about zooming towards manhood had all cut and run. The socialising in the garden was more my mother's thing. She gave the impression that she was having a ball. But me, I felt out of my depth.

Later, Louis drove my mother and me to the hotel where my aunt worked; and where we were staying during our visit. Though my mother had bust her back for years working in a hotel, this was the first time she had actually stayed in a hotel room herself. Louis was very civil and checked us into the accommodation and showed us to our room. It was a large room with a sitting area and a sofa bed for me and a huge bed around the corner for my Mom. Seeing the layout, I felt easier about being in the same room as her. We had our own space. The room was very stylish and up to date, just like Louis' home.

'Well, dis real living! And, I not got to make de bed in de mornin' or clean de bath,' laughed my mother.

'Ace,' I agreed, as I nosed inside the small ice box to see if there were any eats inside.

'You not to eat de snacks inside, I gotta pay for doze. Dey not free. You waits 'til we eats dinner. Louis pay for dat.'

So my stomach continued to rumble.

That evening, we all met up in the hotel restaurant. It was a real family happening. My cousins, my aunt, as well as some of Louis' family, were invited. The young people all sat together at one end of the table. My cousins had changed dramatically in the two years since I'd seen them last. They had changed from children who I used to hang-around with; to looking and behaving much more like worldly-wise adults. I realised immediately that they had become far more sophisticated than me. They chatted about going to university; about perhaps being educated in France. Amongst them, I felt way out of my league. I was like a fish out of water. It was not only because of the conversation, but because of the environment of the restaurant, the white table cloth, the shiny cutlery, together with the menu in French. What on earth were 'Rillettes, Emince de Volaille and a Pavé de Merlu?' Were they trying to finish me off? My cousins seemed quite comfortable with the language and even conversed with Louis' son in French. Thank Christ that one of my cousins came to my rescue and helped me out. I was grateful. The French food, well, it was OK. Everybody else seemed to think that 'on a très bien diné' and that it was worth talking about. But for me, the rillettes tasted much like an everyday pork dish my mother made at home and the Pavé turned to be a fairly boring, bland piece of white fish – with not a drop of hot sauce in sight.

$$$

This was a visit of eye-openers. And there were several more the next day. We went into Fort de France to buy the things we needed for the wedding. The last thing I really wanted was to be dragged around after two middle-aged dames, following them like a puppy dog. But I didn't really have too much of a choice. I knew I couldn't go to the wedding in shorts and a T-shirt.

We started by going to buy the blender for our wedding gift to the married couple. A blender was something that we didn't have at home. I didn't see my mother wanting one, but we were told that it would be very useful to make soups, blend seasonings, and make fruit drinks. We make all of that stuff at home, but still don't have one. The electrical shop was definitely the best stocked store that I had ever been into. It was glitzy and modern, much like everything else I'd seen so far on the island. I'd only seen anything like it on TV. There seemed to be dozens of blenders to choose from. They all looked much the same to me, but their price tags varied a lot. They chose one which seemed like a lot of Euros to me, even though it may have been cheaper than back home. Aunt Bella explained that in Martinique the prices were similar to those in mainland France. France subsidised the goods that were imported into the island. Unlike goods in Sainte Marie, all of which had a heavy import tax on them. That way, the government of Sainte Marie could make money to run the country.

After the blender, it was my turn. What an embarrassment! My mother and her sister had decided the previous evening that they would buy me a plain white shirt for the ceremony. I could choose a bow tie and then, wearing my school pants and shoes, I would look just fine. Unfortunately, the boutique was run by a very pretty and young Martiniquaise, who only seemed to speak French. She looked a real doll. Wrong!

'On cherche une chemise en blanche pour ce jeune homme,' stated my aunt in her best French.

'Oui, bien sûr, en quelle taille?' she asked looking me up and down without smiling.

'What size?' translated my aunt.

'Medium,' said my Mom before I had time to open my mouth.

'Mais, en taille Francaise?' she queried. She went to look for a tape measure then, without a by your leave, she started measuring my neck and around my chest. She pulled the measure tight around my chest. What was this chick doing to me? I could feel myself blushing. What humiliation in front of all to see! I didn't know where to look. I looked down and that was wrong too! I looked straight down to the doll's ample French sweet melons displayed in her low cut dress. I raised my eyes again.

'Je crois une taille trente huit,' she said looking me straight in the eye. No smile! She had been watching me.

'Trente huit en blanche......... nous avons deux models. Je propose que vous essayez les deux.' She pushed the two shirts towards me.

'She want ya to try dem,' explained Aunt Bella. I took the shirts and scurried for the changing room.

'Ya to come an' show uz,' stipulated my mother. 'An' we needs a bow tie,' she continued, talking to the assistant. 'Un noeud papillon,' translated my aunt.

Eventually, like a good boy and a dummy, I was forced to stand in the middle of the store in my beach shorts, plastic flip flops and a crisp white shirt, whilst three females tried various colours of shiny bow ties against my neck. They picked out a red bow tie and some red socks. They knew that they were the ones to choose, as the shop chick told them that 'En ce moment, le rouge est très à la mode.'

They all told me that I looked very smart, very smart apart from my hair. I remember touching my braided hair which hung around my shoulders. Part of my braids held up in a ponytail on the top of my head. I'd paid a guy a fist full of fivers to braid all that hair. It had seemed really cool in Prosper. In Fort de France, I wasn't so sure. It was a relief to bail out of the store, and not have the young shop girl glaring at me throughout the whole pantomime.

My mother was next. She opted for a creole-style madras check skirt with a white blouse to wear to the wedding. The outfit was completed by a tiny check hat with a fabric fanned-tail standing up at the back. Even though I say so myself, my mother looked half decent in the clothes. They were similar to the clothes that she worked in at the hotel in Prosper, but this creole costume was brighter and the blouse was more stylish and looked great against her chocolate brown skin. It made her look quite eye-catching for an old lady.

I remember distinctly that, during our tour of Fort de France, for the first time I had a feeling of being an observer of what was around me, and at the same time felt alien to it. However, I felt all fired up by what I saw and knew that I was thoroughly enjoying myself, despite following my mother and aunt around like a little lamb. I was discovering a different world, a different way of life, and a different language. As we wandered from store to store, it became noticeable that the inhabitants of Martinique were very unlike those I met at home. The people in the shops were far colder and less friendly. I suppose that you could say they were more business-like, but they didn't seem to want to chat, as they did in Sainte Marie. They knew by our conversation that we didn't live on the island and it seemed that they couldn't be bothered with us. The salespeople would leave you standing around in the shop, whilst they had a chat amongst themselves. My mother and aunt didn't take too much notice, as they were too busy doing the same thing – chatting. From my situation as a silent 'puppy dog', I clocked that the store workers seemed to give more importance to their own conversations than taking care of the clients who would be paying their wages.

After an uncomfortable and awkward morning, we headed for lunch of more French food. I was dead beat after a hard time shopping. I felt as hungry as a horse. We strolled towards the sea and found a lively sidewalk restaurant which was full of tourists and young people. This was more my scene. They even had the menu written in French and English. I chose what you and I would call a 'cheese toasty'. But it seemed that the French gave it far more class by calling it a 'Croque Monsieur'. Either way, it tasted pretty damned good and didn't stay on its plate very long. Whilst the two oldies continued to chat, I feasted my eyes on all that was around me. There was an enormous liner docked some way down the bay. On the other side was a large old building looking out to sea, which looked like an old fort. I liked the way many of the shops and cafes were painted in sharp colours. The multi-coloured city filled the flat land by the sea, and then mounted up the hills towards the tall peaks which were covered in clouds.

After our lunch, Aunt Bella showed us the ferry docks, which were crowded with people waiting to catch ferries to other parts of the island. In Prosper, the wharf was a simple planked walkway protruding into the sea. In Fort de France there were parking lots, ticket offices, several jetties, shelters, timetables, attendants and lots of noise. The place was heaving. Aunt Bella told me that I needed to know where it was, as the next day some of the young people in the family planned to take a visit across the bay to a beach for swimming, whilst the adults prepared for the wedding. I silently praised the Lord that my 'puppy dog' leash was being let loose, and that I even might get to party! I just hoped that Yannick wouldn't be there.

4 Taking chances to achieve a dream

Cassandra - 2009

The next day Cassandra did not have a migraine, despite her misgivings on the previous evening. Not only was the boat far more splendid than either of them had imagined, but it was skippered by a local man. Mr Janes only seemed to be in charge of the drinks cool box. The skipper was introduced as Darius. He seemed to know exactly what he was doing on the sailing boat. Another couple were on board. They were from Ireland and had encountered Mr Janes when he had been selling at a holiday home exhibition there. The day was a glorious one. Just a few fluffy clouds and a light breeze. Perfect for a sailing excursion.

After setting sail and heading for the south of the island, Mr Janes, or Damien as he insisted on being called, started to indicate features of the coastline. They passed tiny beaches, trapped between sheer cliffs that showed evidence of volcanic eruptions from millions of years before. The cliffs were topped with tropical vegetation and occasionally they could see signs of habitation at the top of the sheer rock faces.

The very large cool box in Janes' charge was soon raided for cold beers and punches. After downing a few beers, Damien started to boast about his catamaran. How it had been sailed over from Florida. How it had four berths, and a very streamline roof. How the lower mast and boom helped to reduced pitching. How the engine was perfectly insulated from the cabins. And loads of other stuff that Cassandra didn't understand at all. The 'Lagoon 450' was an impressive boat, but she didn't feel they needed to know all this 'sales talk'. It was just another of Damien Janes' long lists of irrelevant information, as well as a session of bragging.

Cassandra was really only interested in the amazing seascape and the beautifully warm, sunny day. Her exasperation got the better of her. She decided to leave Janes and the rest of them. She would sunbath on the taut netting between the hulls. There, in relative peace, she formed her own opinions about the virtues of the boat. The island was so different seen from the sea. Perhaps even more stunning. She felt an unexpected joy rise in her. The craggy coastline was astonishingly beautiful. The strong sunlight showed every aspect of the landscape in sharp detail. The waves broke against the huge boulders at the base of the cliffs. The surf tossed in a lacy pattern that was unique to that moment. Huge, black seabirds glided over the sparkling ocean searching for food. Occasionally, she spotted flying fish leaping over the surface of the calm waters. It was a true paradise. Cassandra knew that she wanted this island to play a part in her life.

Despite the poor start to the trip, the excursion was much more of a success than Cassandra had anticipated. The other couple were very good company. They also loved the island. As they approached the town of Prosper from the ocean, they could see it laid-out across a basin, with a back-drop of hills and mountains covered in tropical vegetation. A few of the houses clung to the slopes of the hills either side of the basin. The habitations were all low and multi-coloured. For Cassandra, it was quite spectacular. Darius brought down the sails and used the motor to navigate the catamaran into the bay. He tied it up at the long concrete wharf in the middle of the cove. A few local boys greeted them all and asked if they could guide them around the town. Darius declined their help. He firmly told them he knew all there was to know about the town. As he was well built and strode around forcefully, the young boys soon stopped their pestering. Unsociably, Janes stayed on the boat with the cool box. Darius took charge of the guided tour.

The first stop was Prosper's large stone church in the centre of the community. The interior was imposing with its white columns and arches, the sun streaming through the gothic style arch-shaped windows, highlighting the simple wooden pews. The town was much quieter than bustling Bourbon. It had a sleepy air about it; an ageless feeling. There were a few of the familiar sights that they had seen elsewhere on the island. School children dressed in their smart uniforms. Lots of stray dogs curled up in the shade. An assortment of ladies selling produce from trays on the pavement. Perilous and extraordinarily deep storm gutters. The Christmas tree of numerous junctions of electrical cables all radiating from the same pole. But, in Prosper, there was more of a feeling of going back in time. The majority of the houses were constructed from wood, with steep corrugated metal roofs. There were a few people carrying goods balanced on their heads, bananas or a box with fish in. They even saw goats tethered outside the town's police station. The shops exteriors were dilapidated and old-fashioned. They only displayed a few goods for sale in their windows.

Unlike Bourbon, Prosper had more people sitting around. They were in the church grounds and outside the shops. Darius told them that it wasn't easy to get jobs in this part of the island. They were doubtless unemployed. Walking up the hill, on close inspection, they discovered that some of the brightly coloured Creole style homes hadn't been painted for a long time. Some were in desperate need of repair. Some had tattered curtains hanging at the windows. Cockerels and hens pecking for morsels of food invaded the gutters and the pavements. There was far more evidence of poverty than in the capital. Cassandra's heart went out to the local people.

Darius tramped them up the hill to a bakery. The delicious odour of baking told them they were getting near. On entering the small-scale commence, they were greeted

39

by a very well-built, rounded lady. She welcomed them with a very broad and friendly smile. The long wooden counter, a metre inside the shop, was covered in bright blue oil-cloth. It was secured by drawing pins. Only a few rustic loaves and pastries were displayed on the oil cloth. The white shelves behind were stocked with a few bags of flour, a variety of bottles and a small selection of tins. Darius explained that the bakery not only sold conventional style bread, but also cassava bread made from the local root vegetable. This had been retained from the old Arawak culture. The proprietress showed them the unleavened mixture and how it was pressed down into a pan to be cooked. She told them about how the flour was prepared, as raw cassava was, in fact, poisonous. Cassava bread was traditionally eaten with meat or fish mixtures. As the cassava flour absorbed a lot of moisture, it filled up hungry stomachs quickly.

Walking back down the hill, each of the women clutched their supply of bread and pastries. Comments were made about how unlike it was from buying a sliced loaf in a plastic bag in Sainsbury's. Descending the hill Cassandra remarked that the style of housing changed. The homes were more contemporary, built in concrete. They were to find out the reason why a little later in the day.

At the bottom of the hill, Darius asked, 'Who likes rum? Who's for visiting the local distillery?' They were soon all in a local taxi, heading away from the sea.

A guide greeted them on arrival. She was not only an expert on the distillation of rum, but also turned out to be a bit of a historian as well. She was able to answer all the queries they had about the town of Prosper. They began to realise how important the town had been in the past. It had once been very affluent, hence its name, because of the sugar grown there. The guide talked of plantation owners, slaves, battles and riots. They learnt of a fire which had destroyed many homes in the centre of town, hence the new concrete replacements. She reminded them of the extensive emigration from there and other islands in the Caribbean to Europe in the 1950s and 60s. They started to see their visit to the town of Prosper in a different light. Cassandra delighted in learning something new. For her, the history lesson was preferable to sipping half a dozen different rums.

Another small group of boys was there to greet them back at the catamaran. They were hungry to earn a few dollars. Darius and Damien tried hard to get rid of them. But luckily for the boys, the tourists felt benevolent, having enjoyed their excursion. The boys left the wharf a few dollars richer. Back on board, Damien was very subdued. To Cassandra's relief, he was not his usual garrulous self. He left the conversation to everybody else. She suspected that it might be something to do with the cool box being far emptier than when they had left the catamaran. During the journey back to Bourbon, Cassandra was quite clear in her mind that, despite their feelings about Damien Janes, Fortune Bay on Sainte Marie was the place for her.

$$$

Three days before the end of their visit on Sainte Marie, Cassandra and Mark dropped in at Mr Janes' Real Estate office. Their decision had been made. They wanted to ask what the next stages were in buying a villa. They were ready to buy their little slice of paradise.

As Janes was unavailable, it was Angel who welcomed them to the office. Cassandra knew Mark well enough to immediately take on board that he found her very attractive. Her tall, curvaceous form clad in a clinging blue dress dominated the room. Her black wavy hair bounced on her slim shoulders as she moved about the reception area. Angel explained that she was new to Tropical Island Villas. She introduced them to the other employees; and directed them to one of the squashy leather sofas.

Efficiently, she contacted Mr Janes by phone, to inform him of their intentions to buy. Cool drinks appeared and she commenced her sales chat to try and sell them the proposed furniture package. Photos and catalogues appeared. Mark was a captive client and was soon persuaded.

'I'm sure the package will be fine,' Cassandra stated after several minutes. 'Just as long as it isn't as ostentatious and as inappropriate as the stuff you have got here.'

Angel stopped, a little taken aback; she then smiled broadly. 'I think maybe you are right,' she answered in a lowered tone, 'but don't tell Damien that, he thinks that it's all superb.'

Fabric, tile, light, and rug samples were soon put aside. They chatted about life on the island and its improving economy. Cassandra found her very well informed and interesting. As usual, Mark sat on the side lines of the dialogue and just threw in a few occasional comments, whilst watching every move Angel made.

Mr Janes appeared on the scene about an hour later. Cassandra was disappointed. She would have much sooner dealt with Angel. She found her salesmanship much easier. Mr Janes, (please call me Damien) gushed his apologies for being so late and showed them into his office. His eyes lit up when they told him of their decision to purchase at Fortune Bay. He pledged that they would never regret their decision. He promised he would make every effort to ensure that the villa would be ready in eighteen months' time. He assured them that, by then, the management company would be up and running. Mark retorted that they would certainly be back on island in eighteen months. They would expect to be able to spend a holiday in the villa. Other promises were made, all accompanied by Janes' smooth, smarmy smiles. 'Yes, they would definitely be using local labour. But of course, the furniture package would be in situ once the home was ready. Naturally, they would up-date them on all of the progress during the construction.' Cassandra and Mark would recall this conversation and Janes' list of promises vividly in the future.

After negotiating a final price for the villa and its furniture package, Janes spelt out, needless to say in considerable detail, the legal aspects that had to be done whilst they were still on island. He asked Angel to organize taking them to the Police Headquarters to obtain an Alien Land Holder's Licence. Angel also made an appointment at the solicitors to sign the Act of Sale. Unfortunately, the only appointment that could be made at the solicitors was at the end of the morning just before their departing flight.

Mr Janes packed them off with Angel in the direction of the Police Headquarters. The event turned out to be quite an experience. Cassandra and Mark found out that anywhere you went with Angel, she was noticed. The Police Headquarters was predictably male dominated. Angel caused a lot of heads to turn. However, she didn't bat an eyelid. She ushered the couple into the dingy atmosphere of the old fashioned headquarters. She clopped down the sombre corridors in her high-heeled shoes. She remained intent on getting the land holders' licence. She blanked out the stares and the nudges from the employees with their tongues lolling out.

Cassandra was highly amused. If she had judged Angel correctly, this was one very confident young lady. She would be going places and certainly wouldn't be interested in any lowly police sergeants. Why was it, she wondered, so many of the male species were so vain and conceited and convinced they would be found sexually attractive by someone like Angel? Someone who, any one in their right senses could see, was obviously way out of their league. Cassandra had initially been married to such a male for nearly twenty-five years and still didn't comprehend it. She rated Angel's approach. She liked her spirit of being detached from all the attention and finding it all rather tedious and pathetic. Disinterested she might have been, but inefficient she was not. Finger prints taken, forms completed and signatures in triplicate were all polished off in a record twenty minutes. Clutching their stamped licences they were soon back out in the blinding sunlight.

5 One day

The Girls - Sainte Marie - 2000

'Woo, woo, woo, it amazing how ya knock me off my feet,' sang Angel as she danced and skipped down the hill. 'Every time you comes around I gets weak, woo, woo, woo,' she sang and waved her arms in the air. Her lanky body swayed from side to side, as she sang the words of one of her then favourite songs.

'I practicing,' she grinned, 'I practicing for Friday. Vini sé-fi, dâsé' (Come on girls, dance), she shouted in Creole to her two friends.

Her braided hair bounced up and down on the shoulders of her white, school blouse. The pleats of her gym slip flounced up and down around her long, thin, brown legs.

The three dancing school girls gyrated along the pavement after leaving school. The passers-by took very little notice of them as they whirled down the hill, jumping over the very deep gutters when they crossed the roads. They bounced past the colourful shops where they looked at their dancing reflections in the large plate glass windows. Giggling and laughing at one another, they jived past the seated ladies selling coconuts, golden apples, or spices from large trays at the edge of the pavement. They headed towards the large metal framed building at the bottom of the hill which was the covered craft market in Bourbon. They entered and wove their way through the numerous stalls. Past the dozens of bottles of flavoured essences, the plastic sachets of local spices, and the brightly coloured jewellery, hats, and bags fighting for attention next to mangos, plantains and yams.

Merle paused to look at a T-shirt on a stall adjacent to one with ginger and jerk sauce.

'Hello Mrs Laurence. Nice T-shirt,' commented Merle.

At a large stall selling bags, bowls, hats, baskets and bins, all woven from dried grasses and banana leaves, they stopped.

'Bonjou, se-fi,' Angel's mother called to the girls, 'Kouman ou ye?' (Hello girls, how are you?)

Angel kissed her mother on the cheek. 'Hi Mom, been a good day? We wants to leave our bags wit' you? We wants to go and see the cruise ship.'

Angel's mother got up from the white plastic garden chair that she had been sitting on, took the school bags and stored them under the tables displaying her wares.

'Now, ya all behaves yaselves,' she warned.

The friends crossed the busy road outside the market building and started to walk in the direction of the huge cruise ship anchored in the harbour. The heat bounced off the pavements. The sun beat down, its light reflecting off the calm waters of the bay. There were just a few open fishing boats dotted across the water. The girls took no notice of them; they were more interested in the huge ship tied up next to the duty free shopping area. The girls talked about what they thought it might be like on board, and pointed towards the many rows of rectangular windows and the streamline front that their teacher had told them about. As they got closer, they passed a couple taking photos of themselves with the ship in the background.

Angel turned and pointed to the cruise ship. 'So mister, what it like? What it like inside?'

The couple surveyed the three West Indian school girls, each with their hair braided in a different manner, each in the same school uniform of a white blouse and a maroon gymslip and each grinning from ear to ear.

'It new, the cruise ship?' persisted Angel.

'Well,' replied the man, 'well, yes it was launched this year. This is its maiden voyage. It's very fancy inside. It's all glitzy, with lots of sparkling glass and lots of new ideas.'

46

'Dat nice,' commented Merle, 'very nice.'

He went on to explain about the features of the ship, relating how many cabins it had, how many passengers and how many crew. He told them about the bars and restaurants, shops, spas and the casino. He said that his cabin had an enormous curved bed in it and large windows that looked out over the sea. He said that he had swum in all of the swimming pools. He seemed pleased that he had been asked and was impressed by the fact that the three local schoolgirls seemed interested.

Angel stared at the anchored ship. 'One day, I going to have a holiday on a cruise ship.' She smiled and asked, 'Where you from?'

The woman returned the smile and told them that they were from the States. She asked them what their names were.

'I'z Angel, she'z Merle and that Laura Rose. She the quiet one,' added Angel. 'Our teacher tell us about the cruise ship. He say it be here until seven o'clock dis evening.'

'You enjoyed visiting Sainte Marie?' enquired Angel. The couple replied that they had. 'And what about Bourbon? You seen the market? It's the best bit of the town. My Mom say "it full of de life of Sainte Marie". My Mom, she work in the market. It just over there. It full of lovely things, all made in Sainte Marie. All de tourists go there to buy their presents to take home you know,' she paused, 'we can show you.'

The couple looked at each other in a dubious manner.

'You not have to buy anything, you just looks. Look, it only over there,' Merle pointed towards the metal framed building.

Laura Rose tried to reassure them. 'You safe wit' us. Lots of tourists goes to the market. We even get you a cheaper price, if you wants to buy something.'

47

A little reluctantly, the couple crossed the road with the local girls and they all entered the covered market building which was full of noise and local colour. The girls introduced them to the different stall holders, sharing a joke with a few of them. They told the tourists about the products and where they came from; the names of all the local exotic fruits and vegetables, and even how to cook some of them. They showed them the bold jewellery made from local stones. Merle held up inexpensive T-shirts with Sainte Marie printed on the front for them to see. They were even persuaded to buy some spices to use in their kitchen back home. And of course, as chance would have it, they ended up at the stall selling basketry. There, Angel introduced the tourists, who turned out to be called Linda and Dave, to her mother.

Merle and Angel started to pick up the different types of woven goods on the stall to show them to the Americans. Angel was clearly viewing them as potential customers, whilst Laura Rose looked at them in another light. Linda wore a very pretty floral dress with a halter neck. The material shone in the light; it wasn't like the fabric of the T-shirts that Merle liked in the market. The dress fitted Linda well; her open toed sandals toned with the colour of the dress. Pink varnished toe nails protruded from the open shoes. They were not at all like the plastic flip-flops that Angel's Mom wore to work every day. Laura Rose also noticed the thick wallet that Dave had taken out from his pocket when he went to pay for things. The couple obviously didn't live the same sort of life as her and her friends. They were nice, but from another world.

Much to Angel's delight, they decided to buy some basketry coasters and a bowl, woven from a banana leaf. Angel's mother told them that she hoped the children hadn't been a nuisance. The adults then entered into conversation about the three girls. Lucilla told them how hard they all worked at school. Dave said that he thought

Angel had already developed a lot of 'people skills' and that she should go a long way with her charming smile and her persuasive chatter.

'I knows she look tall, but she not 13 yet,' explained Lucilla, Angel's Mom. 'My Angel, she talk for Sainte Marie dat one.' They all laughed.

Laura Rose waited for the laughter to subside, 'One o' our teachers say that Angel the number one noise pollution on the island.'

Amidst their laughter, Angel protested, 'I knows I talkz too much, but I got too many ideas and questions in my head just bustin' to get out.'

The conversation turned to the school that the girls attended, and Linda displayed curiosity about the education on the island. Lucilla volunteered the girls' services as guides to show them their school. To Lucilla's surprise Linda said that they would like that.

Angel, Laura Rose and Merle ascended the hill with much more sobriety than they had descended it around an hour earlier. Dave and Linda found the climb up the hill far more of a struggle, not being used to the heat and the humidity. Angel's gregariousness stood her in good stead. She kept the conversation going throughout the walk.

She took the opportunity to show them everything that played a part of her life. She pointed out to the tourists the different establishments she knew. The school uniform shop; their doctor's clinic; the church where they went with their parents every Sunday; and the tiny boutiques in brightly painted wooden huts with sharply pointed corrugated roofs, where they bought clothes. The tourists got to see it all.

Linda, who was a bit of a talker too, was in her element. When Angel took pause for breath, Linda jumped in with her comments. She was quick to tell the girls that their tour of Bourbon was far more enlightening than the one organised by the cruise ship that morning. The tour had been in a bus with at least 20 other American tourists. They had had to stop where the guide wanted them to stop. They had to take photos where they were told, and they had to stop for a drink when and where the guide wanted them to. She congratulated them as guides; with them, they were actually getting to meet local people and finding out a little about life on the island.

When they reached the school at the top of the hill they went in through main entrance hall. The girls were very proud to show the Americans around their school. Not too many tourists showed an interest in local schoolgirls.

'Well, here we are then,' Angel opened the door for the visitors. Linda and Dave gazed around the dark and uninviting space. It was divided by a run of painted green wooden trellising which had just a few notices pinned to it. There were no pictures or photos adorning the walls, no flowers or children's art work.

'And that's the principal's office,' whispered Merle pointing to a door at far end of the space.

'I sure hope you aren't sent to that office too often!' Dave laughed.

Angel was indignant, 'Oh no. I've never seen the inside.'

The girls led the visitors through a door to a large rectangle of classrooms surrounding a recreation area. The yard was filled with pupils practicing volley ball. The school rooms were housed in rather dowdy concrete blocks. Each classroom was ventilated by open wooden louvred 'windows' at the top of the walls to try keep the rooms cool. The openings had meshing on the inside, but no glass, so the sounds would travel from classroom to classroom.

Linda looked around, 'Wow, it's much bigger than I expected. And it's nothing like the school where I teach.'

'But, there's over six hundred of us,' explained Angel. 'We stay here until we are fifteen and then we go to the

Community College. And this is our classroom.' She opened the door with a flourish and skipped inside. 'Well, Laura Rose and I, Merle is in the first year.

Inside the room was gloomy, stark and surprisingly cool. The rows of students' desks and chairs were made from very well-worn wood. But, there was little else. The room was painted a drab grey tone. As in the entrance hall, the walls were not enhanced with students' work or stimulating material. There was an island flag on the wall above a blackboard, with a map of the island to one side, and a map of the world on the other. The lack of scholastic equipment was very evident. There were no ceiling fans and of course, no air conditioning.

'It's nice and cool in here girls,' said Linda. 'Say, there aren't any computers in here. Has the school got computers?'

'Oh but of course, they are all in the library. We all get a turn to use them.' Angel stated proudly.

'Gee, girls this is so interesting for me, it is all so different from where I teach at home. Thanks so much for taking the time out to show us around.'

Laura Rose showed the tourists the piles of text books on a Formica table at the front of the room. The books were in neat piles, but were all very well-thumbed. She showed them all the drawings in the history book that they had studied that day.

'We had History today. We learnt about the Arawak Indians. And then we have Math and English,' explained Laura Rose. 'Angel, she good at English,' she boasted.

'But, Laura Rose, she good at EVERYTHING!' grinned Angel, making Laura Rose hang her head in embarrassment.

To conclude their tour the girls accompanied the tourists to the recreation and sports area. Very soon, Dave reminded everyone that the time was flying and they had to get back to their cruise ship before it sailed. The girls

51

volunteered to escort the newly enlightened and perhaps slightly less insecure travellers back to the harbour. As they all walked back down the hill, the girls quizzed Dave and Linda more about their voyage and the cruise ship. In return the Americans probed more about life and education on Sainte Marie.

They all reached the end of the bay where the liner was moored. They walked past the duty-free building together with many other passengers who were returning on board. They were dwarfed by the enormous, white cruise ship with its strange-shaped funnel.

As they parted, Dave congratulated the school girls on their tour of the capital and told them how much he and his wife had enjoyed it. He told them that they had learnt more from them about the island than on their organised coach tour earlier in the day. He cheerfully told them that it would probably turn out to be the highlight of their holiday and something they would remember for a long time.

Dave unbuttoned the pocket of his shorts and took out his thick wallet again. He gave each of them five dollars for their time. The girls were thrilled with his gift. Laura Rose thanked them for the money and said that they had learnt things about the cruise ship too. As a parting comment, Dave told them he thought that if they continued to work hard they should all do well in life. He hoped that one day they would meet the girls in Miami. He congratulated Angel on her persuasive abilities and being able to make people like him say "yes" when they would probably normally only say "maybe".

They were all smiles. As the couple started to walk towards the gated entrance exclusively for the passengers, Angel called after them, 'Dave, you never say what job you does in America.'

Dave looked surprised that she should ask. 'Oh, I'm in real estate.'

'Dat nice,' Merle called back, not a hundred per cent certain exactly what that really meant.

6 Pointe du Bout

JR - Late 2005

I had hoped that Yannick wouldn't be tagging along on the day trip to the beach. But he was of course there. Despite that, the visit the next day was all that and even more. We all had a pure awesome time; a fab day, one that I would re-play in my head for some time afterwards.

The six of us had to jam up together in Louis' car. My cousins were squeezed between Yannick's friend and me in the back. Louis's car was large, but not big enough for four folks to be comfortable on the back seat. My cousins wriggled and giggled during the journey to the ferry terminal in Fort de France. Even Yannick was chirpy, which wasn't surprising as he had my cousins' cute friend on his lap in the front seat. She was a real looker! He was holding her rather like some fragile parcel, as she clutched her bag, her bare knees bent double in front of the windshield.

'Allez Papa, fonce au ferry!' whooped Yannick.

'In English, in English, Yannick, so that we can all understand,' she thumped his arm.

'Oh, OK sorry. Hurry Papa, we have a ferry to catch.'

Louis replied in his thick French accent. 'You can come to see us again. He does not obey me like that.'

'What a naughty, naughty boy,' she said in a provocative tone, hitting Yannick playfully over the head this time. 'Thank you Louis, I would like to visit you again.'

'Quelle femme fatale!' laughed Louis. We all joined in and for the rest of the visit the friend was nick-named 'La Femme Fatale'.

At the ticket office, Louis generously bought the ferry tickets for all of us and gave Yannick a wad of Euro notes to buy us all drinks at lunchtime. My opinion of him started to soften. Perhaps he wasn't such a bad guy after all. I thanked him as he handed me my ticket.

'Je vous en prie, jeune homme. Amusez-vous bien.'

I pocketed the ticket. 'I hope that your preparations for the wedding work out OK.'

'I will see you all again this evening.'

'We will take the five o'clock ferry, Papa.'

'See you then.'

We were heading for a place called 'Pointe du Bout'. We all raced up to the upper deck of the ferry and installed ourselves at the front of the boat. We sailed straight out from the ferry docks, the wind in our faces, the sun beating down on our heads, and the salty smell of the sea all around us. I started to feel relaxed and enjoying myself for the first time since I had arrived on Martinique. I knew all about the sea and boats; I found it less difficult to cope with than the plushy food and drinks and adult socialising of the day before. On board, again I sat next to my elder cousin. She explained that they had visited the town of Pointe du Bout lots of times since they had been living on the island. She added that, if I wanted, she would show me around. As the gap of sea between the ferry and our destination started to narrow, she moved to the railings of the ferry and started pointing out the different places that we could already distinguish.

As I moved up alongside her, I asked her if she preferred life on Martinique to her life on Sainte Marie.

She smiled at the question. 'It isn't that I prefer it here; I miss my home and my friends, but this island has given us all a future. My father let us all down big time. You know that he did. My Mum decided she wanted to get away from him completely. It was very difficult for her you know. She had to leave everything, her family, her friends, her home and her job and start all over again.'

'It must have been a tough decision for her to make,' I sympathised.

'It was a good decision and I'm very proud of my Mum. She made up her mind about how she wanted to spend the rest of her life. She knew she wanted a completely different life, not just for herself, but for all of us. She stuck by it, despite all the problems that we had. Finding a new home, a new job and a new school for my sis' and me, it wasn't at all easy. And of course, we all had to learn French.'

'Your French is good now Coz. You put my school French to shame.'

'No, not good, but I get by. Mum meeting Louis has helped of course. He has helped us all with our French. He corrects our mistakes for us. He's an OK guy, you know, he gives us more of his attention than my father ever did. Can you believe that?'

'Yup, that's very sad.'

'He is talking about us going to France to be educated. Because as you know, my Mum will become a French citizen when they are married. It frightens me a bit, going to France alone, but I'm sure that I'll be able to cope OK after a bit. Other people manage, so why shouldn't I? ......Hey, look, we are at Pointe du Bout. The beach is just over there,' she said pointing to her right. She smiled at me. I returned it, whilst scrutinising her and trying to find any hint of the timid little kid that I had teased just a few years ago. She was now a confident and animated, but natural young woman. Moving to Martinique had done her a lot of favours.

They were tying up the ferry as we all descended to the lower deck and disembarked. I took to Pointe du Bout straight off, in fact I was rather wowed by it. As we walked through the marina, it was decided that we should all have a drink in one of the cafes before going for a swim. The town was nothing like anything I'd seen in Sainte Marie. The buildings were mainly of Creole style architecture, but all smartened up. All painted in attractive, pastel colours with white trimmings, but nothing like those back home. 'La femme fatale' was over the moon with the boutiques and the fashionable clothing displayed in the shop windows. Yannick explained that there were lots of Parisians who made Martinique their holiday destination, and therefore the boutiques had to cater for their fashion expectations. They were what the French would call 'boutiques chics'. For me, the whole place was 'chic' and not at all like the basic shopping area in Prosper, with its poorly stocked shelves and the shabby shop facades.

In the café, I experienced again the cold and rather unwelcoming attitude of the staff that I had encountered in Fort de France. I put it down to them seeing so many visitors, but then we had lots of tourists in Sainte Marie too; there most of the workers wore a continual smile. During our drinks, I took the opportunity to size up Yannick. He was the centre of the conversation; he was lively, amusing and confident and switched very easily from speaking French to English. I felt certain that some of it was that he was putting on a show for 'La Femme Fatale'. I knew one thing though; he wasn't at all like me. He was like his father; very sure of himself and giving the impression that he had everything under control. No, I admit that I wasn't at all like that.

Our afternoon on the beach passed all too quickly. The small beach was great, with white sand and lots of trees to give plenty of shade. The bay was also protected by a concrete wharf on one side and a row of rocks in front, making the water very calm. The wharf belonged to a hotel which was behind the line of palm trees. So, because of the hotel, the beach was fairly packed, but we managed to find a good spot for our towels. The shallow sea was unbelievably warm; it was rather like swimming in a warm bath. After leaving the warmth of the sea, it was good to laze on the sand and relax. I was pleased that I had another opportunity to talk to my cousin about her life in Martinique. She explained that leaving Sainte Marie had made her see life rather differently, that it had opened her eyes to the possibilities that there are around you, and that you only have to make the effort to reach out and grab them. She told me again that she hoped to go to university and become a teacher.

We sat on the warm white sand after our swim whilst the others still splashed and laughed together in the blue water. We stared at the boulders protecting the beach and the distant horizon beyond. My cousin wriggled her toes into the fine sand and watched the waves flop one after the other onto the beach. Despite all the noise around us, there was a silence between us that was comfortable and for me, it almost felt as if it was just the two of us, sat side by side on that beach, surveying the ocean.

As she had told me so much about her future, I started to tell her about my working on the water taxi and how, at the start, I had thought something might come from it. I got a kick out of the line of work and meeting the tourists from all over the world. We had high tailed it up the coast in a green, red and yellow open speed boat named 'Paradise on Earth'. We skimmed past the empty bays, volcanic mountains and a couple of fishing villages, which I'd only seen from the land before. I liked all that and the spray on my face and the exhilaration of speed. I described how I used to hand out the beer to the clients and make sure that they were all as happy as clams. In Bourbon, I'd help the skipper tie up the boat. Trouble was I would then have to stay there to look after the boat whilst he went off to his business in the port. My Mom was flying high because I was bringing in extra cash; but I didn't I stick with it. Though I basically liked the skipper, following his strict rules wasn't always easy. The worst thing though was to have to lie back in the boat alone. I hung around for hours doing nothing except watch the clouds and the world go by when I knew I could be elsewhere having fun. Much to my Mom's aggravation I packed it all in. I'd figured out after that perhaps I could always earn a few dollars by showing tourists around Prosper or by selling coconut water in plastic bottles on the beach or in the town. I confessed that I was beginning to realise that I need more to occupy my mind.

'But, what will YOU really do?' she asked suddenly, without looking at me. 'What will you do in this big, wide world? Mess around in a boat? Sell shells?'

I didn't reply for several seconds. My thoughts were churning. I looked out towards the horizon, and then said, 'I could tell that when I told Louis I might work on a water taxi, it didn't go down a bundle. You know what, coming to Martinique, meeting Louis, and hanging around with you and your friends – it's been a new experience, a discovery. I've been blown away! I'd like a life like that! Full of new experiences and meeting different kinds of people, discovering their ideas and their personalities. I'd like to be proud of what I do and do something a bit more meaningful than selling shells or coconut water. But Coz, I'm not sure how I'm going to achieve it.'

'You ain't going to get too many great experiences or too much discovery in Prosper, especially working on a water taxi, doing the same drudge every day for the rest of your life. Doing the good stuff in life can be very expensive. Seems like you need to get yourself a damn good nine to five!'

'Mm, I know you're probably right.'

'You just need to get your ideas figured out and get yourself motivated and inspired by something and then have enough courage to see it through. If I can do it, you can do it! I always thought you did good at school. Sounds like you need to give yourself a good kick up the arse and get yourself sorted.'

I told her she already sounded like a bossy old school mam, but I laughed at her frankness and grabbed a handful of sand and threw it in her direction.

'Hey, you mind my hair, you. I don't want it full of sand.'

'I think I have already made some serious decisions and I have definitely found a lot of inspiration these last few days,' I grinned, throwing another fistful of sand towards her.

'Kouyon! (idiot) Pesky boy!' she screeched. She grabbed her wet beach towel and tried to smother me with it. 'You ain't going to live long enough to change them decisions into a future, if you keep on throwing the beach at me.'

It was at this moment that 'La Femme Fatale' decided to join us after her swim. She joined in the scrap as she learnt about the sand fight.

'Another naughty, naughty boy,' she beat me playfully about the head.

I didn't stand a chance against those two high spirited females, with them both at me, beating me with their wet beach towels.

'OK, stop your fooling around,' I held my hands to protect my head and trying to defend myself from their doing over. It didn't really hurt; in fact, I loved every stroke. I could stand them doing that ANY day of the week!

'This ain't no fooling around boy. You're ruining my friend's hair. This is serious war!'

At this, I fell about on the beach laughing. La Femme Fatale pressed her sandy foot onto my stomach and took the stance of the Statue of Liberty.

'You just watch out boy! You got to learn that the chicks rule the world!'

That memorable visit to the beach; that visit to Martinique; the people who crossed my path during those few days; the experiences I was immersed in; were all to be things that made a lasting impression on me. They brought me to the point of looking at myself in a way that I had never done before. That visit brought me to a moment of decision that was to be the start of a very long journey for me and the start of a very long story.

7 Racing towards Uncertainty

Cassandra - 2009

Their last day on the island, Cassandra and Mark were surprised when Darius was waiting for them in the hotel reception. He was to be their taxi to the solicitor's office in Bourbon and then on to the airport to catch a plane home. Up until then, they had only associated him with the catamaran and the tour of Prosper.

Darius stacked all their luggage into the boot of his scarlet BMW saloon. He then dropped them just outside the solicitor's office, telling them that he would be waiting in the car park at the back of the building. The office was in a wooden, creole style property right in the centre of town. The old fashioned hyacinth blue and white exterior gave no clue to the fact that the inside of the building was contemporary, air conditioned and high tech.

The appointment at the solicitors took very much longer than anticipated. It was just their luck that the solicitor was running late and they had to wait for over half an hour to see him. Everything had to be signed three times and explained in detail, dotting the i's and crossing the t's. The solicitor was eager to chat about the improving tourism on the island. Three and a half hours before their plane was due to take off, Cassandra started to get a bit fidgety. She knew that it took around two hours to reach the airport because the roads were so bad. It was getting very late.

Scurrying out of the offices, they found Darius in the car park. Tinted BMW windows wide open and the radio thumping out one of the latest hits. They said that they were getting rather perturbed. They needed to get to the airport as fast as possible; otherwise they were going to miss their flight.

Having lowered the volume of the radio, Darius assured them that it wasn't a problem, the car was very reliable. Mark was then rather fazed when he then told them that they would need to go to the service station first to fill up. That was just outside the capital, and unfortunately there was a queue for fuel. Darius stepped out of the vehicle and started to chat to the petrol pump attendant, a rather attractive young lady. 'Chat up' would perhaps have been more precise.

Inside the car, Cassandra became very agitated. 'Come on, come on! We would appreciate it if you leave the organisation of your love life until another time.'

Even Mark was getting a little fidgety. 'Why on earth didn't he get the fuel whilst we were with the solicitor?'

One by one, the queue of cars diminished and Darius got his petrol. Throwing himself back into the car, Darius was transformed from a laid-back, relaxed man into a demon.

He swung the car out of the garage forecourt with a screeching of the tyres, 'Here we go.'

'Go, go, go!' Cassandra seethed under her breath.

From where Cassandra and Mark sat in the back seat they could see the speedometer dial on the dashboard suddenly spring to the right. Darius started over-taking all the vehicles that were in front of him whenever the road was clear. He was obviously concentrating entirely on his driving and seemed to have become almost unaware of his passengers. They swung from side to side. They heard the roar of the engine revving. There was a squeal of tyres as he swerved to overtake. Cassandra looked at Mark and raised her eyebrows and screwed up her face. Mark just shrugged his shoulders and said, 'You want to get the flight don't you?'

'Yes,' she murmured, 'but I'd like to get on the plane in one piece!'

The red car flashed past the land marks that Cassandra recognised, the gas works, the new general hospital that was under construction, the supermarket in the middle of nowhere, the water cattle paddling through marshland and the people selling fruit and coconut water at the side of the road. They soon came to the long, straight part of the road which had been named 'Banana Straight' by the locals. There was a banana plantation on either side of the road. The speed dial was tipping over 100 mph as Darius put his foot to the floor and his car streaked past all the banana trees with their bunches of fruit protected by their blue plastic bags. Cassandra's hands started to grip onto the leather of the car seats. She knew that this was the last stretch of straight road before you came to some very tight bends.

Mark put his hand over hers clutching the seat and smiled at her. She got the impression that Mark might even be enjoying the 'formula one' type ride. Darius changed down as he sped up a steep hill. Then the bends started, many of them hair pins. He swung the car into each bend. Tyres shrieked. Passengers were tossed sideward. There was rainforest on one side of the road and a sheer drop on the other. Tropical vegetation cascaded down the slope of twenty or thirty metres. The car brushed the overhanging plants on the inner part of the bend. Cassandra held her breath on the outside curve. She was praying that they wouldn't meet any heavy vehicles. Overtaking a car was frightening enough. Her hands were pouring with perspiration. It was obvious that Darius could have no idea if there was any oncoming traffic around the other side of the bend. He was putting all their lives in the lap of the gods. She gripped the car seat tighter.

Then, of course, they did! They did meet a heavy goods vehicle, full of construction workers sat in the back. It was progressing slowly around the bends. It was too much for Cassandra. She just closed her eyes and hoped! She heard the change in engine noise as Darius changed gears. She felt the car swerve again as her body was thrown sharply first to the left and then to the right. She then felt her body move forwards as they descended a hill.

Mark speaking to her made her open her eyes a couple of minutes later.

'Look, look, it's a boa constrictor.'

She was relieved to see that they were on a straighter strip of road. They tore past a man holding a fairly large snake wrapped around him. Cassandra knew that a few islanders captured them in the hope that the tourists would stop and want their photos taken with the reptile; for a small fee, of course. The islander stared after the BMW as it flew past him. He wasn't going to be earning anything from them that day.

As they shot through a hamlet of small creole cottages, Cassandra sneaked a look at her watch. It was now less than two hours before take-off time for their flight home. She looked at the car dash board and saw they were still racing along at around ninety miles an hour. She supposed the speed limit on the island was much the same as back home. However, there were certainly not many police around to enforce it and even in the capital she hadn't seen any speed cameras.

'Not far now,' said Darius.

'Thank goodness for that,' thought Cassandra, relieved that the ordeal of the journey was nearly over.

As they turned into the airport car park about ten minutes later, Mark leaned forward to question Darius.

'Where did you learn to drive like that?'

'In Sainte Marie, of course,' replied Darius. 'It was great, wasn't it?'

'At times, I felt as though we were in a James Bond film,' gulped Cassandra. 'I can't say that I enjoyed it, but I think Mark did. Anyway, we got here safe and sound. Thank you. You didn't seem like the same person that sailed us to Prosper.'

'I love cars. Driving can be so exciting; you have to use all your senses. The car becomes a part of me. Sailing, for me, is just my job.'

'I prefer you in the catamaran, you are less aggressive,' replied Cassandra as she helped to put their suitcases on the airport luggage trolley. 'And on the catamaran, if I see another boat coming towards us, I can jump overboard and swim to safety.'

They thanked Darius again and walked into the airport building, still talking about their memorable journey.

Cassandra still felt very tense. 'I thought we were not going to get to the airport alive.'

'Got the adrenalin going!' Mark said in reply.

'You know what Mark, you learn a lot about somebody when you let them drive you somewhere. You are a good driver. You are patient in traffic and let people in at junctions and don't get aggressive with people on the motorway. You are a good person. I wondered when I saw the red car, if Darius was going to be a boy racer. He was very reckless, taking far too many chances, and like a child, thinking nothing is ever going to happen to him, or us. He enjoyed himself, but didn't think that I might be scared out of my mind in the back seat. I'm sure that he must be like that in his life. He may find that his recklessness will end him up in trouble one day.'

'Are you saying, "Bad driver, bad man"?'

'Maybe I am,' said Cassandra. 'Perhaps we may find out if I'm right in time. Anyway, let's go check in these suitcases.'

8 Isadore and Lili

The Girls - Sainte Marie - 2002

Angel woke up. It was the heavy rain beating on the metal corrugated roof and bouncing against the windows that shattered her dreams. The noise thundered through the room. Water was gushing from the guttering. It was at the end of the small house, next to her room. Rain was washing down the outside timber walls. Plop, plop. Water was dripping from the open glass louvres onto the wooden floor of her bedroom. From under the bed clothes, she could faintly hear that the birds had started to sing. She knew it must be morning, but her mind and her body clung to sleep. She pulled the pink cotton bedcover further over her head. She refused to open her eyes for another few minutes.

It was the fourth day. Only the fourth day after they had started back at school following the long summer break. She was not yet in her routine of getting up early and getting ready for her day at school. She felt slightly concerned. She was going to get very wet on her short journey that day. She could hear her Mom through the wooden partition, moving around in the next room. She heard the radio and indistinct voices mixed with the resounding beat of the rain.

Her metal-framed bed creaked as she rolled herself over. Angel slowly opened her eyes. The room looked very dark, but she could make out the plastic chair with her underwear on and the small mirror which hung above it. She threw a slim arm over the coloured cover. The air felt humid. She sensed a wind blowing through the open louvres. It chilled her skin.

'Get up,' she said to herself. 'Get up. It only rain!' She thought about how the islanders told the tourists that the rain was only liquid sunshine. Today, it didn't sound much like sunshine to her.

She threw back the cover, sat up and dragged her feet to the edge of the bed. Angel pulled on her underwear and padded across the floor in her bare feet. By the window, her toes felt the dampness of the floor. She pushed shut the glass slats, walked around her bed and slowly opened the door of her tiny bedroom. Immediately, she could smell the familiar odour of fried food. It smelt of onions and peppers. Usually, her Mom served them with sausages for breakfast.

'No baskets an' no school today my Angel,' called her Mom. 'I needz ya to help me with de storm shutters. Dere'z a storm warning last night. Hurry up an' put on ya jeans. I can't put dem shutters up at de windows all byz myself.'

Her father had made some rectangles of timber to fit over the glazed areas of the house. They were held in place by planks of wood. They protected the house from things that were carried by the strong winds in a tropical storm or a hurricane.

Angel fumbled amongst the hangers hung on hooks next to the door to find her clothes. Reluctantly, she pulled on her jeans and a T-shirt. She unzipped the large, blue shopping bag under her bed and got out her sports shoes. Angel was dressed, but not really mentally prepared for working outside in the torrent of rain.

The storm shutters were stored at the side of the house. Lucilla and Angel lifted each heavy piece of wood. They fought against the increasingly strong wind and rain as its force tried to snatch the mass of wood from their grasp. They lifted each shutter up in front of the glass louvres and dropped it into the brackets below the window. Whilst her Mom held the shutter in place, Angel went to find the plank which was placed horizontally across the shutter to hold it in place. They also were forced into brackets.

When all the shutters had been installed, Lucilla shouted, 'Se-pul (Chickens),' above the noise of the wind tearing at the broad leaves of the trees on their land.

Angel's father had built a chicken coop between theirs and their neighbour's house several years ago. It was much like a dog kennel with a door on it. It was placed on a concrete base to stop the rats entering through the base to eat the eggs. One hen was sensibly already installed in the shelter. However, there were still two that were pecking for insects on the ground around it. After scrambling around after one of the brown, sodden birds for a couple of minutes, Lucilla enveloped it in her arms. She bundled it into the coop. Angel didn't have as much luck. The last chicken was chased around the plot of land. It scuttled away every time Angel got near her. Just when she thought that she had succeeded, Angel, with the hen in her grasp, tripped over a stone. She fell flat on her face. The creature pecked her hand and succeeded in fluttering away.

'Stooopid bird,' screamed Angel, 'I don't care if the wind blow her all the way to South America. Ain't she got no brains in her little head?'

Her Mom laughed and helped her up. They looked at one another and laughed again. They were both drenched with the torrential rain; their clothes clung to their bodies; the water poured down their faces; their black hair glistened with rain droplets; Angel's face and front were covered with mud.

Lucilla was determined. 'Vini mwe fi, one more try. We go get dat chicken.'

This time, with the two of them, they managed to catch the elusive chicken and flung it into the coop with the others. Lucilla slammed the door shut and turned the fastening, yelling at the hens that they would have to look after themselves for the rest of the day. As they rushed up to the covered veranda, the rain squall stopped. On entering the main room of the house and smelling the food fried earlier, they realised that all the activity had made them feel extraordinarily hungry.

With all the windows shuttered, the entire house was very dark. Fortunately, they still had electricity. Puddles appeared on the worn wooden floor as they both peeled off their saturated garments. They both towelled themselves dry before going to get a change of clothing. Her Mom was reheating the vegetables over a gas ring when Angel re-entered the living room. Lucilla tossed the sausages into the pan and the smell immediately made Angel's mouth water.

Her Mom broke into laughter. 'Ya look so angry with dat chicken,' Angel started to see the funny side of their escapade in the driving rain.

'She so stupid, she should go in the pot. Chicken today, feathers tomorrow!'

'She not so stupid,' laughed Lucilla, 'Ya not catch her.'

With the shuttered windows and the heat from the gas ring, the small living room felt uncomfortably hot. Nevertheless, the fried breakfast tasted like nectar and promptly disappeared from their mismatching plates. Angel felt the moment was right to ask her Mom something that had concerned her for several days.

'Mom, what you do if Pa lost his job and turn to drink and joints 'cos of it?'

Lucilla didn't reply immediately and thought carefully what she should say to her daughter.

'I don't think he go do that Angel. Your Pa, he like his work. If he lose his job, he go try real hard to get another one. Dat why he working in Grenada now. But, if it happen, I tries to help as much as I can. I tries to make 'im see sense.'

'What if he drunk and high all the time though and not fit for work?'

Lucilla knew why Angel was asking these questions, but didn't let on. She had seen the father of Angel's friends

Laura Rose and Merle on the streets or under a tree. He was away in his own drunken world, clutching a rum bottle and puffing on marijuana. She felt sorry for the girls and their mother. They all had to survive on her wage. This sort of situation wasn't uncommon on the island.

'It difficult to say my Angel 'till it happen to ya,' Lucilla paused, 'but, I tries not to get angry. I tries to talk with 'im, talk around 'is problems. And I guess, I tries to get money for 'im to see a doctor.' Lucilla glanced up at the wall clock and cried, 'Angel gets yourself sorted! We needs to get to dat church hall. Dere a storm coming.'

The official Storm Warning during the night had told of a tropical storm that may turn into a hurricane and hit the island. All of the inhabitants who lived in a wooden home, like theirs, or on low lying land, were advised by the authorities to lock up and evacuate their homes. They had to sit out tropical storms and hurricanes in solid concrete structures such as churches, or church and school halls. This was the first warning of the season, though there had been other storms and hurricanes elsewhere in that part of the tropics. They all knew not to take any chances as sometimes the storms were strong enough to lift off the roofs, spewing the house contents around the surrounding area.

Their pots and pans were stacked away. Lucilla and Angel unplugged the television and stored it in a built-in cupboard. They dragged out and checked the large shopping bag for their emergency supplies. Bottled water, tinned food, changes of clothing, a large torch with extra batteries, a portable radio, and a first aid kit were all inside. They both pulled on long, see-through plastic rain coats, even though the rain had momentarily stopped. The house locked up, they struggled down the hill with the large shopping bag, the wind fighting against them. Mother and daughter were silent, but Angel's thoughts drifted to Laura Rose and Merle. She wondered what they would be doing.

Living in an apartment block prevented them from having chickens. They would doubtless be staying in their home, as it was far more robust and more modern than hers.

Angel noticed that, as was usual, some people were moving their cars into the protection of concrete buildings and away from poles and tall trees. Shop keepers were pulling their metal blinds down in front of their shop windows or securing large sheets of wood over them just as Lucilla and Angel had done.

When they arrived at their destination the church hall was already crowded. The official 'Completion of Evacuation' order, issued 24 hours before landfall, had already been broadcast some time before. Everybody knew everyone else. Lucilla and Angel were greeted by one and all. Nobody looked melancholy. They knew they were safer in the hall than in their homes. This type of gathering could happen several times during the hurricane season. Waiting the storm out could be a long one. You got to know people quite well if you had to be shut in the same building with them hour after hour. Here there was a sense of community amongst the inhabitants of Bourbon. Together they felt stronger facing the potentially disastrous situation. They may all be from different back-grounds, have different problems at home, but there they all had the same problem; one that none of them could do anything about.

As Angel tossed aside her raincoat, one of the women remarked on her developing womanly figure.

'She soon have a line of boys knocking on de door, will dat one,' she chuckled.

Angel appeared to have been insulted. 'Not me,' she retorted. 'I not be opening the door to no males. I not going to be at their beck and call! There more interesting things in life than males that always wants to tell you what to do!'

The woman laughed. 'We see.'

'We will,' Angel replied sharply, getting out her school books.

'She got very strong ideas about life, has my Angel,' emphasised her Mom.

Angel took her school things with her and went to sit where the rest of the young people had congregated, leaving her mother to talk to her friends.

Later that day, the crowd congregated in the church hall heard on their radios that the storm had turned west and was heading up towards Jamaica and Cuba. This time the island had been spared from the devastation which hurricanes and storms can bring. They could all pack up their emergency bags and trudge back home. Life could return to normal.

The following Sunday, when many of the same people met at the church for the morning service, they were praying for the poor souls who had lost their homes and even their lives when the storm turned to a category three hurricane, Isadore, and hit land over Jamaica, Cuba and Mexico. This time the island of Sainte Marie was unscathed. Just a few days later however, hurricane Lili was rattling the doors and beating against the windows of the Sainte Mariens. Things were rather different with Lili. She was a far more vicious and deadlier being.

The storm tore at the lives of the islanders for two days and two nights and put fear into the hearts and souls of many. The wind pummelled and lashed at all structures across the island, destroying some buildings. It screamed and moaned through the towns and villages. Rain thundered across the island. It blasted into the islanders' homes and flooded their land. Lili thrashed her way through the island; the inordinate quantity of rain destroyed 75 per cent of that year's crops. The plantation owners were left devastated. Dozens of millions of dollars were lost. Lili destroyed roads and bridges. Island transport was seriously disrupted. Many homes were deprived of electricity and telephones for days.

And the girls, Angel, Laura Rose and Merle, what happened to them after they were sent home from school before the onslaught of the storm. Well, this time they all stayed together in the relative safety of Laura Rose and Merle's concrete built apartment. They knew to follow the hurricane advice to the letter. They had been indoctrinated from a very early age that their lives depended on it. During the day, their mothers tried to distract them with games, competitions and stories. At night, they clung to each other on the mattresses dragged into the centre of the living room floor. The girls took turns to sing their favourite pop songs to each other, as Lili deprived them of their slumber. Her melancholy song whined and wailed. Her music of howling and hollering filled their ears. She had shattered many lives on the island, but had firmly soldered the relationship of Angel, Laura Rose and Merle. It was a time that they would long remember; a time when their friendship was strengthened.

Lili had overstayed her welcome on the island of Sainte Marie. In her fury, she gained in strength and hit Cuba as a category two hurricane, taking the lives of innocent citizens, before causing severe damage in Louisiana. Her rampage of destruction cost the lands she had visited around one billion US dollars.

9 Going to where the Money is

JR - London 2006

Oh Lord, I missed my home.

I missed my mother's small, brightly painted, wooden house nestling on the side of a hill over-looking the bay and the sea. I missed the cool breeze wafting through the open louvres, cooling my clammy skin; and the constant drone of the electric fan in the summer months.

I missed the warmth of my friends' smiles, their hugs or their amicable slaps on my back. I longed for the fierceness of the sun's heat on my head and the warmth of the island's sea enveloping my body.

I missed the battering of the rain on the wooden walls and corrugated metal roof which resounded through the house during a tropical downpour or the sharp 30 second showers. I missed the clatter of large raindrops, which at night would wake me as they bounced off the roof.

I even missed those god-damned blackbirds that would start their shrill and raucous lament at the passing of the day as soon as the sun started its descent behind the horizon. Those blackbirds, whose song was soon followed by the calls of the tiny tree frogs. Then, as dawn crept in the next day, I cursed those same birds, who squawked so loudly as soon as there was a ribbon of light appearing over the sea. I had cursed them when they had stopped my sleep, and erased my dreams. But, in London, I yearned to hear them again.

Oh Lord I missed my home.

As I lay in my bed, my mind played over and over what I'd left there. Flashes of my past invaded my thoughts. They were my companions that kept me from sleep; but also helped me struggle towards my future. They kept me company in the London that was, initially, so empty for me.

In London, my days soon settled into a strict routine. Gone was the freedom I'd had until my change of direction. The freedom to do what I pleased, when I pleased. My past reminded me that I had even absented myself from school. On some days, the relative calm and order of the classroom had seemed less attractive to me than the sun beating down on my head, the warm breeze licking my skin, and the squeals of laughter of my friends. With my Mom at work, I chose our own way of filling the days. My dark, home-made pants, white shirt, lace-up shoes and obligatory school tie would be hastily thrown into a plastic bag and then buried under a convenient bush. We, we rebels, the club of truants, selected the old jetty as a meeting place as it was now rarely used by the locals. A new concrete wharf had been built right in the centre of the bay after the old wooden version had taken a battering in a hurricane in the early nineties. The vulnerable wooden framework was in a state of decay, but still had sufficient of its original structure remaining to cater for our needs. It was well out of sight of nosy, prying eyes. Out of sight of acquaintances of our parents, who would doubtless inform them that we were not where we should be, or where they thought that we were. On the occasions though that my truancy was discovered and my mother was informed, she would beat me for breaking the rules, playing hooky, and for lying to her.

My journey over the Atlantic had made those days seem a universe away, rather than just an ocean. I loved my home and Sainte Marie but, they could not give me what I now really desired. So, my choice had been made. I was set on changing my life. And man, it had changed very quickly. Throughout, I knew I had to be unfaltering in my optimism, and in my feelings of hope to pursue my path to achievement. Self-belief had got me to London, and I was determined to win through.

London was so bewildering. Accepting my new world was at first real tough. In the first six months, it would have been so easy to bail out. In fact, I must own up that, even on arrival at the airport, the environment was so alien to me, that I wanted to turn around and run to get on the next flight going back to the Caribbean. The differences that I had experienced in Martinique were one thing, but those in Britain were mega in comparison to my island home. It was so difficult to find ones feet. But decision was stamped on my new passport. This passport very rapidly opened up many new vistas and possibilities. That stamp on my passport at immigration let me enter into a world of changes; changes that would fashion my future. The process of learning and self-education started from the minute I stepped off that plane. To begin with it all seemed surreal, like something in a dream or I'd seen in a movie.

In London, I would awake most mornings to a flat, grey light that made everything look dull and lifeless. Even the living things looked lifeless. In my lodgings, there was a constant din of traffic, day and night. This was interspersed by the sirens of the emergency vehicles. I soon took on board that there were a lot of emergencies in London. It was not only the street noise, but during the day there seemed to be noise from constructions sites, the continuous whine of electric saws and pounding of hammers and churning of cement mixers. There always seemed something new being built. This tumult first off offended my ears. However, someone explained to me that continual rebuilding was symbolic of a changing and a progressive, affluent society. I learnt to accept it and appreciate the racket.

In London, there were many trials to bear. I think that perhaps the worst of these was to learn to accept the cold weather. During my first year there, as the autumn turned to winter, the temperatures dropped lower and lower. I had to clad myself with more and more layers of clothing.

It wasn't the fast food that made me quickly rotund; it was the five sweaters I had to wear. My poor body took a long time to adjust. It hated the cold. I shivered and shuddered and it made me feel chilled to my bones. Returning home from uni, I'd dash from the bus, rush to my room, and cling to its hot radiator until I stopped trembling from the damp cold of outside. When I felt warm enough, I would start to peel off my layers of cheap, charity shop knitwear. My room was small and basic, but at least it was warm.

At home, I had been used to looking people directly in the eye, to holding my head up high, and looking all around me where ever I went. I would smile directly at anyone and everyone and usually greet them in some way. I quickly discovered that this was not the accepted practice in the busy metropolis.

As I left my lodgings each morning, there were crowds everywhere. But those people did not see me. Their eyes were cast downwards or they were engrossed in a newspaper or absorbed with their phones. They seemed to see nobody, but lived in their own private universe, blinkered to the world of others. I waited for the number 267 bus in silence, clutching my bag of books and folders. The wait in line could be very long, the passengers could get very cold or wet, but those in the queue did not reach out to those in the same predicament. Most were indifferent to their neighbours.

And the buses, they were so unlike the buses in Sainte Marie. Back home, the small buses were so full of colour and chatter and overflowing with baggage. The warm breeze blew through the open windows. The passengers would bang on the inside of the bus roof when they wished to descend or they would politely ask the driver. In my home, the adolescent proudly wearing his school uniform would give his seat up to a wizen and very thin old person; a seated passenger would help one standing by taking their baby or a very full shopping bag on their knee; a

Rastafarian in his grubby working clothes would chat to a smart office girl; and islanders, no matter their colour or ethnic origin, would help out a bewildered tourist. Those London red buses were just oh so different.

In the City of London, the red number 267 would wend the same slow tour each day to my university destination, following the slow moving traffic, passing ugly brick buildings, dirty identical houses and a myriad of shops. More shops than I could ever have thought existed, selling every possible thing one could imagine. There were even shops selling things one would not have imagined.

Mostly, the passengers didn't smile. In fact, they didn't communicate with the other travellers. Sometimes, I saw the same faces, but they came and they went and I never learnt about their worlds. I also heard many languages I couldn't identify.

Whilst travelling, my mind would frequently slip to my tropical birthplace, its blazing sunlight, its forest of a thousand different greens, and its undersea world of a flashing kaleidoscope of marine colours. Then I would have to force my mind to concentrate on my day, my studies and my goals.

I was always glad when I arrived at the university, the LSE. The buildings were so immense, so impressive. Each time, I immediately felt a pride that I was a part of the establishment, and that I was being educated there.

Now, you are going to say for yourself, 'LSE, the London School of Economics! How does a waster from the Caribbean get to be at the London School of Economics?' Well, there are thousands of students from all over the world who go to London for further education every year.

You might ask me, 'How come you managed to earn a place there, one of the best universities in Britain? The last thing we knew, you were thinking of driving a water taxi for a hotel!' You would be right. I had thought that my future might be as a 'beach bum'. However, once I got a taste of the world, once I saw what possibilities could lay ahead of me, my ambitions developed. I really have to thank my old mother for getting me the place. When we returned from my aunt's wedding, I chewed over the idea of further education with her. Immediately, she thanked the Lord that I might no longer be a millstone for her. She telephoned her friends and colleagues, my school, my teachers, the Reverend at the church, the human resources manager at the hotel where she worked and the education authorities. You name it, she phoned them. Her phone bill went skywards.

We visited my school and listened to their suggestions and advice. The island education system already had links with colleges and universities in Britain. We completed the forms; we made the applications; we applied for a scholarship with the hotel chain where my mother worked, and then we waited. I took my examinations. I had interviews, more examinations and then more interviews. My head spun; my days were very full and passed as fast as Superman speeding from Krypton.

My mother sighed with relief when we received the letter of acceptance from the university; she praised God when we learnt the news from the hotel chain about the scholarship; but she cried at the airport before my flight. She stood embarrassing me as she clung to my shoulders and sobbed as though I was going off to war. There were so many tears that the front of her dress became wet. After that damp farewell, I boarded the plane and headed towards my new life alone in a vast continent.

Change of continent; change of life style and a change in me. My first real change was my hair. Unfortunately for me, at that time the series the 'Pirates of the Caribbean' were block buster movies in the UK. On my arrival, my hair was long and braided. To the British eye, I looked much like Mr Johnny Depp as Jack Sparrow. I rapidly became the butt of numerous wise cracks and criticisms from my student peers. To me, I looked nothing like the pirate with his dreadlocks, but I solved the problem by becoming the victim of grade two hair clippers. I also went to a local supermarket and invested in a pair of 0.5 horn-rimmed spectacles. I wanted to fit in. I wanted to be accepted by the society I had chosen to be the start of my future.

For me, fitting in with the other students wasn't easy. I had come from a tiny corner of the world, where my social skills had been limited to a few family members, a developing world community college, and the guys on the beach. From my experiences in Martinique, the young people that I had met there, and the many students at the university, I knew that my social skills had a long way to go. I knew what I wanted to be like. I knew I had to do a complete turnaround. I was quiet and slightly shy. I needed to be lively, confident and fun.

Toby was like that, confident and fun. Toby was one of the other students who also had a room in the house in Fulham. He was worldly, dynamic, self-assured, and people were attracted to him like bees to a honey pot. He had plenty of friends, but I wasn't amongst them.

The first week in the student lodgings, he knocked on my door to introduce himself. I was working at the small table in my room, still dressed in a couple of second-hand jumpers to stave off the cool autumn weather. He charged into the room, his slim form dressed in a white T-shirt printed with the name of a sports club, tailored jeans and some coloured suede boots. His dark blonde, spiky hair was accessorised by a pair of rimless sunglasses. To me, he looked like someone who had stepped out of a fashion magazine. He immediately started a narrative about himself. Within two minutes flat, I'd heard about his mates, his flash wheels and the babes of the moment in his life. He didn't really need to ask about me. He could see what I was like; young for my years, unworldly, and a picture of comparative poverty. His intention was to find somebody to go down the pub with. He was polite enough to ask me, but I'm sure that he was relieved when I said that my meagre funds couldn't run to drinking down at the pub.

He more or less ignored me from that day on. He would say, 'Hi, JR,' 'Watcha JR,' or 'How you doing JR?' if he passed me on the stairs. I wasn't somebody he wanted to spend time with, or would ever likely to be. I was a universe apart from him and his circle of friends. However, I soon became indebted to him. It was all thanks to Toby that I went to The Golden Bell. This was the real start of my life in London.

After two or three weeks of worrying how I was going to manage financially, I decided that I had to get a part-time job. I was getting through my grant money much quicker than I had envisaged. Just about everything in London was costly. I went backwards and forwards to the LSE five days a week and over the weekend wandered around discovering a little of the city all by myself. I couldn't afford to do anything but visit free attractions. I hadn't at that point really made a single friend, so I wasn't too sure how to find myself a job. I had looked at the noticeboard in the local supermarket and in a newspaper, without very much success.

As I was arriving back at my room one evening, I met Toby who was just on his way out.

'Hi JR, all OK with you?' he called out.

'Hi Toby. No, I'm desperately looking for a weekend job,' I said, 'You got any ideas?'

He stopped, perhaps a little surprised that I had confided in him. 'I think they are looking for help at The Golden Bell. If you're quick, I'll give you a lift down there. It's the pub down in the back streets.'

I threw my bag into my room and followed Toby down the stairs. I'd seen his car parked in the street, but this was the first time I'd seen it close-up. It was sleek, shiny, silver and low. Toby told me that it was a Mazda, but this didn't mean a thing to me. He made small talk about his course at uni and that he was going to a party later that evening. He didn't ask me anything about myself; I suppose that he wasn't interested. The pub wasn't far. He parked down the street from it and pointed it out to me. I liked the pub immediately. I liked its solid brick building, ascending out of some flat uninteresting apartments which straddled it on either side. It spoke of ancient times. He told me that it had been built in Victorian times and that it had a garden where they served food in the summer. We could see that there were already plenty of customers outside chatting in groups.

The long tables inside were full with people eating. A semi-circle of customers were waiting around the large curved wooden bar in the corner of the room. Toby greeted a couple of his friends as we entered and then pulled me towards the bar to introduce me to the landlady. We waited a few minutes.

'Toby, what can I get for you?' she asked.

'Hi Lil, a pint of lager please. I can see you are very busy, but Lil, am I right in thinking you are looking for part-time help? This is JR and he's at uni with me. He's kind of desperate for a job.'

Lil looked me up and down. She was a woman of around forty, with short, bleached hair. She grinned at me. 'You're desperate for a job; we're desperate for some help. You can see! You ever worked in a pub before?'

I told her that I hadn't, but that I learnt things very quickly. She asked me when I could start. I told her I could help her straightaway if she liked. Toby told me that I'd just had the most rapid interview ever and left me to join his friends. Lil and I, after she had seen to a few customers, came to the arrangement that I could help her for a couple of hours in exchange for an evening meal. This way, she could see if I was up to the work. She took me into the kitchen and handed me a long black apron, telling me that it would help to hide my ghastly jumper. I laughed, and she then explained how to identify an order, and the table it was to go to. All within a space of about three minutes, she showed me the menu and instructed me how to write down the order that the clients gave. She told me that if I had any questions I was to ask Zuze who was working in the kitchen.

I did, in fact, stay all that evening. I enjoyed the lively atmosphere of the pub and the interaction with the customers. As I chatted to some of them, I told myself that it was better there than hugging the radiator back in my room and studying some of the economic books which were on our syllabus. The 'ghastly' jumper was abandoned within an hour as I become so warm rushing backwards and forwards from the kitchen to the bar. Zuze took a shine to me right off. She fell over herself to be charming. I had to go to her several times during the evening to ask questions. She was all smiles and grabbing hold of my arm.

Around ten o'clock, Lil asked me if I was hungry. As I hadn't eaten since lunch time, I told her I could eat a horse. When I sat in the hot kitchen, eating my steak and chips and sticky toffee pudding on the stainless steel counter, I remember thinking it was the first time I'd felt happy since being in Britain. I had been accepted immediately and the people in the pub were nothing but great to me.

Lil came up to me a bit later, whilst I was helping to clean up the mess in the kitchen. She asked me what I had thought of the evening.

'It was ace,' I replied, 'especially the steak and chips. No, I enjoyed it; busy, but the customers were very tolerant of the fact that I wasn't sure what I was doing some of the time.'

'I assure you that they aren't all like that JR. You were just lucky. So, do you want to come back?' asked Lil.

'Oh yes please, I can't manage on my university grant.'

Lil laughed. She took my face between her hands and landed a wet kiss full on my mouth. 'I love this boy. He said yes before he even knows how much we will pay him! You can tell that you haven't been in the country long! You know what JR, you were indispensable this evening. We were run off our feet tonight. You were a blessing sent from heaven. One thing though, you will have to get rid of that dreadful jumper.'

We agreed on my hours for three nights a week and the wage. We mutually agreed that I should wear jeans and a white shirt. Lil said that she would give me a meal as well each evening. As it turned out, whilst I was a student at the LSE, I was to spend far more than my scheduled pub working hours there. The Golden Bell became my local and almost my second home. More importantly, it served as a second university; a socio-university where I acquired many social skills and learnt lots about London and its very diverse population.

10 Re-inventing myself

JR - 2006

As the surrealism of London started to evaporate and the hard reality of life there started to slap me in the face, I commenced taking a hard look around me. The vastness of my new environment and my insignificance in it initially filled me with alarm. I was a tiny solitary speck in such an enormous society of over seven million souls, so unlike the comparatively tiny population of a couple of hundred thousand on the whole of my tropical isle. I promptly experienced a loneliness which cast heaviness into my heart. I had to find distractions to compensate for this and mask my trepidation. The distraction wasn't difficult to find; it was all around me. I was living in one of the most famous cities in the world, my diversion became London. I found myself dropped into a society of countless historic buildings, a Royal family, and the remnants of centuries of wars, uprisings, social and political changes, and a legacy of history and culture totally different to what I'd been born into. I eventually learnt to love being immersed in the mishmash of the deeply civilised and cultured London. Initially, I explored this vast domain alone. My diversions not only gave me purpose, but educated me to knowing what London was really about.

I started my first term as a solitary soul; because of this, I began to organise my life. I had my studies which opened many new doors for my mind. The more I learnt in maths or accounting, the more I came to realise how little I knew about my chosen career. I was stimulated to read the mass of associated text books during my study time. I had made no real friends, just acquaintances. I had little money to spend on going out socially. My spare time and my week-days became my time to discover the capital. To start with, I walked. I walked to explore the churches, museums and libraries and other historical sites; I watched the people, their interactions and conversations with one another; and I listened. I learnt a different and new vocabulary. It was all English, but not precisely the same English I had used at home. A garbage can was a dustbin, a crosswalk was a zebra crossing, the trunk of a car was a boot (a boot?) and Boots was a chemist not a drugstore. Do you understand my confusion?

I didn't have a camera, so I wrote notes. I also drew little sketches of the things that I saw that interested me, or took pamphlets from the places I had visited. I soon had quite a collection. I sent letters home to my mother and friends and told them all about my findings and included some of my little drawings or a pamphlet. I walked between my lectures if there was enough time; I walked during my lunch break after grabbing something to eat; I walked part of the way back to my room, and I walked at the week-ends. I soon had a reliable map in my head of the districts around the LSE and my digs. Perhaps I would have been better staying in the refectory, coffee bar or student lounges; perhaps I would have fitted in better if I had done some of the optional leisure activities; perhaps I would have made friends much quicker; perhaps I wouldn't have felt so detached from those around me. But instead, I chose to walk; it meant I was always busy.

My job at The Golden Bell though changed my routine and my spirits. I learnt to appreciate the various characters who worked there, and soon became a part of the team. They accepted me immediately for what I was. They were not like Toby, who wanted to associate only with those of a similar outlook and of his own class. I gained an understanding of what their lives were really like. For some of them, their lives were as difficult, maybe even more so, than mine. Some of the team became important to me. The closest of them, and who influenced my existence, were Lil and Zuze, whose full name was Zuzanna.

From evening one, Lil had decided she was going to be a second mother to me. She had no children of her own, just a child-substitute little dog. Lil officially ran the public house with her husband. However, he was rarely on the scene. And he definitely didn't share the work load of running the pub. I was promptly filled in by the other staff that he drank excessively and frequented local bars and clubs with his mates. Hence, the entire business of the bar, restaurant and bed and breakfast rooms on the second floor were all down to Lil. She was committed and hardworking and expected her staff to do the same. Lil was a strong personality and very firm with her employees, but she also had a soft heart. She was quick to find out about me being away from home and missing my family and friends. She was always ready to listen about a problem or explain how things should be done. It didn't take long before Lil was giving me hand-me-down clothes. These were usually things that she said her husband didn't want any more. I suspect that she thought his taste in clothing was superior to mine. His pullovers were certainly more sober than I would have chosen, but he invested in wool and cashmere, fibres I couldn't even consider buying. Lil gave me strict instructions about how to wash and dry the clothes she donated to me, because of course I didn't have a clue. I remember once Lil screaming at me, because I asked why one of her woollen jumpers was no longer wearable. I confessed to putting it on the radiator to dry.

It was on that occasion that I told Lil that I'd always seemed to have problems with my attire and when I went to junior school. I explained that my Mom had always left very early for work, so I was walked to school by our neighbour when I was a kid. I accompanied her with her own son every morning. There was no school bus, as I only lived on the outskirts of Prosper. We walked down the hill and then the mile and a half along the coast road, come rain, come shine. My mother never accompanied me; she was too busy at work. She had worked for as long as I could remember. As my Mom left before me, the state of my school uniform was for me to deal with. I frequently had one of the female teachers telling me that my tie wasn't straight or my socks were not the same.

I recounted some of the phrases I had had ringing in my ears on occasions. 'Jordon young man, please ensure you wear a PAIR of socks tomorrow.' Or, 'Jordon, what have you done to your shirt? It looks like you screwed it up into a ball to play football with! You must take a pride in your school uniform.' I explained that the rest of the class would snigger and laugh at me. Of course, I had failed to notice any problem with my clothing. I felt I was far more important than the school uniform. Lil thought this very entertaining and told me she sympathised with my teachers. Strangely, I seemed to get a bunch more hand-me downs after that.

And Zuze, well, I wasn't really too sure where Poland was before I met her. She had left her homeland, with her parents, in search of work and to try to establish roots in a society with more possibilities and a better future than there was at home. Zuze, a little like me, was reserved and she admitted that she knew very few people, outside of her family and the small Polish community where she lived. She, also like me, had been desperate for a job when she became a sous-chef in The Golden Bell's kitchen. She had been seeking a managerial position in the hotel industry.

Zuze was a little older than me, in her early twenties. In her chefs' whites and her hair net and hat, she looked rather austere. It wasn't until she was leaving work, and the protective clothing was cast off, that one discovered she had long, glossy brown hair which softened her face. Her overalls cast aside exposed her slim form. I would watch her in the kitchen as she helped to prepare a mushroom risotto or a platter of cheese and pickles. She was well organised, full of energy and didn't panic under pressure.

Very quickly, Zuze and I would organise to eat together before the evening rush. Right away, it became clear that she wanted to add me to her short list of friends. Was I going to object? No way! My list of friends was non-existent. I relished the opportunity of someone to talk to about my day and missing my home, and to find out about her life in London and in Poland. Lil, seeing us together, soon informed me, in her typical Brits' frankness and sense of humour, that Zuze was after my beautiful brown body, and in fact, if she was a little younger, she wouldn't mind my beautiful brown body herself. Zuze and I were both embarrassed. She stared at her plate and turned pink; whilst I made a show of slapping Lil's arm and telling her she was too saucy.

Zuze soon discovered that I had become a walker and discoverer of London. The second weekend that I was working at the pub, Zuze asked me if I had visited Kew Gardens, to the west of London. The elegance of the Victorian buildings, the enormous glasshouse and the immense variety of plants appealed to her, but, as yet, she hadn't found anybody to go there with her. I don't think that I would ever have visited the gardens without Zuze. I would have considered the £12 student admission far too much cash out of my meagre wage. Also I certainly wouldn't have had enough courage to be the one to ask her out.

I own up that I was very tense and sweating about the visit to Kew. It was my first date ever with a woman. I had never felt at ease with the girls of my own age and despite trying, had never got very far with them at home. I was usually lost for words with them. But I amazed myself, right from meeting Zuze at the bus stop; we seemed to have plenty of things to say. The number 65 bus headed for the gardens that Sunday afternoon and we chatted all the way. We both loved Kew and didn't want to leave as dusk started to fall. It wasn't just the phenomenal collection of plants and the amazing glasshouses that that made it such a memorable afternoon, one that we didn't want to end. I think it was also the mutual relief that we had both found someone to confide in, to empathise with, and share experiences with.

Out of work, Zuze spoke more freely about her family and her home. Whilst at Kew, she narrated how they had migrated recently, when Poland had become included as a part of the European Community. However, life was not as terrific as her family had hoped for. Her father, who was a construction engineer, had had to accept a job as a bricklayer on a building site. Her mother cleaned offices in the evening so they had enough money to survive; and Zuzanna had been unable to find a management job in one of the London hotels, and had to accept the poorly paid kitchen job at The Golden Bell. Her family rented a tiny one bedroom apartment in Hammersmith where there was hardly room to move. Zuze slept on the settee in the sitting room. She had hoped to earn enough to rent her own room. The worst aspect for her though, one that the family hadn't anticipated, was the racial prejudice that was prevalent in London. There were some that thought the Polish should not be in Britain. There had been thirty or so ethnically motivated attacks on the Polish community in the short time they had been there. I didn't understand what she was talking about. She was white; living in a predominantly white country. I knew there was some racism in Britain, but had thought that it was only against people of colour like me.

Over a drink in the cafeteria at Kew, Zuze explained about the unsettled history of her birthplace. She told of the centuries of persecution by the Prussians and the Germans and the horrific ethnic cleansing of Poles during the Second World War caused by Hitler's greed for land and his anti-Semitic paranoia. Currently, in the United Kingdom, the extremists who thought that 'Britain should be only for the

British' were having a bash at the Polish because large numbers had immigrated to Britain. I listened in silence and shock. She told me she worried about it. She knew that her parents did too. Sometimes she felt she would give up on London because she felt so unwanted there.

I reached across the table and squeezed her hand. I wasn't certain what to say and how to comfort her. I chose a distraction and said that perhaps we should go as the gardens would be closing. As we moved from the cafeteria, I asked her if we could plan to go somewhere next weekend. She smiled at me and said that she would really like that. However, it would be my turn to choose, as she had selected Kew Gardens. As we made for the bus stop, she took hold of my hand. I still remember the feeling of elation that things were going well, despite my initial jitters.

On the bus back, I had time for reflexion. It was crowded and Zuze and I were not sitting together. I congratulated myself on my first date. Things hadn't been awkward or difficult. I was beginning to comprehend why Zuze was eager to count me as a friend. She had probably thought that I would be like her and experiencing similar problems. I replayed in my mind what she had said about anti-Polish feelings. I wanted to try to reassure her, to attempt to get nearer to her. As we neared our stop in Fulham, I realised that I didn't want the date to finish. I wondered if I had the nerve to ask her to come back to my room for a coffee or drink. I glanced towards Zuze, to find that she was watching me. She smiled. I decided there and then that I would dare to ask her.

To my amazement, she accepted. So, after buying a pack of beers at the corner shop, we returned to my lodgings. I now know that Zuze had been hoping for my invitation. I felt awkward for a couple of minutes, being shut into that small space with a young female for the first time. So, I started talking, eighteen to the dozen about the things we had seen that afternoon to try and hide my embarrassment. Rapidly, it became clear that it wasn't the first time that Zuze had been in a locked room with a male. She may have been reserved, but she knew what she wanted that evening. And Zuze knew how to get it. She was far from embarrassed. She held my face between her hands and started kissing me passionately. I instantly felt the tensions in my body disappear. Our clothes very soon joined the other things that were making the room look untidy. My eyes were agog. Zuze tore off her jumper, skirt and then her underwear. Then she started on me. I was too excited to worry about the fact that it was the first time and to wonder if I was doing OK.

Afterwards, we sat on my single bed and drank our beers. We exchanged confidences about how we had felt about one another since we had met. Zuze confessed to being attracted to me from my first evening at The Golden Bell; she had liked my apparent shyness, my dark voice, but particularly my smile and brown eyes. My confidence was growing every second because of the novelty of being told by a woman that she found me attractive. She laughingly added that even Lil fancied me and would not have pushed me away.

Lil being the topic of conversation, we both agreed that her life was really tough. Fifteen or sixteen hours work every day were the norm for her, so that her husband could go off and spend her hard earned money on booze, expensive clothes and his mates. Nevertheless, Lil was gutsy. She stood up to the adversities. I kissed Zuze and told her that perhaps she needed to adopt a similar approach. She should not feel concerned about the few extremists who tried to persecute her race. She should be strong and not give in. Life wasn't always easy. The anti-Polish faction wanted her to give up. They wanted her to go, despite the laws that said had every right to be there. She shouldn't let them win.

This was obviously the right thing to say to her, as she started kissing and caressing me once more and telling me how thoughtful I was towards her. I was obviously learning fast. Lil was forgotten, the conversation ceased and we concentrated on enjoying one another's bodies once again.

From that day my routines changed somewhat. I still had my lectures, my walks and my work, but depending on how busy she was, Zuze would sometimes come to join me on my treks around the capital. The main difference was that lots of my days became longer. After the evening shift at The Golden Bell, Zuze would transform the loneliness of my room at ten thirty or eleven o'clock to share my bed and tell me about her day. She also listened to what I'd learnt that day at uni, my walks around London, or what my mother had told me in her letters.

The clients in The Golden Bell also enhanced my education of life. There was a cross-section of mankind that frequented the bar and the restaurant. There were the regulars that came after work, the labourers, health care workers, engineers and business people of all ages; and the oldies that would come for a quiet drink or a meal and would welcome a chat. I served the inebriated, the drugged, the lonely, the depressed, a few privileged and many disadvantaged. There were the very noisy groups, romantic couples and plenty of people by themselves.

I digress however. My reason for telling you a little about the clients is there was one client who was going to directly fashion my future. His name was Damien. Apparently he had been a regular customer in the pub over the years, as he had lived in Fulham. Yet, I didn't meet him until I started working for Lil during the Christmas break.

I had asked Lil if she would need a little extra help in the pub coming up to the festive season. She laughed and told me that I would find out that the British went mad at Christmas time. She explained how many Brits would

94

spend a fortune on their Christmas celebrations, drinking and eating to excess, and purchasing unnecessarily expensive gifts for their families and friends. 'A little help?' she said, 'I will need a bloody sight more than a little extra help.' So, my three evenings a week in term time became five days a week for two weeks during the Christmas period. Our first exams were at the beginning of January, so I needed to leave time to revise for these. Nevertheless, I was desperate to acquire a computer to store my work efficiently and gain some skill on the accounting programmes recommended by our lecturers. Working for those two weeks seemed to be the only way I was going to afford to buy one.

Damien came into the pub frequently whilst I was working a full week. He came alone, or sometimes with a friend, or with his wife. He was just an average looking guy of about forty I suppose. He was a real Mr GQ. You could see immediately that he dropped a bundle on his clothes. I soon concluded that the smart clothes were to attract the smart babes. Damien was very sure of himself and he liked others to know that he was around. I met his wife a couple of times, but she certainly didn't stop Damien from eyeing up the females 24/7. He had just returned from working in the Caribbean and was in London for the Christmas holidays. When he found out that I came from Sainte Marie, he latched onto me. This was when he told me he had set up a company on the island.

This man liked to drink. He drank enough of the hard stuff for at least two and a half normal men. The more he drank, the more he became sure of himself, but I never saw him paralytic. He always addressed me as 'his mate', even though I wasn't. I suspect he called me that as he couldn't remember my name. He told me and the rest of the pub how well he was doing, how he was making a bomb and what an ace salesman he was. He boasted he would soon be buying a boat. He definitely wasn't my type, but I adopted the attitude that I had seen Lil use. She treated all her clients with the same approach; always friendly, cheerful and polite, and with a positive attitude. I listened to her chat and emulated her example.

He told me all about his villas with pools and apartments on a beach he called Fortune Bay. He even brought in plans to show me. He reiterated how wonderful the properties were. I didn't really know the beach he was talking about, because it was in the north of Sainte Marie and I had lived in the south. I felt sure that this would not be the island's name for it anyway. He bragged about the profits he would be making and what he planned to do with the money. He talked about himself most of the time, but he did ask me why I had come to Britain and what I planned to do when my studies were finished. He even offered me a job if I planned to go back to Sainte Marie when I became qualified. He said that they already had an accountant, but it was sure that they would need more staff in the near future. He even gave me one of his business cards. As I pocketed it, I asked myself if I could tolerate working for such a character.

Well, Christmas came and went, followed by New Year, and Damien Janes returned to the Caribbean. The world kept on turning, the people kept on coming and going and a multitude of various events kept my life buzzing. I thought nothing more about him for a very long time. He was just added to the long mental list of odd fellows and incidents that were making up my 'Book of Life'.

11 Money Talks

Damien - Autumn 2009

It was around seven o'clock by the time he reached the office. Damien Janes wanted to catch up on what had been happening there during the day. The office was in darkness when he entered. He had to fumble for the light switch on the wall. He walked into his own office. Within a few minutes his designer shirt was sticking to his back. Sweat was seeping out of his skin and running down his neck. It was hotter than Satan's arm pits in the locked up building.

Angel, who would have left a couple of hours before, must have systematically turned off the air conditioning. Damien hated super-efficient women. He searched his desk and found there were no messages there. There were no flashing lights on the office phones. His mobile had been silent. He switched on his computer. There were no e-mails from Dell. What the hell was happening? His calls earlier in the day had been ignored. The meeting at the bank had been a critical one. He was anxious to discover how Dell had got on. He really wanted to know the outcome before he had to return home to the tedium of the wife and kids. It had been a very long day. He definitely needed a drink before he could face going back to the family.

He strode back through the reception area. He surveyed the architect's scale model. Sample boards, photos of stylish furniture, and samples of fabric, tile and flooring, all adorned the room. He was proud and pleased with the area. Clients were always impressed by the level of interior design there. He considered the leather and chrome settees and chairs to be chic. He really got a kick out of them and the glass topped table furnishing the room. All had been imported from the States. He particularly liked the abstract painting in black and white which dominated one wall. He reached for the light switch and immediately the image was erased as the room was plunged into darkness.

Janes drove to the marina and the yacht club. Two drinks later he tried phoning Dell again. Nothing!

'Give me another one mate,' he said to the bar man.

'Sure DJ.' As the barman pushed his drink over the highly polished wooden bar, Damien's phone rang. He surveyed the illuminated panel.

'Hi, honey,' he said whilst smiling at the barman. 'No, I'm just wrapping up a meeting here with some clients and I'll be home in half an hour.'

He slammed his phone onto the bar. The call from his wife had not improved his mood. He swigged back his drink and paced up and down in front of the open terrace of the bar which was draped with nautical flags. A light breeze cooled his face. He surveyed the outlines of mega-yachts, cruisers and sport fishers which were lit up in the marina. All of them were neatly tucked into their individual berths. The moorings safeguarded a mass of wealth in a protected haven. Luxury and fortunes sheltered from the possible adversities of storms; and hurricanes in the summer and autumn months.

The view here was definitely better than the local pub he had frequented in Fulham. Janes had left London a few years ago. He had been glad to get out of there. Things had started to hot-up for him in the capital. It had been a relief for him to discover the possibilities in the developing Caribbean.

Just about to order another drink, he saw Dell. 'Dell, for Christ's sake, what has been happening? I really thought you'd phone me,' he shouted. The tall, slim frame of Wendell Thorner walked rather unsteadily into the Yacht Club bar. He was accompanied by a stunning, very shapely young woman, her clinging, short dress revealing more than a little of her Caribbean assets. Her long, wavy hair bobbed up and down as she mounted the stairs.

'We're all pumped up and ready to go sweetie. We been celebrating! Where're we going now?' she said flinging her bangled arms around his neck.

This was rather unlike Angel. Usually, they didn't see eye to eye. He pushed her away gently. Angel certainly lived up to her name in appearance. But though Damien would have been only too happy to give her one, unhappily for him, she seemed to be Wendell's girlfriend. Only Wendell's girlfriend. He swiftly sussed by their unsteadiness that they had been on a bender. He felt rather hacked off. Why hadn't Dell called him? Why hadn't Dell let him know the upshot of the meeting? Why hadn't he thought that there were more important things than going around each local bar throwing back drinks? Why hadn't they even given him a single thought? He thought he knew Dell better than that.

Wendell was the man who had changed Damien's life. He had changed it from a very murky grey to one with a silver lining. Damien had met Wendell a few years before. He had sought him out after arriving on the island. Damien had learnt that the family owned a lot of land on Sainte Marie. Wendell was the eldest son of one of the leading families on the island. His father, Francis Thorner, had moved to Sainte Marie in the 1970's. He had invested what money he had in setting up a rum distillery. The business had been a big success. The rum was being exported throughout the Caribbean and the States. Francis Thorner was reticent about Damien and his ideas. Despite this, the family had sold several acres to him to develop a small time-share complex. The project had gone well. The pair of them had made a killing out of it. Wendell had bought his new Lamborghini. Damien had made a large down payment on a beach-side residence. Both Wendell and Damien knew how to spend money and spend it fast.

'We did it!' exclaimed Wendell. 'The bank is loaning us another 5 million dollars! Byron at the bank was only too pleased to have our custom. We can now pay for the construction of the commercial buildings.'

Damien whooped and held up his hand to meet Wendell's in mid- air. 'Five million dollars! It's more than most buggers even dream of! You got any champagne behind that bar?' he shouted to the barman.

Damien trembled internally with excitement. He hadn't felt this jubilant in ages. He was silently calculating how much his slice of the action would be. He could definitely afford to take all the family for a holiday in the Bahamas now.

The champagne arrived. That bottle was soon emptied, to be replaced by another, and then another. Very soon all the drinkers in the Yacht Club Bar knew more than they ought to know about the new project of Wendell and Damien. To his captive audience, Damien had explained in immense detail all the features of the proposed buildings. He disregarded if they might be curious, slightly interested or totally apathetic ears. That evening, there were several casual acquaintances in the Yacht Club bar who became 'lifelong friends'. Everybody there was invited to a party at Damien's house the following weekend.

Wendell recapped on his interview at the bank and boasted of his mathematical projections and persuasive powers for obtaining the very large loan. As for Angel, she seemed to be enjoying herself sat at a corner table with another young lady much her own age. Occasionally, she blew kisses over her hand in the direction of Wendell and Damien. All too soon, the supply of champagne at the yacht club was exhausted. The back slapping, squeezing of shoulders and the expressions of congratulations ceased. It was agreed they should move on.

$$$

All three revellers were extremely drunk by the time Damien decided that he should drive home. Despite Angel's protests that he should take a taxi, Damien rolled

100

into his 4X4 and drove the short journey to his home in Anse Argent. It was very late. Fortunately for him and for the rest of the people in the town, there wasn't much traffic on the road. As he swung into his driveway, his headlights illuminated the light blue façade of a large residence. They cast light upon its pillars, arches and white shuttered windows. Damien fell out of his car, leaving it unlocked on the drive, and swayed his way to his front door.

'You bastard! You were supposed to be home more than two hours ago,' screamed Donna. He was bombarded by hostility before he had time to close the door behind him. She pushed him across the room.

'Don't you start woman! I'zz going to bed. Isss been a very long day,' slurred Damien, bumping into the coffee table and then slumping onto the settee.

'Careful what you are doing. Mind the table! Damien you're drunk again. Where have you been all evening?' shrieked Donna.

'Ssssh, you'll wake the kids. I was with some clients and then I met Wendell. We was talking about the loan from the bank.'

'You're a liar! I bet you've been fooling around with that bitch Angel!' yelled Donna, beating Damien over the head with a rolled-up magazine. 'You even turned off your phone so I couldn't contact you.'

Damien was slouched over on the sofa. He was having great difficulty trying to unbutton his shirt. 'It'ss true. It'ss true. I wazz with Dell. Just leave me ALONE!' he complained.

'You leave me all day and all night. You don't even think about me. I've had enough of you and all your lies! You're a lying bastard!' shouted Donna, but her tirade was lost as Damien had keeled over into a pile. He was fast asleep. Donna threw her magazine at her husband. He didn't stir.

Donna mounted the stairs crying and feeling rejected. Amidst her sobbing, she checked on the two children. They were fortunately fast asleep. She lay on the large bed in her bedroom. She could hear the crashing of the sea as it broke onto the shore. People thought that she had such an enviable existence, living in a magnificent house in a beautiful place, where she could buy almost anything that she wanted. But Donna had become aware she was happier back in their modest home in London. She had enjoyed her secretarial job, her friends, and living close to her parents. Back then, Damien had been a loving husband and a good dad.

Donna realised that she had been naïve. She had thought that things would stay the same when they moved to the Caribbean. She had been so excited at first. There was just so much to do. They had to find somebody to rent their house and find an agent to manage it. She had spent hours packing up their personal belongings, crating them and organising the shipping. All of this had been fitted around her daily life, her job, and looking after the children and the house. Damien had been in Sainte Marie, starting work on the time-share project. At first, she was so busy trying to fit everything into the day; she hadn't noticed that the calls from Damien became less frequent and the only real topic of conversation had been about himself and how well he was doing with the project.

She thought about the man that was crumpled up on their expensive sofa downstairs. He was not the man who she had lived with in Fulham. Since he had worked in Sainte Marie he had become a changed person. And she was certainly no longer a priority in his life. What had gone wrong? Was it something she had done? He now just took her for granted. He only gave her and their children scraps of his time and attention. It seemed that now he always chose himself over his family and her. She wasn't even sure that she liked him anymore. She definitely felt that she couldn't believe or trust him. In the past, in London, he had confided in her about every aspect of his life. He had seemed to be satisfied with her and the children. But in Sainte Marie, his only reasons for living seemed to be money and power. The glamourous women and fast living were important, but definitely were secondary to the money and the status.

She wasn't even certain that the money was always entirely legally earnt. She had heard a few rumours on the island. It was a relatively small island, with not a great deal happening, hence people became very curious about those around them, especially those that lived the way Damien did. Donna had learnt that gossip was a great distraction for the people of Sainte Marie, some of whom led very uneventful lives. The gossip was turned into the news of the week. Many of the islanders relished in spreading the gossip as fast as possible from one to the other, be it true or untrue. Nevertheless, she worried about some of the rumours concerning Damien making 'shady deals' and the untrustworthy people that he dealt with.

She lay on the bed unable to sleep. She felt torn apart inside and desperate about her situation; wretched about her marriage. She worried about how things were going to turn out and what was going to happen to her and the children. She wondered how long she could tolerate her present circumstances. After too many hours without sleep, she made the decision that she must make Damien find time to talk to her. She must stand up and fight for his attention and love. She must make him see how she felt. Donna thought that she must make him understand how he had changed towards her and the children since they had moved to the Caribbean. She would try to talk to him after she has taken the children to school next morning.

$$$

Damien was still asleep on the sofa when Donna got up to see to the children's breakfast. They asked why Dad was

103

sleeping on the settee and she told them that he had come in very late last night, so was very tired and not to disturb him. She ushered the children out of the house and drove them to the International School in Anse Argent. On her return from the school run, he was starting to stir.

She felt a cup of black coffee might be what was called for and went into the kitchen. She desperately wanted to talk to Damien before Gemma arrived. Gemma was the local lady who helped with the house and the children. Donna glanced at the kitchen clock. Gemma would be there fairly soon. Then she looked out of the window. She glimpsed the sea and the sand through the garden fencing. Tall palms in the garden fluttered in the sea breeze. Vibrant purple coloured bougainvillea, bright yellow tropical hibiscus and pink ginger lilies adorned the beds at the side of their swimming pool. There was a humming bird which darted backwards and forwards looking for nectar. The pool glittered in the bright sunlight. The kid's inflated toys lay on the sun deck. The children loved their time spent in the pool. That pool held many good memories of sociable evenings with friends and family. It was all so attractive; it could all be so wonderful if Damien hadn't become obsessed by his money-making projects.

Damien struggled to half open his eyes. He muttered something that was incomprehensible. He fought with the sofa to sit up straight and to accept the coffee. His face, as well as his clothing, was as crumpled as a used sweet wrapper.

'Damien, we need to talk.'

'What time is it?' asked Damien taking the cup and saucer. 'I need to get to the office.'

'But, Damien we need to talk. We need to talk about our life here and the children. We can't go on like this. We hardly ever see you,' pleaded Donna.

The black coffee didn't improve Damien's mood. 'Stop whining Donna, there are millions of women who would give their eye teeth to change places with you. Millions! You are so bloody lucky, living on the beach, in a superb house, on a beautiful island. The weather is always warm. And, you're still not satisfied. I'm going to get a shower and then go to the office.'

'But Damien, you are never here. You are always in meetings, or drinking, or with other women. There is little point me being here, except to do your washing and ironing. The children miss you.'

'I'm always out, trying to earn money Donna,' shouted Damien, as he pushed his wife out of the way. He walked towards the hall and started to mount the wide staircase.

'But I'd rather be back in London. We were all happy then Damien.'

Damien turned towards her on the staircase. 'Well, you have a choice don't you. I've made mine.' With that comment, he continued up the stairs to get his shower.

12 Jump Up

The Girls - Summer 2009

'Splash' was crowded. It was Friday, Jump Up night in Doublon d'Or. The very regular rhythm of zouk music belted out from an old speaker suspended above the bar. Angel's one hand of long painted finger nails followed the beat on the bar top. The other hand played with the condensation which ran down the outside of the fluted cocktail glass. To celebrate her recently acquired job, she had treated herself to a colourful cocktail. Wendell was late.

Angel hadn't been able to go to the street party for a long time. She had been far too busy studying. She was looking forward to listening to the kind of music that she loved. She longed for the opportunity to dance and have some fun and relax. She knew that she was sure to meet some of her friends and catch up on their news. But, Wendell was late.

The locals loved the Jump Up. It was the end of the working week. A time to relax. Friday meant they got their wage after the long slog of the week. As dusk fell, they blocked off the roads so the street party could begin. For some the temptation of inviting odours of creole food cooking and the sight of so much hard stuff was too much. Their hard earned wage ran through their fingers. However, the stall holders were grateful for their business. Recently, there were far more tourists. And the tourists were the ones with the cash.

If the tourists expected something sophisticated they would be disappointed. There were no coloured, flashing lights, no fancy dance floor, no smartly dressed waitresses serving drinks. It was just the tarmacked road as a dance floor. The shops, cafes and houses of Doublon d'Or were the décor. Many went out of curiosity. To obtain a glimpse, an insight into the lives of the people of Sainte Marie and to listen to their music.

Angel went to the Jump Up solely for the music. She loved to immerse herself in the beat of the reggae, R and B, zouk, and calypso music that was always played there. Whatever the music, it was always played very loudly; so loudly that it blocked out all the other sounds of the world. The beat from the huge speakers in the streets was so booming that it felt like the ground was vibrating. The music was penetrating from the earth, through Angel's body, to command her form and rule her movements.

Vrrrum, vrrrum, vrrrum. Angel loved to give herself to the rhythm of the music; feel her limbs relaxed and loose; they waved freely in the warm air of her homeland. When she gave herself to the music, it blocked out everything. It made her forget all the problems of her life in one single beat. She danced like she was the only one there; she felt lifted; she felt joy.

'So, how is our new employee?' Wendell interrupted her thoughts by kissing the back of her neck.

'Great thanks. How is my new employer?'

'Sorry I'm a bit late. I had a meeting with Damien, which went on and on.'

'Hey, you look really cool! Love the white jeans.' Wendell was dressed all in white. His clinging t-shirt showing to advantage the results of spending many hours in the gym.

'Thanks. We have been trying to sort out some loans for some new buildings at Fortune Bay.'

'Have you got the loans? How does that work?'

'Another one of those cocktails Angel?' Wendell interrupted. After ordering the drinks, he came back to his explanation. 'Well, let's start at the beginning. As you know, the government here is trying to promote tourism on the island. They see it as our future. The days of the island surviving from sugar and bananas are gone. The banks here have a directive to loan money to companies that are trying to promote the local tourist industry. My father is a friend of the manager of a bank in Bourbon. He has known him for years. The bank manager is very sympathetic to people trying to advance the tourist industry. He knows people in the Department of Tourism. So, we have an influential contact in him. Naturally, we have some money from our previous project, but we need bank loans to get started on the Fortune Bay site. We have to advertise and try to sell the properties to potential owners before we see any money from them.'

'Yes, of course I know all that. You needed loans to get yourself established, to pay for your employees and offices, going to vacation home exhibitions and so on. Once the clients start to buy the villas, you need a loan to start the work. They don't pay you until part of their villa has been built. Is that right?'

'They pay a small deposit, usually around 5% or 10% when they first purchase the villa. Then, when the foundations are completed, they pay another 30 % of the total value. You have to make sure that happens quickly, so that you can get some cash coming in.'

'And this goes to pay off some of the loan, before you start work on the next part of the villa. When the walls and the roof are completed, they pay the next 30 per cent. By the time they pay the final instalment, you can pay back the bank and you make a nice profit with what is left over?'

'That's the general idea. So, are we going talk about work all evening or are we going to the Jump Up?'

Angel drained the very last drop of her cocktail. They then walked towards the centre of Doublon d'Or and the sea. Wendell walked proudly holding his body very straight and his shoulders pulled back. Angel clung onto his hand. They joined the river of people that was already flowing towards the street party. Angel and Wendell chatted easily. She was eager to learn about their forthcoming visit to Miami. They passed an assortment of sturdy, plain concrete houses and shops, and wooden built Creole-style cottages. Rusting corrugated metal fenced in some of the back yards.

Tasty colours, pink, peach, yellow or lime decorated the external walls which were topped with corrugated metal roofs. Many of the vibrant shades showed evidence of the extremes of the climate. This was the tropics. There was flaking and blistering of paint on doors and shutters. Most houses opened straight out onto the pavement. They were all built with the Caribbean climate in mind. Louvred windows let a cross-breeze sweep through the house. Decorative fretwork spanned between the slim pillars supporting the roofed verandas. The occupants were boxed in by shaped, wooden balustrades, permitting them to watch the world go by in the shade.

Friday nights, the veranda boards were bowed with the weight of spectators. Music, dancing and tourists became their free entertainment. Private lives became public. The magic of Cassav' serenaded family platters of fish curry shared in view of the street. Jah Vinci was background dancehall raga for work fatigued men enjoying their evening tipple or the clicking and slamming of dominos at the veranda table. And children sat on the boarded floor accompanied Jimi Hendrix rock in their own style. Bashing on saucepans or battering on cake tins.

Angel and Wendell walked towards the beach and the town's wharf. They passed numerous dogs sniffing for scraps of food. The dogs all looked very similar in colour, size and shape. They, the dogs, had learnt that Friday in Doublon d'Or could be very beneficial for their stomachs. Tourists could be very generous to dogs with big, sad eyes.

Both Angel and Wendell had grown up knowing and accepting this environment as the norm. But for many of the tourists, the homes, the people of Sainte Marie, and even the dogs, merited a photo to capture and freeze the moment for ever, so that they would relive the evening of the Jump Up long after they returned home.

The aromas of cooking jerk chicken, roasting pork, fried fish and lobsters attacked their nostrils even before they arrived at the location of the Jump Up. Trestle tables covered with brightly coloured patterned oil cloths lined the sides of the main street. They were heavy with displays of cooked food stuffs in plastic lidded boxes and drink. The stall holders were there to supplement their meagre wages.

Wendell knew in which direction he was heading. He aimed for a stall, protected by a large awning, selling home-made rums. A multitude of bottles was arranged in a neat row at the back of the Formica table. Each bottle had a hand written label telling you who had made the contents of the bottle and indicating its potency. 'Aunty' was scrawled on most of the labels. It transpired that the large, barrel-shaped, middle-aged lady, who stood behind the bottles waiting for her next clients, was in fact Aunty. Aunty was the distiller of the rum. As she saw Angel and Wendell advancing towards her, her large, round face opened into a grin from ear to ear, revealing beautifully white and even teeth.

'So, what can I get ya my dears?' Aunty asked

Naturally, Wendell knew a lot about rum. Nevertheless, he asked the stall holder to explain about the different types of rum that she was selling. Patiently, Aunty gave an explanation of each of her wares. Wendell sniffed and sampled each one that he was interested in. He opted for the spiced rum. Angel was more interested in being intoxicated by the music. She just wanted to dance. She passed on the alcohol and opted for a can of ice cold lemonade instead.

Wendell was sipping and savouring his first beaker of rum of the evening, when he felt a tap on his shoulder. He turned to find Darius and his latest girlfriend. Much to Aunty's delight, Wendell ordered a large beaker of rum for each of them. Just as the four were introducing themselves to one another the music blared. Huge, three metre high loudspeakers started to pump out reggae music. The volume almost hurt your ears. Angel had already met Darius and knew Zari from living in Bourbon.

Soon, the beat of an early Bob Marley hit playing on the loud speakers instantly set Angel's limbs moving. Predictably, the men opted out of the dancing. Their excuse was they had things to discuss. Hence, it was just the girls who skipped into the dancing crowd in the middle of the street. Zari and Angel moved together in harmony. Angel's body became flexible and turned and gyrated in union with the music. Her hands punched the air. Her head went back and a smile formed on her lips. It was evident that she felt at one with the music.

Wendell and Darius watched the two women in silence for a few seconds. Angel wore some dark, baggy shorts. Her over-sized T-shirt declared that she loved Miami; her substantially-sized ear-rings smacked against her long neck.

'Didn't I see you in a T-shirt like that?' asked Darius.

'Same one. I gave it to her.'

'Have to say it looks much better on her than it ever did on you, even though it's probably six sizes too big for her.'

'She'll be able to buy her own in a few weeks, when we go to the Vacation Home Fair,' shouted Wendell over the tumult.

A reggae mix replaced Bob Marley on the immense speakers. The girls continued to dance and their limbs flowed with its rhythm, their forms expressing their joy of the music. Their hips revolved from side to side, as their figures sank slowly towards the tarmac and then circled up again.

'Nice. Cute.' said Darius, 'I hope that she moves like that for you.'

111

'Each time,' smiled Wendell. 'She's quite something, isn't she? She's as cool as the morning. She's not your usual female. She's different and she's proud of the fact that she's different. That girl's a very strong character. She sure likes a challenge. Determined, but a lot of fun as well! One of our dates, she asked me to take her to the zip line. Can you imagine? Most women would have asked to go to an expensive restaurant. Not her.'

Darius scrutinised his boss. He could see his was very taken by his latest conquest. 'How did she manage to persuade you to give her the job?'

'She didn't persuade me, I offered her the job. I think that she could be very useful at the vacation home fairs. There's one coming up in Miami soon. She'll attract the men and be persuasive with the women clients. Business School has given her a buzz. She knows just where she's going that one!'

'One thing's for sure, Damien will make a line for her!'

Wendell smirked. 'Christ no! He came on a bit strong with her yesterday. Angel told him to get lost. She doesn't want to know him. She made it clear that she is only there to work for him, nothing else. She really got his back up yesterday. He went into his office and sulked. Damien can take setbacks in business, but he can't tolerate to be turned down by a woman that he's got the hots for.'

'Man, wish I'd been there.'

'Laverna thought it was rich. I can see she will be taking lessons from our little Miss Angel.'

'Dell, I get the feeling that you like her.'

'Sure, I've been seeing her for over a month. That's three weeks longer than the average woman I've dated on the island.'

As the song faded again, Angel beckoned to the two men to join them for the next dance. She blew them each a kiss over her hand. Wendell finished his rum and put the plastic beaker down on the nearest trestle table.

'Darius, who can resist an invitation like that?' Wendell strode towards the madness of writhing bodies in the middle of Doublon d'Or Main Street.

13 As one door closes..........

JR - 2006/7

My first Christmas away from Sainte Marie was not to be forgotten. After a manic time working at the 'The Golden Bell' in the lead up to Christmas, the 25th of December finally arrived. Where does all that money to spend on booze come from, I had to ask myself? After closing time, Zuze took me to meet her parents and to share their Christmas meal. It was a wonderful, memorable experience. Zuze hadn't exaggerated when she told me they lived in cramped conditions. Even with the sofa bed moved out, there was very little space for the six hungry people sharing the meal. Two of her parent's friends had joined them.

The contrast of the frenzy of the pub to that of the Kaminski home was a marked one. They kept to the Christmas traditions of their home land. The dining table was decked with straw under the table cloth. There was a Nativity scene on the sideboard. What with that, six chairs, a twinkling decorated tree, tinsel and decorations strung across the room, six adults, and pieces of furniture all squashed into the limited space, it was very cosy and intimate. They took it in turns to explain to me about the Polish way that Christmas was celebrated; and I told them a little of what I had been used to at that time of the year. We all started by wishing one another season's greetings. Then came all the traditional Polish Christmas food. It was all amazing! There was just so much of it. They served twelve different dishes, apparently one for each of the apostles. Surprisingly, there was no turkey. In fact, there was no meat at all. There were three lots of fish and then lots of different vegetable dishes. The food just kept on coming, but I couldn't do justice to all of it.

As the wine flowed and inhibitions faded, Zuze's mother, Mrs Kaminski, asked me, as she topped up my wine glass, 'Well JR, how do you like living in London?',

Being forewarned by Zuze where this could lead, I thought carefully about how I replied.

'It's still all very new, I still see myself as an observer,' I replied.

'It must be very unlike your life at home,' added her husband.

'Sure, the culture, history and modern environment here are very different. Those are things I love about London,' I said, 'but there are some similarities. For example, both are places of extremes.'

'What do you mean?' asked Zuze.

'Back home, I live in a small wooden house. Here, some would say it's not much bigger than a garden shed. My Mom and me, we don't have much, and some islanders have even less than us. They live in very run down conditions, you might even say squalor. Sometimes right next to this, you get homes that are worth hundreds of thousands, even several millions of dollars. There is a great divide. I see London is much the same. Naturally, it's a much bigger picture; it's on an immense scale. But on Sainte Marie you also have a few haves and a lot of have nots. We see it in the pub, don't we Zuze?'

'Yes,' she confirmed, 'there are some who think nothing of spending several hundred on bottles of champagne, which they piss away an hour later. Then others who can't even afford a second pint.' Trying to change the conversation, Zuze finished by asking, 'JR, did you enjoy the herring and apple?'

But her mother was insistent, she wanted to keep the topic going, even though she was getting cold looks from her daughter. The rest of the group remained silent. 'We know that there are all sorts here. But, we find that London isn't liberal, it is dominated by a certain class of people. In

English, I think you say elitism. So, do you think you will fit in here?' asked her mother, 'I believe your course at the LSE is three years.'

'I know that I'll have to adapt. I've already had to do so, but surely you have to do that where ever you go. London has its problems. But what capital city doesn't. Me, I have to remain positive. My first few weeks away from home were very difficult. I had to keep a positive attitude because I want to be here. I need to be here. I need London and the LSE to change my old life. I need them to show me the path to a new one.'

It was as if Mrs Kaminski was ignoring what I'd just said. I don't think I'd said what she wanted to hear. She was determined to make her point. 'Do you think that you have been welcomed here though JR?' persisted Mrs Kaminski.

'Zuze can back me up on this, working in the pub, you met a real cross-section of society. Most are likeable and have been very friendly. But, of course there are always the exceptions.'

'You haven't heard any racist comments against you then?'

'Mum give it a break, it's Christmas Eve. You're getting a bit heavy here.'

The coloured lights flashed on and off repeatedly on the artificially frosted Christmas tree. I tried to lighten things up by saying, 'My old Mom used to tell me that people like that need to get their heads sorted out. They are unhappy folks, self-deluded, trapped in their own little worlds, with their brains too full of false fantasies about themselves.' However, I failed. Fortunately, Zuze and her dessert succeeded in doing so.

'Who's for some Kutia (wheat berry and dried fruit pudding)?' she asked and then went on to explain which ingredients had been used to make it. Mrs Kaminski remained silent for a few seconds, and then continued her

116

role as the good hostess and started to serve out the Kutia, which she explained had been made for many centuries in Eastern Europe. Afterwards, the meal continued in a much more unruffled atmosphere.

When Zuze and I left the tiny, hot apartment together, we returned to my room. As we walked back there, we carried on the discussion about the Polish community's feeling of oppression. We put forward our differing opinions of how to cope with it. Zuze said that she had liked my Mom's way of describing racists as self-deluded, negative thinking people. She told me she would remember that and hoped that she would look at them rather differently. I tried to cajole her into thinking more positively about being in Britain and not to let the problems get her down. I made her promise not to change her name to something more British, as she was threatening to do in order to help with her job applications. I also made her promise not to give up trying to find a more suitable job.

We cuddled up together under my duvet, and suddenly the problems of London were forgotten and we celebrated Christmas in our own very private way. I whispered to Zuze that I was very pleased that I had her as a friend and lover for my very first Christmas in Britain. I told her she gave me confidence and made me feel wanted. In return, Zuze told me that I had made her Christmas the best ever.

$$\$\$\$$$

After my exams in January, we celebrated by visiting the Tate to see the newly acquired Turner paintings. I adored the opportunity to envelope myself in so much culture and history, something that was rather lacking at home. After seeing Turner's amazing storms on canvas, we opened the doors to exit the building, Zuze and I discovered a London storm, a world full of white stuff. It was a first for me! The snowflakes were falling heavily and there was a covering of snow everywhere, making the

117

usually noisy capital a quiet and cleaner looking world. But good Lord, the cold! As we ran to the underground station, I can still remember the bitter chill of the wind and my hands hurting with the icy cold temperatures. The next day it was difficult to get to the LSE, the roads were chaotic. It may decorate the city with a bewitching veil and look great in photos, but for me the snow is a purgatory that bites at your body and inconveniences everyone.

Suddenly, Zuze was no longer there. She was no longer in the kitchen at The Golden Bell creating chocolate mousse or slicing potatoes. Just after the Easter break, the inevitable happened; she got one of the jobs I'd been encouraging her apply for. She became the assistant events co-ordinator in a four star hotel near Heathrow Airport. I was pleased for her, but I missed her enormously. We saw one another a couple of times a week for about another month. I went to see her at the hotel and she came back to the pub to see me some evenings. Gradually though, the visits became less frequent and then she found herself a room to rent nearer the airport. Then she got herself another boyfriend. Her exit from my life left a big gap in it. We had shared so much. I felt very much alone again. But this time, I started to spend more time at the LSE; first in the library, then the cafeteria. Then I joined a music club, and a club called 'Itchy Feet' for backpacking and walking weekends around Britain and Europe. I even signed up for a cheap weekend in Paris at the end of the summer break. I started to get to know more of my fellow students. Then, very quickly the end of my first year was looming up.

I had two months in front of me without lectures and without Zuze. Lil, who I suspect felt even sorrier for me after Zuze left, offered me full time work over the summer period. I took it. The only things that were in my diary were the visit of my old mother and my weekend in Paris.

I don't really know how my mother had scraped the money for the fare together, but she had. I got a special deal from Lil for her to use one of the bed and breakfast rooms and I said that I would cover the cost from my wages. My Mom wrote to say that she was so excited about seeing me again and discovering all the places I had told her about in my letters.

I took the airport bus to meet her from her flight. She seemed to take forever to come through the arrivals gate. Then I saw her. She was looking all around, trying to find me amongst the crowds. I waved and my Mom walked slowly towards me.

'JR it really ya?' she asked. I assured that it was and gave her a big hug.

'Ya seems so different. Ya hair, it all gone. Ya'ze all growed up. Just look at ya!' she exclaimed. Then, I could have guessed it, she started to cry. 'Oh, sweet Jesus, ya just so changed. Ya looks like a man, not my little JR,' she sobbed.

'It has only been ten months Mom,' I told her. It had only been ten months, but I knew that I was not the same JR who had left Sainte Marie just that relatively short time ago. I had left as a child, a child who had been satisfied with chasing dogs down the beach and exploring with a curiosity the marine world of fish, sea urchins and jelly fish. Then, just ten months on, after reading millions of words in books, magazines and pamphlets, living a thousand varied experiences, and meeting hundreds of individuals very unlike me, I had changed into an adult who knew more or less which direction he was going in.

My mother settled in immediately at The Golden Bell. Fortunately, Lil and Mom hit it off big time. I thanked Lil later for making my Mom feel like a VIP. I'm not sure what they found to talk about for those ten days that my mother was there, but they seemed to talk non-stop when they were together. Naturally, I was frequently the topic of conversation.

119

She told Lil what a difficult child I had been. I would take no mind of her list of instructions about doing the chores around the house and my homework. She explained how as she had left for work she would call to me, 'JR ya not to forget to feed dem chickens. And pick up all dem eggs.'

Or she would force the broom into my hands with instructions, 'JR afores ya go to school, ya go clean dat porch. But God give me strength Lil, he not do de work.'

'Well, despite what people say, this leopard definitely seems to have changed his spots.' Lil told my Mom. 'He has worked really hard for me'.

'I real glad he change, cos I thinks he be the death of me.' Not wanting to let the topic drop she continued, 'You knows Lil, I gets him a job, for de vacation, working on de sea. What he do? He runs out on it. He leave after three week. I tells him dat money real useful. He not thinks of me. He a real punk kid. I tells him a real spoilt brat!

'Yes, it's tough bringing up a kid by yourself,' sympathised Lil.

'Dey not all difficult like JR! He been a real WOS! A bloody waste o' space! Jus' like his father!' she complained.

'You know what, I think he'll turn out all right. You wait and see, you'll be proud of him when he's an accountant. He'll be able to look after you.'

'I hopes ya right Lil.'

I remembered how I rarely had heeded my mother's demands. As a school child, I was totally self-indulgent. I would sneak out of the house and grab a stick from our front yard. I would then beat my way through the dense vegetation; go banging on neighbours doors and running my stick down their wooden shutters to make as much clatter as possible. I'd then leg it as fast as I could to the old jetty, grinning and well-pleased with myself. There were always kids there to enjoy life with. There were boys my own age to chase lizards, geckos or each other up coconut palms; run down the beach after stray dogs; and turn somersaults off the old jetty into the warm sea.

My preferred amusement had been to discover the fishy world under the ocean. I loved to pester the silver flashes of jacks as the schools all turned simultaneously this way and that, seemingly without a leader's warning. I loved to watch the behaviour of the various parrot fish with their stripes and spots; and to lift up rocks to disturb the toad fish or the frog fish from their hiding places. Occasionally, we saw turtles. Sometimes, we dived for coins that tourists threw into the waters for us to retrieve. From the sea bed below the structure of the wharf, I would look up and see the dapples of sunlight filtering through the constantly moving waves, and the vague shapes one could detect above the water. I relished that fishy underworld. I felt it was a part of me. I had a snorkel that I had 'acquired' from the beach. We swam in our underwear. My mother's miserable wages didn't run to such niceties as swimming trunks in those days. Having retrieved the nickels and dimes, we would immediately spend our 'treasure'. We'd dash to the Daily Bakery to buy a 7UP, gulp it down greedily and then use the cans as footballs for as long as their rigidity allowed.

To this day, I feel ashamed to admit that it wasn't my mother's reprimands that straightened out my head. Though bless her, she tried real hard. I confessed to Lil that perhaps I had been a little slow to help around the house.

But I digress. The palaces, art galleries and museums of London had to be on the list of things to show to my Mom. Buckingham Palace. The Tower of London. The Houses of Parliament. We did the lot. I knew most of them fairly well by then. And of course, it was important that she shared the majestic buildings and the enormity of the LSE. She was rather over-awed by everything. Mom told me that London was nothing like she had imagined. During her visit, I realised that our relationship had changed. It was

121

noticeable to me that she was no longer the mother who tried to direct my mind and behaviour; she had become more of a friend. She was more inclined to accept advice from me.

The last evening, Lil went to town and organised a special meal for the three of us. She had arranged for us to be served all the dishes that she knew were my favourites. We laughed and joked and my mother admitted that even though I'd been a problem, she still missed me. She told Lil that it was only because she worked in a large hotel that I had gained my scholarship to go to the London School of Economics. She had persuaded the hotel to sponsor me. On Sainte Marie, it's not what you know, but who you know.

As the evening came to an end, Lil told Mom that she would be very welcome to return the following year. I presume out of politeness, my mother returned the offer and said that Lil would also be very welcome to visit her in Sainte Marie. Strangely enough, Lil actually took up the offer some time later and went to explore my tropical paradise and to visit my mother. I believe she went in order to get away from her difficult home circumstances and the pressure of work. I found it difficult to imagine her in our tiny Creole cottage and Lil using my tiny bedroom with its old creaky bed and the louvered shutters overlooking the Caribbean Sea. I was sorry to see my Mom go. I knew that most probably I wouldn't see her for at least another year. Although I missed her, I had my trip to Paris and the new term to look forward to.

14 Finding the Right Solution

Damien - Autumn 2010

'Fine,' he thought, 'I look fine. In fact, better than fine.' Damien Janes looked at his reflection in the large mirror hanging on the wall of his air-conditioned office. He ran his fingers through his short, light brown, spiky hair several times. He had recently had it cut so that the top stood up at ninety degrees from his scalp. He liked it. He considered that it made him look younger. He inspected his shaven chin, his cheeks and then his teeth in his mirror image. He straightened his designer shirt and tightened his belt. He thought that he didn't look bad for a man of his age. It was a pity that he was only going to the construction site at Fortune Bay.

In the middle of his scrutiny, his mobile rang. He checked the number on the phone display. It was Darius at the construction site. He told Damien that the supplier from Miami was there waiting to see him. Darius had picked the supplier up from the airport and taken him directly to Fortune Bay. He had already been there half an hour.

'I've been busy Darius. I'll be there in fifteen minutes.'

Janes checked in the reception area that everything in the office was running smoothly. He made another couple of calls. Sunglasses were donned. Iridescent bronze lenses masked his eyes. Then he set off in his 4X4 for Fortune Bay. He had made this journey literally hundreds of times. The car headed away from the commercial area of the town, bound for the very north of the island. He drove through the upmarket residential area. The impressive houses stood alone in large plots. Each home had its own identity. Each property was planted with its own meticulously manicured tropical garden. Damien knew each of the houses by heart. What's more, after several years on the island, he knew many of the people who lived inside them. He could even imagine what might be happening in some of the large, grand villas.

After the luxury houses, the landscape changed dramatically. He turned down a very uneven track, full of ruts, bumps and dips. His 4X4 slowed to a walking pace. As he descended the hill, he could see the bay in front of him. The state of the track had deteriorated immensely since the building work had started. There must have been hundreds of heavy goods vehicles that had passed that way delivering building materials to Fortune Bay.

He parked on a rough area of land next to the building site. A jungle of undergrowth camouflaged the activities behind it. The site had become very muddy and churned up with the recent rain. Doc Martins replaced his handmade leather Derby shoes. Squelch, squelch they went through the mud to the site office. The sticky air was almost humid enough to cut. He surveyed the partly finished villas and apartments that were emerging from the mire. His arrival was acknowledged by local tradesmen who busied themselves with concrete, wood or glass. Pride flushed through him. Three quarters of the units had been sold. Selling property had become part of his being. It had given him everything he now owned. It had given him his boat, his cars, his home, even his new friends. He was aware that he had changed since he had been on the island. He thought differently. He knew he behaved differently because of the two projects that he had been involved in. He lived, slept and ate selling holiday property. His mind was now trained to look at a building and see a balance sheet of how much it would cost to construct it. And very importantly, how much money he could make out of it.

He reached the small Portakabin site office. The supplier was drinking his second coffee. As there were no major suppliers of building materials on island, the materials all had to be imported in containers from the States.

'Hi, DJ. You doing OK? I've had a quick look around and things seem to be going fairly smoothly. I talked to your site manager briefly. He said everything is good. So, what can we do for you this time?' asked Greg, the construction material supplier.

'Yeah, the site manager, that's my cousin Rick. Good guy! He knows his stuff.'

'Keeping it all in the family then,' laughed Greg, 'what's his work background?'

'He worked for a large construction company in Britain. Anyway,' said Damien wanting to change the subject, 'I have a list of the supplies we will need very soon. You can see that the apartment blocks are well on the way. First on the list are the casement windows and slider windows for the bedrooms and lounges.'

'You need hardwood frames, either Oak or Meranti, just the same as the ones in the villas. The price depends on the dimensions.'

'I was thinking that we would go for something a lot cheaper. The last lot, with the import duty, were too high budget.'

'I wouldn't recommend it DJ. You need the site to look uniform. Most importantly, you must have frames that won't warp in this climate. The soft wood, spruce frames might only last four or five years before they need to be replaced. You've seen what the heat and the rain can do to soft woods!'

'Greg, I don't care if they only last four years. That won't be my problem. The owners will have to pay to replace them themselves if they are rotten. Spruce windows it will be and I'll get them all painted. The owners won't know the difference. That'll more than halve the cost.'

'I assure you there will be lots of owners that WILL know the difference DJ. People who can afford to buy villas in the sun usually know chalk from cheese. They aren't stupid; you won't be able to fool them for very long. This may come back and bite you. Plus the buildings have to be inspected by the Department of Works,' declared Greg. He was trying hard to be persuasive, but he knew he couldn't make Janes buy the most appropriate materials.

'Do you want this order or not Greg? We can always find another company to supply us with the stuff. I've told you, I'm sticking with the spruce windows,' said Damien, raising his voice.

The meeting went on in this fashion. Greg gave Damien sound advice. Damien refused to accept it. He continually went for the cheapest option; the most unsuitable option. Greg became exasperated. He felt all of this was very frustrating, unprofessional and short sighted. Damien was, after all, only a salesman. He was not an expert in construction in the tropics. Greg quickly gathered that he was wasting his breath. Damien Janes was adopting a frugal approach across the board. Heaven only knows why! This man was some kind of deluded fool. Greg knew how much the villas were selling for. There should be plenty in the money pot to pay for the best quality materials. He drew his own conclusions as to where all the cash was doubtless going.

After a couple of hours, Greg's back was really up. He had his order. But, it certainly was not the one that he had hoped for. As a result, he didn't feel he wanted to hang around socialising with Damien. He asked if Darius could take him to his next appointment. As he left, he momentarily watched a couple of workers. They were supposed to be building the walls of the spa. They were laughing and joking. They were not concentrating on the task in hand. In his opinion, their work was trashy. He said nothing. There was nobody there supervising them. And Damien, he wouldn't know whether it was a mess or not.

After Greg had left, Damien wanted out of the muggy Portakabin. He started a tour of the site. He wanted to come up to speed on the site's progress. He stopped at one of the near-completed beach front villas. His cousin Rick was there talking to one of the foremen. Plumbing was the matter in hand.

'We were talking about the plumbing contractor DJ. He is scheduled to leave here tomorrow,' explained Rick. 'We really need to keep him for another week because we haven't pressure tested his work yet. We don't know if all the plumbing functions properly in these villas.'

'Another week, just to test his work,' said Damien 'No way! That'll cost us another slab more money. You can test it Rick, it can't be that difficult.'

'No way, DJ! I can't do that. I don't have the equipment. The plumber's team does. It'll only take a few more days. He has the equipment to find out if there are any leaks or blocked pipes and so on,' pronounced Rick.

'I'm sure it will be fine,' proclaimed Damien. 'He's a reliable workman. We will NOT be keeping him here for another week.'

Rick, by then, was feeling rather short-tempered. 'It may be a dammed site easier and cheaper in the long run Damien.'

The foreman had listened to the dialogue in silence. He then interrupted the proceedings. 'You know boss, he right. There could be all sorts of problems there.'

Damien started to turn and marched away from the two workers. 'I've told you that it will be all right. We are not dishing out more dollars for the plumbing team for another week.' He carried on walking and stomped his muddy boots back towards the Portakabin. He wanted to make a run from the situation he found himself in. He felt vulnerable and threatened. Janes had an aversion to situations where he was not totally in control.

'Boss, I needs a word with you about something else?' asked the foreman, hastening after Damien. His boss, who was still good and mad after the plumbing confrontation, gave his foreman a scowl.

'Now what?'

'Well boss, I'z a bit worried.'

He explained his workers had discovered that their social security payments had not been paid for the previous couple of months' work. They had all been paid their wages, and the social security deductions were showing on their wage slips. Damien became very fidgety and he edged away. He could do without this additional confrontation.

The foreman continued that last week, one of his workers, after being ill, had been to the Social Security Office to find out why his sickness benefits had not been paid. He was told his social security payments had never been paid by his employer. The foreman asked if Janes knew any reason why this should be. Damien clenched his jaw. He had had enough altercations for one day. He would put a stop to this interrogation.

'You'll have to sort that out with Wendell, Mr Thorner,' he said in an irritated tone. 'He is the one who deals with all the wages. Why would you think that it was anything to do with me?' he added aggressively. 'I can't sort everything out.'

The good day was turning into one hell of a day. Damien Janes felt ready to have a punch at something or somebody. He was in dire need of a drink. He returned to the empty Portakabin, entered, and slammed the door shut. Inside the air was roasting. The foreman knew better than to follow him in. Very quickly sweat exuded from every pore. The small fan oscillated ineffectively one way, then the other. Damien slumped into the well-worn office chair. He could feel his chest tightening. His muscles were tensing and his heart racing. Perspiration made his spiky hair style cling to his head. Sweat discoloured his expensive shirt which stuck to his damp skin. The office was a refuge from the foreman, but the interior sizzled his temper and fried his cool. He needed to calmly think through the monetary problems that were starting to slap him in the face. He wasn't sure which way to turn, who to talk to or confide in. He had to find a rapid way out. The resort had to be finished. It had to be finished soon. There was very little money left to do it!

The temperatures in the office became too much for him. He trudged his way to the beach and dropped onto the hot sand. A breeze wafted from the calm blue waters. It immediately cooled his skin and his temperament. He inhaled the fresh, clean air. His head started to clear. On Sundays, the locals came to picnic on the sand and swim in the protected bay. That day there didn't appear to be anyone else around. From his sitting position, he glanced up and down Fortune Bay. No, he was wrong. Further down the beach he could see somebody clearing vegetation. The area being cleared had once been a sugar plantation. A man seemed to be making a clearing for some reason or other. Janes could hear the man's rhythmic hacking at the foliage with his machete. Janes assimilated the sounds for several minutes. Slowly a smile spread across his face. 'That was it!' he thought. 'It was simple. Why hadn't he thought of it before? That was the solution.'

$$\$\$\$$$

Several weeks later, Damien was back on Fortune Bay beach again. This time in a very different guise. He went as a family man. He was clad in shorts, T-shirt and flip flops. His iridescent sunglasses were perched on the top of his head. He was carrying a large cool box. He was being followed closely by his two children, each of whom was carrying snorkel and flippers wrapped in a towel. Donna, his wife, was bringing up the rear.

It was Sunday. On the island, Sundays were sacrosanct for the inhabitants. Everything stopped at the weekend. Sunday was a day for going to church and then relaxing with friends and the family. And what better place to relax than on the beach? By the time that Damien and his family arrived, there were already several local families there. Several children and self-conscious mature, well-rounded mums were paddling, flicking water at one another near the water's edge. The really organised families had placed folding tables and chairs in the shade of the palm trees. Everyone was equipped with their obligatory large, bright blue plastic cool boxes.

The main aim for Damien's family visit was no different from the other families that were there. They wished to enjoy the pleasures of the beach and to swim in the warm protected waters. However, he couldn't help himself briefly showing his family the progress that had been made with the resort. His children had made a few expected, appreciative noises about the villas. 'Great Dad, they're real awesome. Nice Dad! Now can we go for a swim?'

They were far more interested in enjoying the liberty of the sea and the sand. Looking at houses was not cool. But Donna, the dutiful wife, displayed her delight in the beach front villas and showed her appreciation of all that was pointed out to her. 'I really love the space in the kitchen DJ.' Or, 'You have done a fabulous job with the en-suites darling.' Donna made all the right noises.

The Janes family found a spare palm tree to install themselves under. Mum and kids were eager to throw their bodies into the embrace of the cooling sea. Damien opted for the shade, the view and a chilled beer from his box.

The outing to the beach had been Damien's idea. He felt that he deserved a well-earned day off. Recently, his life had been dominated by organising and attending

130

meetings. He was very satisfied with the way most of them had turned out. His ideas for the future had been discussed. His game plan was already beginning to turn from imaginative thoughts into actuality. His idea to start a new development was under way. Wendell had easily been persuaded to draw up the new proposal to take to the bank. The architect was busy drawing up plans and checklists. These would be submitted to the Ministry of Development and Housing as soon as they were finished. During the last few weeks, Janes had virtually lived at the office in Anse Argent. It had all taken over his life. Examining various possibilities and considerations relevant for his third project became the reason he got up each morning. All available phones had been in constant use. He was now confident that the first villas at Fortune Bay would very soon be finished. They would be completed with an influx of money from their third project.

Contrary to a few weeks ago, Damien felt far more comfortable with himself and life. He felt extremely chuffed with himself as he had master minded the whole thing. He had found a solution to finishing project two - Fortune Bay. His greed having caused the dilemma in the first place was not even a consideration for him. He didn't see a problem with the fact that he had had his fingers in the till. He thought of it as his till. Naturally, he had only temporarily solved their financial crisis. He had been able to divert funds from management fees at Diamond Point, the time-share resort. The repairs that were needed there would not be done yet. This, as well as investment money for 'Sapphire', project three, meant they were solvent again.

Damien Janes sat under the palm watching his family in the sea. Life at home had returned to its everyday routine. Things had quietened down. Donna had started to work at the Anse Argent office. She now had far more distractions in her life. She had less time to think about personal problems. Donna had replaced Angel in the office. Angel had gone to work in Miami. She had been snapped up by a Miami real estate agent who she had met at a Vacation Home Fair. Angel had been very good at selling property, as well as being very organised. Damien felt put out that his relationship with Angel had not been what he would have liked. Angel had missed out because she didn't want to start an out-of-office relationship with him. Even so, he missed her methodical, business-like manner around the office; and her in a clinging dress really brightened up the office. Donna, on the other hand, was fine for doing the secretarial work and 'meeting and greeting' potential clients, but those were her limitations. Donna's presence had its plus side, but there was a big down side as well. Whilst in the office, he now felt a like a gold fish in a bowl. Being there was claustrophobic. He imagined that he was constantly being watched. Damien was no little fish. He was his own man, a shark! Hence, he tried to be out of the office as much as possible. He organised meetings elsewhere, well away from his wife's scrutiny.

Damien finished his beer. He threw down his empty can on to his beach towel. His flip-flops joined the can. He progressed, as fast as the dry sand would allow him, up the beach. His family were all face down in the water exploring the submarine wilderness beneath them. He couldn't resist taking another look at the roughly cleared area where the next planned project would be built. He gazed at the mass of cut tree stumps and tangled underbrush which had been roughly torn up by an excavator. He could visualise the buildings. He could almost see the complex in his mind, the planned apartments with their swimming pools that were now proposed for this part of the bay. He was sure they would be easy to sell. He already had a few clients who were interested. The deposits from them would soon be coming in, together with loans from the bank. Seeing the plot again gave him a real buzz. He and Wendell would be making mega bucks from it and it would be all thanks to him.

Reluctantly, he turned back towards the shore line. He identified the backs of his wife and children turned to the sun whilst they shifted slowly through the tranquil, sparkling water. They were totally oblivious to his activities, lost in their underwater world. He thought that it was a pity that other aspects of his life weren't the same, so that he could get on and do what he liked in life, without being scrutinised by interfering busybodies.

He had revelled in his egotistical period of solitude and reflexion, but knew he was obliged to tag along with his family in their aquatic exploration before attacking their picnic lunch.

15 Snake in the Grass

Damien - Autumn 2010

Damien felt quite at home dining in smart restaurants. Usually, he dined either with prospective clients or with his new-found island friends. 'At the Water's Edge' was his preferred venue. It was expensive, which meant the clientele was mainly top-notch. It was a restaurant that attracted many of the local business people rather than the tourists. A wharf protruded from the restaurant into the bay. The music of lapping water was constant. The sides of the wharf were open, except for a wooden balustrade. Several gas torches had been installed there. At night, they sent arcs of light across the dark watery mirror of the bay. Dinghies were often illuminated. They chugged to and fro, carrying yatchies back and forth to their anchored boats. Routinely, boats laden with piles of laundry came into view. They ferried supplies to the large beach-front hotels. Fish were seduced into the glow of the torches. They jumped in the lit waves.

Damien had reserved a table on the wharf. He and his wife were dining with some ex-pat friends. That evening, he was dressed to impress. Navy blue silk shirt, suede shoes to match and trousers of white linen. A real peacock! He loved to be noticed. Next to this peacock, his wife was a mere sparrow dressed in a simple cotton dress. Damien insisted that they drive to the restaurant, though it was only a five minute walk from his home. Sartorially elegant men could not get dirt on their costly handmade footwear.

The ex-pat friends had expressed an interest in the resort at Fortune Bay. They had already been to see the progress with the beach front villas and seemed to be suitably impressed. They wanted to buy one as an investment and for the rental revenue. Consequently, Damien had suggested a social evening to try and iron out any concerns. Damien also wanted to propose his help with trying to finance the purchase.

The evening had started badly for Donna and Damien. They had had a bust-up before leaving the house. Damien had let slip that he would be going to Toronto with Dell for a property fair to promote their third project. He would be away for around a week. Donna had to hang around at home to look after the kids. She wouldn't be able to accompany him. Donna had heard rumours, from several sources, about what the two men were like together. She knew they would drink excessively. She had heard tittle-tattle about Wendell and Damien with the girly girls. As many girlies as possible.

'Toronto, I'd like to see Toronto. Why do you have to go with Dell?' shouted Donna. 'We could get somebody to look after the children and I could go. You and he will turn the week into another one of your 'whore tours' otherwise.'

'It won't be a 'whore tour' Donna. I'll be working most of the time! You don't know enough about the project. You are not a sales person. Dell is used to selling property.'

'You don't want to be with me anymore or the children! I'm only here to bloody well iron your fancy shirts and look after the children. You want to continually chase skirt. Do the bars; party and do the night clubs to pick up women. You have wanted a jet set life style since we came to Sainte Marie.'

'It's just not true Donna! You know I enjoy being with you and the children. It's just not practical for you to come to Toronto; end of story. Are you ready? We are supposed to be at the restaurant in ten minutes. Please try and be supportive. I'm hoping to sell Charles a property this evening.'

'You and your bloody villas! They have taken over your life Damien!'

'Don't you dare complain woman!' shouted Damien. 'It's what gives you your life style. The Caribbean, the

135

beach, a beautiful house with a pool; I've told you before, there are millions of women who would love to change places with you.'

'And you are checking them all out to find a replacement for me, I suppose!'

'Don't be so ridiculous! Just finish getting yourself ready.'

At the restaurant, it wasn't until the dessert course in the restaurant that Donna started to feel a little more relaxed. Her anger after her confrontation with Damien had begun to subside. She thoroughly enjoyed her three different chocolate crème brulées. Each spoonful tasted divine. She found pleasure in talking to their friends. They had recently visited Britain. They found a lot to talk about. When the coffee was served the ladies stayed at the table chatting. The men went to talk business at the bar. Donna almost felt pleased that the men had moved away. Damien was explaining to Charles how he knew somebody at an island bank who could organise a loan. Enough of a loan to purchase a villa with a bit left over to buy other things. Charles could have the new car he wanted. Donna felt this idea didn't sound quite legit. She felt she was better off not knowing about all of that. She hoped that Damien wasn't getting involved in something that wasn't above board.

The two wives leant over the wooden railings watching the fish jumping in the torch light. They chatted freely. The two women became engrossed in their conversation. The minutes slipped by pleasantly before Donna looked towards the bar. She could clearly see her husband with a women draped around his shoulder. A young attractive woman. Her temper immediately returned. She stared at the young female; it wasn't any one she recognised. Donna's mind emptied. She wasn't quite sure what she should say or do. Her companion had by then noticed the compromising situation Damien had got himself into.

'If you don't mind, I think I'm going to walk home. I'll leave Damien to drive the car.'

'No, no don't do that, go and see who it is. Donna, don't jump to conclusions.'

'It was good to see you and Charles again. See you soon.'

'But Donna...'

But, she was gone. Donna dashed past the threesome at the bar. She pushed out through the main door of the restaurant. A young waitress, in a long black apron, wished her a good evening. Donna didn't return a word. She hastened out of the restaurant grounds. Her eyes were stinging. Sobs clutched at her throat. Tears misted her vision and her path home. She clutched her bag tightly to her stomach. The passers-by went unnoticed. She was in pain and in turmoil. She was weeping for what she knew she had lost. Lost, never to be mended. She grieved for the close relationship she had had with her husband. Her security and that of her children, dissipated in just a few seconds. She felt as though her heart had been torn out of her. She felt like a wounded creature caught in a trap.

At the front door, Donna could not find her house keys. She rummaged in her hand bag. Confusion clouded her mind and her vision. She felt the dampness of her summer dress as her trembling hands held her bag in front of her. Keys found, she didn't even bother to wipe away the salty stream as she entered the house. The baby sitter came to the hall as she heard Donna enter. She stopped in her tracks. She took in the bloated red eyes of her employer.

'Oh Mrs Janes, don't cry,' she said. 'He not worth it.' She held Donna's hand. 'Mrs Janes, don't cry.' Donna didn't need to explain.

'Oh Gemma, what am I going to do?' Donna squeezed her hand.

'De wife, they always the last to find out. You needs to think real hard. You young. You can start again.' This made the tears recommence. She put her arm around Donna's shoulder. 'You like me to stay a bit?' offered Gemma kindly.

'No. No, that's very thoughtful,' Donna blotted her eyes with a tissue. It was soon sodden.

'De children is fine. Dey fast asleep. You sure you OK?'

'Thank you Gemma. I think I'll go to bed.'

Donna turned off the television and mounted the stairs. She checked on the children, and then went into her bedroom. She locked the door behind her. He definitely wasn't going to share the same bed as her tonight. She carelessly threw her clothes onto the couch at the end of the bed. She rapidly pulled on her cotton nightwear and threw back the sheets to get into bed. She froze. The tears stopped abruptly. She stood staring at her bed, their bed. And then she screamed. A boa constrictor was slowly moving on the white sheet. A very large boa constrictor! A writhing reptile exactly where she had been going to lie down. Another scream rose in her throat. Donna knew about this snake. She knew that it could leap in the air.

It made a fearful contrast. The wild against the man-made; a zigzag of a long dark brown body glistened against the stark white of the cotton bed linen. The saddle–like markings down the length of its body spread horror through Donna. The snake raised its elongated head and hissed at her. It then thrashed to the edge of the bed and flopped to the floor. Donna saw its yellow belly. It fell just in front of her bare feet. Donna's panic forced her to the door. By then, she had no breath to scream. She fumbled with the locked door. The key, the key in the lock wouldn't turn. Her hands were shaking too much. Her insides were churning. The snake thrashed around on the floor.

'Gemma, Gemma!' she shrieked. But Gemma had gone home. She had told her to go. She floundered with the key. At last it turned. The door opened. She pulled the key into her hand, slipped out onto the landing and slammed the door. She locked it from the other side. Donna rushed to the children's bedrooms. She had frequently seen local men with a constrictor wrapped around them like a living scarf. They took the risk in the hope of attracting snap happy tourists. They paid to have their photo taken with the creatures. She knew that they were not venomous. But she also knew that they suffocated their prey by wrapping themselves around it. Crushing and crushing the breath from their victim. With the children in the house, she was taking no chances.

'Wake up, wake up!' she yelled at the children. 'We have to leave. Leave now. We have to go. We must go to see Timmy next door.'

'But, mummy he will be asleep,' said the sleepy eyed Jade.

'Just get up Jade. Don't argue.' In exasperation, she shook her daughter. 'Do as you are told. Put on your slippers and go downstairs. We are going next door.'

Donna slammed the front door of her home behind her and the children. Despite the tropical temperatures, she was shaking with cold and fear. Her bare feet ignored the grazing textures of the drive and garden. She ushered her bewildered children through the gloom towards the light of her neighbours' house. When the door was opened, brightness illuminated Donna, in her strappy nightie and the children in their pyjamas and slippers. They were welcomed by an amazed Louisa, her neighbour. The drowsy children were soon embraced by the comfy sofas. Donna opted to recount her nightmare of an evening in a corner of the room away from their earshot. Slowly and hesitantly, with a trembling mouth, Donna detailed her reason for being there.

Louisa and her husband were islanders. They knew about the local vengeance and black magic of Sainte Marie. They were not so surprised when they heard about the Tet Chyenn (boa constrictor). They installed the two children in one of their spare bedrooms. Donna was given a large glass of rum and a dressing gown, before they started their explanation about island revenge and black arts. Donna failed to understand. Why it should happen to her?

'But what have I done to upset the islanders?' asked Donna

Louisa looked at her husband. They were reluctant to tell her. Unwilling to expose all that they had been privileged to recently. Gossip and rumours about her husband. They had anticipated what effect it could have on her. 'It's not you, my darling. It's Damien.'

Donna still did not comprehend.

Being as considerate as possible, they exposed some of the misdemeanours they knew about. Donna was aware that news travels fast on such a small island. Once one person knew, it didn't take long for it to race along the grape vine. They give a list of thing they had knowledge of; bad treatment of workers and unpaid social security payments. There were local suppliers who were struggling because their bills had not been paid. They had heard about building work going unchecked and using substandard materials at Fortune Bay. They understood that one bank's loan so far had not been reimbursed. They confessed that it didn't take a genius to add things up. There should be plenty of money for everything considering how expensive each unit was. The tales of Damien's womanising were left untold.

Donna's head sunk lower and lower. But the list of offences had clarified her mind; had stopped the flood of tears. She finally masked her face with her hands. She muttered through them that she had wondered about things herself. Damien currently told her very little about his work. She was distraught. How could her husband descend to such depths? And how could she live with such a man? She told herself and her neighbours that she could not be a part of the cheating. The vivid image of the

140

powerful snake replayed in her mind. The danger contorted in front of her feet. Such acts of revenge put her children at risk.

'How could he use the islanders so badly? I've never liked snakes. But at least you know that to expect from them. I never expected this from Damien. He's more deadly than that boa constrictor in my bedroom. That's it!' choked Donna. 'I've had enough. The horror of the constrictor, I can't take any more of it. Of Damien, his deception and lies. It's finished.'

To which her neighbours kindly assured her, that in fact, it was far from finished. This would be just the beginning of what would be a very difficult time for her and her children.

16 The Start of Another Life

Cassandra - Late 2010

Cassandra raised her head to the sky and stared at the canopy above her. A canvas painted a bright turquoise blue. That day, the colour seemed uniform, without a single fleck of white cloud. Where the heavens met the horizon, the sea shaded to a darker tone of turquoise broken by flashes of white breakers. She briefly reflected about home. There were flat grey skies and rain there. The December sunlight seared her bare arms. From behind her she could hear a faint rustling. The vegetation fluttered and whirled in the sea breeze. Before her, lazy waves lapped upon the rosy-coloured flat sand.

She had waited for this moment for what seemed like a very long time. The anticipation of it had kept her going to work every day, to a job that she really didn't like very much. It was so stressful. She had waited almost eighteen long months to feel this velvety warmth enveloping her. Waited for the blinding sun to make her squint without her sunglasses. She sensed an internal exhilaration. She was back on the beach at Fortune Bay.

Little had changed there. Now, in front of the strip of tropical plants, there were a few wooden and palm leaf 'parasols'. A line of simple structures stood waiting for those wanting to hide from the sun's rays. The rest was natural. Everything was just as she remembered it. Except, of course, concealed behind the vegetation were the new villas. Each had their small gated garden which backed onto the beach. One of these would soon belong to her and Mark.

Three weeks prior to their departure Janes informed them that their villa wasn't ready. She had been very disappointed. Mark had been furious. Janes had e-mailed to say that there were a few interior things to be finished off. Some of the furniture had not been shipped in from the States. The e-mail told them that arrangements had been made for them to stay in the time share resort, Diamond Point. Cassandra and Mark had visited Janes' first project in Anse Argent before. She wasn't too sure about staying there. However, now that she was back on Sainte Marie, her love of the island had returned and she still felt euphoric about their new adventure.

They had come to inspect the progress on their property. Mark was currently talking to the site manager, someone called Rick, whilst waiting for Mr Janes to arrive. He was already forty minutes late.

Arriving at the site, they were in for a bit of a surprise. They could immediately see the lack of progress with the complex. The main swimming pool was currently just a very large cemented hole in front of the apartment blocks. The decking around it hadn't even been started. The bar and restaurant were only at the foundation stage. The exteriors of the villas hadn't been painted and the plants for the landscaping were still at the island nursery in Bourbon. The whole resort lacked tarmacked roadways.

There was a large team of construction workers working diligently. They were concentrating on the apartments and communal buildings. Cassandra noticed that many of them were not local. They were speaking in Spanish to one another. They had done the tour with the site manager. Cassandra could not fail to notice that Mark became more and more agitated by what he saw. At the time of their purchase, Janes had assured them that everything would be completed in eighteen months. That time had elapsed, but Rick was telling them that it would be at least another six months before it would be ready for guests. Rick started to explain in detail the agenda for each stage before completion. This had been when Cassandra had wandered off to the beach.

She was impatient to see their villa, or rather the villa that was seventy per cent theirs. They had yet to make the final payment. This would be paid when all the snagging had been done. Then they would finally get the keys. It was going to mark the start of a new stage in their life. They hoped to go to the island for a few weeks every year. When they weren't there, they had been promised a rental income. A rental income to help pay for the high condominium fees, internal repairs and, last but not least, their forthcoming retirement.

Cassandra sat herself on the warm, shifting sand. She stretched her sandaled white feet in the direction of the sea. She took a handful of the heated sand. It ran through her fist like that in an hourglass. Cassandra reflected on how lucky she felt. Lucky to be able to buy a property in the Caribbean. It was something that was beyond many people's dreams. But, it had only been possible because of her divorce. The settlement at the end of her first marriage, at first, had not atoned for all the sleepless nights. The nights of grieving, mourning the past, and anxiety about her future. The money had not recompensed her for her shattered life, her tormented dreams. She had loved Grant so much, too much. The divorce had traumatised her and made her lose all confidence. But then, thanks to her friends, she met Mark. The developing relationship with him had slowly, very slowly, masked and then blocked out the blackness that had become her existence after the marriage break-up.

Mark was so different from Grant. So different from her, but somehow, they seemed to get along. She had, at first, liked him because he made her laugh; something that she hadn't been able to do much after Grant had left her. She gradually learnt that, despite their differences, they saw much of the world from similar perspectives.

As Mark had his own home, they considered that the divorce settlement should be invested for their future. It had been Cassandra's idea to buy a secondary home abroad. Initially, Mark was reticent about the whole project. He had had concerns that the resort might never get built. Even so, he was very pleased to be back on the island. He was relieved to see for himself that the majority of the villas had been virtually finished.

The second hourglass of sand brought Cassandra out of her contemplative mood and made her recall that Mr Janes was very late for their appointment. She glanced at her watch and saw that he was, in fact, sixty-five minutes late. Late, even by 'island time'. She was disinclined to leave her haven on the beach. She forced herself upright, brushed the grains of sand off her shorts and wandered back to where she had last left Mark.

He was still talking to Rick. The topic of conversation had by then moved on to Rick's previous work in Britain. As Cassandra approached them she raised her eyebrows, shoulders and her hands. She simply asked 'Mr Janes?' Mark looked at his watch and discovered exactly how late Damien Janes was for their appointment.

'Well, we can't hang around here all day in the hope that Janes is going to turn up,' he said to Rick. 'It was good talking to you. Our holiday is too precious to waste it dallying here. If you could pass on the message to Janes that we are far from happy that he didn't even phone us. Well, he knows where to find us.'

With that they walked back to the hire car and drove back towards Anse Argent.

'A very interesting conversation,' explained Mark as they bumped their way along the unmade road heading away from Fortune Bay. 'I'll tell you more about it over lunch.'

They headed for Anse Argent marina. Cassandra's sandals made a clopping sound as she walked along the wooden boards of the quay. Lunch was to be in a little café they had discovered there. It had become one of their favourite haunts. There, they found a form of escapism from their mundane city lives. There was perpetually something to interest observers.

The display of boats seemed to change daily. These went from the multi-million dollar ocean cruisers down to simple little wooden fishing boats. They delighted in the odours and the sounds there. They inhaled the salty, sulphuric, fishy odour of the sea. Listened to the flapping of the rigging against the masts; and the continual splashing of the sea against the boats and the pontoons. The creaking from the wooden vessels as they rolled constantly with each incoming wave was music to their ears. There was always lots of toing and froing along the quays. Trolleys of supplies were frequently dragged to large cabin cruisers or motor yachts by the young crew. Cassandra and Mark knew they would never own their own boat, but they both took great pleasure in surveying other peoples' and the cinema of activities related to the island's marine life.

A wonderful aroma of baked bread welcomed them to the café. Fluttering sunshades, cost-effective garden furniture and nattering clients were installed on the boarded walkway. Cassandra and Mark sat themselves at a table in the middle of the café. Whilst deciding between a ham and pineapple Panini or a mozzarella and hamburger, Mark started to pass on what he had gleaned from Rick, the site foreman.

'I wasn't filled with confidence when I discovered that Rick had only had a minor job at a small house construction company in Britain,' explained Mark. 'I'm certain that he is not very qualified. I'm sure he's where he is, simply because he is Damien's cousin.'

'Oh no, that's all we need. That gives me a lot of faith in the building work.'

'Only time will tell. Rick is a nice enough man, but I'm not certain that he has sufficient experience for a project like Fortune Bay. He has quite a large team of workers to manage.'

'I noticed that some of the construction workers now are not islanders. There were some that I heard speaking Spanish. After all the reassurances we had from Mr Janes that the workers would be from Sainte Marie.'

'Mm, I know. I asked Rick about it. He said that they had had to get rid of some of the islanders, but he didn't go......' Mark stopped in mid-sentence. 'Christ, I don't believe it! Don't turn round. Janes is walking this way with his arm around an attractive young lady.'

'She is obviously more important to him than our appointment at Fortune Bay. What do we say if he sees us?'

Mark paused, 'He won't. He's turned to go to the car park. Anyway, he was too engrossed in their cosy conversation. What a cheeky bastard!'

'Well, that says a lot about him! We'll wait and see what excuses he can come up with. He's taking chances, isn't he? I thought that his wife and family lived on island.'

At that point, a smiling waitress came to take their order. Mark asked if she knew what the building along the quay was. He pointed to the white, two-storey building that Mr Janes had come out of. She explained immediately that it was the Anse Argent Yacht Club. Mark thanked her before ordering his hamburger and fries and a Caesar salad for his wife.

'The man is so unprofessional and just not serious,' remarked Cassandra as the waitress walked away with their order.

'Oh, I'm telling you, it all looked pretty serious to me,' smirked Mark.

A shady garden and a swimming pool called to them after lunch, so they retreated to Diamond Point. During their relaxing afternoon, they did receive a call from Janes. He told them that something very urgent had come up that he had just had to deal with right away. Mark, torn between a feeling of anger and amusement, said nothing on the phone about seeing him at the marina. He rescheduled the appointment for the following day, having decided that perhaps it was better to deal with the situation face to face.

'Something urgent came up,' mocked Mark as he turned off his phone. 'I bet it did! I wonder how you are going to worm your way out of this one Janes?' He started making a mental list of all the problems that he wanted to discuss with him at their next meeting.

Lazing around the pool, Cassandra soon started to talk to the person who was on the next sun lounger. From their dialogue, Cassandra learnt that Alice was a time-share owner of one of the apartments. Cassandra's book was soon neglected. She preferred to chat. The two middle aged women, being sociable human beings, exchanged info and compared notes. The afternoon was filled with their very different lives, the island, and its attractions. They both considered it very stimulating; and that they had spent a very pleasant afternoon together. Their men, on the other hand, preferred to pass their time either in the pool or soaking up the sun in silence, content that their wives were otherwise occupied. They only showed an interest when the topic of discussion turned to drinks together. Sundown drinks were organised with Richard and Alice. Cassandra would take the nibbles and Alice and Richard would supply the drinks.

Over pineapple daiquiris they watched the sun dip swiftly to the horizon. The sky took on shades of orange, red and then amethyst. The sea was transformed from topaz to tones of citrine and garnet. Tree frogs in the hotel gardens welcomed the dusk with their incessant night song. Their glasses chinked. They raised them to the end of another beautiful day.

Mark asked about Alice and Richard's investment in the time-share complex. They explained that they had bought a month's usage of the apartment. It was much cheaper than staying in a hotel each year. That year, they had also exchanged a fortnight with some other time share owners and gone to another Caribbean island. Generally, they felt that, up until then, it had worked out very well.

'Has to be said though,' explained Richard, 'that we are a bit concerned this visit. Things aren't running as smoothly as before. The manager who was here has left. The person who has replaced him doesn't seem to be here fulltime or as efficient. We have to pay an annual maintenance fee, which pays for any breakages or repairs in the property and for painting the exterior. This visit, there are several things that need to be repaired, including the roof. Also the television doesn't seem to be working. We are going to the developer's office to talk about it tomorrow. We'll let you know how we get on.'

'Who do you deal with?' enquired Cassandra.

'We usually speak to Damien Janes, but he doesn't seem to be available this week,' replied Alice.

'We can perhaps explain why that is,' informed Mark. He related the story about Janes and their appointment that he had failed to keep. Then, about seeing him with some eye candy in the marina. 'She was too young to be his wife,' commented Mark, 'and, the way they were wrapped around one another; it certainly wasn't a business colleague!'

'We have been told that his wife, Donna, has gone home with the children. We met his wife a couple of times. She used to help out in the office,' said Alice.

'Whilst the cat's away,' smirked Mark.

149

'Oh, we got the impression, when we talked to the hotel manageress here, that she wasn't coming back. It seems he has cheated on her too many times,' informed Alice.

'I know all about men that cheat and lie,' declared Cassandra in a low tone. 'Problem with them is, if they cheat and lie to their wife, they're a cheater in life too. It becomes a part of their nature. In lying, they diminish themselves; they lose their own self esteem. They seem to think that by having exactly what they want, they are improving their life. I feel they are doing the reverse. I don't understand why they think that people are stupid enough to be taken in by their fiction.'

They all turned towards Cassandra. There was a short silence; Mark tried to make signs to her that perhaps she was getting a bit emotional.

'I try to adopt a modern attitude towards deception,' continued Cassandra, 'but, for me, honesty shines through, even though it's maybe now considered rather old fashioned.' She then took on board the signals that Mark was making at her and tried to lighten up the conversation. 'I read somewhere, that Chinese women in Hong Kong have been proven not guilty of murder if they kill their unfaithful husbands. Only trouble is, they have to do it with their bare hands. Don't know how true it is!'

'Not stupid those Chinese! There aren't too many of their petite ladies who would have the strength to finish off a grown man. I've felt like killing Richard myself often enough,' joked Alice, 'but I think I'd resort to arsenic in his tea, rather than with my bare hands. But I'm planning to wait until he ups his life insurance premiums.'

Their laughter rang through the warm air of the dark garden. They had all failed to notice that twilight had fallen and the sky over the tropical plot had turned to the colour of lapis lazuli. It was littered with thousands of tiny, glistening stars. The choir of tree frogs continued their lively chant in veneration to the ascending moon.

The following day dawned just as beautifully as the previous one. But Cassandra and Mark's holiday spirit became more and more dampened as the day unfolded. The morning meeting with Damien Janes turned out to be one of disillusionment and disenchantment with him and his development company. It had started the previous evening over drinks and aperitifs. They felt concerned by the lack of management at Diamond Point and the deteriorating state of the buildings. They asked themselves if there might be a repeat performance of this at Fortune Bay.

They had laughed and joked, but the true picture of what was probably happening at Tropical Island Villas was gradually becoming unveiled to them. They were learning what sort of a character Damien Janes really was. They had also learnt a little about how the time share hotel was managed, or rather mismanaged. Suspicions about where their money, and that of the other investors was going, started to niggle. Alarm bells had started to ring. Initially, when Mark saw Janes in the marina the previous day, he had thought that he would go into their meeting the next day with all guns blazing. He had planned to ask what the hell was he doing missing their meeting because of a date with a woman. In fact, Mark didn't even mention it.

On arriving for the second time at Fortune Bay to inspect their beach front villa, Mark decided he was going to be cautious and so completely changed his strategy. He warned his wife to do the same. They wanted something from this man and his company. They had already paid him a considerable amount of money. They wanted their villa completed and so it was perhaps more prudent to stay on the right side of him.

Outwardly, during the visit, Janes was still the enthusiastic and the over-talkative sales person, full of promises and exaggerations, who they had encountered eighteen months before. He didn't even seem to notice the

151

couple's quietness and lack of interaction. They had established the previous day that the exterior of the villas had not been rendered. This gave them a very unfinished and unattractive appearance. But, when Mr Janes unlocked the front door and showed them in, Cassandra couldn't hide her delight in what she saw. The walls were not painted, but still a raw plaster colour. But the rooms were filled with light. They were all spacious. Best of all, from the sitting area, across the small garden, one could glimpse the beach and the sea. Cassandra could then imagine the final, furnished rooms with all the furniture that they had chosen in them.

'Oh, it will be so beautiful,' she enthused. 'It will be the most beautiful place I have ever lived in.' As soon as she said it, she thought that it must have sounded rather pathetic. But it was her instinctive reaction to seeing the inside of their villa for the first time. Janes seemed pleased at her reaction.

'When do you think that it will be ready to move into it?' Cassandra asked Mr Janes. 'We were so disappointed that it wasn't ready for this visit.'

This started a monologue from Janes about what there still was to do. He seemed to disregard the fact that they had spoken to Rick, his site foreman, just the day before. He had also failed to apologise again for the missed appointment the previous day, or for not having kept them properly informed about the completion date of the villa and the rest of the resort. He did, however, remind them that the keys wouldn't be handed over until the final instalment was paid and cleared in the bank. It was difficult for Mark to suppress his anger about the lack of communication all-round. Cassandra and he had established by then that the company was far from professional about keeping clients informed, despite the fact that there seemed to be sufficient staff to deal with it.

They didn't get a direct answer to the question Cassandra had asked about the completion of the building. So, Mark asked the question again.

'You are like a politician,' he joked 'You never can get a direct answer from them either,' he laughed. 'But, we need to know, because we will want to come and inspect the building before we make the final thirty per cent payment.'

The smile fell from Mr Janes's face. He seemed rather taken aback. 'Oh, that's not usual! But, yes of course. Usually though, most clients take our architect and site manager's word for it. Usually, it's them who signs off the building. We send you the 'Completion Certificate' so that the final instalment can be made.'

'Perhaps we aren't your usual clients. That thirty per cent is a lot of money to us. We have no intention of handing it over until we have seen that the building regulations are adhered to and that the villa is one hundred per cent complete. We will need to organise our lives so that we can come out to Sainte Marie for at least ten days. We need at least three months' notice to do that. There is also the furniture package too; we won't pay for the totality until all of the furniture is installed.'

'Yes, yes, of course. We will keep in contact and let you know in plenty of time. The furniture package is rather problematic at present. Some of the suppliers are proving to be very unreliable.' By the look on his face and the tone of his voice, it didn't take a genius to see that Mr Janes wasn't too happy about this financial arrangement.

Cassandra and Mark stood in their new villa and looked at one another. They now knew one another well enough to know more or less what the other was thinking. They both knew they didn't like or trust Damien Janes. They hoped that their thoughts were not as apparent to him. The initial feelings of elation that Cassandra had felt on entering had faded, just as rapidly as they had appeared. There was a silence between the three of them. Cassandra brought it to an end by asking about the bathrooms. As they continued their tour of the villa, she tried to restore that fantastic momentary image of the finished villa that she had seen just a few minutes previously. She prayed that it wouldn't turn out to be a complete illusion.

17 At the Water's Edge

Cassandra - 2010

On a whim, after leaving the site, they opted to eat lunch 'At the Waters' Edge.' Alice and Richard had recommended it the previous evening. Mark wanted to mull over what had happened at the construction site. Things that Alice and Richard had mentioned were also niggling him. He needed to be clear in his mind how they should deal with the situation that they found themselves in. Damien Janes, and the development company, needed to be put under his microscope.

Cassandra and Mark were foodies. The menu seemed innovative, though expensive. It was their style of eating place. Cassandra was also captivated by the garden. It was a kaleidoscope of colours. She sensed that it must have been created by someone who found a great joy in nature. It was full of vibrant pink bougainvillea, fuchsia, ginger lilies, and some waxy looking scarlet and yellow plants neither of them knew the name of.

A young waitress welcomed them. She was clad in a very long white apron that almost reached her ankles. They were directed across the restaurant, to a table set on a wooden quay right at the waters' edge. They were obviously the first customers that day. All the tables were unoccupied.

'Wow,' cried out Cassandra as they seated themselves. 'I bet this is spectacular at night.'

From their table, they could see through the numerous masts of the boats anchored near the shore, across to the headland at the other end of the bay. Nearby, a fish jumped out of the shimmering waters attracting their attention. They failed to notice they were not alone.

'Well, if the food is only half as good as the view, we are in for a treat,' declared Cassandra.

'Oh, it's almost as good as the view on most days,' said a grinning lady, who stood next to their table, 'and if the chef is having a really good day, it's even better.'

'We really look forward to our lunch then,' replied Cassandra returning the smile. 'We hope he's having a really great day!'

'What can I get you to drink?' asked the woman.

From her soft, relaxed accent Cassandra judged her to be a native to the island. Before they gave their order, Cassandra couldn't help but ask about the garden.

'Well, thank you my dear, the birds and insects like it too. It's just one of my little projects. We have such a spectacular view at the rear of the restaurant; we felt that we had to make a bit of an effort out at the front too.'

'You certainly succeeded,' congratulated Cassandra. 'Would you be so kind as to tell me the name of the bright red plants, edged with yellow, that hang down from the stem?'

'Ah yes, that. That's called a Crab's Claw here, or a Hanging Lobster Claw on other tropical islands.'

'Great name for it. Thank you.' Mark was eager to cut the conversation and get a drink, but Cassandra continued to chat about her love of the island's flowers.

Drinks were finally ordered. The lady, who seemed to be the proprietor, disappeared to get them. Mark's conversation quickly turned to Janes and Tropical Island Villas. The more they learnt about Janes, the more they came to dislike and mistrust him.

'Another thing,' added Mark, 'It became very obvious that Janes was uneasy about us insisting we personally inspect our villa before paying the last thirty per cent. I get the feeling that Janes may have financial problems. He needs to get his hands on as much money as fast as .....'

'Janes, do you mean Damien Janes?' asked the proprietor who had returned with the drinks.

156

'Yes. Damien Janes, the property developer. We have bought a villa from him.'

'I hope you don't mind me saying, but I heard a little of your conversation. You really need to stay as far away as possible from that man. The "Pirates of the Caribbean" have got nothing on him. He's your worst type of twenty first century pirate there is. Unfortunately, there are too many greedy developers like him on the island. They are giving Sainte Marie a very bad name.'

'How do you know him?' asked Cassandra.

'Know him? Everybody on the island knows him. He has an appalling reputation. I also have the misfortune of seeing him as a frequent customer here at the restaurant. I see him most weeks. Unfortunately, we can't refuse reservations from people who we detest. My only pleasure is that I try to make as much money out of him as I possibly can.' She placed the drinks on the table. 'If you have got five minutes, I can tell you plenty about him.'

'I think its best we know what kind of person we are dealing with. We are investing what for us is a large sum of money in our villa. Since returning to the island, we have had several suspicions about him and his company. We'd be only too pleased to hear your opinion,' Mark replied anxiously.

The proprietor put her hands on the table and leaned forward. 'He came to the island four or five years ago and formed a company with one of the sons of a local rum producer – the Thorner family. They had invested some of their profits from the distillery in land on the island. Well, the island was trying to expand its tourist industry. Janes convinced the Thorner family to sell him land for a tourist development. They took advantage of government incentives and tax relief on imported materials. He also used the Thorner's influence on the island to get loans from the local banks. They have had directives from the government to assist. The Thorner son, Wendell, and Janes got permission to build Diamond Point, just here in Anse Argent.'

'That's where we are staying at present,' interrupted Casandra.

'Well, it was all done on borrowed money. They used local labour to start with. Then the rot started to set in. It soon became apparent that the money from the huge bank loans was going elsewhere. First, they weren't able to pay the social security payments of the workers. Then they couldn't even pay the wages. Why was this, my dears?'

'I can guess,' uttered Cassandra.

'Yes, my dear, I'm sure you can! Well, Wendell Thorner now owns the most expensive car on the island. A low, high-class, shiny thing. Totally, unsuitable for the island's roads.

'Might have seen it,' admitted Mark, as the proprietor seated herself at their table.

'And, my dears, Damien Janes has bought himself a large villa on the beach, here at Anse Argent. When they first started, the world economy was booming. The units sold fairly well. Even sold off plan. They charged an exorbitant price for the time-shares. They had pots of money pouring in from clients. But, the enormous loans from the banks, you guessed it, were not being re-paid. Instead of the time-share money paying off the loans, where is it going? Well, it seems to be lining their pockets. And so the story goes on. Do you want to hear more?'

Cassandra and Mark looked at one another. Cassandra nodded.

'Then they started another project at Fortune Bay. A load more units. Even more expensive ones this time. I believe the biggest ones are around one and a half million US. And my dears, unfortunately, Janes isn't the only developer here. It's happening at several other locations on the island.'

Cassandra interrupted her, 'Fortune Bay, that's where we have bought a villa.'

'Yes, it's a beautiful bay. So, the same things are happening again there. They took out huge loans from the banks. The island banks were trying to be competitive with international banks, as well as aid the tourist industry. They also had money from the people buying, but despite all this, there was not enough money to pay the workers at Fortune Bay. He has now started another site to get another source of funds. I believe it's called pyramid selling. Unfortunately, the banks don't get their loans repaid. The islanders suffer. You can imagine that the interest on loans for Mr Average on Sainte Marie goes up. It has to go up to compensate for the enormous debts the banks have had to write off.'

'I hadn't thought about those repercussions!' gasped Cassandra.

'No, people don't. Well, that's the story very briefly, but there's another side to it,' continued the restaurant owner. 'There's the story of local revenge. Janes screwed enough people to buy a fancy boat. Some of your money will doubtless have paid for that, I'm sure. But, my dears, that fancy boat is now at the bottom of the sea.'

'What! What happened to it?'

'It has not been proved, but it is thought that the workers, who never had their social security contributions or wages paid, towed it out of the marina. They wouldn't want to harm anybody else's boat, would they? They towed it into the bay here and blew it up. That's island-style vengeance for you.'

'Oh my God! Incredible! We actually sailed down to Prosper with Janes on that boat,' Mark declared.

'Well, believe me, you won't be doing that again. Janes also found a boa constrictor in his bed one evening. In fact, his wife found it first. It was the same thing - islanders' vengeance. That finished his wife off, poor soul. Even she

159

couldn't put up with him after that. I think that the shock made her see sense and realise what a scoundrel she was married to. She recently went home to Britain with the children.'

At this point, some other customers came into the restaurant. The waitress in the long apron welcomed them and showed them to a nearby table. The proprietor smiled, 'Will you excuse me, my dears? I'll be back for your order in a moment.'

'I don't feel much like eating, after having heard all that,' muttered Cassandra.

'Look, Cassie, that's the past. I know it influences the future, our future, but the villas are near completion. Janes and Co. will need the resort to be finished to be able to sell their next project successfully. We have seen that they are still working on completing the apartments and the commercial buildings. I think that it's better that we aren't blind to such information. It opens our eyes. It gives us ammunition to cope with these people.'

'He makes me so angry! How can he descend to such depths? Using the island, the islanders and the investors in such a despicable way.'

'Quite easily my darling! You and I know that there's a lot of Damiens out there. The proprietor said there are several on the island. Unfortunately, we have the misfortune to have got involved with one. They are greedy, totally egotistical and make money their god. But, there's so much in life that their money can't buy them. Just look at the hatred for him that has developed amongst the people of Sainte Marie. His money can't buy their respect.'

'I wouldn't want to have to live with all that hatred. I hope that he has difficulty sleeping with his conscience every night.'

'He won't have one, will he?' Mark took her hand. 'Anyway, what are we going to try from this wonderful menu? The duck with banana chutney and sweet potato crisps sounds good.'

'Mm, I think I'd prefer some fish.'

It was at this point that the proprietor returned with her order pad. Mark explained that his wife had lost some of her appetite and was worrying about the development company and Damien Janes.

'No point in worrying about it my dear. It doesn't take away your troubles. It'll only make you feel miserable and sad. Enjoy your lunch. Think positive and come up with a plan of action of how you are going to cope with the problems.'

'That's very good advice,' Mark agreed.

'That man Janes, he thinks he's so smart, that he can fool and manipulate people for his own good,' jeered the restaurant owner. 'But he's not so clever. One day soon, he'll meet somebody who is much more intelligent than him. They'll expose him for the lousy fraud that he is. They'll gradually strip him of his riches and he'll be the one who is in the mire with nothing. I wish it could be me, but I ain't got the time, I've got to run this restaurant.'

'Yes, I hope you're right. Well, I'm getting quite hungry,' retorted back Mark. 'I'm going for the duck please, I'm sure that will make me see things in a different light. I'm certainly not going to let worrying spoil my lunch.'

18 The Time Will Come

JR - 2011

'Would you like red or white wine with you meal Sir?' smiled the air hostess as she handed me a tray of what I knew would be plastic, nondescript food. I considered it to be a strange question. It was trying to give the boxed tuck undeserved status. Most passengers would consider that it was questionable whether the meals were really fit for human consumption. But I smiled in return to the question because I was very pleased to be on the flight, despite the poor food.

At last, I was going home! I was flying back to Sainte Marie. I had been in Britain for nearly five years. It seemed like an eternity ago that I had flown across the Atlantic, going in the opposite direction, to an unknown future. The cost of the airline tickets had prohibited me from returning to Sainte Marie whilst I had been studying in London. Even though I was now counted as one of the office slaves and earning money, there always seemed to be other things that had to be paid for. After nearly two years of very full time work, I decided that I had to get my priorities right. I finally decided I could wait no longer. So, I put the cost of the ticket on my newly acquired credit card. Unfortunately, I'd had to buy a return ticket. I had to go back to work in Britain to pay for my holiday at home in the Caribbean.

The world had moved on five years. I considered I had moved with it. I'd gone through a whole bunch of change! I had metamorphosed. I had cast aside the garb of an unworldly kid. Slowly, gradually had taken on the outfit of a stronger, more rounded individual. I strode from task to task rather than meander. The LSE had straightened out many of my academic wrinkles. I got to encounter many intellectuals and pedagogues. They upgraded me; remade me. Their wisdom enlightened and inspired me; gave me the ability to transform abstract ideas into concrete projects. Like many of my peers, I had been stimulated to try out new ideas, to learn to accept failures, and start up again more intelligently. But the city of London had also refashioned my personality. I'd worked real hard on my social skills. They had seriously come along. Working in the Golden Bell could take credit for much of that. London had also made me into an advocate of change. I now enjoyed challenges in life; it kept me heads up.

I guessed that the passage of time would, equally, have made my friends develop into different characters. I was hoping however, that beneath their adult guises, their adolescent temperaments would still shine through. I felt that that was still true of me. I knew those five years had transformed me; I saw the world through different eyes, but it had not altered me out of all recognition.

Technology had helped shrink the miles between Sainte Marie and Great Britain; and had enabled me to keep alive many of my island relationships. My mother never was a real 'techno' bod, but she now had a friend with a computer who helped her out each week. In my absence, she had been promoted to hotel housekeeper. Though the extra dosh had improved her lifestyle a little, as frequently happens, the hard work meant far less time for herself and had ushered in a multitude of additional problems for her.

Joining the LSE 'Itchy Feet Club' had been a great move. It had taken me to several places in Europe. I'd seen Paris, Bordeaux, Amsterdam and Vienna and numerous towns in Britain. 'Itchy Feet' had taken me to Bath. I loved the graceful, historic buildings there and the chatty, friendly people, so different from Londoners. I had been successful in acquiring a job there. I found life slower and calmer in the West Country.

'Itchy Feet' had also widened my circle of friends, especially female ones after the break-up with Zuzanna. Each girlfriend was so totally different. They also influenced and re-formed me and added sparkle and music to my life. The experience of being with some of my exes was like listening to jazz, some were reminiscent of lively pop music and the real memorable ones were like the 1812 Overture. With bloody explosions nearing the finale. I favoured the babes that left you with similar emotions to listening to Vivaldi's Four Seasons; spirited, slightly unpredictable and something you want to hear time and time again.

I was renting two rooms on the edge of Bath, near the university, and working near the centre. I could see distant hills from my first floor windows. I found it far more pleasant than the brick houses, construction work and the scaffolding I had seen from my room in Fulham. I chose to cycle to work to save money. I'd started to stash away a bit, although it certainly wasn't easy. I was saving for my future and when I would return back to Sainte Marie for good. I'd decided I would try to get myself another part-time job at the weekends, if only for a few months, to help pay off my credit card bill and to augment my savings. It would mess up my social life, but I would benefit long term.

I was half way through my CIMA course to become a chartered management accountant. A distance learning course had worked out cheaper. The qualification would mean my wage would virtually double compared to what I could earn as a standard accountant. It meant studying most evenings and some of the weekend, but having come straight out of uni, I was used to it. The colleagues who I worked with in the Bath office were an affable lot. They helped me where they could with my studies. There were a couple of other employees that were doing exactly the same thing.

'Can I take your tray sir?' asked one of the air hostesses, as she reached to remove the remains of my grossly over-cooked chicken dinner. The flight was passing very slowly despite the book I had bought to read. I was so impatient to set my feet on Sainte Marie soil again. I guess I was expecting too much of the plane's pilot. He could only go at the plane's cruising speed, but he was flying at too much of a leisurely pace for my liking. To me, it seemed like he needed some coaching from Superman.

I kept staring out of plane window hoping that the clouds beneath me would speed up as they did in some of the movies. They didn't; but to my relief, we did arrive on schedule. Much to the annoyance of the woman who was sitting next to me, I was the first to jump up from my seat and get my hand luggage from the overhead locker.

'Sweet Jesus! The Lord be praised,' cried my mother as she saw me wheeling my case through the arrivals gate. She didn't have very much confidence in the ability of airlines to convey their passengers safely to their chosen destination. She rushed up to me and made far too much fuss. The very first thing that I noticed was that she looked much older than when I had seen her two years previously. She had visited me in London for the second time. It seemed that her job was taking it out of her. She'd more grey hairs and wrinkles.

One of Mother's colleagues had acted as a taxi to drive her to the airport and then take us back to Prosper. I felt on top of the world. It felt so good to see all the regular, typical features of my island home again. I appreciated every second of that transfer from the airport. Palms. The occasional sparkle of the sea. That cloudless turquoise sky. It beat London or Bath. I smiled constantly and my mind was in a state of euphoria. I sat in the back of the old car listening to my mother's constant chatter, whilst I kept my eyes fixed on what was on the other side of the car windows. However, on arrival at our home, the small creole style cottage seemed to have become even smaller, even shabbier, even more unmaintained than I remembered. The picture of it hit me full in the face. The

165

romantic vision I'd had of my pretty home in the sun, overlooking the sea, crumbled instantly. I said nothing, but knew that the time had come for me to consider altering this situation.

$$$

For the next seven mornings, I swung my legs out of my old single bed (which needed a new mattress) feeling on top of the world. Whilst my mother went to work at the hotel, I'd had a great time catching up with old friends. Then, at the end of the day, I would go, clad in my Marks and Spencer's swimwear, down to the beach at Prosper. I clutched my snorkel and flippers that, this time, I'd had to pay for. After putting on my equipment and plunging into the luke-warm waters of the Caribbean Sea, I revelled in the enchantment of becoming a spectator to that other world. The world beneath the waves. On a couple of evenings I was joined by a friend. It seemed quite like 'old times'.

I was all jazzed up by catching up my island friends. They fitted into two categories. Category one, they were the ones who still lived in and around Prosper. On the whole, they had not done too much with their lives. They just got by doing casual work. One of them seemed to be relying on his babe to bring home a wage, whilst he spent days on the beach selling shells he had retrieved from the ocean. I thought, I could have been like that. I was sure thankful I wasn't. Category two, they had moved to the north of the island, where the majority of the commerce and tourist outlets were. They were more ambitious. They had chosen a career. Two were working in hotels and one had become quite big in real estate.

I'd kicked out with my mates all week, but this day was for my Mother. We were going to speed up to Bourbon on the hotel water taxi. It was the quickest way to go. From there, we could get around on the local buses. I had told her we were going out for lunch. We were, but I'd a

166

surprise for her first. We got off the bus on the main road outside Anse Argent. I walked her down a quiet road with a bakery on the corner.

'Where ya taking me JR? There ain't no restaurants down this road! Where we going?' asked my mother.

'It's a new one Mom,' I reassured her, 'It's just a bit further.' We walked past a mix of newly built houses, all painted in sharp, bright colours.

I stopped at a plot of very overgrown land. There was a large mango tree growing in the centre, emerging from the wilderness of weeds.

'Here you go Mom. This is where we are heading. What do you think? There's no sea view, but you have a great view of the hills.'

'Where de restaurant JR?' asked my confused mother.

'Patience! I wanted to show you this before we had lunch. It's half an acre of building land Mom. I bought it from a friend this week. I'm going to have a house built here when I've got a bit more money.'

'But JR, where you get the money from?'

'I took out a loan Mom. I've got an OK job now in the UK. I've saved a little money and I will pay the loan off from my wage. The house will be for us, you, me and my wife. I shall be coming back to Sainte Marie when I have finished my studies.'

'I don't understand. You ain't got no wife. And I works in Prosper.'

'No, I don't have a wife now, but I will have one.'

'Who ya thinkin' of?'

'Don't know as yet, but I'm sure that there will be somebody that will have me,' I laughed. 'And you, you don't have to work for ever. You can give up your job; may be you can get a little job in Anse Argent.'

'I don't knows what to say JR. When ya thinkin' of coming back home to live 'ere?'

167

'In a couple of years maybe. I'll have finished my studies by then and I will be able to earn big money. I'm planning for the future, our future. I thought you would be pleased!'

'Ya a good son JR!' she took my hand. 'God will bless ya; ya thinking of ya old Mom like dat! I thinks ya done de right thing buying de land. De price go up each year. We see if I ready to live up 'ere in a couple of years. But, no, ya a good boy, thinking of me like that. You better than ya father! He ain't done much for me. He left me to struggle on me own, after he gone run off wit' dat floozy Janice.'

'I don't want you to have to work for ever Mom. I know you have to work real hard to get through life and my father has done nothing to help.'

My mother stared at me. I noticed that her hair pulled back in a bun showed up all the lines around her eyes and perhaps made her look much older than her years. 'Dat not exactly true JR. He not really help me, but he help you.'

'But I don't remember him; I was tiny when he left home you told me. How did he help me?'

'JR, he got ya grant for de LSE. He work for de hotel. I apply for de grant, but he convince de hotel to give it to ya; ya and one other student. He manage de hotel JR. Ya father the hotel manager now.'

My mind was racing. I didn't know whether to be furious because my father, who worked just a few miles away from our home, had ignored my mother and I for most of my life, or thankful because he had at last faced up to some of his parental responsibilities.

'But, why didn't you tell me before Mom?' I asked.

'Ya needs to know? It not make any difference to tings? I's waitin' for the right time to tell ya. I sees him nearly every day now, ya know. He ask me how ya are sometime, but he never ask to see ya JR.'

'I'm not interested in my father. It's you that's had to work real hard to bring me up. Thank you for doing that for me Mom, and for getting the grant.' I gave her a hug. 'It has changed my life.'

'I's glad to get rid of ya,' she laughed. 'Ya's getting to be a punk monkey at home. It's best ya do something wit' ya life! Now what about dat restaurant? I's starving!'

'Yeah, we are going to a restaurant. Let's go back to the bus-stop. We are going to a restaurant on the beach in Anse Argent.'

'I hope they got plenty of real food, I's as hungry as a lion. I could kill a plate o' fish head and Dasheen.'

19 Distorted Reflections

Damien - Summer 2011

In Anse Argent the sun burnt down. The sky was a topaz blue. Its light played across the surface of the ocean, reflecting a shining palette of a thousand shades of lavender, turquoise and sapphire. Though the temperature gauges were reading thirty-two degrees centigrade, it seemed hotter, as it was exceedingly humid. There had recently been a torrential downpour of rain, the roads and pavements were still running with water. The leaves on the vegetation still dripped heavy droplets of rain after the deluge. Clouds had cleared quickly. Steam rose from the pavements. Pedestrians had put down their umbrellas, but their shoes remained sodden.

Inside the Tropical Island Villas building the air conditioning hummed quietly. It blocked out the traffic noise. The large contemporary mirror in the reception area reflected the images of three men working diligently. They seemed to be labouring in a sense of camaraderie. They were oblivious to the exterior weather conditions. There was a large, growing pile of empty beer bottles collecting in the centre of the table. They were near the end of a meeting in which they had been discussing the latest villa sales and the monthly accounts. Adrian was busy calculating something on his computer. Wendell and Damien discussed the forthcoming visit of one of Damien's friends to view a villa.

'My mate Pete arrives on Saturday. You'll like Pete. He's a good guy. I've known him for years. I used to live near him when I was living in London. We used to go out drinking together. We've shared some good times. Pete has done very well for himself in the construction business. I'm hoping that he'll be tempted by one of our three bedroom villas.'

'You like the guy, but you like his money more, eh?' asked Wendell sarcastically.

'Not at all, he's a good mate,' Damien retorted. He looked at his Cartier tank watch and addressed his accountant.

'So, what's the final figures Adrian?' queried Damien 'I'm not quite finished yet.'

'I'm glad it's you doing that,' declared Wendell. 'You are good at math, but not me. My brain goes numb when I'm faced with a mathematical problem. I know there is only one correct solution. But me, I can't even get my calculator to come up with the right one. Give me any other subject but math!' declared Wendell.

'I'm OK with the basic stuff, but give me any maths where you have to use theorem and I'm lost!' added Damien.

'So,' interrupted Adrian, 'this month, outgoings of wages, building materials, plus import duty, advertising costs, rental for this building and so on, come to 278,754 US dollars. Incomings from stage payments and the payments we have had from the banks for the mortgages on the two beach front villas and the three apartments that were sold are, as near as damn it, 2.7 million US dollars. You will now be able to start paying back a good slice of the large bank loans.'

'We were lucky to get nearly 600,000 dollars for that two-bed apartment. Who is the greatest real estate agent in the Caribbean then?' boasted Damien. 'What was the sales value of that per square foot?'

'For the two bed apart, you got around 430 dollars a square foot,' calculated Adrian, 'and building costs were around 95 dollars a square foot.'

'So, if we can sell at that price per square foot, just think what the biggest beach villa can be sold for.'

'Building costs are higher per square foot for the larger individual properties,' Adrian informed them.

'I want to buy the large beach front villa. I've always thought that I'd like it for entertaining my friends and for having the family over for holidays,' boasted Damien.

Wendell cut him short and asked, 'By the way DJ, how are your kids, now that they are back in England?'

'They are finding it difficult to settle back into school in Britain. They're coming over in the school holidays. It will be good to see them again. I'll have to take a couple of weeks off when they come.'

'Are they coming with Donna?'

'No, they are coming with my parents. Donna won't be coming. She'll be staying in London.' Damien paused. 'Going back to the large beach front villa - I'd like to use it for the family and I thought it could look very impressive for prospective clients to stay there and for entertaining VIPs.'

'So how are you going to pay for it DJ? We can't afford just to give it to you,' enquired Wendell.

'I'll get a mortgage from the bank. If we can prove that we can sell the villas to clients for so much per square foot, I thought that I might be able to get a larger loan. For more than the building costs. Then I could buy all the furnishings from the loan. Maybe even have a bit for a holiday too. I thought that I would try and get a loan of a million dollars. I think that we can show that it is worth that and more.'

Adrian raised his head. He stopped looking at his computer. A loan for a million US! It was perhaps more than he would ever earn in his lifetime. He studied his boss's face for several seconds. He then returned to the work he was doing. He remained silent. He had learnt that it was wisest not to express his opinion of some of the things that went on in the office. He valued his job too much. He was earning a good wage compared to many on the island and he'd like to keep it as long as he could.

'But the bigger the loan, the bigger the repayments DJ. How you going to pay for that? Pay for that and your other house in Anse Argent?' quizzed Wendell.

'Dell, I don't see it as a problem. We are on a roller now. We are doing great! With my selling skills, we'll soon be making millions. We'll make enough with Fortune Bay and the next project to more than pay for that! I thought that I could set up a company on the island. I'd buy it through the company to avoid paying the sales tax if I ever want to sell it. Why should I give ten per cent to the government, when I can keep it myself? I think that I'll be suggesting that to Pete. Buy the villa through a company, that is.'

Adrian looked up again, surveyed DJ and then Wendell. Again he stayed silent. He knew that if the company failed to keep up the payments, it would be Damien's new company that would be bankrupted. It wouldn't be Damien. He would be able to keep his other assets. In fact, judging by Damien's previous performances, he suspected that Damien would try to avoid making the repayments. Personally, he considered that to be rather devious. He tried to change the topic of conversation.

'Are we going to discuss the repayment of the existing bank loans? The loans for all the building work?' asked Adrian. 'Initially, you stated that once you started to get substantial amounts coming in, you would start to pay them off in larger amounts than the regular monthly repayments to keep the interest level down.'

'Let's wait for a bit, and see what happens. There may be some unforeseen expenses. Wait a bit before we start paying it back in large sums,' stated Damien.

Adrian hoped that the 'unforeseen expenses' would not be anything to do with Wendell's and Damien's developing taste for extravagance. Damien's catamaran had been one of his 'unforeseen expenses' and now it was at the bottom of the sea. Now he wanted the biggest villa at Fortune Bay. Whatever happened, however they squandered the company money, there was nothing that he could do about it. It wasn't his company. He was just paid to do the accounts. He just did his best to advise them about their finances. It wasn't his problem if they chose to ignore him.

'Who is for another cold one?' asked Damien. He made his way to the large refrigerator in the corner of the reception area. He passed by a large mirror. Out of habit, he studied his reflexion.

Adrian refused the beer. He then asked if they had finished the meeting. He felt that he wanted to get away from the meeting.

As he walked to his car, his mind was still whirling from the thought of Damien taking on a million dollar loan. He started his short journey home to his wife and children. He asked himself if he was jealous. He decided that that wasn't the emotion that was upper most in his mind. He felt worried. He was worried for himself and his future. He understood all the finances of the small company. He knew how much they had on loan. He knew that they needed to start paying some of it back from their recent sales. It was obvious that Damien and Wendell didn't understand this. No, Adrian thought. It was rather that they didn't want to understand. He could see that he must make the most of his good wage whilst he could. If they were going to spend too much money, too fast and too soon, Tropical Island Villas may not exist in a few years' time.

$$$

Saturday soon came around. Damien had promised to drive to the airport to pick up Pete. He never liked the drive down there. The roads were hazardous at the best of times. They were not well maintained. There were masses of potholes, twists and turns. The rainy season made the journey worse. A storm prior to leaving home had made the roads wet and slippery. Acute concentration on the road would be essential.

The rainy season wasn't Damien's favourite time of the year. He found it hellish to cope with. He hated, with a passion, feeling hot and sweaty most of the day. He loathed the incessant perspiration that trickled down his neck. His shirts sticking to his back. Grime clinging to his moist skin. Feeling continually thirsty. He tried to stay in an air conditioned environment as much as he could. He was always pleased when December loomed and the weather became drier.

The rainy season could also play havoc with construction work. Torrential rain had stopped work at Fortune Bay several times. Storms or even hurricanes could do untold damage on construction sites. Despite all the problems of the rainy season, he knew that he preferred life on Sainte Marie to cold, damp and wet London.

Damien grabbed a quick beer at the airport bar before meeting Pete in the arrivals area. Pete's suitcase was thrown into the back of the 4X4. Damien buckled himself into his car, checking his appearance in the rear view mirror as he did so. Then he inhaled. He mentally prepared himself for the difficult journey back to Anse Argent.

'You are looking really great DJ,' acclaimed Pete 'the tropical life-style must suit you.'

Damien turned the key in the ignition and made his way out of the airport car park. 'Thanks, yes I'm feeling good. When is Emma coming out? I thought that she was going to be with you today.'

'Emma couldn't get the time off work to come with me. So DJ, we thought that I could try and get all the business side of the villa settled. Then Emma and I can have ten days holiday when she comes out next Saturday.'

'Will Emma be staying at my house when she comes over?'

175

'No, I hope that you don't mind DJ, but we thought that we would stay in a hotel for those ten days. We thought that it would be a bit more of a holiday. In a hotel environment, there's a bar and the spa and so on. Emma wanted to go somewhere where she could get spa treatments.'

'Oh, I see. OK,' Damien was rather taken aback. 'Has she spoken to Donna since she was back in London?'

'Yes, she went over to see Donna a couple of weeks ago. They went out for the evening.'

'So, that's it. Donna has been telling her tales. Explaining why she packed up her suitcases and boarded a flight to freedom for her and the kids. She'll have told her how unhappy I made her! She'll have said how awful and uncaring I was to her. Now, Emma doesn't want to stay in the same house as me.'

'No, DJ it's not that at all. We thought that staying in a hotel would be more of a real holiday. We haven't had one for several years.'

The car sped through tropical rain forest which grew right up to the edge of the road side. The route was fairly narrow. Pete noticed its state of repair. He was glad he wasn't driving. They started to steadily climb up a mountainside. The road snaked first one way and then in the opposite direction. Damien took each of the hair pin bends with care. He had on occasions turned a bend only to meet a large truck that seemed to be thundering towards him. Generally, the islanders had the reputation of not being prudent drivers.

'Well, fine if that's the case. Just so long as Emma will talk to me when she arrives on the island,' replied Damien. 'But you know what Pete, Donna just became far too difficult. She was too demanding; a real misery. She cried a lot of the time. Of course, she said that all the problems were my fault. Everything was my fault! She couldn't seem to take on board that I was working for her and the kids as well. She was too possessive. She moaned. She wanted me at home with her too much. She failed to see that I had to spend most of my time at work. She wouldn't accept that if she wanted a fabulous life style out here, she had to make allowances for that. It wasn't until we moved out here that I realised how incompatible we were.'

'She told Emma that there were lots of other women in your life.'

'Well,' Damien paused, 'well, when things started to go wrong, Donna didn't want to know me. They were just casual relationships, nothing serious and only occasionally. What was I supposed to do? She wouldn't let me near her! I have physical needs like every other man.'

'I don't think that Donna would quite see it that way DJ. However, I'm not going to be judgmental here. I ain't going to take sides. It's your life DJ. It's your marriage and your family. Emma says that Donna has found herself a job. She is starting to make a new life. She's aiming at a new future for herself and the kids. I have a strong suspicion, from what Emma has said, that she won't be coming back to you.'

'If that's what she wants, it's up to her. I have established a good life out here now. I've become an important figure on the island. I'm doing really well selling property. If she doesn't want to be part of it, that's fine by me.' Damien decided it was time to change the topic of conversation. 'What about you Pete? Are you too tired to go out this evening, after the flight? We won't get back to Anse Argent for well over another hour. I don't mind if you prefer to have an early night.'

'Tell you what mate, let's go out for a few drinks, like we used to. I think it's best to stay up to try and get over the five hours' time difference; rather than go straight to bed because you feel wrecked from the flight. Then wake up at some ungodly hour and have to lay there for hours until it's morning.'

'Fine! We'll throw your luggage into the house and then head for the Yacht Club to down a few.'

The 4X4 started its descent down the mountain. The two men swayed from side to side as they swung into each of the sharp bends. Pete remarked on how different the driving was on the island. It was nothing like driving in London. Battling against thousands of agitated motorists. Getting stuck in a jam for hours on the M25. The light quickly started to fade as the evening approached. Pete noticed that the few villages they passed through were certainly colourful. The architecture was like nothing he had experienced before. Each village boasted a dominant church, indicative of the strong religious belief of the local people. They eventually reached the flatter terrain of the north of the island and approached the more touristic and built-up area. They passed supermarkets, commercial areas, and restaurants, including some international fast food outlets.

The car swung into the long sweeping driveway of Damien's villa in Anse Argent. Pete couldn't help but be impressed. The tall white pillars supporting the roof at the entrance immediately caught his eye. He liked the large shuttered windows. The tidy garden planted with tropical trees and bushes; all was illuminated by the automatic lighting as they drove towards the double garage door. It was all very different from the small house Pete had in the suburbs of London. That had a tiny frontage, just big enough to park his car. The back garden was overlooked by dozens of identical homes. His home was small and without character. Nevertheless, he still had to pay hefty mortgage repayments each month for it. Life in London didn't come cheap.

The sound of crashing waves bombarded his ears as they climbed out of the vehicle. The sea sounded rough, and also very close. Pete began to comprehend why it was that Damien enjoyed the life style he had established on the island. The interior of the house was just as stunning. Large, spacious rooms decked with expensive-looking contemporary furniture. He guessed it had been imported from America. He was shown to his bedroom. The super king size bed was illuminated by several recessed spots around the bed alcove. Damien slid open the patio doors of the bedroom to reveal the large swimming pool in the back garden. This was also lit. The pool shone a turquoise, glittering hue.

'Very tasteful DJ! You're certainly living the life of luxury.'

'Nobody gave me all this Pete. I had to work bloody hard to get it! OK, let's get you to the Yacht Club for a drink. Do you mind if we leave the car in the garage? It's only a short walk away.'

'No problem. I'll enjoy my Rum Punch even more after a bit of a walk.'

$$\$\$\$$$

'Let's go Pete. I'll show you Fortune Bay. I know you'll be impressed,' exclaimed Damien after an early breakfast the next day. 'We'll have to go to the office first to collect all the keys that we'll need.'

It was with great pride that, shortly afterwards, Damien drove up to the security booth at the resort entrance. He asked the security guard to open up the electric gates to give them access to the site. As it was Sunday, the security staff were the only ones working. Most of the construction of the villas and apartments was now complete. Many of the plants and trees had been installed. The rainy season had encouraged the plants to develop and form a lacy pattern around the base of the buildings, softening their austere form. Damien now thought that the site was starting to look quite imposing and aesthetically pleasing. He drove to the end of the road. He stopped his car as near as he could get to the beach.

'I'll show you the beach first. That, in its self, is impressive. It's a natural beach, and the sand is soft and pale pink.'

As they stepped out of the 4X4, they were enveloped in a velvety, humid warmth. They sauntered down the recently constructed boarded walkway to the beach. Tropical greenery was growing on either side. It formed a tunnel of vegetation. This hid the beach from view. As they reached the end of the boards, Damien stopped. The sea breeze immediately cooled their skins and the sunlight made their eyes narrow. The entire large bay could be seen from their vantage point. The light from the fierce summer sun danced across the water. At either end of it, the land rose sharply up. Several dark seabirds with extraordinary long wings and deeply forked tails soared effortlessly over the large expanse of water. The palms descending over the sand at various angles arrested Pete's perception of the bay. Waves rolled gently onto the silvery, rose pink sand. Man, it was something straight out of a travel brochure! Pete could see immediately the reason why the force of the sea there was not the same as it was by DJ's villa. Perhaps a quarter of a mile out from the beach, there was the clear line of a reef right across the bay.

It was still early in the day and the middle of the rainy season. Consequently, they were the only people on the beach. Damien remained silent, but stepped onto the sand. He knew the beach was breath-taking. He realised it sold itself. He remembered how he had felt the first time that he had visited it. Pete looked up and down the beach; he stood awe struck for several seconds.

'DJ, I never imagined….. It's like something out of Robinson Crusoe! It's mind-blowing…… unbelievable! I can only say WOW! Impressed? Yes, I am impressed.'

'Just wait until you see the villas Pete!'

'Sorry DJ. A villa is just another building, but this beach is something else, something really special. It's a million miles away from where I live in London.'

Slightly taken aback, Damien informed his friend 'But, there are several other very similar bays just down the coast. Anyway, let me show you the villas.'

The two men explored the site, viewing the beach front villas, the large main swimming pool, the communal areas, the apartment blocks and the villas further back in the resort. Despite the fact that Pete was his mate, he still used his sales techniques. He laboured the facts about the villas being superior products. 'They are very prestigious and could earn you a good income once the management company is established at the resort.' Damien didn't seem to have mastered the skill of listening enough to his clients. He bombarded Pete with facts and figures about potential income being able to cover mortgage costs, even before Pete had the time to think that far ahead. Pete's head was spinning. He knew he liked what he saw. He had been seduced by the exotic vista, the '"mposing and glamorous" villas, and the possibility of spending part of his future on the idyllic isle. However, he felt that he needed a little time for reflexion. He didn't get it. Damien tried to close the deal and talk about making appointments at the bank in Bourbon to set up a mortgage.

'DJ, do you mind if I do another tour, but, this time by myself?'

'OK. I'll go and sit under a tree for half an hour and then we can go into the marina and perhaps get a bit of lunch.'

$$$

At the marina, Pete took in all the extensive acreage of berths. He figured that there were fortunes anchored there. It seemed evident to him that the island attracted people with money. Damien explained that there were plans to extend the marina to allow even larger, super yachts to moor at Anse Argent. From what he had seen so far, Pete felt excitement about the island and the prospect of possibly buying his own tiny part of it.

Whilst he consumed his beef burger and chips, Damien commenced another of his long-winded monologues about selling property on the island. How well he had done so far, how much money he had made, and what he hoped to achieve in the future with the next project. He then embarqued on his personal plans. He explained about buying the largest villa himself. He tried to sway Pete's opinion by showing he had confidence in the project at Fortune Bay.

'I've applied for a loan to buy the large beach front villa that we saw,' Damien told Pete. 'So far, there doesn't seem to be any problems about that. The bank knows that I'm earning a very good wage. They know that the properties will be worth considerably more than their current value in a few years' time, and that each property is a phenomenal investment.'

Even after the last chip had disappeared into his continually moving jaw, Damien still had more to say about his talent for selling property. He re-iterated how many clients he had convinced to invest with them. But, Pete had mentally switched off from the spiel. He was reflecting about his own circumstances and if he could afford to buy something at Fortune Bay. He nodded at Damien at the appropriate times, whilst surveying the vessels in the marina. He was thinking about how he could get used to this lifestyle for several months a year. His construction business was doing well. He could buy himself a little boat and Emma and he could perhaps eventually spend the winters in the Caribbean away from the biting cold of Europe.

'Would it be a good idea to phone the bank tomorrow to make an appointment to talk about a loan?' asked Damien.

'Yes DJ, I think it would. I think that I would like to buy one of the three bed villas at the back of the complex. I like the idea of the small, private pool and the small enclosed garden. I think Emma will love it.'

'Great! Incredible! I'm really pleased. I knew that you'd be convinced when you saw the complex and a bit of the island. As you are a mate, we can let you have the villa for 430,000 US. That's a reduction of 70,000 on the listed price.'

Damien got up and moved to slap his mate on the back. 'Let's get another beer to celebrate or even a bottle of champagne? On seconds thoughts though, maybe wine. I don't think that they will have champagne here.'

'Wine is fine. That would mean that I need a loan of around 300,000 US,' calculated Pete. 'As things are at present, I can afford to repay that each month without any rental income from your management company.'

'Another mate of mine is doing the same thing, but he is going for a beach front villa. What he is doing is getting a mortgage for more than the real value of the property. We up the sales price for the bank. This gives him money for things that he needs at home and for an interior designer to furnish the villa.'

'No DJ, I don't want to do that. I can make the repayments for the 300 grand. I don't want to over-stretch myself.'

'Think about it! With the rental that you will earn from letting out the villa, you could afford a larger loan. That way, you could get some of those little extra things that you and Emma would really like.'

The bottle of wine arrived. They celebrated beginnings of a new home for Pete, raising their glasses to the changes that it would make to his life. They toasted the adventure of Pete discovering the island and the Caribbean. Time was spent discussing all the money that they would both be making from renting out their tropical dream homes.

20 The Only Way is Up

Damien - Autumn 2011

The bell boy inserted the room card into the lock of the hotel suite. He wheeled the luggage to the padded luggage stool at the end of the king size bed. He carefully installed the suitcases on it. The housekeeper followed him in. She methodically smoothed the bedcover, embroidered with a very large hotel logo, and straightened the rose-coloured bed throw. Both employees were dressed in white cotton uniforms trimmed in an identical pink. She unlocked and threw open the balcony window. The view of the colourful hotel gardens and the ocean invaded the suite. Immediately, the flimsy under curtain fluttered in the sea breeze. The bell boy took a bottle of pink champagne from the mini-bar. It was placed in the silvery ice bucket next to the orchids on the coffee table. The housekeeper checked the marble clad bathroom, straightened the towels, the bath robes and the slippers, all in house colours. She then nodded to her colleague, who picked up the phone to say that the suite was ready. Their movements were automatic and performed without speaking. It was a choreography that had been developed through working together in the same hotel for many years. They stood in silence next to the door waiting for the clients to arrive and to be thanked by the conventional method for their fastidious preparations.

A third member of staff had accompanied the two guests to one of the best rooms in the hotel. He opened the door to reveal a very spacious and well-lit room furnished with extravagant looking dark furniture. Everything shone. The contents of the room were juxtaposed to give any observer an image of opulence and perfection. A tall, slim, white man in his forties and a young West Indian woman of equal height, but nowhere near equal age, were ushered into the room. The entrance caused all three members of staff to smile automatically. They politely wished the guests an excellent stay on their island and at the hotel. The male guest, as a matter of course, reached for his wallet and withdrew three notes, of large denominations, to give to the staff. The young lady, on the other hand, raced to the open window and cooed about the 'great view of the sea'. She then lifted the bottle out of the ice bucket to examine it, before dashing into the marble bathroom to scrutinise the complimentary products that were lined up in front of the large wall mirror. By then, all the members of staff had exited the room each looking very pleased with their gratuity.

'I never seen anything like this before! This is real living!' cried the girl, kicking her high heeled shoes off and bouncing herself onto the recently smoothed bed cover.

'Champagne?' enquired the man.

'It French, isn't it? It all so awesome, the hotel, the room, the view and pink champagne all in one day!'

'You can show me your appreciation later,' Damien raised his champagne flute towards his companion. 'Cheers! Here's to a great week in Barbados! Lots of sun, sea and sex.'

'I never stayed in a deluxe hotel before. Glad it not me who pay the bill!'

'Don't you worry about the bill! I've got plenty of money to pay that. I make more money than you can spend my dear. I've got plenty of bread tucked away. You're going out with a very rich and successful man. I'm on the up and up,' boasted Damien, who was spending a chunk of the loan which he had obtained to buy his villa at Fortune Bay.

She took her champagne glass from his hand and kissed him lightly on the nose. 'Sure DJ, the only way in life got to be UP. I know that you done real good and your villas makes a lot of bucks. Everyone on Saint Marie know about you and your company.' She looked towards the balcony and asked, 'Can we go and sit outside and watch the folks in the garden?'

'Fine, just until we've drunk the champagne. Then I've got other plans.' He stepped onto the balcony and placed the ice bucket on the glass-topped garden table.

'I love the pink cushions! Look, they are the same colour as the ones on the chairs in the garden. Hey, DJ! Look at her dress! The blue one! Isn't it really something?'

'If you're a very good girl, I might buy you one,' smiled DJ.

'But DJ, you say that you like me best when I a very bad girl. How I going to get my dress sweetie?' she grinned whilst sipping her champagne.

'Don't try to get clever with me. You be nice to me and I'll be nice to you. That's the rules of the game, isn't it?'

'You really special to me DJ. You treats me real good. I very proud I going out with you.'

The conversation was cut short by the ringing of DJ's phone. He looked at the display.

'Hi Rick. How's things? ....What do you mean - bad news? It's a great day in Barbados, let's keep it that way! ....Yes, Barbados. I told you I was going on holiday.... Yes, with Ayanna. I am allowed to have a holiday!'

Damien smirked at Ayanna as she blew him a kiss and raised her glass to him.

'What do you mean? The sewage pump isn't working. Can't you sort this out yourself? ....Why do they want money in advance?.......How much do we owe them?..... Shit, we haven't got enough to cover it! ...... No, I don't want to phone up the installation company. I'm on holiday for Christ sake! Can't you ask Wendell and Adrian to sort it?'

Damien concentrated on what he was being told on his mobile phone. He put his elbow on the table and his hand to his forehead. Suddenly, he looked worried and his face looked strained and much older than he had five minutes earlier. He muttered several obscenities under his breath and sighed.

Ayanna listened attentively, trying to understand what was going on. She said nothing. Although there was a cool breeze blowing from the sea, she became aware the beads of sweat that had appeared on Damien's slightly lined forehead. The smile on her pretty face remained fixed, but inside she was beginning to feel rather disconcerted. She could see that her idyllic holiday and her expensive dress may be in jeopardy.

'Send me their contact details Rick. I'll try to sort it out when I can. Rick, you're interrupting things here…. Yes, interrupting things.' Damien threw his phone onto the glass–topped table. He looked at Ayanna and said, 'I've only been away for about five hours and they want me to sort their problems out! I'm not there for the day and they can't cope. What a cock up! You employ all these incompetent people and you end up doing the work yourself.'

'Where'd they be without you DJ? What the problem honey?' she asked getting up and putting her arms around Damien's shoulders.

'They have a problem with the bastard sewage pump. Nothing for us to worry about. Let's finish the champagne and then try to relax.'

But this was not to be. The champagne was sipped. The marked differences between Barbados and Sainte Marie were discussed. Plans for the holiday were made. However, just as the contents of the extravagantly-priced bottle of champagne disappeared and the couple were heading for the bedroom, Damien's phone started ringing and vibrating on the table top. He looked at it in disbelief. Ayanna smiled and continued her way into the bedroom.

'YES RICK,' shouted Damien into his phone. 'Oh, it's not Rick…… OK…. Yes….. Do I really need to have my bloody holiday interrupted again? Villa 5B....Yes, I know they are coming out next week to inspect their villa. What do you mean the kitchen isn't complete?........What can I do about it in Barbados?......... Yes, I know that they won't pay the final instalment if the kitchen isn't complete.... Yes, I know we need the money to pay for the sewage to be sorted.' Damien wiped the sweat from his forehead, uttered several more swear words and looked into the hotel suite. Through the glass Damien could see Ayanna was changing into a bright pink bikini. She covered it with a beach dress and then lay in the centre of the very large bed. She turned to watch Damien on the phone.

'Look, there's a simple solution. Why couldn't you bloody well think of it? I don't know, what do I bloody well pay you for? Take the units and the dish washer from Villa 3, they are the same spec, and put them into 5B. Villa 3 has already been signed off. The owners will never know. By the time they visit the island again, the replacements will have arrived from the States. Simple! Yes, I know it's a lot of work, but you wanted a goddamn solution!'

Damien could see through the window that Ayanna was beckoning to him from her spot on the bed. 'I'm not going to be a prisoner to my phone the rest of the day. I'm turning it off. You'll have to sort things out yourself or with Wendell.' Damien moved into the bedroom.

Ayanna held out her hand. 'Give me the phone. You need to relax now.' She dropped the offending article into her beach bag which was at the side of the bed. 'When we get to the beach, I going to drop it into the sea,' she laughed. 'It real beautiful here; too beautiful to spend your time working on the phone.'

For once, Damien did as he was told.

21 Embracing an Unknown Future

Cassandra - Autumn 2011

Cassandra left her shoes on the walkway. She ran towards the sea. She was still dressed for the flight. Woollen jumper. Tweed pencil skirt. Elasticated stockings. She felt unbearably warm. But she was determined to paddle in the sea at Fortune Bay before they drove on to the hotel to check-in. She could have changed into something cooler at the airport. But Cassandra was filled with excitement. She was back in Sainte Marie again. All that she could think about was seeing their villa and the beach again. She stopped at the waters' edge; bent down and peeled off her stockings. And almost fell over in the process of doing so. Jumping up and down in the cooling sea. Waving her stockings above her head. She started to dance to a music that was only in her mind. There were very few people left on the beach. The sun was descending towards the horizon. Those that were there took no notice of the middle-aged woman, with a middle-aged figure, wearing unsuitable middle-age style clothing, cavorting about in the white surf.

She kicked one leg as far as her skirt would allow. Pirouetted to face the land. She could see it from where she stood. She could see their new home, well the top part of it anyway. Its painted wall was tinted a beige pink shade from the fading sunlight.

'Yes!' shouted Cassandra, waving her stockings above her head like a football supporter at a match. 'Yes, our new home is finally ready! At last! At last! Let's go and peek through the fence to see it.' She kicked the seawater towards her husband as he approached her across the beach.

'Cassie, you're just like a kid at Christmas.'

189

'Fine by me. A kid at Christmas is good. Full of optimism, hope and exuberance. Not like adults. They've long stopped believing in Father Christmas. Time has gifted them with fixed ideas, set ways and even predictable presents. Often their presents are as unsurprising and boring as they are. Dreary socks or scarves that nobody will ever wear.'

'Goodness you are waxing lyrical after the long flight. But I'd rather have you like a kid too. And nobody could ever say that your behaviour was predictable.'

Cassandra danced across the beach towards their newly finished home. Dry sand stuck to her feet giving her ballerina shoes of sand. She sang at the top of her voice.

'Definitely unpredictable behaviour,' he repeated, laughing to himself.

Mark followed her holding his footwear in his hands. They reached the fence marking the rear of the villa's garden. Cassandra put her face to a gap in the fence. She parted the foliage to survey the small garden with its patio area and plunge pool. The plants were all very young and recently planted. This left the garden looking surprisingly 'untropical', as usually everything grows with great abundance. From where they were, the building looked impressive, pristine and perfect. But the colours and details of everything were being transformed minute by minute by the fading light and the approaching nightfall. They were soon unable to see everything with clarity. Unexpectedly, a large brown insect ran over Cassandra's hand. A tiny cry of surprise and she withdrew it rapidly from the fence. Mark laughed.

'Better than a pair of socks eh?' They left their station by the fence.

'But you can't buy many Caribbean villas for the price of a pair of woolly socks, especially if you're buying it through Damien Janes.'

'We have that pleasure to look forward to tomorrow,' added Mark sarcastically. 'Better get going to the hotel.'

They were staying in a hotel for a couple of days whilst checking that all was well with their villa. They would not be acquiring the keys until the final thirty per cent was handed over to the developers. The couple had splashed out on five star luxury. The hotel was only 10 minutes away from the villa. They had discovered it on a previous visit. They had been wooed by its cliff-top location, next to a small bay. Cassandra was delighted by their room and the view of the sea. She relished in its luxury and elegance. She had a liking for being pampered.

But the anticipation and elation throughout the long journey to the island and flying across several time zones had left her feeling exhausted. Consequently, at dinner, contrary to normal, she soon lost interest in the wonderful gourmet food. The main course put away, Cassandra informed Mark she had to head back to the room.

'I feel exhilarated, but elation makes my batteries run low,' Cassandra took her husband's hand. He told her that he would be along in just a minute, having finished off the bottle of wine.

'Let's hope that your happiness isn't premature, as we haven't inspected the villa yet,' declared the ever cautious Mark. As she wandered back to their room, those words were ringing in her ears.

Cassandra felt too dead tired to start worrying about potential problems. She reached their room in a daze. Her clothes and shoes were soon piled on a chair. She felt exhausted. She needed to sleep for a week. She crawled between the smooth, cool sheets of the huge bed. The lullaby of croaking tree frogs drifted on the warm night air. She loved their chorus. After fifteen seconds, she became oblivious to everything in the world, including the tree frogs. She didn't even hear her husband enter the room some five minutes afterwards.

After the miracle of a long night's sleep, and dreams of calm crystal water disturbed by sea serpents, Cassandra awoke ready to face the world. She was well prepared for the meeting with Damien Janes and any surprises that that might bring. On arrival at the Tropical Island Villas office, neither of them were astounded that he wasn't there. Adrian, his accountant, met them. Mr Janes had been detained. Rick, the site manager, would show them their villa. Mr Janes hoped to join them later.

Mark was privately pleased about the arrangement. Rick was a far more appropriate person to show them the construction. He was far more knowledgeable. He was not a tedious personality.

'Janes seems to be making a habit of not turning up for our appointments,' said Mark.

'I'm very sorry about this. I'm sure that Mr Janes will be along soon.'

Taking advantage of the situation, Mark thought he would try to find out a bit more about the complex. 'Adrian, can you tell us how many properties are now complete and paid for?'

Adrian looked rather taken aback. He hesitated about replying. 'Well....... um, I'm not certain of all the details. I believe around a third have received their Certificate of Completion. And they have been paid for in full.'

'And are any of these occupied?'

Again Adrian looked dubious about answering, 'Um ...well, to my knowledge, I don't think any are occupied, but I may be wrong.'

'We will be spending the rest of our holiday in our villa,' piped up Cassandra. Did she imagine it, or did Cassandra see the accountant's face change slightly at this comment? 'We discussed it with Mr Janes.'

'Oh really! I know nothing about that. I'm only the accountant. I just know that Rick has signed your Certificate of Completion for 5B,' he paused. 'As the building is complete, shall I set up a bank transfer for your final payment?'

Mark was fazed by the suggestion. 'Oh no Adrian, I think that is rather untimely. Our villa has to be inspected before we will transfer any funds.'

'It's just that the keys are not handed over until we have the last thirty per cent. And you have just said that you intend to stay in your villa.'

'All in good time Adrian.'

After the exchange of several niceties, Cassandra and Mark left the office. They walked to the hire car in silence. Mark started up the car and then just sat looking through the windscreen into space.

'I'm not happy,' he said in a low tone. 'What did you notice about Adrian?'

'He was not his usual cheerful, talkative self.'

'He was as transparent as a two year old. He was concerned about something. I hope that he never wants to have an affair, because his wife would know about it within five minutes.'

'You think that he knows something about our villa? Something that he couldn't tell us? I did notice his reaction when I mentioned about us staying there.'

'I'm pretty certain he knows something. Info that he would have liked to have told us, but couldn't for professional reasons. What with that and Janes not turning up again, it makes me feel rather wary.'

'Well, we know that we are dealing with some dubious characters here. Let's go Mark. Come on, let's go and face the music.'

They drove to Fortune Bay feeling rather flat and deflated. However, they agreed that they should behave as though everything in the garden was rosy. Rick was awaiting their arrival.

'Well, I'm pleased that somebody is punctual about keeping their appointments,' Mark said snidely. 'To be

193

frank Rick, we consider that Janes is very unprofessional. This isn't the first time he hasn't turned up for a meeting. AND he doesn't even apologise afterwards. There you are, I believe in telling it like it is.'

'I believe Damien has a bit of an emergency with another client,' responded Rick. 'I'm sure that he will be along as soon as he can. Shall we go and have a look at your villa? I think you are aware that you haven't got all of your furnishings. However, the basics are there. The installation of the kitchen was only finished last week.'

'But, we've paid for the majority of the furniture package Rick. We paid at the same time as the initial deposit. Why isn't it all in place?' queried Cassandra.

'We don't have enough storage to keep all of the furniture on island. We have to order things as they are needed. Everything comes from the States. Unfortunately, some of the suppliers are very unreliable.'

'But, Janes has known about this visit for three months,' said Mark whose patience was becoming frayed. Rick didn't respond.

As they approached the front door of their villa, Cassandra reflected that she had dreamed of this moment for what seemed like an eternity. She took a deep intake of breath as Rick turned the key in the lock and let them into the entrance hall. With a sense of relief, she looked around her. No cracks in the wall, the flooring looked great and there was even their chosen pendant lighting in the hall. The telephone however was stowed on the floor. Mark immediately opened the note pad he had been carrying and started to note any problems. The sitting room looked exceedingly bare as there was only a sofa and a rug in it. Cassandra noticed with disappointment that the wrong tiles had been put in one of the bathrooms. There were no locks on some of the external doors. The pool had not been filled, as the pump hadn't been installed. There were several things that were not completely finished off. Mark's list grew quickly, but they didn't actually encounter anything that would stop them staying in the villa. Cassandra could feel her inside starting to relax. Perhaps they had been wrong. Perhaps there was no major problem.

'We will come into the office and pay the balance tomorrow. We will retain a small amount until all of the problems on the list are rectified and we have all of the missing furniture,' stated Mark. 'Then we plan to move in.'

'Oh, we advise you not to stay here at the moment. You would be the only ones here. We couldn't guarantee that you would be safe. You will have to sort out with Damien and Adrian about the finances,' said Rick.

'There are security staff here 24/7, aren't there?' asked Cassandra. Rick affirmed that there was. 'So, what's the problem?'

'You have seen that there are some doors that don't have proper locks. There is also the noise in the day of the workers at the far end of the complex. The place is still partially a building site.'

They hadn't been mistaken. Cassandra knew that their suspicions were on track. There was some problem that they were not being told about. Something that wasn't immediately obvious. It was a pity that they couldn't be left alone in the villa in order to have a really good look around.

'Well, you have been warned. You really might be better in a hotel, at least for the next few days, until we can get all of these problems sorted out.'

'Rick, we have looked forward to staying in the villa during our holiday. There has been delay after delay with the construction. One problem after another has stopped us from coming here. We have waited far too long. When we pay you tomorrow, this villa is ours to do what we want with.' As Cassandra said this, in a flash, it came to her. 'They want us to pay the money,' she thought. 'For some reason they need our thirty per cent. They're running short of funds. Yes, that's it! They definitely need our money! They need it to fix something in the villa. Even Adrian had asked us to settle our final payment.'

'My wife is right,' added Mark, 'we have waited far too long, for what after all is only a medium sized house. We are fed up with waiting. We will be coming here tomorrow with our luggage after we have paid at the office. If you could be so good as to get one of your men to install the locks before we arrive.'

'We are really going to enjoy making this our second home,' said Cassandra. 'We just need to go and get a few supplies in Anse Argent.' As they were in the kitchen, Cassandra went to one of the kitchen units and surveyed inside. It was filled with plates and cups and saucers. 'Great, we've got something to eat off,' she smiled.

She opened each of the cupboards whilst making her way towards the sink. There she lifted up the tap. Water splashed into the stainless steel sink. 'So, it's not the water supply,' she thought to herself. She looked out of the kitchen window towards their pool. She wondered if it could be the pool and walked out onto the patio and looked into the pool again. It looked fine; it wasn't leaking, as there was a quantity of stagnant rain water in the bottom of it. The men had come outside to join her. 'When is the pool pump due to arrive? It would be great to have it useable before we go home.'

'Sorry, I've no idea. You will have to ask in the office about that,' responded Rick.

'Shall we go back to the hotel then Mark? It would be nice to have a swim. Thank you for your time then Rick. I suspect we will see you around the site, as we are here for nearly three weeks.' There was silence from Rick.

As they walked out of the front door, Cassandra said 'I'll see you back at the car Mark. I'm just going to use the bathroom.'

'Eh yes, OK,' said Rick, 'I hope you enjoy your holiday.'

She went back into the villa, rushed to the nearest bathroom and checked the lights, the shower, washbasin and toilet. To her surprise, they all seemed to work fine. She was running out of ideas. She was convinced that there was something they weren't being told. On returning to the car, she started to explain her misgivings about their villa to Mark. He was in agreement with her.

'Look Cassie, we're in a catch 22 situation here. We both know there is something wrong. But they aren't going to give us the keys, so that we can find out what it is, until we pay the final balance. I suggest we withhold 5 per cent of the villa money and also refuse to pay the rest for the furniture package.'

'Yes, we only have around a third of the furniture that we ordered. It was also very obvious Rick was very much against us using the villa. We will have to wait to see what tomorrow brings.'

$$$

Above was a palette of turquoise; a collage of tropical images filled the small enclosed garden. The blackbirds squawked their shrill cry from the overhanging palms and a red throated finch bounced around between the newly planted bushes searching for scraps. A full bellied dove strutted up and down the stone patio which surrounded the empty plunge pool. Its pink and purple iridescent chest feathers gleamed. A bright yellow butterfly flitted from immature plant to plant. Several khaki-coloured geckos could be seen chasing one another up the newly painted garden fence.

The cacophony of waves breaking onto the adjacent beach and then ebbing back dominated the compact area. A bikini clad woman was stretched out on a sunbed next to the useless pool. Only her white lower legs were exposed to the fading sunlight. The upper part of her body was protected by the shade of a large multi-coloured parasol.

It was nearing the end of the second day that Cassandra and Mark had been installed at their brand-new address. Cassandra was on cloud nine. She loved the space, the luminosity and the contemporary architecture. Even though they had very little furniture, she was a fan of what they had. She was ecstatic about the exotic plants and unusual birds in their garden. She adored the perpetual rhapsody of the sea pounding in her ears. Compared to the three bed 'semi' that they had at home, it was like a palace, a dream home. Despite several other problems with the villa having come to light, which were added to the already long snagging list, the lady of the house was in raptures over their villa. They had done a thorough investigation. They had not found any major default.

She had lain awake during their first night in the villa. A mixture of the hum of the air conditioning and the crashing of the surf outside filled the starkly furnished bedroom. Mark slept soundly. Not Cassandra. She worried that there must be something they had missed. She became anxious that they may not get all the snagging in the house rectified. She was perturbed that the rest of the furniture package would never be theirs. She was frightened that because of this, they would be unable to rent out the villa. She fretted that they may have unexpected expenses that they would not be able to pay for. In spite of all this, she finally fell asleep. Two hours later, she was woken by the squeal of the birds. Then she heard the whining of an electric drill in the neighbouring villa. Through the window, unclad by curtaining, sharp shadows from one of the palms flicked across the ceiling. Cassandra turned to look at the window and could see a clear aquamarine sky. A smile spread across her face. The worries of the previous night evaporated into tropical thin air.

They were nearing the end of their second day, and the light was growing dimmer. From her supine position on the sunbed, Cassandra squinted through her sunglasses.

She espied Mark bring out two glasses full of a coral coloured liquid. There was no garden table to put them on. Consequently, he put Cassandra's cocktail on an upside down crate. He had purloined it from the construction site earlier in the day.

'Rum punches to pay tribute to the sunset.' Mark raised his glass to the sky.

'You wonderful, wonderful man!' sighed Cassandra. 'A perfect end to a perfect day,' she toasted.

They had decided to cook their first meal in the villa that evening. They started discussing the logistics of the operation. The kitchen was so ill-equipped. The dialogue was interrupted. Someone was calling through their open front door. Mark investigated. He discovered two construction workers.

'Good evening my friends, I bring mwen jan, my mate, about the carpentry job you needs. He work at Fortune Bay some time ago.'

The previous day, Mark had asked one of the workers if he knew any local carpenters. They wanted a little lock up cupboard built at the side of the villa to put their small garden furniture, parasols and cushions in.

The two workers entered in an unsure manner. They were still dressed in their working attire. One was tall and slim and around thirty. The wood worker was much older. The site worker pulled off his woolly hat to reveal medium length braided hair.

'This Tim. He good guy and real good wood worker.'

'That's great; thank you so much,' Cassandra welcomed them. 'Mark has done a simple drawing with dimensions of what we want.'

'You welcome, mi lady.'

'Can I offer you both a beer whilst we talk about the cupboard?' she asked.

What workman would refuse a cold beer at the end of a long hot day? Mark directed Tim, clutching his bottle of beer, to the side of the house. Cassandra chatted to Zakari, the construction worker. He reluctantly sat on the sun bed opposite her. Basically, there was nowhere else to sit. It was obvious he didn't seem comfortable with the seating arrangement. Zakari sitting on the sunbed. Him in his working clothes. Her in her bikini.

She sensed this. She promptly put on her beach dress to hide up her roly-poly bits. Conversation led to Zakari telling her that he had helped to build their house. Zakari spoke very softly and with a heavy local accent. Cassandra had to listen very carefully to be able to understand what he was saying. She enquired if he enjoyed working at the Fortune Bay site. He replied that it was usually fine, but there were sometimes problems.

'What sort of problems?'

Zakari hesitated. He looked around before replying. He explained that they didn't always get paid on time. Also, in the past the developers hadn't paid any money to the Social Security Department for the workers. Cassandra admitted that she had heard about that during their last visit to the island. She told Zakari that she thought it was scandalous and asked if that was the reason why Tim had stopped working there. He confessed that it was partially the reason. But there were other reasons. He preferred not to discuss them, as they were more to do with Tim. This sparked Cassandra's curiosity. She offered him another beer hoping that it might loosen his tongue a little. Zakari accepted the beer, but changed the topic of conversation.

'Is ya happy wit' ya new house?'

'Happy is not the word Zakari, I'm over the moon. There are things that still need to be done, but I think overall, it is superb, so thank you for helping to make it so terrific.'

'Ya very welcome, mi lady.'

'Zakari, my name is Cassandra. I'm not really my lady.'

'OK, Miss Cassandra. Ya happy wit' de bathrooms? I helps wit' de pipes in de bathrooms ya know. Dat what I do.'

By this time Cassandra's mind was starting to race. Perhaps the second beer was working after all. She felt that Zakari was perhaps trying to tell her something about the bathrooms. She asked if he would like to see one of the finished bathrooms.

'But, mi lady, ...Cassandra, dis what I try to tell ya.' He looked around again and lowered his voice even more. 'De bathrooms not finish mi lady. They not commissioned. De lifting station here not installed. De plumbing company not get dere money. Dey refuses to install de lifting station here. Dey wants de money first. But, mi lady, I never done told ya dat. Ya understand?'

'I don't really understand Zakari. Lifting station? What is it? What does it do? Why do we need it?'

'It take de slops, de sewage to de tanks in de service area, at end of villas. Up there.'

'Zakari, show me. Where should it be?'

'Miss Cassandra, I not sure I can do dat. I works here. I needs my job. I not like my boss, but he my boss. He pay me. Well, usually he pay me.'

'OK. You tell me where it SHOULD be.'

'In front of de house next door, dere a square of metal in de ground. It smell real strong when ya near it.'

Cassandra grabbed hold of Zakari's arm.

'Zakari, just stay exactly where you are.' She chased into the kitchen. Cassandra found her purse. She emptied all the dollars on the work surface. She knew that it wasn't a fortune. She wanted Zakari to see that she appreciated him taking a risk. She rushed back and pushed the money into his hand. 'That's all I have at present Zakari. Thank you so much for telling us. We were suspicious that there was a problem, but we couldn't find out what it was. I suppose we would have known for sure in a few days.'

'For sure, mi lady.....Cassandra. I not tell ya for de money. Dey not treat people right mi lady. Dey cheats on everybody. Dat why Tim leave.'

'Take the money Zakari. I want you to take it. I know you are risking your job. Mark and I will sort this out. We won't mention you or Tim. We will say we have discovered it ourselves.'

At this point, Mark was just finishing talking to Tim and was shaking his hand and making arrangements for him to return the following week. Cassandra saw little point in repeating the story in front of Tim. They saw the men out.

'I think you need another drink Mark. A very strong one. Come into the kitchen and I'll make it for you.' Cassandra closed the sliding door behind them. The ruby-coloured cocktail was put on the kitchen work surface.

'Shame we haven't got any seating in here. I think you will probably want to sit down when you hear what I have to tell you. I hate to say this Mark, but we are in the shit.'

'That's not like you Cassie.'

'I mean it. Well, in a couple of days, we will definitely be in the shit, in the sewage, in the bathroom waste or whatever you like to call it! The problem we thought was there, but couldn't find it, is the sewage. There is no pump to pump it away from here. It is just lying under a manhole in front of the next door villa and it's gradually backing up.'

Mark didn't take too long to understand what his wife was trying to explain. 'That bastard Janes! I'm going to kill him! Where's my phone?'

22 Confrontations and Compensations

Cassandra - Autumn 2011

It had been dark when the couple had investigated the problem. They very quickly found that Zakari had been correct. As soon as they stood to the far side of the villa next door, the predicament became blatantly obvious. They rapidly moved back to the shelter of their new home. Mark immediately phoned the office of Tropical Island Villas. Wendell answered the phone. Mark told him that if Janes didn't get his ugly face in front of their villa in half an hour, he was likely to rearrange it for him next time he saw him. He didn't care what Janes was doing. He didn't care which woman Janes was with, he had to be there.

Cassandra had never seen Mark so furious. He was not a violent man. He was usually so placid and calm. However, she understood; she felt equally livid. She felt exceedingly tense. Her emotions told her she should be lashing out at someone. They had been used. They had been made a fool of. She knew from her knowledge of the island that they had paid a very high price for the villa. She had calculated that the development company was making a very good profit from the units at Fortune Bay. Adrian had reluctantly told them that around a third of the clients had already paid for their properties. So why the hell didn't they have enough money to pay the construction company's bills? It didn't take a genius to work that one out. She felt sure that Janes and his companies had several off-shore accounts. She understood more fully why it was that the islanders hated Janes together with his development business so much. It was sad, but comprehensible, the islanders would do anything to get back at them. It was such a small island. Everybody knew what was going on.

A short time later, there was a knock at the door. Mark opened it. Wendell Thorner and Damien Janes. They entered. Mark remained silent. Cassandra was also tight-lipped. She stood in the doorway of the sitting room.

Janes looked around and started talking, 'Your choice of lighting works very well in the hall. I think you....'

'This is not a social occasion Janes. I'm not going to offer you drinks. I'm sure that you both know why I asked you to come here,' Mark interrupted. His voice remained calm.

'I have no idea,' said Damien. Wendell said nothing.

'Then you are a liar, as well as a cheat,' said Mark raising his voice slightly. 'I will be contacting my lawyer on the island to instruct him to take action against you. You had your site manager sign the Certificate of Completion. You let us pay our last thirty per cent. You did all this. And you knew the villa was not in fact ready for habitation.'

'We knew from your accountant, Adrian, and from Rick, that there was a problem. Adrian is transparent as air. They aren't as used to lying as you. Rick tried very hard to get us to stay in a hotel for a few days,' Cassandra joined in.

'It didn't take a genius to work it out Janes. We knew there was a problem when we moved in. We knew, but just couldn't find it. After two days of living here, it was easy to find. It hits you in the face. Or should I say the nose!'

Damien Janes and Wendell Thorner spoke at the same time. 'I still don't know what the problem is,' stated Janes.

'So, what would you like us to do about things?' asked Wendell. Damien looked at him sharply.

'It would seem that perhaps Mr Thorner has slightly more of a conscience than you Janes.' Mark maintained his serious face. 'What I want you to do is to find us a hotel that we can move into from tomorrow morning. It should be of the same standard as our villa. You will pay for the hotel until all of the problems in this villa are sorted out. Rick has a list of all the snagging. The list is long. We will pay for our own food during this time. The longer it takes, the longer you will be paying our hotel bill.'

'We can probably find room for you at the time share hotel, Diamond Point, in Anse Argent,' Janes responded.

'Definitely not!' Cassandra cut in. 'We want a proper hotel. You won't have to pay for Diamond Point. We have just paid you a sizeable amount of money. You can get us a good hotel from some of your profits. We are not fools Mr Janes. Don't treat us like them. You can phone us in the morning to explain what has been organised.'

'It would seem then you have conceded that there is a problem,' interjected Mark. 'You get this sorted, or you will find your name all over the local newspapers and on the internet. I'm sure that the papers would be interested in the story, knowing how popular you are on the island. My wife is very good at writing. She would do a very good job of writing an article for the papers.'

'We will sort something out for you in the morning,' Wendell muttered.

'Cassie, do you have anything to add?' queried Mark. She shook her head.

Mark strode to the front door and opened it. Wendell made his way towards it. Damien stood where he was.

'Janes,' Mark said brusquely, 'you are not welcome here.' Damien went to open his mouth to say something. He decided against it.

'Good evening Cassandra. Come on DJ,' prompted Wendell.

Damien Janes left without another word. The door was shut behind him. Cassandra moved towards her husband and put her arms around him. He knew that she was desperately upset. She loved the villa and didn't want to stay in a hotel.

'Don't worry Cassie. We've got the upper hand here. We'll get all of the snagging done. The pump will be installed at the speed of light. They won't want to pay our hotel bill.'

'What have we got ourselves into? We seem to be dealing with a load of crooks. It doesn't look good for the future.'

'Look Cassie, let's not worry about the future. We can create our own future; we will sort out each problem as it arises. That bunch of bandits is not going to get the better of us.'

'You're right. I know none of this is amusing my darling, but we actually saw Janes lost for words. That must be a very rare occurrence. And another thing, he capitulated without us actually mentioning what the major problem with the villa was,' giggled Cassandra.

'That's my girl. See the funny side of it. You know something Cassie; I've got a very long memory. I'm going to get that Janes. However long it takes, I'm going to see him fall.'

$$$

The next morning, it hadn't taken them long to pack up their suitcases and leave the villa. They drove to the hotel that Tropical Island Villas had reserved for them. Before they checked in, they asked to see the room. Even before they got there, they could see that the hotel was barely living up to its three star rating. Cassie squeezed Mark's hand and whispered that she didn't want to stay there. The room was spartan and basic. The furniture had definitely seen better days. When they returned to reception, they told the receptionist that they wouldn't be taking up the reservation. She informed them that Tropical Island Villas had already paid for the first night. Cassandra apologised. She hoped they hadn't inconvenienced them, but they had decided that they wouldn't be staying there. She declared that she was certain the hotel could sort things out with the development company.

Installed back in the car, Mark was on his phone again.

'OK Adrian, give me Janes please. ......Janes, you are really testing our patience here. How dare you think you can brush us off with that run-down hotel! We have told you, we are not fools. We are going to drive to the Calabash Tree........ Yes, I know it's one of the most expensive hotels on the island.......... You had your chance. We have taken the decision out of your hands. You had better send somebody down there to pay for the first few nights...... but Janes, you are the one that created the problem........ We'll wait for somebody to meet us in the hotel bar. If they aren't down at the bar in an hour, we will drive to the 'Harbour Lights' and that's all-inclusive, so will cost you even more.'

'What happened to my quiet and reserved husband? You used to say so little,' declared Cassandra. 'These problems are obviously very character building for you.'

'I don't usually lose my temper and get angry, but that man pushes me to the limits of my patience.'

As they approached the bay and drove through the village of Calabash, they commented on how different life was there from the north of the island. The village spanned the top of a ridge, which dropped down sharply to the sea. The vast majority of the homes were small, wooden creole cottages. They faced directly onto the road. The cottages were all painted in bright cheerful colours, much the same as they had seen in Prosper. It appeared that much of life was lived outdoors. Many of the inhabitants sat on their veranda steps. Their children, many of whom wore no shoes, played together in the road. There seemed to be no modern shops. Several of the village people had old-world type stalls. They sold goods from their verandas. Cassandra noticed drinks, local fruit, vegetables and eggs for sale.

They drove through the village and down a steep slope towards the hotel and the shore. Within a few hundred yards from Calabash, they found the five star hotel which ascended from the water's edge up a steep slope. Further round the bay, perched along the top of the ridge, they could see some enormous villas. They made theirs look like a doll's house. The bay was a dichotomy of twenty first century luxury against Caribbean poverty, both sharing the same phenomenal view over the ocean.

They waited in the bar of the Calabash Tree. Darius arrived within the hour. He made no comment about their situation. He behaved as though this was an everyday phenomenon. Perhaps it was for him. He informed them that the company would not pay for their meals. Mark and Cassandra were soon installed in a hotel room that cost more per night than Cassandra earned in a week.

The couple's suite overlooked an exquisite tropical garden, the marina and Calabash Bay. The marina was small, but the vessels moored there certainly were not. The whole complex exuded an ambiance of affluence and wealth. On exploring the facilities of the hotel, they found that there was an arcade of up-market shops, cafes and restaurants. From the marina, they were able to take a very rustic-looking ferry over to a small beach on the opposite side of the cove. Cassandra loved the idea. It was so unlike anything that she had encountered before. The ferry was a flat pontoon-type boat with a bright red wooden canopy. They were given a pass for the ferry at reception. The ferry man would take them backwards and forwards to the sandy beach and other places around the bay.

They had already decided that they could not eat at the hotel restaurants. It would be way beyond their budget. They had the car. They would have to eat out in the local restaurants. In retrospect, they realised that this decision added so much to their experience at Calabash Bay. However, they didn't need the car. Whilst exploring near the hotel, they found a small restaurant and bar called the Bullion Bar. Like many of the facilities not attached to the hotel, it was painted up in bright, almost garish colours.

The rustic wooden bar area was painted in gold. International currency was pinned to its ceiling. In the adjoining restaurant, there were life size tropical birds. Silent birds made out of felt. On phony perches, strung from the ceiling. In addition, lots of cheerful sayings about life were posted on the pillars holding up the ceiling. "I'm like a good red wine, I'm best when I'm drunk." "I only drink beer on days that end with a Y." Quotes that one might only find amusing if you had consumed too much alcohol. The decking of the floor of the restaurant was built over the water. The view from its open front went right around the bay. One could see over to the beach they had visited the previous day. There, numerous palms soared upwards. Enormous long trunks topped with just a few ragged leaves and bunches of coconuts. The little red ferry toing and froing. Yachts sailing in and out of the marina passed very close to the dining platform. Spectacular!

Compared to the hotel facilities, the place was really native. The menu was very simple. It was mainly consisted of local foods. Jerk chicken, salt fish with green figs, fried local fish, accra and fried plantain. Of course, Cassandra loved it. It seemed that many of the local inhabitants did too. On a couple of occasions, they were the only tourists eating in the establishment. It was filled with lively chatter and laughter. Cassandra being Cassandra, soon got to know the waitresses. She chatted to them when they weren't too busy. She asked them about the island food, about where they lived and their families. They shared lots of jokes and laughter. She found them naturally very amusing. The restaurant played Caribbean-style music. Cassandra didn't recognise the melodies, but appreciated them. More than once, a waitress would come up to their rustic wooden table dancing to the piped music. One of the young ladies had a very ample behind, which jiggled from side to side as she danced. Cassandra could see from his facial expressions that Mark was very taken by this 'erotic' dancing. One day, this young waitress served their food and as she was about to leave asked if there was anything else they needed.

Immediately Cassandra said, 'Yes, you can teach me how to dance like that. My husband's eyes were out on stalks watching you!'

'Sure,' retorted the waitress, 'You finish your dinner and I go teach you.' They both collapsed into laughter. The waitress cheekily danced away to the rhythm of the music, her behind wiggling as she went, singing 'Shake ya business, shake what ya Mama gave ya.'

One lunchtime they were impressed by a very large mega yacht anchored in the bay. Cassandra and Mark watched as four people descended from the yacht into a dinghy. It headed towards the Bullion Bar. The four were a white American, aged around seventy-five, who spoke loud enough for all of the restaurant to hear, two West Indian crew members, and a young and very beautiful Afro-Caribbean girl of around twenty. The relationship between the American and the young lady was very soon obvious. The American helped her from the dingy. He held her closely. He draped his arm over her shoulder. As she strolled along the wharf, Cassandra could see immediately that her clothes definitely didn't come from a chain store like her own. She was very elegant. Classy swim suit and wrap. Bespangled sandals. Designer sunglasses. The ensemble was topped with a very becoming straw hat. Also unlike Cassandra, the girl was bedecked with masses of jewellery. Diamond bracelets, diamond droplet earrings and a diamond pendant. Plus a monster-sized gold watch. She looked very stunning, but totally out of place in the simple, rustic environment.

Apart from ordering her meal, the young lady said nothing. She amused herself with what looked like a computer game. The men talked loudly about boats and their proposed voyage. They didn't address the girl at all during the hour whilst they ate their lunch. She was beautiful, but she definitely didn't look very happy. As Cassandra and Mark were finishing off their lunch; and the group was leaving, the young waitress came up to speak to them.

She chuckled and said to Cassandra, 'It your turn to have eyes out on stalks!'

'Oh, was it that obvious? I was fascinated! They just ignored the girl.'

'But she there for one thing. She not there to chat about yachts.'

'But she looked so unhappy,' remarked Cassandra.

'Is sleeping with man of his age a lot of fun? I think not. But, she make her choice. She gotten compensations. She gotten all them diamonds. She see the world. When he stop giving her diamonds, she leave him. She go find some other old fool.'

Cassandra laughed, 'It wouldn't be for me.'

'Nor me,' laughed the waitress, 'I rather have my friends and my job than all that bling.'

'I bet you really see life here.'

'Sure do! I loves my job. We sees the world here, it come to us, we laughs a lot and dances a lot..... You needs anything else for lunch my darlings?'

The incident started a conversation between Cassandra and Mark about some of the islanders who they had encountered. They were so full of joy and laughter and yet didn't seem to have very much. The waitress, the boys on the beach looking after the beach chairs, the man guarding the cars in the car park, the ladies trying to sell cheap jewellery on the beach. They all smiled very readily. They laughed and joked with anyone and everyone. This was in contrast to some of the foreign tourists in the five star hotel. They complained at the bar, complained at reception, complained by the pool, they complained to other guests, and they complained in the cafes. They did nothing but complain. Complain in that island paradise. They obviously had a very different attitude to life than the people of Sainte Marie.

Though Cassandra had initially been very disappointed about moving out of their villa, they had such a wonderful time at Calabash Bay that they wouldn't have missed that time for anything. For Cassandra, it was a period of learning. Understanding much more about the island and islanders. It changed her view of them and perhaps even slightly her view about life in general.

They stayed there six nights before returning back to their villa. As Mark had anticipated, the majority of the construction problems were rectified. They even had a few more pieces of furniture in place. After those initial problems, they anticipated that they may be only the beginning of the trials and tribulations that were to follow in the future. How right they were.

23 Working with a Soul Mate

Damien - Spring 2012

Donna would have been very upset. She would be upset if she could have seen the state of the beach house at Anse Argent. She liked everything to be in good order. Spick and span. The cushions had to be plumped up on the settees. The glass tops of the coffee tables had to gleam. The towels in the bathrooms had to be folded and hung straight. Ornaments had to be displayed at just the right angle. All the utensils in the kitchen had to be put back in their designated place.

None of that was the case. That evening, Damien didn't care about any of it. He was having a party and Donna was in England. Ayanna was looking after things. The coffee table was filled with empty bottles and glasses. A couple of the bathrooms seemed to be permanently locked from the inside and the last thing that mattered in there was the towels. The kitchen was filled to overflowing with people laughing and engaged in loud conversation. It was fairly obvious that a large percentage had had too much to drink. Some of the other guests were also high on weed. There was a thick haze of smoke that filled the room. Scraps of food had been left all over the house and garden. They were on floors, tables, seats, beds, work surfaces, and even in the swimming pool. There were a few people dancing to very loud music on the patio next to the pool.

Damien had invited about thirty people, including some of his neighbours and a couple of villa owners who happened to be on island. However, there was more than double that. The noise and the music had attracted others who thought they would help Damien consume his bottles of champagne, rum, whisky and wine. And eat up the trays of food that had been ordered from the local caterer. Damien hadn't seemed to notice that there were people in his house that he had never seen before in his life. He also didn't seem to notice the large statuette that lay in slivers on the hall floor. Or observe the sad state of his usually smart home.

Ayanna wasn't any better. She came out of one of the bedrooms. She smoothed down her close-fitting pink dress that Damien had recently bought her in a shop of a local five star hotel. She knew that she looked good in it. She walked down the stairs, disregarding the household problems that she saw on the way, but surveying her finger nails that had been painted in a salon. Ayanna knew that it wouldn't be her that had to clear up all the mess the following day, though she had been calling the house 'home' for several months now.

She found Damien in the sitting room. Despite the fact that he was pontificating about something to a guest who she didn't know, she went up to him and kissed him lightly on the mouth.

'Great party, honey. Everyone is enjoying themselves,' she remarked.

He turned to face her. She had had a bit to drink, but nevertheless noticed that his eyes were very blood-shot. His breath smelt of a foul mixture of stale alcohol and spicy food. He was perspiring excessively, his shirt clinging to his lean form. He looked very much older than his years. His words were run together. He had become rather inarticulate.

'Ayanna, come and meet my friend......... I'zz been telling him all about Fortune Bay. Tell him how smart it izz.'

'Yeah, the villas are real high end.'

'They been sooo very easy to sell. The beach is perfect and the facil ...teas are excellent. You should reee...ally take a look. I'zz.. can meet you for lunch first.'

'I real proud of Damien, he sold so many beautiful homes. There's so many happy people.'

214

The 'friend' nodded, excused himself and then left the pair, saying that he would perhaps contact Damien tomorrow to visit the villa complex. Damien glugged back the drink that he had in his hand. He suddenly fell backwards. Fortunately there was a settee to catch him; but unfortunately, there was already somebody else sat on it. After some howling and cursing, the initial occupant of the settee succumbed to its owner. Damien lay back on his settee and told Ayanna that his 'friend' had been very impressed.

'Izz a great salesman. You know, I can ssss..ell anything to anybody. It's like Wendell sayzz "You can fool eeeverybody all the time and that'zz enough to make a bloody good living."' His befuddled brain, from his earlier joint and too much alchohol, made him misquote and slur the well-known saying. It didn't matter, as Ayanna had heard it from Damien several times before during their relationship.

Even though Damien was as high as the stars, Ayanna was always careful how she replied to him. She knew that it was important to try to boost his ego, maintain his confidence, and stay on the right side of him. Occasionally, she took chances and was ambiguous in what she said, hoping that her sarcasm would not be noticed. This was one of those occasions.

'Sure, DJ, we all know you a great salesman. You tells everybody. You knows all there is to know about selling; you told me. You chases the deal even after the guy he say "no". You never gives up.'

This time she need not have worried about either his sensitivity or his ego because when she looked at him again, he had passed out. His head was supported by the settee back, his mouth wide open. The mixture of alcohol and pot had obviously got the better of him. She surmised that he would be there until late the next morning. As she looked at him, she wondered if he would think he was so

215

great if he could see himself now. His face looked worn and tired, despite the help he had had from Botox. There were deep lines around his eyes and his hair was starting to recede and turn white. Ayanna looked around her. She surveyed the multi-million dollar house. She knew why she stayed. She smoothed down her dress again and took the opportunity to go and really enjoy the party. Perhaps she might even find somebody a lot more enticing.

$$$

Damien slammed his beer bottle down on the plastic table top in the Yacht Club bar. They were the only customers there that afternoon; just them and the young lady behind the bar. This was the reason that they had chosen the venue.

'Christ Dell, no! We can't do that! Take no notice of him Van. He's got no idea. He only does the job for the fast cars and fast women he can get with his money.'

Van looked at Wendell and laughed, 'Could be worse reasons for doing a job! '

'You need me for my family name DJ. You wouldn't have got as far as we have without me. On this island it's who you know that's important and my family know all the influential people of Sainte Marie. Don't you forget that!'

'But Dell, we wouldn't have achieved anything without my prime ideas,' said Damien.

Wendell felt rather annoyed about being put down in front of his mate. He leaned back in his chair and displayed his broad chest and shoulders and remained silent whilst drinking his beer.

Damien considered that it was time to start renting out the owners' units he had sold. He wanted to establish a management team and someone to do the marketing in the States and Europe. They needed to start receiving a rental income from the development. Damien had already registered a new company to deal with the management of

Fortune Bay. This was only one amongst many companies that bore their names; each being set up to for different aspects of their projects. Wendell had suggested that perhaps Van might be the right person to set up the management team for the complex. They had discussed it at a Tropical Island Villas meeting. Van and Wendell were old friends. In fact, they had been at college together. However, this occasion was the first time that they had seen each other in several years. Van had been in Miami managing a small hotel.

Van was much the same age as Wendell - around forty, but unlike Wendell, who spent hours in the gym perfecting his shape, Van was well rounded and fleshy. Van liked his food and drink too much. He had flown in from Miami. The partners had shown him around Fortune Bay. They presented each type of villa and apartment; then the spa, the shops, the bar, the reception and offices. The restaurant on the beach was nearing completion. Damien and Wendell explained to Van that they wanted the whole of the complex to be set up like a hotel operation. They were looking for some-one to head it up.

'OK boys, you would like me to market the units to tourists and set up maintenance, cleaning, security and hospitality staff and so on?' Van seemed quite taken with the idea.

'We already have security and cleaning in place, but yes, whatever it takes to get it up and running,' Wendell clarified. 'We are too busy selling the next project, Sapphire, to deal with it ourselves.' Tropical Island Villas had already started clearing a plot of land on the same beach as Fortune Bay, and plans had been drawn up. He and Damien were both very involved in selling apartments and villas there, and collecting deposits in order that building work could commence.

'We want someone who has experience in the hotel trade, but also someone who is flexible and can adapt to what we need here,' added Damien. 'We think we can pay you an attractive salary, find you a home nearby, and perhaps even include an additional incentive, a percentage of the profits.'

'Sounds interesting! I'd like to ask a few questions about the contract with the purchasers. You said that the rental profits will be split fifty fifty between the owners and the Management Company. The marketing costs will be very substantial to start with. Do they come off the overall profits or from the management company's share? '

'That's a good point Van. Obviously it's better for us if marketing is deducted first, before the profits are divided. It means the owners and the management company are paying for the marketing, rather than just the management.'

'And the owners,' asked Van. 'Can they rent out their villas themselves?'

'No,' answered Damien. 'When they purchased their villa, they signed a contract to say that they could use them for up to four weeks a year and then they would be put into a rental pool, which is managed by us, for the rest of the time. The owners are supposed to receive fifty per cent of the net profits.'

'What does it say about the four weeks they can use themselves? Is it in blocks of two weeks at a time or a block of four weeks? The thing is you don't want them all coming out around Christmas for four weeks. This is real high season, when you can get the maximum for the accommodation.'

'Good point. I don't think it actually stipulates if it can be a block of four weeks. It just says four weeks within each year. This is why we could use someone like you Van, who can point out how we can maximise the profits,' stated Wendell.

'Some resorts' contracts state that owners can only take two weeks in high season and then two weeks in mid or low season, other establishments give a lower percentage of the profits if the weeks are taken in high season - say forty or thirty-five per cent. You want owners at the resort as little as possible during the peak season,' pointed out Van.

'Another way of bringing down the owners' percentage,' he continued in a lowed tone, 'is to take an amount off the top of the owners' profits to buy replacement furniture and for improvements to the interiors when they are needed. Things like painting walls and minor repairs. Say five to ten per cent.'

'I hadn't thought of that,' commented Damien. 'That could be a good move.'

'We can always change the Bye Laws, as we will have somebody on the Condominium Board. We will own a couple of the villas, so will in fact be owners as well,' Damien said thoughtfully. 'I'm buying the biggest one of them for myself.'

'Are you indeed? That could prove useful,' smiled Van.

Damien leaned over and patted Van on the shoulder, 'I like this guy. He's a man after my own heart.'

'Any friend of mine is a good guy and good guys are hard to find these days,' grinned Wendell proudly. 'Can I get you another cold one Van?'

Wendell stood up to go and buy some more beers from the bar, whilst Damien and Van continued their discussion, their voices lowered.

'Has the Home Owners' Association been established yet? Have the Bye Laws been written?' asked Van.

'It's called the Condominium on the island. No, we haven't had a meeting yet. There are no Condominium Board members yet,' replied Damien. 'We can call a meeting between ourselves to establish and change anything in the Bye Laws. We are owners ourselves and I have mates who are also owners, enough to make up a Board.'

'And the fees, the condo fees, who is responsible for collecting them?' asked Van.

Damien was rather unsure of the answer, 'Well, the Condominium committee, I suppose.'

'Why not organise it all under the same team, the management team?' queried Van. 'The management team could collect in all of the dues, rather than the Condominium.'

'You know Van, you're right; there could be real big advantages for us by doing that. Let me think this one through.'

At this point, Wendell returned clutching three beers. He placed them on the table before handing them out.

'You are right Dell. This friend of yours, he's a real good guy. I like him a lot. He has some excellent ideas. I think that he's definitely the man we need,' smirked Damien.

'I told you he was one of the best,' proclaimed Wendell, who wasn't too certain why Damien had come to that conclusion so quickly whilst he was getting the drinks in.

24 Duplicity?

The Girls – Summer 2012

'It's Mr Janes isn't it?' enquired Laura Rose. 'You may not remember me, but I'm a friend of Angel.'

'How could I forget such a pretty face? Yes, of course I remember you. You came into the office several times to see Angel when she worked for us,' replied Damien. 'You're Laura Rose aren't you?' He was sitting in the departure lounge at Miami airport waiting for his flight to Sainte Marie. He was studying something on his lap-top. He had been in Miami with Van attending a Vacation Home Exhibition.

'I suppose we must be on the same flight. I've been visiting Angel during my vacation,' Laura Rose told him, 'and I'm heading back home. Is it OK to sit here?'

'Yes, of course.' Damien put away his computer. 'Is this your first time in Miami?'

'No, it's the second time I've visited Angel. I've had a wonderful time. We go to the beach and the shops. Angel, she shows me around and takes me to some of the properties that she's trying to sell. You wouldn't believe the size of some of them!' Laura Rose enthused.

'How is Angel doing in her job?'

'She's doing real good. She drives her own car now and she's gotten her own apartment that she rents. She just loves her job!'

'I thought that she would do well. She's got the chat. And what about you? You're a teacher aren't you?'

'That's right, I teach in a junior school on Sainte Marie. Being in Miami makes me realise how different life is on Sainte Marie from life here. Angel took me to a school in Miami and showed me the facilities that the children have here. It's all swish modern buildings and high tech

221

classrooms with lots of computers. My Education Authority can't afford all that.'

'Yes, the classrooms in Sainte Marie can be rather basic. When my children were at school on island they went to the International School. They really liked it there.'

'Yes, but Mr Janes, the International School is fee paying. Sainte Marie is a small island with a relatively small population, so the state schools have to be run on a tight budget. A few schools now have modern buildings, but not the school where I teach in Doubloon d'Or. I have very few modern aids in my classroom.'

'I would like to visit your school. Maybe I could help in some way. We are just about to start a rental operation at Fortune Bay. There will be lots of tourists in the near future. I'm sure that we could start some sort of fund or collection to assist, even if it is only in a small way.'

'That's very kind. Would you really like to see the school? That would be wonderful. There are so many things that the school needs. I know that a couple of the large hotel chains on the island help the schools and colleges. The Lions Association helps as well. I'm aware that they help with scholarships overseas and awards for certain pupils.'

'Yes, even if it is only a few computers, televisions and books to start off with.......listen, Laura Rose, I think that is our flight being called.' Damien and Laura Rose listened to the flight announcement. 'Yes. I'll come to find you on the plane and we can organise when I can visit you at your school.'

'Thank you Mr Janes, I'll look forward to that. I'll phone Angel when I return and tell her that I have met you,' responded Laura Rose.

'I tell you what, perhaps we could go out to dinner next week and discuss how we could help you and your school.'

'That's very kind Mr Janes, I'm very grateful. I'll give you my phone number.'

A smile of satisfaction crossed Damien Janes's face as he headed towards the plane.

$$$

'Rosie, DO NOT GET INVOLVED WITH THAT MAN!' Angel screamed down the phone. 'You know what he is like. He doesn't care who he hurts.'

'I'm not getting involved with him. He just said that he would help the school. The school is in dire need of teaching aids Angel. You know that Doublon d'Or isn't like Miami. He offered to help; I didn't ask him,' shouted Laura Rose. 'You don't have to teach those kids everyday with barely a book between them.'

'Sure, I know it's difficult, but you can't trust that man. Try to find some other way of getting help for the school. Even Janes's own mother doesn't trust him.'

'Angel, you don't know that,' Laura Rose yelled down the phone. 'He said that he could get the resort at Fortune Bay involved with the school. That maybe the villa owners might help and donate money for books and new equipment that we desperately need.'

'That may be true Rosie, but if Damien Janes is behind it all, he'll have some ulterior motive. Damien doesn't do anything unless he is going to benefit from it. Rosie, I know him. I worked for him for over a year. Wendell Thorner isn't perfect, but he's the Angel Gabriel when put next to Damien.'

'He told me that he would come to see the children at school. And we could perhaps organise some sort of activity for them at Fortune Bay. He thinks that the owners would really like that and would doubtless contribute to a collection......'

'They would Rosie,' interrupted Angel. 'Everybody likes little kids and they love to see them enjoying themselves. Some of the owners who I met were really nice people. Rosie, ask Wendell to help, but don't ask Damien.

223

Pleeeee...ase, don't ask Damien,' pleaded Angel. 'I promise you, you'll get more than you bargained for.'

'I'll have to think about it Angel. I'm not a kid anymore. I do know what men can be like!' Laura Rose declared more quietly to her friend down the phone.

'Not this one you don't,' replied Angel.

'But, I have arranged for him to come to the school next week. He said that he would try to bring the children a present.'

'Oh, my sweet Jesus! Rosie, don't ever say that I didn't warn you.'

'Let's change the subject Angel. I have to decide for myself. Did I tell you about Merle? She really loves the new job that she's got. They have made her responsible for all the new seedlings at the plantation. She has to enter all the data onto a computer program and then........'

Angel sighed, 'Rosie, can I just say one last thing? You are a very good person. You gave up a half decent job to go and work in an under privileged school. You want to try and help those less fortunate than yourself. You deserve a really good man, an honest man, a man that is like you. You will meet him. Don't ruin things in the meantime by getting involved with Damien Janes. He is really bad news! OK, I've had my say. Now tell me about Merle.'

$$$

Laura Rose immediately thought that Damien Janes looked alien in her classroom. He didn't seem to fit in somehow. His tall form looked smart in a short sleeved shirt, dark tailored trousers and fashionable leather shoes. She wished that he had come in shorts and a T-shirt. He would have been more in keeping. Her class of seven year olds was silent. Their little faces regarded him with eyes wide open. They had very quickly stopped their activities in the poorly lit classroom to stare at the strange foreigner. Even Sally-Ann, who normally talked from the second she came into the classroom to the moment that she left, sat on a floor cushion with her jaw open, speechless.

Laura Rose introduced Mr Janes. She told them that he was interested in their work and what they were all learning. Damien Janes put down the large black plastic sack that he was carrying and asked the children if they could explain to him what they were doing that day. There was silence. Not a word.

'You should come more often Mr Janes, they are not usually so quiet,' Laura Rose felt a little embarrassed.

Damien took in the rectangle of well-worn desks with the frayed piece of carpet in the centre which housed several floor cushions. He surveyed the lines of string crossing two of the walls that held some of the children's drawings and paintings. He looked at Laura Rose's Formica topped table in one corner with several piles of books and a few pieces of equipment on it.

'Your teacher has told me that you visited the Fort and National Park last week. Did you all enjoy that?' asked Damien.

Nothing! Damien moved along the wall looking at the paintings. 'This is very good. I like the Fort on the top of the peak. Who painted this?' he asked. No reply. The wide eyes continued surveying the tall, white man walking around their classroom.

'Miss, he one real tall guy. Even 'is hair's tall,' piped up Sally-Ann. She stood up as some of the children sniggered at her remark. Her over-sized checked gym slip covering her cream blouse dwarfed her. Her head was a mass of braided pigtails finished in coloured beads. 'My Pa tall, but he not as tall as 'im!'

'Mr Janes, Sally-Ann. His name is Mr Janes. How tall do you think he is Sally-Ann?' asked Laura Rose.

'Dunno. How tall you mister…. Janes, Mr Janes?'

'I'm not too sure Sally-Ann,' answered Damien.

'We got a measure. We can measure you? You stands over there. Right near the door. No, by the measure. We all got lines. Then, I gets a chair. Leon, I needs the chair,' Sally-Ann was in control mode. As frequently happened, she tried to take over the organisation of the classroom activity. A few of the pupils did look as though they might be interested in helping Sally-Ann.

'Sally-Ann, we need to ask Mr Janes if he objects to being measured. It is only polite,' directed Laura Rose.

'Sure.' She turned towards Damien 'You like to be measured? Sure, you needs to know for when you buys your new jeans.'

'What you got in that bag over there?' piped up a voice from the back of the room.

Damien stifled a smile. 'She's a smart young lady. She knows that I need to buy some new jeans. That would be very useful Sally-Ann. Then, when I find out my height, I'll show you all what I have in the bag.'

'Let's go,' said the enthusiastic Sally-Ann. She conducted him to the wall measure, Mr Janes towering above her. She instructed Leon to bring the chair for her to stand on; directed another pupil to find the ruler to put across the top of Damien's head. She then looked on Laura Rose's table for a piece of chalk. Laura Rose left her in charge of the task, whilst she asked the rest of her class what they estimated Mr Janes's height would be, and then she did a little revision of the measurements they had learnt so far.

'I drawing the line! He........ he... one metre ninety-two centimetres!' exclaimed Sally-Ann. 'He one tall dude! What's you eat to be that tall?' she asked him.

'Thank you children. Well, my Mum used to feed me on carrots and greens when I was a kid,' Damien laughed.

'There a guy in America and he two metres thirty-five centimetre tall,' interrupted Zak, a young boy with spectacles. 'My Mom say he never find a wife.' Laura Rose

226

showed them all where two metres thirty-five was on the height chart and mentioned that she had seen some very tall basketball players on the television as well. She then told all the children to go back to their seats. Laura Rose questioned Mr Janes about what he had in his bag. The atmosphere had changed and it seemed that the children were now more relaxed with the stranger in their classroom. Several of them tried to guess the contents of the bag.

Damien gradually undid the large bag to reveal various sized coloured balls, including footballs, and lots of tubs, much like waste paper baskets, all stacked one inside the other. Using some pupils to help him, he demonstrated how the equipment could be used for throwing, catching, aiming and dribbling. Laura Rose watched him carefully. He seemed perfectly at ease with the children. She knew from Angel that he had two children of his own. Mr Janes didn't let the children get the better of him. He kept them all under his control, even though the children were enthusiastic to go outside and try the skills they had seen in the demonstrations. He then started to ask individuals about their favourite outside activities. He enquired the name of each child before listening to their response. Most of the replies were what one would anticipate, football, cricket and swimming; but bespectacled Zak told them all that he really liked kites. His grandpa had taught him how to fly a kite.

This was the type of response that Damien had been waiting for. He informed Zak that he thought it was an excellent activity. He mentioned to the class that perhaps he would be able to put together some sort of kite competition at Fortune Bay, the place where he worked. That was it. The classroom that had been so silent only fifteen minutes before hand was suddenly filled with zealous, chatting pupils.

Laura Rose and Damien escorted the children outside and put them into small groups, so that they could practice using the balls and the tubs. Whilst they were overseeing the youngsters, Laura Rose praised Damien's efforts in the classroom. She told him that she was very impressed.

'Oh, I enjoyed it,' Damien told her, 'anything is better than a day stuck in the office. But, it was all thanks to Sally-Ann. She saved the situation. I will get the women that run the Kids' Club to put together some kind of Kite competition. We need something that we can do around the pool and then on the beach, so that it gets the visitors involved as well.'

'That would be great! I know that the children would love it. I'm so grateful. It gives them something different to think about and it also gives them the opportunity to visit different places and meet a variety of people. Watch out! Here comes Sally-Ann.' Sally-Ann and her friend were walking their way.

'You coming again?' Sally-Ann asked Damien.

'I would like to Sally-Ann,' he responded.

'What you bring next time?' asked her friend.

'Oh my goodness,' cried Laura Rose, 'girls, you should never ask people for presents. It isn't considered to be polite.'

'But, my Mom, she always asking for….' started Sally-Ann.

'No, Sally-Ann,' insisted Laura Rose who was mindful of the type of embarrassing things she was capable of saying in front of Damien, 'you never ask for presents.'

'You will just have to wait and see, won't you girls?' declared Damien. 'That way, it'll be more of a surprise.'

$$$

Laura Rose's phone rang one evening around three weeks later. It was Damien Janes. He wanted to talk about helping the school and a possible Kite Competition. He invited her out for dinner. She wasn't certain if her hesitation was detectable on the phone. With Angel's warnings still fairly fresh in her memory, she thought that perhaps there would be safety in numbers. Laura Rose told him that perhaps it would be best not to meet in a restaurant, as she thought that her Principal of the junior department should be involved in the discussions as well. Without hesitation, he told her that he would be delighted to take both of them out. He asked if the Chinese restaurant in Anse Argent would fit the bill. Laura Rose explained that she would have to let him know, as naturally, she would have to ask her Principal first.

Mrs Felix, Laura Rose's principal, was a lively and friendly person who took her job very seriously. She was very supportive of her staff. She knew that Damien had visited the school several weeks before and had given the school some sports equipment. Like most of the island, she knew all about Damien Janes and Fortune Bay. She was also very aware of Damien Janes' reputation with the local women. This being the case, she was rather taken aback when Laura Rose asked her if she would be willing to discuss raising money for the school with him. She immediately told Laura Rose that it seemed quite out of character for Mr Janes. However, she agreed that he could come any day after school to discuss how he could assist. Like all head teachers, Mrs Felix was continually very busy. She was committed to improving the school and trying to drag its facilities and teaching methods into the twenty-first century in order to give her pupils the best education possible.

Laura Rose smiled sweetly. A little embarrassed, she explained quietly that Mr Janes had suggested they all meet together at the Chinese restaurant, where they could discuss financial aid for the school. Laura Rose also explained that they were thinking of holding a kite competition at the resort just before the Christmas school vacation. It was the season when there were the most visitors.

Laura Rose was taken aback when Mrs Felix laughed. 'Well, did he indeed!' she smiled. 'The Chinese restaurant! A kite competition! I think that the kids would love that! It's certainly something the school couldn't afford to do without financial aid. Do you think he would mind us taking Celia along as well? She's good at organising events. If I've read Mr Janes correctly, I think he could rather enjoy dining with three ladies. Do you know, I think we should accept?'

'I will have to ask him about Celia, but as she is the school secretary, I don't think it would be a problem,' returned Laura Rose.

'You're not being naive here Laura Rose, are you? It's not just his way of hitting on you? Do you really think he will go to all of this trouble just to help a few kids?'

'Mrs Felix, so far he has been very professional. He really seemed to enjoy the time he spent with my class. Everyone is very ready to run him down, but you know what they say, "everyone has a heart of gold", especially where little children are concerned.'

'Sorry Laura Rose, but I think that there are plenty of folks that would disagree with that. But anyway, let's give him the benefit of the doubt for the moment. Tell him that we accept, but it will have to be early and a quick meal for me. I've got a hundred and one things to do when I get home.'

$$\$\$\$$$

Kites, kids and cash were discussed over Peking duck and chicken sizzler several days later at the Anse Argent Chinese restaurant. Mr Janes had brought along a children's kite kit and a pack of felt tip crayons, which seemed to keep them enraptured for some time. They enthusiastically discussed the merits of decorating the kites, and whether the decorating could form part of the

230

competition. The other diners possibly thought that it was a strange occupation for four adults in a restaurant. But none of them stared or made any comment. In Sainte Marie nearly anything goes.

True to form, Celia wrote down how everything was to be organised and who should be responsible for what. Damien volunteered the staff of the Kid's Club at the resort to help. He thought that perhaps some of the resort guests' youngsters might wish to join in as well. He also volunteered himself to go around with the credit card terminal. He felt he could be good at encouraging the visitors to part with their money. Mrs Felix felt it was appropriate that she should accompany him as a representative of the school. Damien suggested that he telephone the island newspaper. It would be first rate if the event and the resort could gain a little publicity. By the time they had all finished their deliberations, three bottles of wine had been consumed. They were all relaxed and getting on fairly well. Ideas were contributed by all; and nobody had dominated the meeting.

'Oh my Lordy,' said Mrs Felix, 'It's nearly nine o'clock. I really must get going. Thank you Mr Janes for a very enjoyable and productive evening. We look forward to the competition in a few weeks' time.'

It was on that note that the ladies, who were all heading home in the same car, started to get ready to leave. Mr Janes was left to pay the bill.

$$$

Laura Rose reached her small apartment after the Chinese meal. Lesson preparation for the following day weighed on her mind, but she decided she was going to call Angel. It was well over a month since they had last spoken.

'Hi Angel. How are things babe? Have you got time to talk for five minutes?'

'Things are going great, Rosie. Property has been selling better than we had anticipated.'

'Have you sold that large villa with the enormous infinity pool yet? The one that you showed me in August,' asked Laura Rose.

'Oh yes, that's gone. Somebody who owns a chain of hairdressing salons bought that. I might even be able to afford to have my hair done in one of her salons soon,' laughed Angel. 'I'm earning enough now. I'm so glad you phoned, I've been longing to tell you all about my latest Bo.'

Laura Rose was bursting to tell Angel about Damien Janes, but listened to Angel's news about her latest boyfriend instead. Angel was never without one. She attracted all types of men, but Angel only kept the ones with good prospects. She was very ambitious.

'So, is he that special one Angel?'

'He's got distinct possibilities. He's taking me to see the dolphins at Blue Lagoon Island the week-end after next.'

'Blue Lagoon?'

'It's off Nassau. We have to fly from here to Nassau and then catch a boat. Hey Rosie, what about you?'

'I think all the eligible men on the island left when you did Angel. There's nobody special. Anyway I'm always too bloody busy for men. But I must tell you what has happened about Mr Janes.'

'Oh no, Rosie, he is not a man, he's a monster, a lying cheating demon.'

'Just listen Angel! Listen to what has happened at the school and at a meeting that we had this evening. Then tell me what you think.' Laura Rose went on to explain in detail how Damien had visited the school with a big bag of equipment and had played games with the children. She also told her about the meeting that evening to organise a kite competition. Damien had been charming. She felt he had been charismatic with the three of them. Angel was very quiet on the other end of the line.

'Rosie, that is completely out of character for Damien. He must have some hidden agenda here. There must be a reason he is doing this.'

'That's exactly what Mrs Felix said. Mrs Felix is my principal. But, cross my heart, he hasn't been anything but professional. The school couldn't afford to buy fifty kite kits. They are more than thirty dollars each and then there are all the crayons and paints. He said he was going to contact the newspaper. So, the school and the event could get a bit of publicity.'

'Let me make a few calls Rosie and try and find out what is going on at Fortune Bay. I can contact some of the people that I worked with.'

'Personally, I'm very wary of him after all the warnings you gave me. I know you think I'm rather naive, but I like to see the best in everybody. If somebody is nice to me, I'm inclined to believe them. I just want to help the school and the children as well Angel.'

'I've told you before Rosie, you are too good, too trusting. If that man hurts a hair of your head, he'll have me to deal with.'

'Look Angel, I've got to go. I've still got things to prepare for tomorrow. Let me know if what you find out anything about him. Have a great time with the dolphins!'

25 Let's Go Fly a Kite

The Girls - Late 2012

Laura Rose was not used to butterflies in her stomach, but the countdown was on for the kite competition. As it came nearer, she felt more and more tense and nervous about it. She hoped that she wasn't making a dreadful mistake in trusting Damien Janes, and that the whole thing would not be a tremendous flop. The children in her class were becoming very excited. She was anxious that everything should go well for them and the other seven year olds in the school who were participating. Laura Rose had spoken to Damien several times on the phone about the competition. He informed her that there were around 175 people who would be staying at the villas and apartments that weekend. They had all received flyers informing them of the kite competition and that small donations for the local junior school would be gratefully received.

At their meeting in the Chinese restaurant they had decided that a suitable prize for the winning pair would be a voucher from a toy shop in Bourbon. However, all of the children would leave with some sort of gift. She had volunteered to purchase the vouchers herself. On her expedition to the toy shop, she wandered around for some time wishing that she could have some of the learning toys and books in her classroom. All those bright, colourful boxes called out to her. She played with some of the toys and games as eagerly as any of the seven year olds in her class. She knew that her pupils would learn so much from them. They would extend the children's imagination. Leaving the store with her vouchers, she felt rather frustrated about not being able to buy more.

A couple of days before the planned event, Mrs Felix called Laura Rose into her office. Laura Rose was just about to leave for home. She pointed to two televisions, a DVD player and two lap top computers that were on the floor of her office.

'Praise to the Lord,' chanted Mrs Felix. 'These were all delivered this afternoon with a note that said they were surplus to requirements. I think we misjudged that man.'

'I can't believe it,' cried Laura Rose. They had all been on Mr Janes' list of things that the school desperately needed. 'Oh Mrs Felix, I'm so pleased.'

'I did a double take when I saw them arriving in the back of a van. Well, it's all thanks to you and your meeting with him at the airport. You can see that they are not brand new, but they aren't that old either.'

'I must phone him this evening to thank him.' Laura Rose was so thrilled for the school.

'Done. It was done pronto. I left a message on his phone. Alleluia, we can now change the old TV in the library.'

Laura Rose left school that evening feeling less stressed about Damien Janes and kites. Unfortunately, that was the last thing Laura Rose should have done!

$$$

Noise and commotion invaded Fortune Bay. It was the Saturday of the kite competition. Sixty children, and as many adults, milled around the very large swimming pool area. Laura Rose didn't have time to have butterflies in her stomach. Or a minute to feel nervous; she was far too busy. The ladies in the resort's Kids' Club had done an admirable job. There were restaurant tables laid out for the kite making. Some were around the pool, and others in the shade of the beach restaurant. The ladies welcomed the children, parents and staff with drinks of fruit juice. As had been anticipated, many of the youngsters were a little over-awed to start with. Some immediately wanted to know where the toilets were. Opportunely, there were a few of the tourists' children who wanted to join in with the fun.

235

They were soon chatting to the pupils. This helped them feel a little less apprehensive. Mrs Felix started the proceedings by explaining to all of those present about the aims of the competition. She expressed how grateful she was to Mr Janes and his staff for their help; and for giving the school the opportunity to visit Fortune Bay that morning.

Janes was there, amidst the children, wearing a continual beaming smile for all and sundry. The promised journalist was amongst the crowd. Mrs Felix kept her introduction short. She realised that all the children would be getting fidgety. They wanted to get on with the task they had come for.

Soon the children were all working away at their allocated tables. At school, Laura Rose had already talked her group through what they had to do and shown them the simple construction of the kite. The children had also brain-stormed what type of designs could be drawn onto the front of them. They had also practiced kite flying in the school yard. Animals, spiders, birds and even witch drawings, appeared on the front of the kites. There were also strings of bows and ribbons being stapled onto the bases. Some worked in pairs. Other children decided to be independent.

The adults were as bubbly as the children. The place was alive with encouragement and praise. Laura Rose was in her element. Some of the holiday makers came up to talk to her about her work in the school. She made a point of chatting to the ladies who ran the Kids' Club. They told her that they thought it was a great idea; they hoped that they had helped with the fundraising. The clicking of cameras and photos was plentiful. A party atmosphere prevailed.

'I think that we have met before,' said a voice behind Laura Rose. She turned to see a man in his thirties holding the hand of little girl. 'You are Angel's friend aren't you? I used to work with her. My name is Adrian.'

'Oh yes, Adrian I remember you. You work as the accountant in the Tropical Island Villas office. Great to see you again! And who is this very beautiful little princess?'

'This is my daughter Cara. We have come to see the kites and give the children our support.'

'That's very kind. I was talking to Angel last......'

'Yes, I know she phoned me,' interrupted Adrian. 'She asked me to speak to you, but I don't really think that this is the time or place. I'll give you my phone number. I've written it on a piece of paper for you.......'

'Look Miss! Whatduyathink?' said a child's voice behind Laura Rose as she put the paper in to her bag. Sally-Ann and her side-kick had come to show her their decorated kite. It had been turned into a fish with enormous eyes and coloured ribbons as a tail.

'Wow girls, I really like that! You have done very well.' exclaimed Laura Rose. 'What do you think Cara?'

Cara just smiled shyly, but her father inspected the kite and said, 'Well done girls, I hope everybody else likes it too.'

'We got cake now. Banana bread I hope!' chipped in Sally Ann. 'And another drink. It hot work makin' kites.'

'It will be even hotter on the beach when you are flying your kite,' Adrian told them. The girls left them to seek and then devour their slices of cake. 'You can phone me any time. As I told Angel, there may be a reason for all this show of philanthropy.'

Soon, all eyes were turned skywards. The children ran along the beach in their attempts to get their kites airborne. They all knew the theory of putting their backs to the wind, holding it above their heads and reeling out the line. Even so, lots needed help. But there was plenty of advice available. A few of the adults even wanted to monopolise the kites themselves. Gradually, more kites sailed above the sands. Laura-Rose watched all the children running around, many with the breeze tugging at their kites, and she could see that they were all enjoying themselves. She felt elated that she was a part of it all. Despite her previous apprehensions, the morning seemed to have been a great success. She also knew from Mrs Felix that several of the holiday makers had been very generous with their donations.

During the launching of the kites, Laura Rose was unaware that there was somebody there watching her. Pink shorts, white blouse and tennis shoes, she darted from one child to the next. Aiding the children, encouraging them and giving them praise. Someone was smiling to himself. He took in her slim form. He appraised her short tightly curled hair. And studied her abundance of enthusiasm and energy.

Four judges had been selected. Mrs Felix and Celia from the school, and Damien Janes and one of the British tourists. They knew that some of the children would find their decisions disappointing. Decisions finalised; the children were asked to go and sit under the sunshades with their kites. There was so much hustle and bustle on the beach that nobody noticed what was happening right at the end of the bay.

Two riders had descended the trail over the ridge at the end of the bay. They had dismounted their horses. Suddenly, as if from nowhere, two large dogs bounded up to the horses, barking and yapping around their legs. One of the riders managed to restrain and calm his mount, but the other was unable to. The tan-coloured horse tore up the beach towards the group in front of the hotel. The dogs followed. Snap, snapping around the horse's legs. It was totally out of control. The rider ran futilely after it. Only one other person seemed to see all that was happening. Damien Janes. All of the other adults were still involved in organising the children.

Janes glanced rapidly towards the shoreline to see if there was anybody in the path of the galloping animal.

There was Zak. He was right in its path. His little head was tilted upwards watching his kite drifting higher and higher. Zak had been very pleased with himself. He had enjoyed all his work that morning. His kite had flown higher than all the rest. The judges had already decided that he was going to win one of the prizes.

'Oh my God,' shouted Damien. Instinctively he rushed down the beach towards Zak and his kite.

'Zak, Zak! The horse! Behind you!' Before anyone really knew what was happening, Damien had thrown himself on top of the child. He pushed Zak into the sea. The horse hurtled past. One of Damien's legs jerked with pain as the horse's hoof caught it. The horse galloped on further down the beach. Yelping dogs followed. The pair, Janes and Zak, were entangled together; kite string around them. Zak lifted his head out of the shallow water. He still didn't really understanding why he was drenched. Why had his kite been ruined? Why had Mr Janes pushed him around the way he had? He put his hand to his face.

Zak screwed up his face. Damien wasn't sure, but perhaps there were tears on the boy's wet face. 'I lost me glasses, Mr Janes.'

'Don't you worry! I'll buy you a new pair,' consoled Damien. 'Didn't you hear the horse Zak?'

By this time, they were surrounded by adults and children all talking at once. They helped to untangle the kite's twine. They pulled the child out of the sea. Some started to look for Zak's glasses along the waterline. The reporter was occupied taking photos of the incident. Damien remained sitting in the sea.

'Thanks be to God that you are both alive,' declared Mrs Felix. 'Oh Mr Janes, what a thing to happen! Thanks to the Lord that you acted as quickly as you did. Zak, are you alright? No broken bones? Excellent. What a lucky escape!'

'It was lucky that I saw it all happening in time!' gasped Damien.

Zak's glasses had been found, not completely intact. There was chaos at the shoreline. Everyone was trying to help, but they were only hindering progress.

'Take Zak and all the other children back up to the top of the beach. Let us get Mr Janes sorted out. Find out what has happened to that horse and the dogs!' ordered Mrs Felix. She repeated her commands. The crowd started to move away and walk back up the sand.

'Thank goodness for bossy school teachers Mrs Felix. I'm not sure I can walk. The horse clipped my leg as I threw Zak into the sea.' They looked down at his leg. His ankle was already swollen. It was starting to change colour. 'You might need to find a strong man to help me up the beach,' said Damien. 'My ankle hurts like hell; it feels like I've got a knife stuck in it.' Mrs Felix went to organise help for Mr Janes.

Adrian appeared with a couple of the children's fathers. They were all in admiration of Damien's quick thinking. They praised him for his actions which had possibly saved a child's life.

'For God's sake, cut the chat, and help me up the beach,' moaned Damien to Adrian. 'You need to get me to the bloody hospital.'

26 Little Miss Goody Two Shoes

Damien - Late 2012

Damien Janes listened to all the chatter as he was supported towards the car park. His helpers told him that they were amazed at his courage. However, there was nobody more amazed than he was. Had that really been him who had rocketed down to the water's edge? Really him who ran in front of a galloping horse? Had that really been Damien Janes sat in the sea with that little kid? Was it him who told Zak he would buy him some new glasses? Yes, he had amazed himself. Was that really Damien Janes who had been applauded as he hopped up the beach? Had he really told Mrs Felix to carry on with the competition? He had been amazing! He was a real hero!

It had been Van's idea to try to gain publicity for Fortune Bay, and improve Damien's image on the island. Van thought that becoming involved with the local community, and trying to raise funds for some sort of charity, would perhaps portray them all in a better light. They were being taken to court for not paying the National Insurance payments again. One of the local contractors was doing the same thing because they had never settled his bill. Their reputation was at a low. Van had been right; a bit of positive publicity could do a lot of good. Van was also right in saying that any donation to charity needn't cost them too much. Up until now, it had cost him next to nothing. The Kid's Club was paying for all the kites and the colouring stuff. Van would see that it was paid for out of the Condominium dues. Van had given him the tellies which were left over from what they had ordered for the owners' villas. The computers were old ones from the Tropical Island Villas office. He wasn't too sure where the DVD player had come from. Never mind, the school's needs were definitely greater than that of the villa owners!

No sooner had Van implanted the idea into his mind, than Damien had met 'Little Miss Goody Two Shoes' Laura Rose at Miami airport. It had all slotted into place. It had all worked out like a dream. All except he now had a smashed-up ankle; and there was nobody at home to look after him. Ayanna had stormed out of the house last month after an enormous row.

The three men gently manoeuvred Damien towards Adrian's car. One of the staff from the resort rushed up to them with a bundle of towels tucked under her arm and clutching a bag of frozen peas. She gave the towels to Adrian to protect his car seats from Damien's damp clothes.

'Peas! I don't need goddamn peas girl,' scowled Damien.

'It's for the swelling Mr Janes. They suggest that you put an ice pack on the swelling,' she informed him.

'She's right. When you are in the car, hold the peas over your ankle,' nodded Adrian.

Damien was helped into the passenger seat. 'Shit Adrian, mind my bloody leg,' moaned Damien.

'DJ, my daughter is in the back of the car, I wonder if you could mind your language,' asked Adrian. 'She is only five. I'm going to take her home on the way to the clinic. It's not much of a detour.'

Damien said nothing as he strapped himself into the seat. Adrian thanked the fathers and the member of staff who had brought the peas, and suggested that they all return to the competition on the beach. He assured himself that his daughter was safely strapped-in in the back of the car.

'It's such a pity that the accident had to happen, everything was going so well. The kids were having such a good time,' acclaimed Adrian as he started the car.

'S-H-I-T!' whinged Damien under his breath as he placed the bag of peas on his ankle. 'Yeh sure. It was great!'

242

he replied in a sarcastic tone. 'I could do with a bloody drink Adrian.'

'Not a good idea DJ. You don't know if the doctor will give you pain killers. Alcohol and drugs aren't always compatible. Let's get you to the clinic. Shame we haven't got a blue light on the top of our car, eh Cara? We might get there a bit quicker!'

'Cut the crap Adrian. None of this is f'ing amusing,' grimaced Damien.

'Am I laughing? I can empathise with you DJ; I broke my arm a few years ago. Wow the pain!' sympathised Adrian. 'OK my princess? We'll soon have you home Cara!'

$$\$\$\$$$

The health clinic was heaving. There was a long queue of patients waiting to see a doctor. Janes was none too pleased. He had had to wait for nearly two hours before having his leg X-rayed. They were hanging around in one of the curtained cubicles waiting for the results when Adrian's phone rang. He wandered into the reception area to take his call.

It was Laura Rose. She wanted to know how Damien was. He told her that he was in a foul humour and that they were getting on one another's nerves. Laura Rose asked if there was anything she could do to help. Adrian gave her a negative reply. Once they had finished at the Clinic, he would take Damien back home. He'd be on his own from there on. Laura Rose said that she would grab something for Damien to eat and meet them in the clinic in half an hour.

'Hey Laura Rose, that's not really necessary. He can hop around and get himself something. He really is spitting blood here and is hyper irritable. Are you sure that you want to have to put up with that?'

'Adrian, he probably saved Zak's life. It's the least I can do. See ya soon.'

243

'Laura Rose, you be careful of him.'

'Adrian, I'm a big girl. I can cope.'

'Yeah, but he likes big girls, especially the pretty ones. I know what he's like.'

'See ya Adrian.'

Damien was diagnosed as having a fractured ankle and had a surgical walker boot fitted. The doctor also suggested that he take a crutch. Damien was adamant that he wasn't resorting to that. Damien was informed that he should return in two weeks for a check-up. However, it would doubtless be at least six weeks before the facture would heal. The doctor's comment about it taking a little longer considering his age was not well received by Damien.

The health service on island was not free. Consequently, Damien was given a list of charges at the end of the consultation. Adrian was very pleased that it wasn't him who had to foot the bill. Damien just handed over his credit card without a second thought. As they walked back out through the waiting area, Laura Rose was sat there clutching a plastic carrier bag.

'Laura Rose, what are you doing here?' asked Damien.

'I've come to see how you are Mr Janes,' she replied.

'Apart from a shattered ankle, I'm fine. I'm looking forward to getting out of these dirty clothes,' smiled Damien.

'Wow Mr Janes, everybody was singing your praises back at Fortune Bay,' Laura Rose congratulated.

'They wouldn't have been singing them if they had been here with him,' muttered Adrian under his breath.

'They were saying that you could have been very badly injured or even killed, running in front of that galloping horse as you did. Poor little Zak, he didn't really know what was happening to him,' continued Laura Rose.

'Should I drive you home then DJ?' queried Adrian. He turned to Laura Rose 'Are you coming along as well?'

They moved out of the Health Clinic and towards Adrian's car. Damien had to hold onto Adrian's shoulder, as he hobbled along.

'I brought something for you to eat Mr Janes, as I realised you didn't get any lunch. I bought it in the Chinese, as I know you like Chinese food.' Laura Rose followed the men to the car.

'That was very thoughtful. I feel ravenous.'

'Zak was so pleased that he won one of the prizes for his "rocket" kite. It kinda made up for the fact that it was ruined in the sea. Mrs Felix organised everything when you left. She got everybody under control and gave out the prizes on the beach. The ladies who work for your Kids' Club were unbelievable. They let the children take the kites and the crayons home with them. The journalist asked me about Zak. He took his photo. The journalist also asked and we discussed how the competition happened.' Laura Rose babbled on as they drove the short distance to Damien's home.

Neither of the males expressed their opinions. Both men were lost in thought about the events of the morning and the possible implications for Laura Rose that afternoon. Adrian would be pleased to be shot of his boss and get home to his family. Damien was feeling pleased that Laura Rose seemed to be prepared to help him out. He was wondering just how grateful she might be that one of her pupils had escaped possible injury. His mood started to improve.

Adrian drove through Anse Argent, past the new commercial area that was under construction, past a couple of small hotels, and then into the select residential district of large alluring houses, some of which backed onto the beach. He swung into Damien's drive and parked right outside the front door. From the back seat Laura Rose looked up at the large colonial style house with white pillars and shutters. It reminded her of some of the luxury residences she had seen in Miami with Angel.

'Amazing house Mr Janes,' exclaimed Laura Rose. 'The garden is lovely too.' Adrian was tight-lipped. He knew he preferred his own much smaller apartment filled with his family.

Damien let them into the house.

'I'll put this food on a plate for you, if you can tell me where everything is,' offered Laura Rose.

'If you don't mind, I'll get out of these clothes first. Can you get us a drink though Laura Rose? Adrian, would you mind going to get me another pair of shorts and a shirt from the main bedroom upstairs. You'll find them in the right hand wardrobe,' directed Damien.

'Fine, I'll put it in the oven,' announced Laura Rose as she walked into the kitchen. 'Oh, you've got a pool too. Choice!'

She put the take-away in the oven to keep warm. She rummaged around in the cupboards looking for glasses, drinks and a plate. Laura Rose immediately discovered that there was little in the kitchen but wine and other alcoholic drinks. She took a bottle of white wine from the fridge. She returned to the sitting room laden with a bottle and wine glasses.

Damien was not there, presumably changing his clothes in the downstairs bedroom.

'Adrian, there's no food in this house. There's just booze!' she told him quietly. 'I'll have to go buy him some groceries.'

'He probably ties one on every night now Ayanna isn't here to look after him. But, Laura Rose, this isn't your problem. Don't get involved,' Adrian added, speaking in hushed tones.

'I'll just get a few groceries and then I must go home. I've got a lot of work to catch up on. I'll come with you up to the shops and then I'll walk back.'

Damien appeared back in the sitting room wearing a clean floral shirt, but the same shorts. He was learning to hobble along on the surgical boot. 'I'll move into the guest room for the time being, so that I don't have to go and down the stairs.'

'I was just saying to Adrian, that I'll have to go up to the supermarket to get you some food. You haven't got anything in the house to eat. You can't drive and you can't walk to the shops yourself, so I'll need to get you a few supplies. I'll go and get your take-away out of the oven.'

'I usually eat out or get something easy to heat up in the oven,' confessed Damien. 'Here Laura Rose, take some money for the food,' he handed her two hundred dollars. 'I can cook steak, so perhaps you could buy me a couple. I think I need some more red wine too.'

They left Damien opening the bottle of white wine and planning to eat his late lunch supplied thanks to Laura Rose. As they pulled out of his drive, Adrian told her that she was being too caring and that Damien would not appreciate her efforts.

'He just uses people Laura Rose. He takes advantage of people's generosity and kindness. He thinks that the world revolves around him. He feels everyone should be submissive to his wishes. Don't waste too much of your time on him, he really isn't worth it. I can tell you have a good heart and feel grateful to him for saving Zak, but be smart and don't let the gratitude last too long. Don't give him too much of your help, he wouldn't do the same for you.'

'Adrian, he has been so good to the children and the school. He has given us equipment and organised this morning. He gave us an opportunity to collect money for the school. He can't be all bad.'

'It might be a ploy to try and improve his image on the island. This is what I said to Angel. The reputation of the company is at an all-time low. He has a couple of impending court cases to cope with. It could be his way of trying to get positive publicity. I noticed there was a journalist there.'

'Yes, that was his idea. Thanks for your advice Adrian. I will take heed of what you've said. And I'm grateful for the ride to the supermarket. It was a pleasure to meet you and your daughter.'

'I can't let you struggle back with all that shopping. I'll wait here for you.'

Damien had finished eating his food and was lounging on the large sofa when Laura Rose returned with his shopping. She noticed that the bottle of wine was more than half empty. She struggled into the kitchen with the bags. Most of the foodstuff was stored in the mega-sized fridge. The rest was left on the work surface. She cleared the plate from the table.

'Laura Rose, how about a glass of wine, just so that I can say thanks for getting the food and the take-away?' asked Damien.

'Only one thanks Mr Janes. I've got a whole load of work to do when I get home. It was a real shame that this morning was all messed up by the accident. It's a real drag that you have been injured. Otherwise it would have been a first class event. On the way back to school in the bus, Mrs Felix told me that they collected nearly three and a half thousand dollars. Your guests were really generous. She was so thrilled and really grateful. So, am I. It was a lot of work, but worth the effort.'

'I'm pleased that you collected so much. It won't be so difficult the second time around,' responded Damien.

'Do you think we could hold another fund-raising morning?' Laura Rose enquired.

'Don't see why not, perhaps before the summer holidays.' There was a few seconds silence between them.

'Mr Janes, do you think I can ask you a personal question?' Janes was taken aback, but said nothing. 'Why did you suggest having a fund-raising event for the school?' Laura Rose asked in a serious voice.

Damien stared at Laura Rose where she sat opposite him. His mind was working overtime. What should he tell her, some concocted story or the truth? After several seconds of reflection, he decided on something down the middle, a little of each.

'Well, what a very probing question! To be honest, the company went through hard times a couple of years ago; we had financial problems. Now, things have started to turn around and I thought it was about time we gave to others and at the same time have some positive publicity,' Damien paused, 'but Laura Rose, I've enjoyed visiting your school and meeting your class and your colleagues. It was fun. I'm pleased that the morning was a success and some good has come out of it.'

'Thank you for being frank with me. That wasn't what I expected you to say. Yes, it was fun. Being with a crowd of kids can be very hard work, but when things go well, it's very satisfying and rewarding.' There was another silence.

'I must go.' Laura Rose stood up.

'Can I ask one last favour before you go? Would you mind bringing a few of my things from downstairs so that I don't have to climb up and down the stairs to get them? It is going to be rather difficult wearing this boot. I feel rather unstable.'

'Oh no, let me show you. I've seen a kid doing it when he had a broken leg,' she claimed enthusiastically. She grabbed hold of his hand to pull him up off the sofa. 'Come and see. It's not too difficult.'

She led him to the wide, open staircase and let go of his hand. She sat on the second step and holding out one of her legs straight in front of her, raised herself up with her arms to the next step.

'It's like this – bump, bump, bump,' she demonstrated, elevating herself up the wooden stair case with the aid of her arms. 'Now it's your turn. Don't laugh. It's the easiest thing to do. There's no chance of falling.' She climbed back down the stairs again laughing to herself.

Damien stood motionless. His ankle throbbed like hell. He studied Laura Rose as she bounced up the staircase. She was so full of energy. He took measure of her shapely coffee coloured leg pointing towards him. He had visually explored her slim body mounting the staircase. His interest in her intensified. Damien considered that he deserved some sort of consolation. Some reward after all that display of heroism. Laura Rose came level with him. Damien grabbed her hand. He pulled her towards him. 'You looked very sexy bumping up the stairs like that,' he uttered. Their bodies were very close.

'No Mr Janes! This isn't a good idea,' announced Laura Rose. But she failed to move away from him.

'Tell me why not. I was watching you this morning as you helped your class. You're lively. Full of enthusiasm and fun. You're beautiful and very appealing.' He held her face up to his. He kissed her mouth very gently.

'No, Mr Janes, I need to go,' she muttered. Again, she made no effort to move. Damien led her back to the settee. He started to unbutton her cheap cotton blouse. He kissed her as he did so.

'I've wanted to do that since I met you in Miami airport,' he whispered. 'I've had to wait a long time.' He kissed her again a little more forcefully this time. This time Laura Rose reciprocated. She did not resist his caresses. Minutes later, Damien put his arm around Laura Rose's shoulder. They left the settee. They walked together towards the guest bedroom. They kissed and caressed one another as they went.

Laura Rose did not get her school preparation work done that evening.

The pain in Damien's ankle woke him up. The sun was streaming through the patio window. The curtains had not been drawn the night before. He was conscious of the sun's glare on the swimming pool. Its quivering reflections illuminated the room. He glanced to the other side of the bed. Little Miss GTS was still asleep. She had probably drunk more wine than she was used to the night before. He contemplated on the previous day. Broken bones were an unwelcome first for him. The whole thing was shitty and terribly inconvenient. He thought perhaps he could work from home for a few days. And the Christmas holidays were looming.

He smiled to himself. Things had gone the way he had hoped when Laura Rose came back from the supermarket. She was not really his type; she was too serious and unworldly. But she was pretty enough. Her main aim in life seemed to be trying to help others. She didn't seem to seek fun for herself. He had the notion that she felt very grateful to him. He had aided one of her pupils and the school. It hadn't taken much persuasion to get her into bed. It soon become apparent to Damien that Laura Rose did not know her way around the bedroom. She was obviously inexperienced in that department. But like a good teacher, she was quick to learn. The second time had been much better, despite the bloody surgical boot. They had laughed a lot that time. She had to go and find a pair of scissors to cut off his shorts because they had been too tight to pull over the clumsy plastic boot. She had clambered over him. She was wearing just his shirt. She waved the scissors around. He had cried out in fake pain. He pretended that she was cutting his skin. They then agreed, as they now knew one another on an intimate basis, that she should stop calling him Mr Janes and that he could call her Rosie.

He was thankful that Laura Rose had looked after him so well during the evening. She cooked them a meal and shared another bottle of wine with him. He had told her an

251

abridged version of how Fortune Bay had happened. She had explained about her previous school and why she left. Yes, they had got along fine. She could prove useful this Little Miss Goody Two Shoes, at least until the Christmas week. He planned to visit his parents and the kids in Britain for the holidays. Damien felt sure that he knew the right sort of things to say to her to keep her interested. He looked at the clock at the side of his bed. It was nearly half past eight. He needed to take two more of the pain killers that they had prescribed for him at the clinic. He reached over. He ran his hand over the naked slim back next to him.

'Hi Rosie.'

'Hi,' she mumbled sleepily. She rolled towards him still wondering exactly where she was. 'What's the time?'

'Half eight,' he told her as she sat up in bed, 'but it's Sunday.'

'How's the ankle?'

'Not good. Thanks for last night. You were great.'

'Mmm. Shall I make some coffee?'

'That would be good, but give me a kiss first,' smiled Damien. She kissed him lightly on the mouth. 'I know that you can do better than that. You were really desirable last night.'

'Damien, was it all a big mistake? Perhaps I shouldn't have stayed.' She sat facing him with the sheet draped in front of her.

'Rosie, we had a good time didn't we?' She nodded her head. 'So, why was it a mistake? I'd wanted you from the minute I met you at the airport. You were so bubbly, pretty and appealing. I was watching you all yesterday morning. I'm surprised that you didn't notice.'

'When I've made you some coffee, I must go Damien. I really do have a lot to do preparing for the last few days of the term.'

252

'Could you do your work here, if we go and collect your school things? We can get a taxi to fetch them. I might even be able to help you with your work. What do you think? I don't want you to go Rosie; I've only just found you,' he kissed her deeply. 'Shall we wait a few minutes for the coffee? I'd rather have you for breakfast.' He started to playfully nibble at her shoulder.

'Yum. Delish. Mmm, much better than toast and marmalade,' Laura Rose laughed and pushed him away teasingly. He pulled the sheet gently away from her, as she acquiesced to his wishes.

$$\$\$\$$$

'Who the super hero then?' asked Melissa as she entered the house first thing Monday morning. Melissa came every Monday and Thursday morning. She cleaned Damien's house. She changed all the linen. Melissa then took away the dirty things for her to wash and iron at home. Naturally, Damien was usually at work when she came. Even so, Melissa had become accustomed to finding different women, or evidence of Damien's tail chasing adventures, in the house. When she opened the front door she never knew what she might find.

Her husband came one day in the week to look after the pool and the garden. Damien hadn't done any household chores since he had arrived in Sainte Marie. There were plenty of the local people who were always very eager to do the work for a relatively small wage. Since Fortune Bay had been up and running he hadn't even paid for the house maintenance himself. He had put his domestic help on the payroll of Fortune Bay, which of course was taken out of condominium dues from the owners. Damien considered that Melissa didn't seem to mind where her money came from as long as she got it.

Melissa handed Damien the newspaper that had been tucked under her arm. 'There a picture of ya on page two. Ain't too good, you'ze all wet. Wish I been there. Don't

253

sound like ya at all.' Melissa was renowned for being frank and saying exactly what she thought. She left Damien in the sitting room to go and clean up the kitchen.

He opened up the paper to find the photo of him and Zak on page two. There were two columns about him saving the boy at the kiting event at Fortune Bay. Damien was still incensed about having his ankle in pieces. He was mad as hell about the inconvenience that it was causing him. Still, he couldn't have wished for better publicity for himself and the resort. He thought that the photograph of him was poor. It made him look rather like a drowned rat, and much older than his years. However, the article included phrases such as "quick-thinking, courageous action, and despite possible grave danger to himself". He could tolerate plenty of comments like that being printed for all to see. Laura Rose was also mentioned, as well as Mrs Felix and the school. There was a photo of her presenting a prize to one of the children. Next time he bumped into the journalist, he would have to buy him a few drinks.

'Any chance of a coffee Melissa? I'm still finding it painful to walk about,' Damien called into the kitchen.

Several minutes later, Melissa brought Damien his cup of coffee. 'Ya forgotten where de dishwasher is Mr J? Dere one god damn mess in dat kitchen. What ya think of de story in de paper? Thanks be to God that de little fella ain't hurt. Ya sure that was ya runnin' in front of de horse?'

'It's exactly as it happened Melissa. And no, I haven't forgotten where the dishwasher is. As I said, I'm finding it painful to walk around.'

'Ya friend got a broken ankle too? I sees dere two plates, two glasses,' she said smiling at her own wit. 'Ya don't train dem right Mr J.' Melissa insisted, being very used to Damien's succession of women friends.

254

'Oh Melissa, I assure you that I do train them right! I don't know why I put up with all your banter? I've got work to do.'

'Ya puts up wit' me Mr J cos ya knows I cleans de house and irons ya shirts real well. Better than all de rest.'

Damien answered his mobile as it started to ring. Melissa headed back to the kitchen. 'Hi Van. Yes, it's true…. It's very painful to walk. It's the reason that I'm not in the office. Could you come and pick me up asap. My cleaning lady is getting on my nerves. I think she's likely to rope me into doing the housework unless I get out of here. A quarter of an hour, that's fine.'

In the car, Van asked Damien, 'So, what's this about you throwing yourself in front of a horse that had bolted? Doesn't sound like you at all.'

'That's what Melissa, the cleaning lady, said. It doesn't seem like me at all. I don't know, nobody else seemed to be aware that the horse was heading straight for that kid. He was totally oblivious. Natural instinct on my part I suppose.'

'It seems like you are getting lots of brownie points. They told me about it at work. I tried phoning you yesterday, but got no reply,' said Van.

'I was rather occupied yesterday. The brownie points may have got me a new girlfriend,' chuckled Damien.

'Oh yeah. Who is it this time?'

'The kid's teacher. She's very grateful for everything! She's a bit serious, but a pretty little thing!'

'How the hell do you manage it DJ? With a bloody broken ankle too! How old is she?'

'Twenty four, twenty five I suppose.'

'Christ DJ, she's half your sodding age.'

'They've got to be young Van. I like them young. They must be full of life and energy! She's enjoying the wealth of my sexual experience.' Damien paused, 'Anyway, we need to get back to the office to talk about how we are going to pay for the f'ing insurance for Fortune Bay. At present, there is no way that we can pay over one hundred thousand US dollars insurance from the condominium fees, there's too many other things we've got to pay for.'

'Including your medical expenses eh DJ?'

Damien laughed and pointed his index finger at Van as he was driving. 'You cheeky bastard! Smart thinking Van, I hadn't thought of that one. There speaks a man after my own heart.'

27 The World Turns Upside Down

The Girls Late 2012 - Early 2013

Laura Rose sat at the end of the wharf in Doublon d'Or. Her flip-flops were lined up beside her. Her bare feet hung down and were splashed by each wave as it hit the wooden structure. The water made a plopping sound as it hit the construction. Behind her, in the strip of low coloured creole style cottages, the cafes were closed as it was mid-afternoon; but she could hear some noise coming from the row of houses facing seaward. They all looked over the narrow coastal road and straight out across the bay. Situated at the end of it were majestic volcanic cores, completely covered in tropical vegetation. In the distance, one could see the National Park that Laura Rose had recently visited with the children in her class. She heard the tapping of wood against wood. She turned to see somebody sweeping up the veranda of the last house on the coast road. She waved in their direction and they responded, waving their broom at her. Laura Rose was becoming a recognised figure in the town. In front of the corner house there were two children, and a sandy coloured mongrel sniffing around. Looking down the narrow beach, she could see a local man fishing and another dog rummaging near him. It was probably one of the dogs that hung around the cafes hoping for scraps. Near them there was a group of noisy, laughing children clad in their swim wear. They amused themselves by screeching as they jumped over the waves as they crashed onto the shore.

Several hours earlier, Laura Rose had said good-bye to Damien. He had taken a taxi to the airport at the southern end of the island. She missed him already. She longed to be in his arms again. He was scheduled to be away for two weeks. She reflected on the last twelve days. She had been to see him each night after school. Then when the term finished, she had stayed in Damien's villa, lazing around the pool or preparing school projects for the next term.

When he returned home from work, they shared drinks and she made a meal for him. Those evenings had been magical for her. Each evening had been so unforgettable. Each one was so different than what she was used to. Damien had helped with her school work. They had laughed at his attempts to draw pictures for her work sheets. They had danced slowly to romantic music. They had watched a movie on TV with their arms around one another on the sofa. They had showered together and then dried each other afterwards. She had enjoyed it all so much. He had complemented her on the way she looked after him. He had enjoyed her cooking. He told her everyday how lovely she was. He knew just how to slowly undress her, caress and kiss her. They had now made love so many different ways, despite his surgical boot, and in so many different places in the house; and she had wanted him each time. She wanted his attention so much. Her head spun thinking of the complements and erotic things he had whispered to her every time they were together. Now he was gone.

Just before he left for the airport, he had given her a necklace as a Christmas present. It had a small diamond in the centre of it. Nobody had ever treated her like this before. Nobody else had aroused her passion so much. Nobody had ever made her feel so feminine or desirable. Damien had told her he was going to see his children and his parents. He said nothing to her about his wife and he didn't tell her what he would be doing in England. He hadn't even promised to phone her.

Tomorrow morning, she was going to leave her rooms in Doublon d'Or to spend Christmas with her family. She knew that she would be thinking about him constantly during her visit. Nevertheless, she had decided she would

258

not tell them about Damien. It was too soon in their relationship. In fact, she wasn't certain that she was going to tell anyone, not even Angel. Angel had decided not to leave Miami and return home for the holidays. She only had a few days off work and had made plans to come for a longer period nearer Easter.

Laura Rose knew that her mother would be surprised if she told her about Damien. No, her mother would not be surprised. Surprised was not the correct adjective, she would be horrified. Her mother would be astounded that Damien was twice her age. She would be perplexed, as Damien was someone who didn't have the best of reputations on the island. On the other hand, she didn't think she would have a problem with the fact that he was white. No, it was best that her family didn't know. Personally, she didn't care about his age, the lines around his eyes and his greying hair. She now felt sure that his bad reputation was mainly malicious gossip on the island. He had been so thoughtful and caring to her. She hoped that when Damien returned, the relationship would carry on as before, but she had taken on board that he hadn't made any promises to her. But after all, they had only been together twelve days. Twelve days and twelve incredible nights.

She looked out to sea. She noted a few small fishing boats moored in the bay. They tossed backwards and forwards with the movement of the sea. By now, Damien would be flying over the same ocean, soaring his way towards London. She wished that she could be with him, but knew in her heart of hearts that it wasn't really possible. She had her family to see and then her job to go back to.

'What ya thinkin' about Miss?' asked a voice behind her. It was Pearl, one of her pupils. She hadn't heard her approaching over the wooden planks of the wharf because of her bare feet.

'I was thinking about all the thousands of fish in the sea,' she lied.

'Ya think they can see us up here?' she quizzed, sitting down on the wooden wharf, beside Laura Rose's sandals.

'Oh, I'm sure that they can. They are probably thinking "who are those strange-looking creatures up there looking at us?"' laughed Laura Rose.

'Ya reckon?'

'We don't know do we Pearl? We don't know because they can't talk to us. We don't know what happens in their brains. Or what they think. But, we do know that they do communicate with each other. When there is danger they tell one another and all move quickly away as one. They all stick together when there is a problem.'

'Shame they can't talk ain't it? It would be good to knows what they thinks.'

Laura Rose changed the topic of conversation. 'So, what is Santa Claus bringing you this year?'

'I send him a letter to ask for a book about animals or a game I seed in the toy shop,' Pearl told her.

'It's saw …..I saw it in the toy shop, not seed,' responded Laura Rose gently. 'I was in the toy shop in Bourbon not long ago and I saw some wonderful toys and games. I would have liked to have bought some of them for the classroom. Unfortunately, the school doesn't have enough money to buy any.'

'It like my Pa, he say, perhaps he not enough money to buy a present for my Mom this year.'

'Yes, Pearl, Christmas can be a very expensive time. Everything costs so much these days, but I hope that you get your present from Santa.'

'What you ask Santa for?' Pearl wanted to know.

'Well, I don't think he will come to me. I'm too old. He only visits children.'

'Well, what you like to get?'

'Me, Pearl, I've got everything I could possibly wish for. I'm very lucky, there nothing that I really need for myself. I would like a bit more money for the school though.'

'Well ya never know eh?' Pearl assured her. 'Ya don't know what happen. My ma say life got plenty of surprises.'

'That's true. Your mom's quite right. Life is definitely full of surprises.' Laura Rose smiled to herself and thought immediately of Damien and her.

Laura Rose picked up her flip-flops. 'Well, I'd better go and throw a few things into a suitcase.' She stood and fitted her feet into her sandals. 'I hope that you really enjoy your time with your family Pearl. Let's hope Santa is kind to you. I'll see you next trimester.'

'Yeah, happy Christmas Miss. See ya soon.'

Her sandals made a clattering noise as she walked back down the worn wooden planks. She touched her necklace; Damien's present. She would have to leave it in her rooms. Her parents would know that there was no way that she would be able to buy such a thing herself. She waved again to Pearl's mother, still outside the corner house. It was the last house on the coast road. The first house on the main street. Its architecture was pleasing. Wooden pillars along the edge of the veranda. White painted fretwork between each of them. There was trellis work on the front door.

Each home had its own personality and very much reflected the people who lived inside it. There were some that were neat, well painted and tidy. There were others that desperately needed attention. Rubbish was stacked outside them. Paint peeled on the construction boards and broken shutters or doors. Laura Rose walked down the main street avoiding the deep storm gutters. They ran with water from the recent rain. Several men sat drinking, playing dominoes and chatting outside their homes. They didn't even notice Laura Rose as she walked briskly up the main road of the village. Past her favourite house of Doublon d'Or. She thought it was reminiscent of something out of a child's fairy story book. A tiny abode, with a steeply sloped corrugated metal roof. Fuchsia pink clapper board walls. The door and shutters coloured a dark turquoise.

Laura Rose reached the end of the main street. She arrived at the two storey building where she rented her two rooms. She mounted the unpainted concrete stair case and entered the small living room. Her rooms were sparsely furnished with basic, cheap furniture. Laura Rose took a cold drink from the table top refrigerator, then went into her bedroom. She dragged her suitcase from under the single bed and flung it on top of the crumpled bed linen. Opening up the scratched and worn wardrobe, she selected a few pieces of clothing to take with her for her visit the next day. Through the open glass louvres a breeze fluttered the thin, faded curtains. She surveyed the slightly grubby walls and tacky, tatty furnishings. It was all a million miles away from Damien's beautifully decorated villa. His home furnished with tasteful imported furniture. His well-tended, colourful garden, filled with vibrant coloured flowers. They were a million miles away, but only seven or eight minutes ride away on the local bus.

$$$

The sun was going down over Anse Argent beach as Laura Rose sat drinking a glass of white wine in the Ancient Mariner. The taste of it reminded her of the wine she had drunk the very first night with Damien. She looked out of the open sided structure of the restaurant to see the tourists leaving for the day. The sun bed man was stacking up metal and plastic furniture at the back of the beach. She was waiting for Angel. Angel, as promised, had returned home from Miami for the Easter break to catch up with her family and friends. It was nine months since they had seen one another last.

Laura Rose placed her glass on the table. She looked towards the entrance as a woman entered the beach bar.

Other people there noticed her arrival. Her stature and attire were attracting considerable attention. The tall, slim figure was wearing clinging cut-off white jeans and a voluminous black top. Her black Afro hair stood out around her oval face. Despite the fact it was dusk, she wore circular gold rimmed sun glasses. She strode towards Laura Rose's table, her stiletto heels clacking on the wooden floor of the Ancient Mariner.

'Darling, sorry I'm a bit late.' Angel kissed her cheek.

'Angel, you look absolutely bloody fantastic! I love your hair like that. You look like a model in a fashion magazine. And your blouse, it's silk isn't it?'

'Oh, that's Shaun. It's one of the many things he's given me. He's very good to me. But what about you? You look pretty good yourself.' She sat herself opposite Laura Rose, and ordered a drink from the waitress who had appeared with a note pad.

'Rosie, you need to tell me all about Merle. Do you think she'll invite me to her wedding? What's her boyfriend like, I know that you have met him?'

During the Christmas family gathering, there had been great excitement when Merle had announced that she planned to marry the man who managed the cocoa plantation where she worked. The wedding plans were already well underway, scheduled for that summer.

'Yes, he's a nice guy,' Laura Rose paused. 'But Angel, I don't know what I'll wear for the wedding.'

'Darling, surely you will be able to find a dress in Bourbon.'

'No, Angel, you don't understand, I will find it difficult to find a dress to fit me for the wedding. I'm three and a half months pregnant. By the time of the wedding, it will be very obvious that I'm expecting a baby.' Angel took her hand across the table.

'Rosie, who's the lucky man? You kept that all very quiet!' Angel beamed at her across the table. Rosie said nothing, but large tears started to trickle down her face. Angel stared at her. Her face changed.

'Oh no Rosie! Rosie, it's Damien Janes isn't it?' Angel asked quietly. 'Please tell me that I'm wrong Rosie.'

Laura Rose remained silent. Angel removed her fashion sun glasses and held her face in her hands. Slowly she lifted her head, 'Rosie, I'm going to go and pay for the drinks. I'll be back in a moment.' She took the paper serviette off the table. 'Dry your eyes darling.'

When she came back, they both walked onto the beach and sat a little distance from the bar. The beach was practically deserted. There was very little light left in the sky. The sea was turning into a dark purple and black mass. Angel put her arm around Laura Rose.

'Tell me all about it; right from the beginning.'

She recounted, for the first time ever, the story of her and Damien. She started with the kite competition, explained about the steamy affair leading up to Christmas, the habitual visits to his villa after her school day. She described how Damien had given her a key to let herself into his home in Anse Argent. However, he hadn't asked her to go and live with him full time. He was currently away at a vacation home exhibition. She confessed that she had known for sure that she was pregnant for around two weeks. She had felt very nauseous in the classroom and knew immediately why she felt that way. Damien hadn't noticed, but she was very aware that her breasts were fuller. She had visited the Well Women's' Clinic in Anse Argent. They had confirmed that her baby would be due around the middle of September.

'I know that it's too late now Rosie, but didn't you think of taking the pill?'

'Angel, I went to the clinic the Monday after the kite competition, but obviously it was too late. I was taking them for three months for nothing.'

264

'I don't really understand though Rosie, why Damien? Did you feel sorry for him because the horse smashed up his ankle?' Angel pleaded with her.

'Feel sorry for him? No Angel, I felt sorry for myself. I hadn't been out with a man for six months. Damien treated me as though I was somebody special, somebody who's desirable. A lot of the island men, they're full of flattery until they get what they want and then they can't be bothered with you. Very soon they are off with someone new. Damien makes me feel good about myself.'

'Darling, you are someone special. You are somebody who's desirable. But Rosie, you need to know more about Damien. I've never told you everything and there's a lot to tell. He cheated my father and other workers out of their wages and National Insurance payments. He wasted the villa owners' money on extravagances for himself. He bought himself a boat out of their money. Why do you think I stopped working with him? But for the moment, we need to sort you out, you and your baby. I'm sure that Damien won't want to take responsibility for his child. I suspect that he may suggest an abortion. But I know you well enough to know that you won't do that.'

'Too damned right. I love children. I'm certainly not going to kill my own child. This may be the only child I ever have, even if his father doesn't want it.'

'Don't think that. We're only young. Does anybody else know about this Rosie?'

The two women sat on the beach for some time. Rosie clothed in her cheap, thin cotton dress. Angel in her couturier outfit. The pop music from the beach restaurant played in the background. It was a clear night and the stars shone down on them. The night air smelt of the ocean and seaweed. The moon came up. It was almost a full moon. It reflected as a silver zigzag over the surface of the ocean and it put the vegetation near them into silhouette form. An arch of yellow lights glinted at the end of the bay as it did every night. The waves rolled continually onto the sandy beach. Idyllic? Alluring? Definitely, but the two women didn't notice any of it. They were too occupied trying to put Laura Rose's world back into a state of equilibrium. They never ate the meal that they had planned together.

28 From Abandonment to Illegality

Damien - Spring 2013

Damien Janes bought a bottle of rum at the airport. He was returning from Montreal to Sainte Marie. He was feeling really down. It had not been a good trip. They didn't make one single sale at the Vacation Home Exhibition. They had had a few punters who had said they were interested, but there had been nothing definite. Damien had gone to the exhibition with Van. Prior to their visit to the exhibition, they had researched the state of consumer spending and the real estate market. Economists had said that Canada had turned the corner after the economic slump and things were on the up and up.

At the exhibition, it was a different story. It was poorly attended and the optimism about spending seemed to be a fantasy. They were told by the other exhibitors there that it seemed that the economy wouldn't improve until the following year. However, Tropical Island Villas couldn't wait until next year. If their current project, Sapphire, was to follow through to completion; they needed to be selling properties now. Van had flown from Montreal via Miami to see some friends. Consequently, Damien returned to the island alone.

As he left the plane, there was an unseasonal downpour. There were no covered air bridges at the airport. Damien was drenched. This added to his depressed and dark mood. He threw his suitcase into the back of the taxi and commenced the slow journey back to Anse Argent. He sat in the back sipping the rum straight from the bottle.

When he arrived back at his villa, he had consumed more than half the rum. He paid for the taxi. As he put his key into the front door lock, he could hear music playing.

Suddenly he remembered that he had given Laura Rose a key.

'Christ no! That's all I want!' he mumbled to himself. 'Hi Rosie,' he called throwing his suitcase down in the hall.

'Oh Damien, I'm so pleased to see you.' Laura Rose threw her arms around his neck. 'I've really missed you. Did you do well in Montreal?'

'No, Rosie, in fact, it was a disaster. We paid out all that money and didn't sell a single bloody thing. Actually, Rosie this isn't a good time for me. I feel very tired and very pissed off. Perhaps you could come back another time. I just want to go to sleep.'

'Can't I stay with you and cook you a meal? It won't take very long. And I've got something I especially want to tell you.'

'It's not a good time Rosie,' insisted Damien.

Rosie was desperate to talk to Damien about the baby. He had been away for a week and the exasperation of not being able to tell him had made her anxious. She understood it was not a good time for him, but she felt at her wit's end that he should know and as soon as possible.

'Damien, I'm expecting your baby. I'm nearly four months pregnant,' she revealed.

'Oh yeah, I've heard stories like that before. I thought you were better than to stoop so low Rosie. You just want some money for an abortion and then it turns out you're not pregnant at all,' shouted Damien.

'No, no Damien. I wouldn't do that. You should know me by now. It's true. I can show you the letter for the appointment at the Well Women's Clinic.'

'That doesn't mean a thing. Get out of my way! You are beginning to annoy me.' Damien tried to push Laura Rose out of his path. The lure of the drinks cabinet was top of his concerns. He had pushed too hard. She fell sideward against a table next to the sofa. Laura Rose lay on the floor crumpled up in a heap.

'Oh no, the baby! What have you done to our baby?' wailed Laura Rose. She slowly picked herself up and sat on the sofa, clutching her front with both hands. 'I want this baby Damien, even if you don't.' She sobbed loudly.

Damien was pouring himself a drink. 'Laura Rose, get yourself sorted out. I'm going to bed.' He picked up his glass, walked towards the staircase, and then mounted them. She heard the bedroom door slam.

$$$

The alcohol kept Damien asleep for nearly ten hours. After showering, he descended the stairs to find to his surprise and annoyance that Laura Rose was still there. His head was still feeling as though it had been under a road roller the night before. His mouth felt furry and as dry as a desert. He wondered how he was going to do anything productive that day.

For Laura Rose the night had been black. A heavy, dark mood had hung over the sofa. Stress had dominated her night. She had worried about the baby being hurt by her fall. She had replayed over and over Damien's aggressive behaviour towards her. She had been astounded and mortified. He had previously been so attentive, so tactile and caring. She remembered Angel had warned her that he could be very difficult. After a tortuous night, her eye lids finally started to droop. As the garden birds chanted-in the dawn, she gave herself up to sleep. She had, by then, managed to organise her problems into neat little piles. Mental plans were stacked up for most eventualities. Laura Rose was an insistent character.

Damien rattled around in the kitchen making himself a cup of coffee. Every noise resounded in his head. He knew that food for breakfast was out of the question. Even so, he considered that a large coffee might improve his hang over. The noise from the kitchen made Laura Rose stir. She straightened her clothing and walked over to stand in the kitchen doorway.

'Damien, can we talk sensibly about things?' she appealed to him. 'I realise you had a difficult time in Canada. All the same, I would like just a little of your time. I am expecting your child. Look, you can see by the roundness of my belly.' She pulled her dress tightly over her rounded middle.

'What do you expect me to do, rush you up to the altar, so we can live happily ever after?'

'I would appreciate it if you took a bit of responsibility for our child. I'm not asking you to marry me.'

'This is your problem Rosie. You knew what you were doing. You're an intelligent woman. You were only too eager to sleep with me. You should have been on the pill.'

'It takes two to make a baby Damien. Are you saying the contraception was purely my responsibility?'

'You didn't tell me you weren't protected.'

'You didn't ask me either Damien.'

'Rosie, you are doing my head in here. I am not marrying you. I am not giving you any money. And I really don't want another child. I have two already who give me plenty of grief. It won't be long before they'll be your age.'

'Please Damien,' pleaded Laura Rose, 'Mrs Felix will only keep me on until July. How am I supposed to manage until the baby is born? How am I going to buy all the things a new baby needs? I only want a bit of financial help for our baby.'

'As far as I'm concerned, this could be any guy's baby.'

'You know I'm not like that Damien. You know that it could only be yours. I've been with you most nights for nearly four months.' Laura Rose looked Damien straight in the eye. 'So, you're saying I have to cope with this by myself without any type of help? You are making me feel very alone in this world Damien.' Stifled a sob. 'I never felt alone or lonely with you before. We seemed to get on so well.'

'For Christ's sake Rosie, don't whine on. We're all bloody alone in this world; from birth to death. We have to learn to manage the problems that the world throws at us by ourselves. We had a good time Rosie, but it's over. You helped me to forget my broken ankle for a bit, but that was about all you were good for.' He heard her cry, but he continued, 'Put the key for the front door on the hall table as you leave.'

'Damien, you know what, I figured you out all wrong. I thought we had some kind of relationship. But people like you deserve to be, not only alone, but lonely as well. I'm never going to be lonely again; I'll have our child to love. And, Damien, you know what, I hope I never have the misfortune to meet such a lying hypocrite as you again,' gasped Laura Rose.

She walked towards the front door. Large, warm droplets trickling down her cheeks. She turned towards Damien again. Through her tears she asked, 'Do I take it that the second kite competition in June is cancelled?'

'Fucking kites! Just piss off Little Miss Goody Two Shoes,' bellowed Damien.

Laura Rose left the key in a bowl on the hall table. She walked to the bus top to take her on the seven or eight minute bus ride back to her rooms. She left Damien alone in his large, beautifully decorated house, overlooking the beach. The villa was left with a heavy air of emptiness hanging over it. It was packed with a resounding silence.

$$$

Van returned from Miami three days later. He was finding it difficult to settle back into work. Despite the disappointment of the Canadian visit, it had been terrific to leave the treadmill of his daily routine behind during the short break in Florida.

There were still plenty of reservations for the villas and apartments at Fortune Bay after the Easter vacations. The resort restaurant had done well in his absence and things currently seemed to be in top form. The bank accounts were looking healthy. However, the reservations for the summer months looked in rather a sad state. The possibility of poor, wet weather, even hurricanes, in the hot season, always made it more difficult to attract holiday makers. Plus, the world economy was being slow to recover. It was still taking its toll in the tourist industry. Some airline companies had even cut back on their number of flights to the island. But, if Barbados hotels were getting fifty per cent summer occupancy, Fortune Bay could do better than they were at present.

He had asked for a meeting to discuss employing a marketing specialist. They needed to improve the room occupancy rate. He was waiting for Damien, Wendell and Adrian to arrive. He picked up his phone to ask his secretary to organise coffee for the meeting. Promptly he decided that, as Damien was going to be there, perhaps she needed to go to the resort shop to stock up with beers as well.

Damien came into his office not looking as well turned out as usual. His shirt was very crumpled and his shoes muddy along the sides. His eyes looked evil, blood flecked and glazed. The image of his face was finished by dark grey and red rings under his eyes. His chin displayed three days of stubble.

'You OK DJ?' enquired Van. 'You get hammered again last night? And looks like your girlfriend forgot to iron your shirt?'

'Just might have had one or two last night. Girlfriend! That slut of a teacher. When I got back from Montreal, the bloody bitch was waiting for me to tell me she was knocked up. They're all the same these local girls. They see you've got a bit of money. They think you're filthy rich. So, they imagine you're going to give them thousands of your hard-earned cash if they tell you that they're up the duff.'

'So, is she in the family way?' asked Adrian.

'Shit, how should I know? She certainly looked a bit more pear-shaped. Could be anybody's brat though, a slut like that.'

'She wasn't a slut when she was prepared to look after you with a broken ankle,' interrupted Adrian. 'Who wants coffee?'

'Got any beer Van?' asked Damien. 'Shut it Adrian; you're only jealous because you didn't get to shag her yourself. I saw you eyeing her up the day of the kite competition.'

Adrian went to rise from his seat to respond to Damien's accusation. Rapidly, he thought better of it, sat down again and stared at his note pad. He started pressing his biro firmly into the top of his jotter, drawing a series of different-sized pointed arrows on the front.

Van pushed a bottle of the local beer towards Damien. 'Hey you guys, are we going to start this bloody meeting or are we going talk about Damien's sex life all morning?'

'I asked for a meeting so we can look at the reservations for the next five months. If you look at the spreadsheet I've given you, you can see that occupancy in September is down to only twelve per cent. Naturally, we can't break even at such a low rate of occupancy. My idea is that we get a marketing specialist to set up some promotional advertising to try and attract more clients over the summer months, and perhaps even going into the high season.'

Wendell learned back in his chair. 'Won't the fee for the marketing guy and the advertising cost more than the profits we could make from putting the extra bums in beds?'

'You've forgotten something Dell; the marketing costs come off the top of any monies taken from the profit made by the rental operation, before the fifty fifty split between management and owners.'

'So, how does that help? We still have to pay for half of the marketing,' Wendell reacted.

273

'Do we?' asked Van. 'Do we have to pay for half of it?'

Another arrow was added to Adrian's art work on the cover of his note book and his other hand became clenched.

'There speaks a man after my own heart,' smirked Damien. Wendell and Adrian remained silent. 'I see where you are coming from Van. We could pay a smaller percentage or no percentage at all.'

'You got my drift. We could get the advantage of a marketing guy and we wouldn't have to pay a cent for him.'

Damien reflected the question in hand. 'In fact, as we have control of the Condo account, it could come out of there, and state that the costs were double what they actually were.'

'And what would you do if there was an audit? How are you going to get the marketing guy to give you an invoice for twice the amount? That will not work,' Adrian stated firmly.

They were all silent for a few moments. 'We could have the monies from the reservations from one or two new agencies going into a separate account,' Van suggested.

'Can you explain yourself Van?' asked Adrian.

'Why do the owners have to know about all of the reservations that we get? We could set up accounts that the funds from certain travel agency sites went into. The owners needn't know anything about it. That's to say, they wouldn't get their fifty per cent of the profits. I know that you boys are desperate for cash to continue the Sapphire complex. I'm only trying to help out.'

Adrian looked at Van in disbelief. He returned to his doodling. He was aware that Van would get a percentage of those undeclared profits. His mind drifted. He had thought about finding a new accountancy job for some time. He had stayed with Tropical Island Villas for so long only because the salary was extremely good. Now, too many things had started to go on that he just didn't want to be part of. In fact, there always had been things that he wasn't happy about being involved in. What with that, and now the latest news about Laura Rose. He felt very sorry for her, but then he had warned her several times. It was decided as he drew another arrow; it was clearly the right time to start job hunting a lot more seriously.

'I can see a problem here,' remarked Wendell. 'The owners are sent a breakdown of room occupancy each month right? Say you have an owner occupying their villa. They'll see that the occupancy level is incorrect? The rate and the profits are all sent to each owner right?'

'Yes, every month,' agreed Adrian.

'There are some owners who are so far up their own arses, they can barely breath. They are certainly not going to notice,' said Damien laughing at his own joke.

'Damien, they are not all like that. Some of them are switched on. You can't treat them like ignoramuses,' insisted Wendell.

Van ran his hand over his large stomach. 'If anybody asked, you could always say that travel agents are getting complementary rooms to weigh up the resort before they send their clients. I think we would have to set up a new account for a percentage of any promotional bookings. Undeclared funds would be diverted into there. It might mean having to have two sets of accounts,' explained Van.

'You can count me out. I'm not doing that as well, I've got my work cut out as it is. You will need to get a part-time accountant,' Adrian grumbled. The front of his notebook was by then nearly covered in his aggressive, sharp pointed doodled arrows.

'Let me get this straight, you would be using the villas and apartments without letting the owners know about a percentage of the promotional occupancy?' asked Wendell. 'And the profits would be going into a special account? Your idea is that we could use those funds for Sapphire. Is that legal?'

'No,' stated Adrian sharply.

'It's only illegal if you're found out,' countered Damien.

Adrian's eyes rolled.

Damien continued 'This idea actually opens up all sorts of possibilities. I need to think this through properly. Finding a part-time accountant should not be a problem.'

$$$

Melissa pushed the vacuum around the entrance hall of Damien's villa, singing loudly whilst she went. She left the vacuum running and stopped to dust pictures and the pieces of furniture around her.

'For Christ's sake Melissa, do you have to make so much bloody noise first thing in the morning?' Damien shouted down the stairs.

Melissa carried on with her work. Damien padded down the wide stair case wearing just his boxer shorts.

'Melissa, the vacuum! Give it a break!' shouted Damien over the hum of the vacuum.

'Mr J, you'z pay me to cleans dis house and dat what I doing,' declared Melissa in her sing-song voice 'And good morning. Good morning to ya Mr J.'

'The noise is a bit much Melissa. Any chance of a cup of coffee?' Damien screwed up his face. The din was too much for him after a hard night.

'Eh, ya forget how to put the coffee machine on? I got my work to do. Oh, ya got a bit of a headache Mr J? Ya been cuddlin' dat rum bottle again?'

Damien ignored her remark, 'I'm looking for a clean shirt as well Melissa. A clean shirt that has been ironed. I had to go out the other day wearing an un-ironed shirt.'

'Oh my good Lord, ya not knows how to iron ya own shirt? What de world comin' to?' pronounced Melissa sarcastically. 'Ya come wit me.'

Melissa put her duster down on the hall table. She walked briskly through the kitchen. Snappily into the utility room with Damien following obediently behind her in just his underwear. There were at least a dozen shirts, buttoned onto clothes hangers hanging on a line. Every one of them was ironed pristinely.

'There! Ya not think o lookin' in 'ere? Why ya not ask ya teacher girlfriend? She know dey dere.'

'I dumped her,' explained Damien taking one of his shirts, putting it on and buttoning it up the front.

'Shame, she a sweetie; the best ya had by far. I shows ya how to work de coffee machine now. So, why Miss Rosie not with ya?'

'Melissa, it's none of your bloody business, but she's getting too fat. She's knocked up. She's expecting a baby.'

'Oh, de Lord forbid, de poor little soul. Ya dump her and it ya baby! She got brothers?'

'How the hell should I know? Why do you ask?'

'I just wondering,' Melissa muttered quietly.

'Let's get that coffee. I must get to the office.'

'Ya not going to da office today Mr J,' Melissa told him, more confidently this time.

'Why the bloody hell not?'

'Ya got no car to go to office,' she smiled. 'Someone cut all ya tyres Mr J. Ya car, it sitting on it wheels outside ya door. Ya knows what it like in Sainte Marie? I'z betting 'er brothers a bit upset wit ya.'

'For Christ sake Melissa, why the bloody hell didn't you say before woman?' shouted Damien, as he rushed through the kitchen, the entrance hall and then into the front garden.

'Cos ya asks me for a cup of coffee and a shirt Mr J,' she smiled as Damien disappeared through the door. 'God, he been so good to me today. My man, he going to love dis one.' She laughed to herself as she headed towards the open front door. She stood in the open doorway watching Damien in his shirt and underpants, and without his shoes. He stood on the tarmac surveying his four flat tyres.

'I wonders why ya not de man of de moment when I sees ya car first thing dis mornin'. Now I knows.'

'Shut up Melissa. I'm going to phone the police.'

'Ya phone the police Mr J, but dere no frenzick department in Anse Argent police station. It don't do no real good. Ya best bet's 'er brothers.'

'It's that bitch Laura Rose,' blamed Damien prodding a ruined tyre of his 4x4.

'Oh no Mr J, it ain't Rosie, she not got no spiteful bone in her body.'

'Out my way Melissa, let me find my phone.' Damien barged through the door, pushing Melissa out of his way. 'Why the hell didn't you tell me about this first thing?'

'It like I say, ya was wanting a cup of coffee.'

'Melissa, you really aren't that stupid. You really are pissing me off! Do you want to work for me or not?' Damien shouted at his cleaning lady whilst looking for his phone.

'Tell ya de truth,' Melissa said seriously 'No, I not want dis job, but I needs dis job. And I thinks that any human being that work for ya, dey feels the same.' She returned to the hall table, picked up her duster and flicked the switch for the vacuum. It started to hum again loudly. Melissa pushed it vigorously backward and forwards over the marble tiled floor.

29 Disaster Six Different Ways

Cassandra - Late 2013

The sun had sunk well below the horizon. Dusk was enveloping the island of Sainte Marie. A few birds made their last flight of the day across Cassandra's line of vision. The shrill cry of the mockingbird assailed her ears. . It repeated the phrases of its perfected melody. Cassandra recognised his call. She'd seen tropical mockingbirds frequently on the garden shrubs. Then there was calm. The canvas of pearly pinks and chartreuse green was dissolving into a dark blue.

It was almost dark, but Cassandra remained on the beach. She sat upright on the sunbed outside her villa garden. She studied the waves just a few metres in front of her. They crashed regularly onto the shore. She was in a comtemplatory mood. It had a seemed like a lifetime ago since she had been able to sit in just that spot. She reflected on the past two years. They were years when they had been unable to enjoy the benefits of their beautiful second home. They just hadn't been able to afford it.

Her second marriage had flourished, and her relationship with Mark had become much closer. It was uncanny that they had become closer because of the problems with their holiday home. They had had to struggle to keep it going. This struggle had improved their relationship, rather than weakened it. They were both determined to sort the problems out. Determined to sort them out together; resolute to win through in the end. Unfortunately, they were still a long way from the end.

They hadn't been able to enjoy the benefits of the villa, but others had. The management company that had been set up to market and manage Fortune Bay had, by then, been well established. The company had attracted tourists from all over the world. They had revelled in the beauty of the island and the beach that Cassandra loved so much. Despite the passage of time, the owners' share of the profits had never materialised. The management team continued to inform the owners that there were insufficient profits from the holiday rentals. They were told, even now, nearly eighteen months down the line that they were still only at break-even point.

Mr Van Joseph had been made responsible for the running of the resort. In his reports to the owners, he stated that there hadn't been enough travellers for there to be any profit to pay out to owners. There had been so many things that had to be purchased to make the condominium into a hotel type resort. On returning, Cassandra and Mark had seen the deterioration in their villa. They were very aware that lots of people had stayed in their home. And they, as owners, had received no rental. Not a cent! Some of those people who had stayed there had not been too careful. There were things that were missing. There were things that were broken.

They had been asked to replace some of these things by the management team - Fortune Bay Management Ltd. They had been asked to have things repaired. They also had to pay their hefty condominium dues each month. A substantial annual insurance had to be paid. They were not affluent people. This left them short of money. They had had to make sacrifices. Cassandra had had to cut back on things that she bought for herself and their house at home. In addition, Mark had accepted consultancy work. He had to work hard on that most weekends. They were thankful that they didn't have a mortgage on the villa. They knew that they would never have been able to pay that as well.

Initially, when purchasing the villa, they had been reassured by Mr Janes that they would soon receive rental income. Rental income that would pay for the condo dues. Rental income that would give them a nice profit as well. They had been told that ten per cent of the profits would be put into a fund, a servicing account, to pay for replacements and repairs. But, there were never any profits and never any servicing account. Therefore, they had to pay for these all things themselves. There were times when they felt they would have to try to sell their investment, but with the state of the global economy at that time, they knew they would nowhere near recuperate their initial outlay.

They had also been informed by e-mail that a Condominium Board had been established. This was to deal with the running of the units and the collection of the condominium dues. The chair person was Damien Janes. He had apparently purchased the largest property at Fortune Bay for himself. So, as an owner, he had the right to be on the Board. This Board had already written some Bye-Laws. To Cassandra and Mark's knowledge, they had not been told about the formation of this Board beforehand, nor been asked whether they wished to be part of it. The four other seats were taken by owners who they didn't know.

When they were furnished with a copy of the Bye-Laws, they were surprised to find that the Condominium dues were to be paid to Fortune Bay Management Ltd and not into a separate account. Mark considered this to be potentially problematic. The owners had no control over their own money. They also discovered they could only use their own unit in two blocks of two weeks. Currently, this wasn't too much of a problem for them, but for their future; they had anticipated that, when they retired they would perhaps use the villa for a month in the winter. This would no longer be possible. The management company had control over all the units for the other forty eight weeks of the year. Forty eight weeks when there could be total strangers in their villa. Most days of each year when, up until then, they hadn't received a single nickel or dime for the privilege. They both felt that the developers and

Management Company were treating the owners like complete fools.

Cassandra looked up as the automatic lighting installed on the casuarina tree behind her switched on. It illuminated the beach and the oncoming waves. Flying insects were immediately attracted to the light source. Cassandra sat mesmerised watching the toppling waves lit by the spot light. The sea had been transformed into a series of stripes. Stripes of pale grey-blue and very dark midnight indigo, before the waves crashed onto the shore. The light had metamorphosed the sea into a fabulous contemporary, living work of art. It lifted her spirits.

Her fascination was short-lived as Mark tapped her on her shoulder. She nearly jumped out of her skin. She had been concentrating so intently on the vision in front of her.

'Tim will be here in a few minutes Cassie. Do you want to come and talk to him about the repairs?' he queried.

'Just look at this Mark!' she exclaimed, as she pointed out the stripy, glittering sea making a moving picture.

Not being a great art lover himself, Mark was not that impressed, 'Cassie, we must have paid the most expensive admission fee to an art gallery ever.'

She laughed. 'You fool. I'll tear myself away from my private art gallery. I'll come and see Tim.'

$$$

There were a few repairs that needed to be done in their villa. It had been previous, careless, disrespectful visitors staying there who had created the problems. Mark had asked Van Joseph how much the repairs would cost for his maintenance team to do them. He was rather dismayed at the quote they were given. Hence, they had contacted Tim who had built them their shelter for storing garden furniture.

The wood worker greeted them like old friends. Rather than discussing the repairs immediately, Cassandra invited him for a drink with them on the terrace.

'So Tim, has the world been treating you well?' Cassandra handed him his beer.

'Real fine, ma'am. Real fine, ya know.'

'It's Cassandra please. Have you been doing plenty of work on the island? I understand that the world economy is making things a bit difficult.'

'It been a bit slow at times ya know, but I not complaining. My wife, she work as well, ya know. And our daughter, now, she not at home. No, things dey not too bad.'

'So, where does your wife work then Tim?' quizzed Mark.

'Bourbon market, sir. She sell baskets to de tourists. And my daughter, my Angel, she work in Miami.'

'Angel, we know an Angel, she used to work for Tropical Island Villas,' Cassandra told him in a surprised tone. 'She's a very beautiful young lady.'

'Same Angel. Dat my Angel. Yes, she like her mother, she clean up real good.' Cassandra laughed at his description of his daughter. 'She de one dat gotten me de job working here some years back.'

'Well, well, it's a really small world,' Mark answered. 'Angel is your daughter. We really liked her. And it's Mark. My name's Mark.'

'Everybody like her Mr Mark. Dat how she gotten de job for herself, easy as pie. Mr Thorner, he think she real cute. Mr Wendell Thorner, of dem rum Thorners. When she start working, she had her first wage, she had a make up in a hotel. I tell ya all. She look like a real film star.'

'A make-up? Tim, do you mean she had a makeover?' asked Cassandra.

'Maybe you right….. Mr Thorner, he take her to Miami for work. He real taken with my Angel. He even show her how to drive. She gotten everything she want from her boss. She ask him if I can work at Fortune Bay. I's real thankful back then.'

283

'Didn't they treat you well?' Cassandra asked Tim, when she already knew what the response would be.

'Dey not always pay de men ya know. Dey not pay my assistance money. Dey, de social security people, take dem to court, ya know. But, my Angel, she found other bad things too. Dem men, that Janes and Thorner, dey real black sheep. Crooked! Dey thinks we islanders lives in de jungle. We eats bananas at breakfast, coconuts at lunch and coconut water as soup at dinner. Dey thinks we not need payin'!'

'Tim, we know a bit about them. We don't like Damien Janes either! We never liked him from the start,' Cassandra explained, finishing off her drink and trying to hide her smile over Tim's explanation.

'My Lord, dat man Janes, he go to church, but he wear horns under his hat,' Tim claimed with a very grave expression on his face. 'Dat man, he go burn in hell.'

Cassandra tried to suppress another smile at the description of Janes. She immediately envisaged him with devil's horns on his head. 'We had better show you the repairs we need doing Tim, so that you can give us a quote.'

'Ya be careful of dat man! I knows enough stories about him, I be 'ere all night telling ya,' Tim paused. 'But me, I talks too much.' Tim stood up and got out his notebook and a pencil.

'Let's start in the kitchen. There are a couple of unit doors that need a bit of attention,' said Mark, as he took Tim's glass from his hand and then ushered him into the kitchen.

Cassandra glanced at Mark, who smiled at her. Her mind was whirring. She would have liked to ask Tim more, but knew that it was inappropriate. Perhaps she could get more information out of him when he came to do the work.

Early the next day Cassandra packed their beach bag. They planned to drive down the east coast of the island, to explore its bays. Tourist information assured them that there were lots of secluded coves there. They were both enthusiastic. They were discoverers; they loved to explore unknown territory. They were always game for a bit of an adventure. Mark threw the beach bag into the 4X4. He had plotted his route out. He envisaged that the roads may not be very good.

He was proved correct. As they turned off the main road and headed towards Teller's Gap, they were soon swaying from side to side as they bumped down a narrow track. It seemed as though it had not been made up in decades. Some of the potholes were so deep, that they had to drive over them at a crawling pace.

'Whose crazy idea was this?' jeered Cassandra.

'It will be worth it, just wait and see,' Mark reassured her.

More potholes. More bumps. Suddenly they both saw, through the tunnel of trees in front of them, the aquamarine of the sea. Blue green, broken up by the irregular pattern of surf. They parked amidst other cars at the side of the track.

'We are obviously not the only halfwits who have braved the road,' Mark joked.

'Wow, just look at that sea!' exclaimed Cassandra. She raced ahead down the uneven steps towards the mass of turquoise. 'Don't forget the camera,' she shouted back to Mark. As she reached the end of the vegetation, she was accosted by a young man selling hand-made local jewellery.

'Hi Mam, take a look at my bangles. I do some real good deals today,' he pushed some of his wares towards her.

'I'll perhaps look on my way back, thank you,' replied Cassandra. She continued to descend the steps. She turned to look at Teller's Gap beach. They had to cross a pathway over some rocks to get down to the sand. A few people were stretched out on towels near the shore line. She looked down at her feet; and decided that her sparkly sandals were not really suitable for rock climbing. She would wait for Mark to help her across the boulders.

She turned to see him descending the path. 'Wait,' he shouted, 'I'll help you.'

As he tried to step past her, he slipped. Cassandra turned rapidly. She screamed. She saw Mark hit his head on the rocks below. He bounced back towards her before falling again. Blood showered around him.

She screamed again. 'Mark, Mark!' She tore off her sandals. And tried to get down the two to three metres of rocks to where he lay.

'Don't, I'll go,' called the jewellery seller. He ran in his bare feet down the path. From nowhere, two other young men raced to try and help Mark. He was lying lifeless wedged between two large stone blocks.

'Mark,' whispered Cassandra. She felt sure that he was dead. There was so much blood. He had fallen straight onto his back. In an instant, she thought of all their hopes and fears. She recalled their love and the fun of their relationship. It seemed one second he was there full of life and enthusiasm. The next he was gone. Then her mind emptied. She stood rigid, watching what was happening on the beach as if it wasn't part of her.

She saw a middle-aged woman of around fifty five. She was standing motionless. Her hands up to her face. She watched the scene on the beach in silence. There were three local young men. Then two tourists, who had rushed from their sun-bathing positions on the beach. All were trying to aid the man who had fallen. The woman's eyes widened as they pulled the body of a tall, well-built man. Dragged him from his trap between the rocks. His entire form was splattered with blood. It ran down his full face. It dripped onto the stones. Gradually, slowly he was pulled onto the sandy beach. His clothes were very torn. One of the tourists salvaged the man's camera. It had fallen into a rock pool. The tourist started a search for its missing lens.

Blood oozing from his wounds, the male was slowly, slowly aided along the beach. He commenced the ascent of the path up from the sand. Abruptly, the inert women seemed to come to life. She rushed down the path towards her husband. He refused her help. There was no point her getting covered in blood as well. She said nothing. The jewellery seller sprinted up the path. He brought back his white plastic garden chair. It was placed on the first step for the man to sit on. From what seemed like nowhere, his friend found his bottle of drinking water and a first-aid box. They started to pour water over the injured man's head, legs, hands and chest. It cleared the blood. They ascertained the extent of the injuries.

One of them told the couple he could take them to the nearest clinic. It was about three kilometres away. The wife was very grateful. She asked him his name. It was TJ. The wife looked down at her bare feet. She spotted that her sandals, bag and destroyed camera were further up the path. She told TJ that she needed to recuperate her belongings. He informed her that these things were only 'vanities that she didn't really need'. She looked at him. He was right. She agreed with him. However, she would need her bag with her money in it to pay the doctor.

They all returned to the hired car. The beach towels were spread over the seats to protect them from the blood still seeping from Mark's wounds. TJ said he felt that it was best if he drove the car. Only he knew the way. He was not insured to do so, but it seemed easiest that way.

At the clinic, they were immediately shown into the doctors' consultation room. The young female doctor assessed all the cuts. She disappeared from the consulting room. She quickly reappeared with an assistant who started to bathe the wounds. The bin beside her was soon full of brownish red, wet gauze.

'Cassie. Cassie, are you all right?' asked Mark.

'Yes, I'm fine.' Cassandra was trying to fight back the tears. 'You concentrate on yourself.'

'She is probably a bit shocked,' said the doctor.

'I thought from the way that he bounced off the rocks, and with all that blood pouring from his head, that he was dead,' Cassandra explained. 'I was amazed when he was helped up and staggered down the beach.' The doctor looked in her direction, and smiled.

Whist the wounds were dressed, Cassandra looked around the doctor's consulting room. It was all very basic, primitive. Nothing like her doctor's office at home. The wooden walls of the room were supported by unevenly spaced uprights, partially clad in what looked like painted chip board. All the furniture was very rustic and possibly home-made. The medical equipment was housed on several wooden shelves on the wall. It all looked very poor. But she was very pleased to be there.

Cassandra suddenly remembered TJ. 'I should go and see the man who drove us here. He will need to get back to the beach. I'll be back in a minute.'

TJ was still in the small waiting room sitting on one of the green plastic garden chairs. He stood up as Cassandra walked towards him.

'His wounds are being cleaned. The doctor will be stitching up the worst ones,' Cassandra told him.

'He one real lucky daddy, man! He real lucky falling on dem rocks like dat,' TJ said shaking her arm. She took his hand.

'Thank you so much for all your kindness TJ. You were a great help. You need to get back to the beach. Please thank your friends too.' She turned to the receptionist sat behind a desk and asked if it would be possible to call a taxi for TJ. She pulled a note out of her purse and handed it to TJ. There was so much that she wanted to say to the young man, but could not find the words. He and his friends had acted instinctively. They had given their time to help two complete strangers. She knew that she would never see them again, but knew that she would always remember them. Always be grateful to them.

Cassandra had a very unsettled night. She kept thinking through the accident. It replayed over and over in her mind. For some reason, she couldn't believe that she still had a husband. She slept fitfully. When she awoke, she wasn't too certain why, but she checked that Mark was still breathing. She was relieved when light filtered through the bedroom curtains.

After a really sluggish start, Mark ate a meagre breakfast. He had decided that he didn't feel inclined to go out and about for several days. The large communal pool on the resort seemed a safer option. Around the pool, he received a lot of attention from the other visitors and owners. Multiple scars, plasters and bandages made it clear that he had had some misfortune.

'Your wife been beating you up has she?' enquired a tall man with a soft American accent.

'It wasn't her this time, but the rocks at Tellers Gap,' replied Mark.

'Wow, that must have been some nasty tumble,' remarked the American. 'How did that happen?'

Mark commenced, yet again, to relate the story of his accident. It turned out that the American knew the beach.

'You were bloody lucky, to come off so lightly,' he sympathised.

'People keep telling him that,' Cassandra agreed. 'Even the doctor said he had been very fortunate.'

'With such luck, you need to go out and buy yourself a lottery ticket pretty damn quick,' laughed the American. He put out his hand, 'My name's Tyler. Which villa are you staying in?

This was the question that led to them finding out that they were both owners of villas. Mark and Cassandra on the beach front. Tyler and his wife further back in the complex. Mark told them that he was pleased to meet another owner. There were so many aspects about their villa and the management company that he felt unsettled by.

'Hey, tell you what. Why don't you come to my villa for a drink to celebrate your lucky escape? You can come and meet the wife.'

Tyler led the way. He seemed like your average middle-aged business man. He was confident, but quietly spoken. On the other hand, his wife, Maddie, was something else. As they entered the villa they could hear music, Caribbean style music. It came from the kitchen. They all headed in that direction.

Maddie was dancing around the kitchen in time to the music. Whilst doing this, she seemed to be chopping up and then throwing fruit into a blender. She wore a short white skirt and a tight fitting turquoise T-shirt. She carried on dancing. She was tall, slim and curvaceous. Her blonde hair, tied up in a ponytail, swung from side to side. It was obvious she was enjoying herself.

'Hi,' called out Tyler's wife.

'This is Maddie. You can see that she lives up to her name!' Tyler laughed. 'No, to be fair, she used to be a dancer.'

Maddie stopped dancing. 'This Zouk music, I just love it! It's the regular rhythm; it's just great to dance to.'

'Hi, Maddie, bet that keeps you really fit.' Cassandra felt rather self-conscious of her own rounded form.

'Cassandra and Mark own one of the villas on the beach,' explained Tyler. 'You can see that Mark had a bit of a fight with some rocks yesterday. I brought them over for a drink and a chat honey. What we got in the fridge?'

'I was just making some smoothie for the kids, but we have juice, coke, wine, and beer.'

'So, where are your children?' asked Cassandra.

'They're on the beach. They're fine. They are fifteen and seventeen years old now. They kinda look after themselves,' explained Maddie, doing a Samba over to the fridge. She returned with several bottles. She lined them up several glasses on the work unit. It was at this point that Cassandra noticed their toaster.

'Maddie, you are going to find this a strange question, but where did you get your toaster?' asked Cassandra.

'No idea. They bought it for me here. The management team told me the other one was kaput and we needed to buy a new one. It was one hundred and eighty dollars. Bloody expensive for a toaster I thought! I could have bought a basic one at home for thirty dollars,' growled Maddie.

Cassandra looked at Mark. She then explained that they had been told the same story. They had also paid out one hundred and eighty dollars for a new toaster. She wondered if the toaster Maddie had was the one that Cassandra had been given as a present. She had brought it to the Caribbean herself in her luggage. She went on to explain that there was several other items that had either disappeared or had had to be replaced.

Tyler wore a quizzical expression on his face. 'Hey, we have had a television that had to be replaced. It was for the kids' bedroom.'

'We are missing a DVD player and a games console,' Mark added. 'This is what I started to explain to you by the pool. There is something underhand going on here. One toaster or a DVD player isn't a lot of money, but sixty of them is.'

Cassandra said that she would go back to their villa to fetch the toaster they now had to see if it was Maddie's. Whilst she was gone, Mark started to briefly relate all the things that they had found out about Tropical Island Villas, Damien Janes and the management company.

By the time that Cassie returned with the toaster, Maddie had turned off her music. She was sitting at the kitchen counter, looking rather more worried than when Cassie had left. She immediately identified that it wasn't her toaster. So, it probably belonged to another owner. Moreover, it didn't really look like a new one.

'Christ Mark, I really didn't realise just how many problems there were here,' Tyler was perturbed. 'Our dilemma is that we are just so busy, we don't have the time to check on our investment as much as we should.'

'I think that Damien Janes relies on that,' commented Mark.

'Everybody is busy with their lives. We just have to find time to make sure that our investments are going smoothly,' pronounced Maddie. 'What he hasn't told you is that we have also invested in the other complex, Sapphire, further up the beach from here.'

'Wow,' exclaimed Cassandra 'When did you do that?'

'Around two years ago,' said Tyler. 'At present, things are going according to plan, I don't know if you have seen the construction. The roofs are just going on. I have to hope that there is enough money to finish it all off.'

'You have to more than hope honey, you have to pray. What he has failed to say is, we have used our home in the States as collateral for a loan to buy a unit in Sapphire. If it doesn't become functional, we will really be in the shit!' Maddie retorted.

'You would be even worse off than us,' Cassandra pointed out. 'I have made cut backs at home and Mark has to work at weekends to pay the dues. But, unlike you we don't have a mortgage to pay for the villa. For you things would be much worse if things go wrong here.'

'There has to be something that we can do to ensure that we get some of the profits. We need a strategy to give the owners power over their own properties,' declared Maddie.

They talked about it for some time. Maddie and Tyler's children came in from the beach, demanded food, consumed it and then returned to the beach leaving the adults to the 'heavy talk'. During their discussions, the couples considered that Tropical Island Villas probably thought that they had everything sewn up. As Damien was an owner himself, he had every right to be on the Home Owners Association, the Condo Board. They had written the Bye-Laws to their own advantage. They had held two Annual General Meetings in Sainte Marie, not giving most owners sufficient notice to organise their diaries to be able to attend. They had appointed their own manager to run the resort. He was doubtless as slippery as Janes and Thorner. He, no doubt, would do exactly as he was instructed. They probably gave him a share of the funds. The management company were receiving not only the owners' condominium fees, but all the monies from the holiday makers who were renting the properties at Fortune Bay. They were treating the owners like a group of imbeciles.

Tyler had lived in a condominium in the States. He knew something about the law there, but unfortunately, nothing about the laws of Sainte Marie. He felt that they needed to get one of them on the Condominium Board. That way, they would have more of an idea what was going on. Tyler pointed out that he remembered seeing in the Bye-Laws that all members of the Board had to have paid up all of their dues. He wondered if this would be the case of all the current members. He also recalled that owners were entitled to see the Condominium accounts, in order that they could see how their money was being spent. He thought that seeing the accounts might give them some indication of those owners who were paying.

'We have met Adrian, the accountant who they use. I don't mind going to him. I could ask him for a copy of the accounts,' offered Cassandra.

'It may be a good idea to consult a lawyer on the island whilst we are here to explain our situation. I don't mind paying, just so long as Mark comes too to give his side of the story,' offered Tyler.

'You know what bugs me the most,' admitted Maddie, 'that we are actually paying people to stay in our villas. We get no share of the profits and yet we have to pay out for repairs and replacement items, AND all the time, strangers are using our homes and making the furniture, electrical stuff and so on, deteriorate.'

'I'm glad that I bumped into you guys by the pool today,' said Tyler. 'You have certainly made me see the complications at Fortune Bay a lot clearer.'

'Sorry we have opened up such a can of worms for you,' declared Cassandra. 'But tell you something, I feel a bit better now that we have shared our opinions with both of you.'

'Well, you know what people say "A problem gets heavier when it's only you that carrying it",' quoted Maddie. 'Here Cassandra, you take your toaster that somebody gave you and I'll keep the one that you had. Next time they ask to replace something, I'll just tell them to take it out of the profits from renting out our villa.'

They all laughed.

'Life has a way of sorting things out, you know. Usually, right and justice shines through in the end,' Tyler declared.

'I only hope your right,' said Mark 'I should hate to think that Damien Janes was finally going to get the better of me.'

30 Spreading Wings

JR - Summer 2013

Warmth, strong tropical light, wide open spaces and Sainte Marie surrounded me. I was ecstatic. I was home. The open windows on the bus from Anse Argent had managed to keep me and its other passengers relatively cool. But as I alighted the thick, humid air of summer enveloped me. I walked purposefully the last few hundred metres to my destination. This was perhaps a mistake because by the time I got there, I was feeling very sticky from the intense heat. It was a blistering hot, hot day.

But this was a day that I had looked forward to for some time. The gods of fortune had been very benevolent to me since my arrival back in the Caribbean. My circumstances had changed. My destiny had taken another direction. A gift from Lady Luck was enabling me to spread my wings further.

I arrived at my plot of land. I automatically smiled to myself with satisfaction. Since my return to Sainte Marie, I had cleared the jungle of undergrowth with the aid of a friend. I had pegged out the outline of my future home from the plans that I had had drawn up. That day, I had come to meet up with my chosen builder. I walked through the area of 'my house' into what would be my back yard. Even though it was getting near the end of the mango season, my mature tree still had a few fruits weighing heavy on their slender stems. I sat down beneath it to await the arrival of the tradesman. It was so welcoming to be in the shade. Whist sitting there, I revelled in the view in front of me, looking out towards the interior of the island.

I lifted my face skywards and reached up to pick one of the mangos dangling over my head. Its ripe flesh yielded to my touch. I removed the mango from its thin stem and laid it carefully on the ground beside me. I looked around myself and felt proud. This was my piece of land; and my mango tree. It felt very fulfilling being able to pick fruit from my own tree. After the house was finished I would plant more trees, perhaps bananas and even an avocado.

My watch informed me that the builder was late. It wasn't unusual in Sainte Marie; the inhabitants were known for their lack of punctuality. I had spoken to him on the phone that morning, so I knew that he would turn up eventually. He was coming to discuss the plans. The first stage being the foundations and the services. My mind was full of the house and what it would be like. Sitting there, I day-dreamed of the time when I would be able to wake up each morning to that same view looking over those distant hills. I hoped that I would not have to wait too long; a lot depended on the builder. Unfortunately, many had the inauspicious reputation of being unreliable.

I was still feeling extraordinarily fortunate the way things had worked out for me after I finished my chartered accountant studies in Bath. I had quit the job to return to my island home to try and find work there. My return coincided with an invitation I had received. A joyful family wedding sometime before. I'd gone with my mother.

Leading up to my home coming, I had been a little worried. I knew that I had to find work on the island on the double. I now had financial commitments. I had to rake in to further my projects; to pay the rent for a modest apartment. But, as things had worked out, everything went just fine and dandy. I had hit the jackpot!

Finding work had been thanks to my friends and contacts on the island. They had come up with several suggestions. Thanks to them, I had managed to swing two part time jobs very quickly. One job was working for a restaurant in Bourbon. The other was a job that was, in the fullness of time, to revolutionize my destiny. I learnt that a Damien Janes, at Fortune Bay, was seeking to recruit somebody to help with his accounts. My contact was only too eager to tell me about the development, but also to warn me about Janes. It seemed that he and some of his colleagues had a very bad reputation amongst the islanders. Mr Janes was considered to be working on the brink of legality. He had also apparently demonstrated that he cared very little for the way the islanders were treated, as fellow men or as employees. But my contacts also told me that he was far from the only entrepreneur that was using the island to make a bundle. To top it all, Damien Janes also fancied himself as the number one play boy of the island.

Immediately I heard about Damien Janes at Fortune Bay, I had said to myself, 'I know that name.' I recalled, all those years ago, that one of the clients of the pub in Fulham had been called Damien Janes. I also remembered that, when I was still a student, he had offered me a job should I return to the island. I recollected that I hadn't liked the man in England. If his current standing was anything to go by, I would like him even less on Sainte Marie. Despite initial reservations, I had to adopt the attitude that work was work, money was money. I wasn't going to get far without it. So, I had phoned him at the resort and asked him if he had already found extra help for his accountancy work.

Strangely enough, Damien Janes remembered me. When I explained to him on the phone that we had met before and that I had worked at The Golden Bell, he recalled who I was.

'Of course I remember you JR, the smiley guy who used to wear weird pullovers. We used to chat about Sainte Marie and the Caribbean. Yes mate, sure, I remember you. So, you're back on island and looking for work?' Damien had asked.

Damien had invited me to go and see him at Fortune Bay. Meeting him again reinforced my previous sentiments about the man. Naturally he had aged, but unfortunately age hadn't mellowed him. He was still loud, brash, over-confident and extremely self-centred. He also seemed to have retained his love of sharp gear. The day of my interview, his slim, tall frame was clad in a boldly patterned silk shirt and co-ordinating shorts. I calculated that his outfit had cost much more than I was likely to earn in a month.

As he briefly showed me around Fortune Bay, true to form, he had talked big of his success with the resort. He bragged about how well he had done from it. Despite my feelings about my prospective employee, I was impressed by the villas and apartments, all set in beautiful tropical gardens. Damien Janes had made it clear that I would be working with his regular accountant, Adrian. He had worked for him for years. I would not be working directly with Janes. That was one aspect to be thankful for. He had taken me into one of the offices and introduced me his accountant. I was told that Adrian would spell out what would be entailed in the work. Damien offered me three hours each evening at a more than generous salary, so naturally I jumped at it. I had to be earning. I had started my part time job working for Damien the very next evening. A job is a job, even if you find your boss as likeable as a rattle snake.

Adrian turned out to be an amicable enough guy. It hadn't taken me long to weigh up that Adrian had no time for Janes either. Like me, he was working at Fortune Bay for one reason only; he needed his ample wage packet. When Adrian had explained in detail that I had to record occupancy rates and rental earned in the owners units, it didn't take a genius to work out that I would be doing a second set of accounts. Things started to click into place; I put two and two together and made one big fat four. I concluded that Janes was definitely trying to pull the wool over the owners' eyes for some reason or another. I said nothing. Initially, Adrian told me that he didn't have the time to do the extra accounting himself. But, as time went on and as I got to know him a little better, he confessed to not wanting to have anything to do with Janes' crooked schemes. He had refused to do the work.

Consequently, for five evenings a week, I took over from Adrian. I worked in his office after he had packed up and gone home. Because of my hours, I didn't see too many people at all. I thanked the stars that I saw next to nothing of Damien Janes. I was left to my own devices. There was nobody there to bother me. I was free to work as I pleased. Having access to Adrian's records, I produced the special set of accounts and presented them to the manager Van Joseph on a regular basis. At the end of each fortnight, he gave me my cheque. Considering the reputation the developers had at Fortune Bay, I was at the bank the very next morning, as fast as light, to cash it.

But, things were to change. I had been working at Fortune Bay for just over a month. One evening I was greeted by a grinning Adrian sitting on his desk waiting for my arrival. Obviously, he was feeling very pleased with life. He told me that he had something he wanted to discuss and asked if he could meet me for a drink after I'd finished my work. This was a first. I kind of gathered it wasn't going to be purely a social occasion. We agreed to meet up in a bar in Doublon d'Or.

That evening was to be one of surprises. The bar was crowded. It was full of tourists and locals, but Adrian had managed to grab a table outside. 'Over here JR!' Adrian raised his hand to attract my attention as I arrived.

'Did you have a good evening cooking their books? What ya drinking?' smiled Adrian as I reached the table.

'A Crystal beer thanks. No, I spent all evening watching a movie on my computer,' I joked.

'Was it "Dirty Rotten Scoundrels"?' laughed Adrian.

'No, I was working really. So, what's your story Adrian? You look all puffed-up about something.'

'I'm quitting tomorrow,' Adrian had confessed. 'I'm going to go and see Damien. I'm going to tell him that I've got another job. I've been looking for something for a long time. I can't stand to be working with that lowlife any longer.'

'Well done Adrian. That's brilliant!'

'I thought that I'd tell you first. I thought that you might want my job. And you could apply for it straight away. With your project to build a house, I know that you need the money.'

'Thanks for that. Where are you going to work?' I asked Adrian.

'I've got a job at the new Casino in Anse Argent. The pay isn't quite as good, but I think I'll be happier there. I asked you to meet up because I think that you have what it takes to do the work. I also think that Janes could easily be persuaded to give you a bigger part in the "Damien Janes Deluxe Property Show". Main problem for you is, you would have to work alongside the pain in the arse.'

'It's a problem; he's real low-life. But thanks for the tip off Adrian, it's very much appreciated.' I told him.

'The pay is very good, more than you could get in most resorts, but be warned, the work can be rather questionable at times. But, I guess that you have already sussed that out JR.'

'Too dammed right, you don't need to be Einstein!' I had admitted. 'If I apply for the full-time job, I'll have the same dilemma as you Adrian. I will have work for someone who I detest. At present, I see very little of Damien and the rest of the crew because of my hours.'

'It depends what you are prepared to put up with to get your house built and get yourself settled. I think Janes will offer you the job if you want it. He knows that you are already au fait with Fortune Bay and its, shall I say, "special book-keeping". That will give you the edge. If you do take the job, be forewarned; don't put your name on anything that is going out to owners. If you take my advice, you bleed him for as much as you can get out of him. Don't make any blatant accusations, just subtle innuendos and see how many bucks you can squeeze out of him.'

Well, that was exactly what happened. He did and I did. He did offer me the job the next day and I did bleed him for all that I could get out of him. I was surprised just how far I could push him.

My newly acquired job enabled me to take out another loan so that my projects could advance far quicker than I had initially imagined. Sure, there came a big down side to this. That was, of course, having to work more closely with a man who I soon learnt to hate and regard with contempt. I had to develop a strategy to cope with the scumbag.

My reflections quickly came to an end as a very muddy pickup truck screeched to a halt in front of my plot. The builder got out of his vehicle, clutching a pile of papers. He slammed the car door and waved at me with his free hand.

'Sorry I so late,' he grinned. 'Let get down to business.'

'Let's go for it!' I agreed. 'The sooner you get started, the sooner I'll have a house.'

31 "It is the Beginning of the End"*
(*Talleyrand - Perigord 1815)

Cassandra - Late 2014

Cassandra was back in Sainte Marie. She sat on the terrace drinking a glass of her favourite white wine. She was alone. Mark had gone to see another owner called Pete.

She was really elated to be back in their villa. It wasn't a large villa as villas go and it wasn't grand, but to her it was her castle, her chateau along the Loire. She loved wasting her time there, just watching the bright light and sharp shadows. She adored the sparkle of the moonbeams on the night water; the tropical vegetation stirring in the wind in their small enclosed garden. Listening to the unfamiliar cry of the birds, and the music of the waves crashing onto the beach. All of it was a rhapsody to her ears. On Sainte Marie she felt at one with nature. If they ate a meal outside, the birds and geckos would soon appear on the table to share their food. They were just so tame. Birds had even sat on Mark's shoulder and hands; it gave them so much amusement and joy watching the tiny creatures at such close quarters.

When Cassandra was away from the island, it called to her. She saw flashes in her mind of fish jumping in tranquil waters. The red disc of the sun descending behind steep hills covered to the top with tropical vegetation. She saw local ladies walking to church in their Sunday best. She saw dark green flashes of a humming bird flitting from one frangipani flower to the next. She wished she could live there permanently, but she knew that it just wasn't possible at present. Mark and she had to keep up their full-time jobs.

She didn't delude herself into thinking that Sainte Marie was a Utopia; in her book, no such place existed. She had seen that there were all kinds of problems on the island, but she was prepared to accept them and appreciate its numerous fine qualities. They had met so many different islanders, the majority of whom had a natural, infectious sense of humour. Many adopted a very different view of life than inhabitants of the Western World. Most had a smiley and sunny nature, so unlike the majority of folks that Cassandra was surrounded by at home. They had given her a very different perception on life.

Her mind meandered one way, then another. She reflected on the present. She saw less of her husband. He had become so involved with the affairs of the condo board and trying to straighten things out at Fortune Bay. They had bought their villa as an investment and for their retirement, but with the current state of things it seemed that it would never be either. But things changed with every visit. Mark had become determined to try and make their investment work. Despite the multitude of problems, never for one moment had she regretted purchasing their villa. Though her admission to paradise was proving to be a very costly one in terms of finance and time.

Cassandra glanced skywards. Wheeling gracefully high above her, on an air current, were two large frigate birds. She took another sip of her wine. Like the birds above her, her mind circled. It spiralled back to the time since their previous visit to the island.

They had kept in contact with Maddie and Tyler and they now felt like good friends. Their e-mails were frequent. Mark and Tyler chatted on Skype on a regular basis. Tyler and Maddie had been frustrated by the problems that had come to light at Fortune Bay. After talking to Mark and Cassandra, Tyler had decided that they needed to do something about them. Tyler had visited an attorney with Mark before they left for home to find out what their options were.

Cassandra also remembered how she had tried, near the end of their previous visit, to get information from the Tropical Island Villa accountant, Adrian. The episode replayed in her mind. It had been a catalyst that had sparked a chain of important events. They needed to verify whether Damien and the other Condominium Board members had all paid their condominium dues. To her surprise, when she had knocked on the door of his office, it wasn't Adrian who answered. She had entered to be greeted by a grinning young man dressed in a bright pink shirt sitting at the desk. He had said that he was helping Adrian out. He introduced himself as JR.

Cassandra had asked if she could have a recent copy of the all the condominium dues that had been paid by owners. The accountant had looked surprised.

'Can I ask why you need a copy?' queried JR.

'Adrian can vouch that I own one of the beach villas. I need to see which owners are delinquent on their condominium dues. You possibly know that all owners are entitled to a copy of the condominium accounts.'

'I don't think that that will be a problem, but I'll have to check with Adrian first.'

'Thank you, that would be very useful.'

'You're most welcome.'

'Let me write down my e-mail address for you, so that you can send it to me.' She smiled at JR. 'How long have you been working with Adrian?'

JR had explained that he had been working at Fortune Bay for several weeks. It had been his first job as an accountant on the island. He was doing free-lance work and already had two clients. He had returned home after working in Britain for some time. This comment had led them to comparing notes about life there. After around five minutes' conversation, when they seemed to be getting along rather well, Cassandra considered that JR seemed to be a likeable character. She had thought that she would push her luck and ask the young man for his help with something else.

'You wouldn't happen to have a copy of the occupancy of our villa over the past year would you? We get the overall occupancy for the whole resort each month, but not a detailed one for each villa. We seemed to have got a lot of wear and tear in our place considering the stated occupancy rates.'

Again, JR said that he would have to ask Adrian. He wasn't sure that such a list existed. It could possibly mean doing a spread sheet from scratch. He told that he hoped she would have the condo dues list by the next day. Cassandra assured him that if she didn't, she would be back again. She had left the office thinking that she had enjoyed her chat and that she liked the attitude of the new accountant.

As promised, the next day Cassandra had received the list of dues paid. The list exposed the fact that Damien and one of his mates were very delinquent. They hadn't paid dues for some time, yet still had their seats on the Board. It wasn't clear if Janes had ever paid any. This was against what was stated in the Bye Laws. Cassandra had not been surprised that she never received the second spread sheet which she had requested. She had wondered if it might be a good idea to pester JR again the next time they were on island.

On returning home, Tyler had instructed the attorney they had visited to put together a letter stating that they wished both owners who were delinquent to resign from the board. Janes and his mate should go. Tyler had proposed himself and Mark to take their places. A copy of the letter was sent to all of the owners. There was no reply to this letter from Damien or his friend. No big surprise. Tyler wasn't prepared to give up on the situation. The next attorney's letter had stated that at the next Annual General Meeting, all board members had to be elected by the owners. This was clearly stated in the Condominium Bye-Laws. A copy had been circulated again to the owners. It had started an inundation of e-mails and telephone calls supporting their action.

But something dramatic had happened before the proposed Annual General Meeting. Tyler had broken the news to Cassandra and Mark. It was their second investment at Sapphire. He had found out that the project would not get finished. There were insufficient funds. The buildings were left without doors and windows. They were just a shell. No internal work had been started. The incomplete constructions had been left to the elements. Initially there had been security to protect the site. Soon, through lack of money, there wasn't any security. Things had started disappearing from the building site. Sapphire Limited, one of Damien and Wendell's many limited companies, had been franticly trying to find an investor to back them. World economy was working against them. Unfortunately, for those who had invested money in the development, the project had failed. The money invested was lost. With the news, the bank demanded immediate repayment from Tyler and Maddie. They had threatened foreclosure if they couldn't replay the loan in full.

Maddie and Tyler had been frantic with worry. The normally lively and bubbly Maddie hadn't been able to sleep at night. She had become prone to bouts of uncontrollable weeping. She became very depressed. They had been unable to find the large sum owed. Devastatingly, the bank had foreclosed on the loan for their investment in Sapphire. Their house, that they had lived in since their children were small, was taken away from them. It had been their collateral. There was nothing they could do. They put their furniture into storage. Maddie, Tyler and their children had to go to live with Tyler's parents for the time being. Naturally, they both felt incensed. They were very bitter about the loss of their home. They had lost nearly half a million dollars.

The rage that surrounded Tyler and Maddie's situation steered them towards investigating who the other investors at Sapphire had been. Tyler discovered that several of the other owners were in similar circumstances as them. Like him, some had lost their homes. For others their pension pots had vanished or even their life savings. His fury had led him to propose to the former investors at Sapphire that they clubbed together to share court costs. The aim was to take Sapphire Limited to court. To try and liquidate them. Tyler had become very preoccupied with organising this. Cassandra felt so sorry for them both. She realised that she would not be seeing them again at Fortune Bay in the near future. They had to save to buy a new home.

Mark therefore had been left to deal with the problems at Fortune Bay by himself. He and Cassandra knew that, one way or another, the Annual General Meeting was scheduled to be a momentous occasion. It had been scheduled to take place at a hotel in Britain. Tyler had said that he would give Mark his proxy vote as he could not afford to attend. Mark had spent many evenings phoning owners to try and convince someone else to join the condominium board. Thankfully, he had persuaded two others. They supported him and wished to stand for a seat on the Condominium Board. If they were all elected, they would have an important voice on the Board.

Cassandra remembered that she had felt rather nervous about the AGM. They so wanted to remove Damien Janes from the Board. They needed to replace him with somebody who had the interest of the owners at heart. She had worried. She was anxious about the reaction of some of the other owners. Janes didn't attend the meeting. At learning this news, Cassandra had breathed a sigh of relief. He had sent his general manager, Van Joseph.

Cassandra recalled vividly some of the owners she had met at the AGM. Once Cassandra and Mark had started to chat to some of the community, they had quickly realised that most of them felt the same way as they did. Some of Cassandra's anxiety dissipated. Most thought that the management company was making an appalling mess at the resort. A few remained ardent Damien Janes' fans. They seemed to think that he could do no wrong.

During the meeting, Van Joseph had addressed the gathering. He was verbose to the extreme. He had spoken about the world economy. He told them all about rising costs. Reminded them how it had affected the occupancy at Fortune Bay. Up until that point, there had not been any profits. Even after employing a marketing specialist, there was no pay back. Disgruntled owners had questioned this. Some recounted that during their stay on island there had certainly seemed to be far more than the stated occupancy figures. Notwithstanding, Mr Joseph had had lots of answers. Answers supported by spread sheets. A response to each of the queries. Solutions and excuses to try and hoodwink all who had been present. They had let travel agent representatives stay in some units. It had cost them nothing. The management team hoped to get bookings from their recommendations. There had not been an audit. There had been insufficient funds to pay for one. There had been no profits, so the fund for the replacement of furniture and decorations had never been established. The delinquent owners had not been chased. There had been insufficient funds to pay for the solicitor's fees. The beach bar had been running at a loss. They had to make large monthly repayments for the new kitchen equipment.

Owners were uneasy. Most had seen instantly through the wool that was being pulled over their eyes. The room became heavy with anger. Tempers ran high. At one point, the meeting had had to be called to order. But, the responses from Joseph were fixed.

The question of losses from villas and apartments was brought up. There was shouting. There was pointing of fingers and accusations. Many owners had been enraged by the topic. It seemed that most people present had suffered expensive breakages and losses from their properties. Cassandra had even stood up and told her story of her toaster. She asked Van Joseph why it was they had had to pay a hundred and eighty dollars for a new one. There was nothing wrong with the original toaster. It had just been moved to another villa. Mr Joseph had stated that he was unable to respond to questions about such minor aspects as the contents of each unit. But, he would certainly try and find out from the housekeeper on his return to the island. Naturally, he had never responded to Cassandra's enquiry.

Discontentment had filled the room. It had visibly affected many owners' stance about the re-election of the board. Nearing the end of the meeting, the voting had taken place. Candidate by candidate. Cassandra had been very tense. The two delinquent owners had not been re-elected. Janes and his mate were no longer on the Board. Mark and the two other volunteers had been voted onto the Condo instead. One of the existing board members was to replace Damien Janes as the Chair Person. His name was Pete. Cassandra vividly recalled how much easier her mind had felt. The lead–up to the AGM had been stressful. After the election, the stress had disappeared instantaneously.

At the close of the meeting, Cassandra and Mark had gone to the hotel bar. Within minutes, Mr Joseph had approached them to converse; to discuss the meeting. Mark was visibly hostile. Not at all eager to spend time with him. He openly showed his annoyance at his presence.

'Well, do I congratulate you, or commiserate with you on your appointment?' Mr Joseph had asked as he had walked towards them.

'Definitely the latter,' Mark had replied brusquely.

'So, why did you volunteer?'

Mark looked him directly in the face. 'Somebody has to sort out this bloody mess!' Immediately, Van Joseph became rather fidgety. Cassandra and Mark had remained silent. Joseph had made his excuses to go and talk to some of the other owners.

'If I was the violent type, I'd have punched him in the face,' Mark had confessed, not all that quietly.

'All those lies and excuses! And did he really have to make his talk so long and tedious? Perhaps he thought that if he made it long enough, there wouldn't be any time left for questions. Or, on the other hand, perhaps he thought that we'd be so bored we would all go to sleep.'

Cassandra and Mark had been re-assured when some of the owners had joined them for a drink. They had thanked Mark for all his efforts. The couple had started to put faces to the names of the small community at Fortune Bay. That had been the AGM. That was all in the past.

Back at Fortune Bay, Cassandra studied the behaviour of the bananaquit chirping in a bush near her sunbed. Her period of reflection was interrupted. The brightly coloured little bird took flight. Her husband touched her shoulder. Mark was back from his meeting with Pete.

'You're going to be walking the plank tomorrow,' he declared.

'Oh yeh! Are you going to bind my arms and legs like the pirates of old?'

'No, worse than that, they will fasten lead weights to your ankles. Then I'll force you to the end of the plank, slashing with a cutlass behind you.'

'My knees have already started to tremble. And then, when I'm at the depth of the ocean, you will run off with the pirate's fiancé. Mark, what are you going on about?'

'Pete has invited us to join him on the ship "Pirates' Ransom" tomorrow. It sails from the marina at ten o'clock.'

'I thought that you considered pirate cruises were for kids.'

'Well, we don't know until we try, do we? Besides, I didn't like to say no.'

32 Modern Day Pirates

Cassandra - Late 2014

'Ahoy, me mateys! Are we ready to set sail on the good ship Jolly Roger?' cried Pete as he saw Cassandra and Mark walking towards him. 'Shiver me timbers, she's brought her own booty,' pointing towards Cassandra's large beach bag. It was obvious that Pete was getting in the mood for his cruise down the coast.

'This is my wench Emma. I think you've met before.' He introduced his wife to Cassandra.

'Sounds like he's already drunk,' joked Emma, 'but he's not really. He's always this strange. And it's the "Pirate's Ransom" Pete, not "Jolly Roger".'

They all joined the line of tourists. All waiting to board the reproduction eighteenth century sail boat docked in the marina. When on board, they all had to remove their shoes. The crew were clad in eighteen century style pirates clothing, porting head scarves or cocked hats. Despite Mark's initial reservation about pirate ships and thinking that they were solely for children, the vast majority of the passengers were adults. Pete assured them that it was indeed only for children, but children of all ages, from two to ninety two.

Cassandra and Emma were attracted to the shade. The men did a tour of the two-mast brig. It seemed that they very quickly discovered the inclusive bar. As the ship sailed out of the marina, they returned carrying four beakers of rum punch. Cassandra declared that it was far too early for her to be drinking alcohol. She had only just eaten breakfast.

All eyes were on the crew when some climbed up the masts to untie the square sails. The motors were cut and the brig continued under sail down the coast of the island. A group of children of all shapes, sizes and ages were entertained by two of the crew on the prow. They were told blood thirsty stories of pirates of old. Brigs, schooners, slaves, cutlasses, blood and thunder enthralled them. Afterwards, mock sword fights (with plastic swords). The two couples from Fortune Bay were entertained by their antics, whilst they chatted about their holidays. Sword fighting over, their conversation swung to their common interest, their investments on the island.

'Why did you buy your villa Pete?' asked Cassandra.

'Well, it's a bit of a story,' Pete told them. 'Damien has been a mate for more years than I care to remember. He persuaded Emma and I to visit the island. Naturally, he was keen to sell us one of his villas. But, he didn't have to sell the idea to us. All his sales chat was wasted. I came to the island a week before Emma. I stayed with Damien. I was bowled over immediately by the island and the beach. I had actually purchased the villa before Emma arrived on the island. Naturally, we had talked about it beforehand. When Emma flew in, fortunately she loved it too.

Emma interrupted and explained, 'We have socialised with Damien and his wife Donna for years. We were sorry to see them move to the Caribbean. We know that before moving to Sainte Marie, Damien had had problems with his selling job in Britain. We guessed that perhaps he had strayed off the straight and narrow. For me, it was really Donna who was my friend, not Damien. I kept in contact with her after they moved. Donna kept telling me that Damien had changed. Making substantial amounts of money had turned his head. He started to chase after other women. Eventually, Donna could not tolerate him any longer. To cut a long story short, she finally left him to return to London.'

'Despite this,' continued Pete, 'we decided to come for a holiday. As soon as I arrived, I could tell that Damien wasn't the old friend I'd known in London. And Emma, when she got here, could also see that Donna had been right. She's not too keen on the new version Damien. Neither am I, if the truth be told. Emma tries to stay away from him as much as possible.'

'We loved the villa, but I certainly didn't like the cheat who sold it to us,' exclaimed Emma. 'He has done very well for himself, but he is so self-opinionated now. To the point of being boorish. Pete only joined the Condominium Board as a favour to Damien. He was asked to make up the numbers. We weren't aware, when you first phoned us, that Damien hadn't paid any dues for his villa.'

'Any more grog for you me hearties?' A female pirate with an eye–patch presented them with a tray of drinks. The men helped themselves to another rum punch.

'I'm like a lot of businessmen,' continued Pete sipping his drink, 'I just don't have a lot of time to spend on thinking about our secondary home and renting it out. I was quite prepared to leave it to the management company. We now know that they relied on that. People are thousands of miles away. They don't have enough time to think about their investments. But this visit, we can see that the villas are falling into disrepair. The outsides need cleaning and painting. The main pool needs new pumps as the water isn't always clear. And the gardens require a professional to sort them out. I have even seen a termite trail going up the front of one villa. No money is being spent on looking after it at all. And this story that there were no funds to do all these things is a fairy story. Just look how many people are at the resort at present.'

'The AGM was an eye-opener for us. All those complaints from owners,' stated Emma. 'The management company say there is no money to spend on anything, but we know for certain that Damien is still squandering money left, right and centre. So, it's fairly obvious where our money is going. It's going straight into his pockets.'

'We think you're right,' Cassandra agreed. 'And the board meetings? What happened at the board meetings?'

314

'Well, there weren't too many of them. They were mainly informational. At the AGM I realised that I couldn't leave things to Damien and his company. I have to look after my own investment. We paid out a very heavy wodge of money for it. Damien may be a friend, but there are limits to what you can tolerate from them. You should also like your friends; but I'm not sure that I do anymore. I shall have to distance myself from him. Mark, I'm pleased that we have you on the Board. We need to devise a strategy to give owners control of their own money and to have far more power in what is going on.'

'Frankly,' Mark confided, 'I think that the only way we will do that is to get rid of the management company.'

'Wow, what a beautiful bay,' interrupted Cassandra.

The ship had sailed into a sheltered bay, Green Monkey Bay. They had taken down the sails and dropped anchor. A silvery sandy beach lay in front of them. It was backed by dense vegetation and palm trees. The crew were securing a plank for diving. They threw bottles full of "treasure" into the sea for people to dive for. Others took a dinghy ashore to set up a small treasure hunt on the beach.

'Looks like good fun!' Pete started to head in the direction of the passengers putting on masks, snorkels and flippers.

The snorkelling didn't last long for the ladies. They were soon back on board. They preferred sitting in the shade, sipping cold drinks. They observed the pirate crew prepare the buffet lunch.

'I'm not a great swimmer,' professed Cassandra. 'A quick dip is enough for me. I really love this bay with.......'

'Cassie, I need to tell you something about Damien. You need to pass it onto Mark,' Emma interrupted her. 'It's something that Pete won't mention, because Damien is still his friend. It's about the loan for buying our villa. Damien offered him the opportunity to take out a larger loan than we needed. Of course for a fee; a pretty hefty fee. Damien

315

could provide evidence for the bank declaring that the villa was worth more than it actually was. I suppose he knows the right people in the bank. Pete didn't take up the offer. But, the reason for telling you this is, Pete found out that Damien fairly recently re-sold a property. He acquired a loan for the man buying it. The guy set up a company on the island. Got a loan for a couple of million dollars. Apparently, this new buyer has not paid any dues. Nor has he made any repayments to the bank, nor does he intend to. He just wanted to get his hands on the cash. The Condominium Board will need to do something about it. They'll need to take the owner to court to repossess the property I suppose. Of course, whilst Damien was chairperson, he was not going to let on that the buyer had no intention of making any payments. Especially as he will have had a large back-hander from the two million.'

'Oh my God! Can you believe it! Oh Emma, thanks for letting us know.' Cassandra was shocked. 'For heaven's sake, what is wrong with that man Janes? He has made money his god and just look at what it has done to him.'

'Since he treated Donna and his own children the way he did, I've got no time for him at all,' replied Emma grievously.

'I understand, I'd feel the same way. I won't mention anything in front of Pete. Looks like the men have had enough now. They want their lunch...... Oh lord, what has Pete got?'

'Yo ho ho, me beauties, I've some buccaneer's booty. I found it with the help of me old sea dog here.' Pete held up a plastic bottle half filled with sand, topped up with coloured beads and a few silver coloured dollars. He gave the bottle to Emma. 'I said I'd find you something special for our wedding anniversary.'

The pirate excursion was more of a success than Cassandra and Mark had anticipated. They both liked Emma and Pete. They had all hit it off. Over lunch, whilst the pirate wenches served nibbles from the buffet, Pete and Mark had started to put together a plan for moving forward with their ideas.

But the sea air, the sun, and the rum punch had taken its toll on them. They returned to their respective villas feeling rather weary.

'I wonder what the accounts departments want?' asked Cassandra as she checked their e-mails on their return. 'They have asked for our local mobile phone number to discuss our condo account. It says they have found an error with it.' She quickly tapped a reply on her phone. 'I hope that they aren't going to ask us for more money.'

But that wasn't the reason at all. Later in the evening, as they sat talking over the things that had happened during the day, their cheap and cheerful island mobile phone rang out. It was JR.

'Oh hello JR. You are working very late. What exactly is the problem with the account?'

'I'm not actually at work,' replied JR, 'I'm phoning you from home. I didn't want to phone you from work, just in case the call was interrupted, if you understand my meaning. I'm sure that you remember, some time ago, you asked me for a list of the occupancy for your villa. I hadn't forgotten. I've been keeping a list since you were on island last time. It's a list with the occupancy nights, the prices paid and the travel agents commission and so on.'

Cassandra's face developed a questioning look. 'Can you e-mail a copy of the list JR?'

'I really don't think that that's a very good idea. I do not wish my employers to know about this list. I have to go to the bank in Bourbon tomorrow morning. Can you meet me in the multi-storey car park then?'

Cassandra was dumb founded. Initially, she wasn't sure what to say. 'Ummm...Yes, we can do that. What time are you thinking of?'

'Say around ten thirty. If you go to the top floor, you can always find a space up there. I have a small 4X4 in metallic red. It has tinted windows.'

'We'll see you then. Thank you for your call. Oh and yes, our hire car is a white Toyota.'

'Yes, I know,' JR stated as he ended the call.

'Mark, I think there is a spy in the enemy camp,' Cassandra told him as she switched off the phone.

$$$

Cassandra and Mark climbed into the back of JR's car. He had kept the motor running so that they still had the air conditioning. It was very sticky with all three of them squashed in together. They thanked him for calling them. They understood why he didn't want Tropical Island Villas to know about the list. Mark told JR that many owners had suspicions that the occupancy rate stated was a fabrication. Of course they had no way of proving it. They were very grateful for his efforts.

'You cannot show this list to the other owners, Tropical Island Villas would know immediately that it was me who gave it to you. Damien can be a very aggressive person and ....well........ I want to keep my job at Fortune Bay for the time being. I think I can be more use to you employed there, than getting a job elsewhere.' He handed Mark an envelope.

'We won't use it against the management company.' Mark opened the envelope. He looked at the end of the spread sheet. 'Oh my god JR! I don't believe it!'

'Yes, I know sir....., but I'm afraid I have to go. I need to get back to Anse Argent. Remember, this meeting did not happen. Just one other thing; your DVD player was given to a local junior school some time ago. The school also received other things like televisions and play stations. Van Joseph gave the things to Damien to give away.' He stopped and got out of the back of his car, he looked

318

around the car park. He signalled to Cassandra and Mark to join him.

They shut the back car door. And stood next to JR's 4X4. JR was soon in the drivers' seat.

'Adrian couldn't stand working with them any longer, so I've taken over his job,' JR told them through his open window. Before leaving he confided lots of things to me. I will have to tell you a little more another time. Got to go. Enjoy the rest of your stay.' He drove away down the ramp towards the exit.

Mark passed the spread sheet to his wife as they walked towards their vehicle. She stopped suddenly. She was still looking at the pages that JR had given them. She looked towards Mark as he opened their hire car door. 'The bastards!' she suddenly shouted.

'Shh.. Cassie.' He opened the passenger door. 'Get in the car!'

Cassandra got into the passenger seat and fastened her seat belt. The tears started to flow down her face. She cried uncontrollably. 'But Mark, you have been working your fingers to the bone for nearly three years to pay the condo dues,' she sobbed. 'I've not been able to buy replacement things for the house because those bastards have been pocketing our money. All that money that we should have received as profits. Over two hundred days' occupancy this year!'

'Yes I know Cassie, but we can't tell anybody. We can't jeopardise JR's job or perhaps even his safety. We just have to work out a way to get rid of them. I need to go and see that attorney again. I need to think this through. I'll try to talk to Tyler again sometime today.'

33 Nearing the End Game

Damien - Early Summer 2016

Damien kicked open the door of the office at Fortune Bay. He slammed it shut behind him. His cantankerous humour was very evident. He swore because the air conditioning had been turned off. He swore because there was only one cold beer in the fridge. He slammed the beer on the desk and swore. He threw his mobile phone after it. Then launched himself into the swivel chair. Minutes later, he was guzzling his beer when Wendell Thorner came in. They had had a very difficult morning. They had just returned from the court rooms in Bourbon. Sitting in the court waiting area, killing time for nearly two hours, had been very nerve wracking. When their case was called, they had followed their attorney into the small bare court room. The judge's raised dais in front; simple wooden chairs before it. They had been followed in by Mr Tyler Thomas, his attorney, and the attorney representing the Bank of Sainte Marie.

'I don't want to have to go through a day like that again. I still can't believe that it's happened. If I could get my hands on that son of a bitch Tyler Thomas, I'd ring his bloody neck,' spat Damien.

'Well, that would really help, wouldn't it?' snapped Wendell. 'He has bankrupted the company through the courts Damien. It was the court and the judge that made the decision. It has been done legally. Wringing his bloody neck would simply put you inside. Everybody would know that it was you who did it. At least, it is only Sapphire Limited that has gone under.'

'What do you mean, only? We have lost a very valuable asset. We could have sold that for millions of dollars.'

'Yes, I know DJ, but we couldn't sell it could we. And we didn't make the repayments for the loan? Perhaps we asked too high a price of the buildings. I really thought the Americans were going to go for it. Perhaps they would, if the price had been lower.'

'It's all hypothetical anyway, because it isn't ours to sell anymore, it will be for the liquidator to sell it.'

'The only way of looking at it is that we have already made a pot of gold from that project. We did really well from it! I got my new car!'

'You and your fuckin' cars! You're pathetic! As long as you got a motor and hot hussy you don't care! Your fuckin' parents will make sure that you'll never be poor!'

'My parents worked bloody hard for their money,' shouted Wendell. He started to pace up and down the hot office. 'They are still working bloody hard. Don't you dare take down my parents DJ! You wouldn't have made a cent on this island without them. They sold us the land to build our projects. You owe them a lot!'

'You make me sick Wendell. You would never have sold any of the property without me. The land doesn't make you any money without my expertise. The land didn't give you your fuckin' wheels. It was me!'

'You still need me Damien. The only way we are going to make any big money now is to start another project. You will need my father again to sell you some land. It'll be more difficult after the liquidation. But with my contacts on the island, we may be able to organise something.'

'I've now got my own bloody contacts on the island Wendell. I'm going. I've had enough of you for one day! I may get a bit more sense out of Darius or Van.'

'Go to hell Damien!' retorted Wendell. Damien left the office slamming the door behind him.

$$$

Damien was in the main office at Fortune Bay. He had spent much of the morning on the phone. He had been going through his online address book contacting people.

321

Contacting anyone he thought might be of some use to him.

There was a knock at his door. Damien finished his call before he shouted, 'Yes.'

'Sorry to bother you DJ. I know you are very busy, but I have several queries about payments. Could you tell me what you would like me to do about them,' JR aked. 'I would ask Wendell, but I haven't seen him for a couple of days.'

'He's probably sulking after the court case. Or he's gone to sell rum for his mummy and daddy.'

'No idea DJ. The problem is we have an invoice from Vacation Marketing Ltd. We haven't paid them this year and they are sending threatening letters. Should I pay them a small part of the amount and say we will pay them the rest later?'

'I don't need this JR. I'm trying to sort out a new project here.'

'Yes, sorry! But it's getting very difficult. They keep phoning me. They have threatened legal action. I wasn't certain what I should do. The thing is DJ, they account for around thirty per cent of our reservations.'

'How much do we owe them?'

'Over two hundred thousand dollars DJ. Should I ask if we could pay it in stages?'

'Give me their number and I will try to sort it out,' Damien said begrudgingly.

'That's great! The other thing is the electricity bill here. There isn't enough to pay the bill either.'

'What do you mean there isn't enough to pay the electricity bill?' snapped Damien, 'Why isn't there enough?'

'You paid thirty five thousand into your BLU account. You transferred twenty thousand dollars from the Condo account into the Karib Ltd. account. The electricity bill is over twenty five thousand dollars. It's for two months.

There isn't enough money left in the Condo account to pay the electricity bill and all the wages at the end of the week.'

'Have you spoken to the guy at the electricity board? We know him don't we? Can't we ask for an extension to pay the bill?'

'I have spoken to a Mr Simons. If we don't pay within thirty days we are charged interest. If we don't pay within sixty days they cut the current. We have nine thousand odd in the Condo account when the wages have been paid. I will see what they say to accepting that as a down payment. Or should I transfer the money back out of the Karib account?'

'You've got my head spinning JR with all those numbers. Yes, pay them the nine thousand. But there is no way you should transfer the money back out of the Karib Ltd. account. No way!'

'What if they cut the current DJ? We have around fifty guests in the units at present.'

'Do I have to sort out every fucking problem in this place?' yelled Damien. 'Just pay them the nine thousand JR. Stop creating problems!'

'It's just that, if there is no electricity, there is no resort. People won't stay here without power. They will want their money back Damien.'

'Just piss off JR. You are getting me all riled up. I don't want to think about this at the moment. Just pay them the bloody nine thousand bucks!'

'Will do DJ. I'll go into the electricity board office later this morning to pay it.'

At the end of the following month, over forty people had to be bussed from Fortune Bay to another hotel resort. None of the units had any electricity. The other hotel resort sent an invoice to the Fortune Bay management company for their additional guests. They never received any payment.

34 Do You Want the Good News or the Bad News First?

Cassandra - Summer 2016

'We have another e-mail from 007,' Cassandra told her husband. 'He wants to know if we can meet him the day before we leave. We can do that can't we?'

007 was the nickname that Cassandra had given JR. He had kept in contact with them from his computer at home. He had sent them the news that the power had been cut at Fortune Bay. He informed them that the disgruntled guests and owners in residence had been taken to a resort in Anse Argent. It must be true that bad news travels like wildfire. Other contacts on the island very quickly let the Board members know about the cut. The management company at Fortune Bay however, were a little slower to admit to the problem.

The Board had held an emergency Skype meeting the following evening. It was decided that their only solution was to ask all owners if they would pay a couple of months of their dues in advance. To prevent the management company having access to this capital, they planned to set up a new bank account in Britain. All the owners would be given the new account details. From this bank account, the Board would be able to pay the electricity company directly. The Board also decided that they would pay for one of them to go out to Sainte Marie to facilitate the termination of the current management company as quickly as possible. Two of the members were very much against it. They warned that the Condominium Board could be taken to court by the management company. They would be breaking the management contract. Strange as it might seem, these members were still friends of Damien Janes.

Because of work commitments, most Board members were unable to fly to Sainte Marie. Mark, however, managed to rearrange his holiday schedule. He left for the island two weeks later. Cassandra would not hear of her husband going to Sainte Marie without her. She managed to wangle time off work.

By the time Cassandra and Mark had reached the island, the electricity had been reconnected. Everything, on the surface, was back to normal at Fortune Bay. Sufficient owners had paid their dues in advance to enable the electricity company to be paid. Mr Janes was back in his air conditioned office. Mr Joseph was accepting paying guests, and money was once again flowing into the management company's coffers.

However, everything was not back to normal. For when the accountant went into the condominium bank account on his computer, he discovered that the account had been frozen. On Damien Janes' instructions, the accountant, JR visited the Bank of Sainte Marie immediately. The bank disclosed that they had received a letter from an island attorney. It was signed by all the Board members and stamped with the condominium seal. It had instructed the bank to freeze all the funds in the account. The Condominium Board was in the process of trying to set up another one in the name of the Condominium. JR returned to Fortune Bay to inform Janes about the account. Fireworks started. The air in Janes' office turned a distinct shade of blue. There was much shouting. Profanities could be heard by all who were close by.

Oh what excitement! Cassandra loved all of this action against Janes and his management company. This visit was something that she would not have missed for the world. It was a true adventure. They were going to get the better of Janes. They were aiming to reshape the future of the complex. They were giving the owners some power. Mark had already set up several meetings for their visit. He had to meet with their attorney. He also planned to see the bank manager. They had interviews with two possible managers to run the complex in place of Mr Joseph. One meeting they didn't look forward to was the one he had set up with Damien Janes and the said Van Joseph. It goes without saying, one person they did not contact whilst on island, was the accountant at Fortune Bay. Though JR (007) was well aware that they were there and what was happening, they kept well away from his office. Cassandra was therefore surprised to receive his e-mail. Despite this, she replied that they would be able to meet him that Saturday.

Cassandra was delighted that the initial meeting with the attorney would be held in a restaurant. One they hadn't visited before. The attorney had told them that the only way she could fit them in was to have a breakfast meeting before work. The restaurant was not far from the attorney's office in Bourbon, but it was up in the hills overlooking the city and the ocean. So that morning, Cassandra and Mark were up with the sun in order that they could get to Bourbon in time. They avoided the main road, which was usually full of traffic jams in the morning. Mark drove the tortuous route across country. The narrow roads, which trekked up into the hills, were full of hair pin bends. However, there were remarkable views over the rainforest. Cassandra was in her element. Mark told her that she wouldn't be so enamoured if she had to do the difficult driving.

The restaurant turned out to be in an extensive old cocoa plantation house. It was constructed entirely of painted timber. When they entered, Cassandra had the impression that they had stepped back at least a hundred years. The tables were set out on an extraordinarily wide raised wooden veranda. To block out the sun light it was covered by a wood and metal canopy. The view from the tables was astounding, down over Bourbon and the busy port. They could see three large cruise ships anchored there that morning. Their attorney, Mrs Monday, was already waiting for them.

'I thought that you might appreciate a meeting here,' Mrs Monday welcomed them. 'It's one of the oldest buildings on the island. I hope you don't mind, I have ordered a traditional island breakfast.'

'Not at all, I look forward to it,' replied Cassandra, 'and yes, the view here is phenomenal!'

Their breakfast of salt fish and cucumber salad, accompanied by floats (small fried buns), arrived quickly. They drank cocoa tea, seasoned with cinnamon, in large ceramic cups decorated with tropical flowers. The discussion about the legal issues was quickly in progress. Mark seemed very satisfied with the options that were open to them. After breakfast, Cassandra excused herself to take a tour of the restaurant house and gardens, whilst Mark and Mrs Monday continued their discussion. Cassandra wandered from room to room studying the antique furnishings and pictures. There was not a single glass window in the house. Painted storm shutters at the side of each of the openings were designed to protect the interior from inclement weather. The elevated position of the house seemed to keep it cool. There was a constant breeze blowing up from the ocean. Only the toilet area had louvered shutters at the window. In the gardens there were still old outhouses. These had presumably been kitchens in the past.

The plot surrounding the plantation house was packed with enormous crabs' claws, ginger lilies, tree ferns and various palms, all of which dwarfed Cassandra. Several enormous sugar cauldrons were scattered around the grounds filled with water plants. It was a veritable gardeners' delight. When Cassandra returned to their table the attorney was packing up her things. She was ready to go to start her day in court.

'Don't forget, if you have any queries, just e-mail me. I will get back to you as soon as I can. I will let you know when the claims and the termination letter are ready to be signed. I can have them sent up to you by a justice of the peace if that is the easiest solution,' Mrs Monday informed Mark.

'Yes I think so. And thank you for your invaluable help,' said Mark.

'And thank you for meeting us here, it's quite magical,' interrupted Cassandra.

After the attorney had left, Cassandra and Mark sat chatting about what Mrs Monday had told him. He shared how he planned to move forward. This visit, they had no time to occupy themselves with the usual tourist things. This was definitely a working holiday.

$$$

Their time on the island was coming to an end. They had both been so busy that the time had taken flight. Even so, they were left with a multitude of uncommon memories. They had had so many meetings and Skype calls. They had met so many different island people. Most knew what was happening at Fortune Bay. It had opened up a new world to them. The fleeting time had been well directed and profitably used. They had accomplished what they had planned to do. They were due to leave in three days, but they still had one important challenge to face - the meeting with Damien Janes.

Mark had asked somebody from the solicitor's office to be present at the meeting. One of their assistants attended, though they were really only there as a witness. There were no pleasantries when they arrived at Janes' office. At least, they were all asked to sit down.

Mark started the dialogue. 'Mr Janes, we, the owners have become very disillusioned by the performance of the current management company. The owners have never received any money, despite having an endless stream of visitors in our units.'

'There have been visitors, but insufficient visitors for us to be able to run it and make a profit,' explained Van Joseph.

'So you keep telling us Mr Joseph,' continued Mark. 'Anyway, as I was saying, the owners have had to tolerate people using their villas for years, without a single cent being paid to them for the privilege. Some units have experienced an enormous amount of wear and tear. You have also stated that there was never enough money to establish a sinking fund for repairs and replacements. Some owners have had items stolen and damage done. They have been asked by the management to pay for replacements themselves. Or been asked to pay exorbitant prices to have things to be repaired or restored.'

'The fees paid for the repairs are average for the island,' explained Van Joseph.

'Not according to the tradesmen who I talk to,' responded Mark. 'As I was saying, there have been numerous items stolen. Far too many!'

'There was a spate of robberies a couple of years ago. We seem to have stopped those by putting barbed wire along the boundary walls,' declared Janes.

'I know that they haven't stopped Mr Janes, because there are still things that have disappeared each time we visit our villa. There is insufficient checking by housekeeping. Even though each unit has its own inventory, it would seem that these are never checked. The interiors and the exteriors of the units have been left to deteriorate dramatically. Some are in a pitiful state.'

'Look, you know that the interior of units is the responsibility of each owner. And you know that there have never been the funds to do any major repairs on the complex,' interrupted Damien Janes, raising his voice. 'We have done the best we could with the funds available.'

'Yes, so you keep telling us,' continued Mark. 'Anyway, the members of the Board have recently phoned owners to try and establish the approximate amount of money that has been paid into the Condominium account each month. According to our calculations there should have been plenty of money to pay the electricity bills. There really should never have been a cut because of unpaid invoices.'

'So, what the fucking hell are you saying we are doing with the money?' swore Damien Janes.

'Really, Mr Janes, there are two ladies present. That sort of language is never necessary,' Mark reprimanded him.

'I don't effing care if there are women here,' shouted Mr Janes. 'There are lots of owners who never pay their condo dues! This is one of the reasons why the place can't be run fuckin' properly.'

'Damien, you won't get anywhere talking like that. We need to discuss this sensibly,' Van Joseph reminded him.

'We are aware that there are far too many delinquent owners and that legal action has never been taken against them. You have stated that this is because of lack of funds. However, we have some good news about that. But I will come to that later. To get back to the reason for us being here; after the electricity cut, the Board held an emergency meeting. It was decided that action had to be taken. We could not have a repetition of that.'

'So you think that you could do a bloody better job?' bellowed Damien. 'It's tough trying to run this place.'

'Well Mr Janes, Mr Joseph, if that is the case, I have some good news for you,' Mark smiled. 'The Board have decided that we no longer require your services. We are terminating the contract with the Fortune Bay Management Company.'

'What the hell do you mean? It's a ten year contract; it has nearly five years still to run.'

'The contract is only valid Mr Janes, if the owners are satisfied with the performance of the management company. And they are not.'

'You do this and we will take the Condominium to court for every cent they have. We will put you all into receivership,' shrieked Janes.

'You can try Mr Janes, you can try. Anyway, you have twenty eight days to vacate the premises. There will be another management company taking over then. We have already appointed them. The clerk from Monday and Mundy is here to serve the notice of Termination of Contract.' The clerk handed Janes a large brown envelope.

'Get the fuck out of my office!'

Mark stood up. Cassandra and the clerk followed his example. 'One last thing Mr Janes, there's the other piece of good news that I mentioned earlier. There has been a distinct lack of funds in the Condominium account because there are so many delinquent owners. After so long, the condominium is owed hundreds of thousands of dollars. The condominium has decided to do something about it.'

'Get out of my sight you bastard, before I wring your bloody neck.'

'Mr Janes please!' said the clerk. All three of them moved towards the office door.

'Yesterday,' continued Mark, 'the solicitors of Monday and Mundy served two claims on behalf of the Condominium on owners of properties at Fortune Bay.' The clerk nodded to indicate that this was true. 'Both properties were bought through companies, so they simply served the claim at the address where the company was registered. We hope to be able to get back most of the delinquent dues owed when the two villas are sold by judicial auction. One of them was served on DJL Ltd. I think you may know who the director of DJL Ltd is.'

'Go to hell!' screamed Damien Janes, 'Go to hell all three of you.'

'Really Mr Janes, after that performance, I think you are more likely to get to know about hell than we are,' rebuked the female clerk as they walked out of the office.

Damien kicked the door shut behind them shouting, 'Get the fuck out of my office.'

Once outside in the warm humid air, Cassandra took hold of her husband's hand. 'I'm glad that's over Mark. But there was something that you forgot to tell him. You forgot to tell him that in twenty eight days, it won't be his office!'

35 A Will Finds a Way

JR - 2016

I typed *'Same time; same place; different reason'* to Cassandra and hit the send button.

I had waited a very long time for this day. Never for one moment would I ever regret what I was about to do. Today was to be the culmination of much scheming, planning and waiting. I was very pleased that it was about to come to an end. I would no longer have to live a lie. I knew that very soon I would be able to be far more content with my life. I could be more carefree. Life may be a little difficult for us for a short time, but I felt fairly confident that I would be able to find more work on the island very soon. I had established some reliable contacts on Sainte Marie and neighbouring islands.

My work at Fortune Bay had been very trying. Only when I was away from there, had I been able to experience any moments of joy. I had had to wear the costume of a charlatan every day. I had had to act out my role of a greedy, hateful, deceitful and lying member of staff. I had to emulate the qualities of my employers. However, I felt that my employment there was yet another era of life's bizarre education; a period of learning; another investment in knowledge for the future.

I may have been the most highly paid accountant on the island, but I wasn't proud of the way that I earned my salary. But, I ensured that every cent was being put to very good use. I had felt no sense of shame setting up my own separate small account and diverting money into it each week. There was so much transferal of funds from one account to another that a few hundred dollars here and there would never be missed. It was labelled as bank charges. I made sure that it was only ever deducted from Damien Janes millions. He had entrusted me with his bank

333

account details as well as those of the condominium and management company. I felt certain though that there were others that I didn't have access to. That man was filthy, stinking rich – at present.

I snatched up the envelope I had left on my desk and prepared for the journey into the capital with everything I needed to show Cassandra and Mark. As it was Saturday, the traffic was light. There were two cruise liners in, so there were crowds of pedestrians. There was also the weekend food market which attracted lots of locals. Bourbon was very busy.

I took a ticket as I entered the parking lot. I drove directly to the top floor. It's always easy to find a vacant parking spot there. Usually there were only half a dozen other cars parked at that level. I had arrived a little early and found a space right at the front. You could overlook the cruise ship docks and the main bay of Bourbon. By good luck, one could see the coming and goings of the town and also see the vehicles as they entered the car park. As I had anticipated, I saw Cassandra and Mark's hire car arriving punctually at the time that I had suggested.

They parked next to my 4X4, got out and slammed their car doors.

'So how are things with you?' asked Cassandra.

'I'm good, real good,' I smiled. 'I have to find a new job, but I shall be pleased to do that. I asked you to come because I have something very valuable for you.' I gave Cassandra the envelope. 'It's a memory stick. It has spreadsheets which show that the management had several sets of accounts for the reservations. It also shows monies that were transferred from the Condominium account and where they were transferred to.'

'Wow, you wonderful person! I could kiss you!' cried Cassandra. She kissed me lightly on my cheek, then put the envelope into her handbag.

'Quite honestly, I don't think that you will need it, but if just by any chance they threaten you with court action, you now have the evidence against them.'

'They have already threatened us with legal action for terminating the management contract,' explained Mark. 'But they wouldn't stand a chance in court. There is too much questionable behaviour against them.'

'Yes, you're right. Also attorneys and court cases can cost mega bucks. Damien will not want to lose big money, especially if he may lose the case and has to pay the court costs,' I added. 'Also, you may not have realised, the commercial units at Fortune Bay were used as collateral for the loan on Sapphire. They are now in the hands of the liquidator, following the winding up of Sapphire.'

'Yes, we know about Sapphire, because we are friends with Tyler and Maddie. They invested there. I didn't know about the commercial units though,' Mark pointed out. 'So, in fact, even without the termination of the management contract, they wouldn't be able to continue the resort without a shop, restaurant, reception and so on.'

'That's right. The liquidator will be trying to sell them as soon as possible. They owe so much money to the banks and companies that have done work for them. They have masses of debts. Then there are private individuals like Mr Thomas. They owe people hundreds of thousands of dollars. However, that isn't the only reason that I have put up with the awful job and lived the life of a lie for so long. I want to introduce you to somebody.'

Cassandra and Mark had been so busy talking to me that I don't think they realised that I was not alone. The tinted windscreen had masked the interior of my car. The noise of the town had disguised any sounds that may have come from the back seat. I opened the back door, 'This is my beautiful wife Laura Rose and this is my beloved son Aimé.'

Cassandra was startled, 'Oh I'm sorry JR, I hadn't realised that there was anybody else in the car.'

Laura Rose stepped out of the car with our son. He blinked at the bright sunlight. He put his arms up to me, 'Dada.' I picked him up in my arms.

It's a great pleasure to meet you,' Cassandra stretched her hand towards Laura Rose, 'and congratulations,' she added seeing my wife's large pregnant belly.

'It's a very long saga, but it is because of Laura Rose that I became an accountant.' I explained briefly that it had been Laura Rose who had, more than ten years ago, made me see that I needed to do something with my life. I should go out to be part of the big wide world, rather than drift along as a beach bum, an insignificant speck on this tiny island. Laura Rose had made me want to succeed in life. She made me want her, though unfortunately I never revealed that to her at the time. I then told them about gaining my scholarship at the LSE because of my mother's job in a hotel. It had been in London that I had first met Damien when I had taken a part-time job as a student. I told them about earning money in a pub to survive. I smiled at my wife.

I gave them my full story. Working in Bath to buy a plot of land on the island. Janes, in fact, paying for most of our home to be built. To keep me quiet, Janes knew that he would have to pay me a very good salary. Though he didn't realise it, he had paid for most the construction of the roof over our heads. We had lived on my wife's wages; my wage paid for the house. My mother had stayed at home to look after Aimé. I proudly told them my wife was a teacher at Doublon d'Or junior school.

'I'm afraid that is where your DVD player went,' confessed Laura Rose. 'To gain positive publicity on the island Damien Janes donated several televisions and other equipment to the school where I work. I was mortified when found out they were stolen. He had told me they were surplus to requirements. He also organised a kite competition at the school. I'm now sure that all the money for the competition came from the Condominium funds. My friends tried to warn me about Mr Janes. They all said that he was to be avoided at all costs. I didn't believe them. I thought that it was all malicious gossip.'

'It's a shame you didn't listen to them.' Cassandra told her. 'But, the school is very welcome to the DVD player. I'm sure that your school's needs are far greater than ours.'

'The kite competition was the reason we have Aimé,' I tried to explain.

'I don't understand,' Mark admitted.

'Laura Rose was taken in by Damien's benevolence. She truly thought that he was a caring person wanting the very best for the school. She fell for his Casanova charms. So, in fact, Aimé is Damien's child, not mine.'

I noticed Cassandra looking at Aimé to see if he resembled Janes. Of course, he is predominantly dark skinned with tight curly hair like his mother.

Laura Rose took over the narrative, 'Yes, all Damien wanted was somebody to look after him because he was injured by a galloping horse during the kite competition.'

'When Laura Rose told him she was pregnant, the son of a bitch refused to accept any responsibility for his child. He refused to help Laura Rose in any way,' I added.

Mark stared at the three of us. 'I'm beginning to understand now. When you came back to the island, you found Laura Rose was pregnant by Janes. You decided to try and see that he had his comeuppance for refusing to accept liability for his own child. You were determined he could pay for a home for his child.'

'Yes, I suppose you could put it like that. But, he also needed to get his just desserts. He has treated everyone, the workers, the owners, the islands' banks, like dirt. He has walked all over everybody. I accept I played him at his own game. I admit I conned him into giving me an extortionate wage by island standards. I admit I took small amounts out of his accounts when I could and put them into an account for Aimé. I am investing it. I'll give it to him when he's older.'

Laura Rose touched JR's hand, 'Naughty Daddy.' Cassandra smothered a smile.

'No Laura Rose, perhaps I should feel guilty, but I don't. The man is a crook. Unfortunately, his money has come from some poor unsuspecting souls who thought that they were investing in a dream. Would you believe, he is still trying to put together a plan for a new project? But Wendell Thorner seems to have given up on him. Consequently, he's going to find it difficult to find land at a reasonable price. I think he is trying to sell his former villa at Fortune Bay, even though it legally belongs to the bank.'

Mark smiled at JR and his family. He added his side to the story. 'Even his friends are getting tired of him, because he uses them to his own advantage as well. Our current chairman of the Board used to be his best mate. Now he is working against Janes. He considers him immoral and greedy. As you say, he doesn't care an iota how he earns his money.'

'I see in him everything I despise,' added Cassandra. 'I see a liar, a cheat, somebody totally egotistical, a womaniser, a bad parent and husband, a spend thrift. All of that would make me feel very miserable with myself. I have to ask myself if he can possibly be happy.'

'JR will be very pleased to stop working with Mr Janes,' my wife said. 'He has already told him that he will be leaving them at the end of next week. JR hopes he will find some more work soon.'

'We'll have to see if we can use you on a part-time basis. The Board will need their own accountant,' Mark assured me.

'That would be great!' I thanked him. 'As for Damien Janes, I think that he realises deep down that he and

Wendell are finished at Fortune Bay. But even yesterday, after your meeting with him, he was saying that the condominium would never be able to get rid of him. He may have stashed away millions, but he can no longer bleed dry the condominium bank account. He no longer has control over the management of Fortune Bay. He will lose his own villa. The villas that he conned his friends into purchasing with loans that they had no intension of repaying will be repossessed by the banks. He will lose the commercial units because they are now owned by the liquidator. His wife left him some time ago. He rejected his own child that Laura Rose was expecting. There is enough hatred from islanders on Sainte Marie for him to drown in. That man gets his shoes made by hand in London, but I would not want to be walking in them. In my opinion, his future looks fairly bleak.'

'Folks like him, unfortunately, always get by,' Cassandra sneered. 'He'll start another project on another developing island and try to fool more poor, unsuspecting people.'

'Yes perhaps, because he has developed an insatiable urge for more and more money. However, personally I feel a great sense of satisfaction knowing that we have been a part of ensuring that he won't do well again on this island. I think JR is right. Here in Sainte Marie he will stand alone. Alone because he has succeeded in alienating all those he thought he could use for his own purpose,' concluded Mark.

36 And the Gentle Surf Breaking onto the Shoreline

The Girls - 2018

Chi-chi-chi squawked a group of black grackles as they flew out of the bougainvillea creeper growing over the wall. They were startled by the noise of Laura Rose slamming the car door next to the boundary of Fortune Bay. She had brought the boys out to play on the beach. She had left JR in peace so he could get on with his work at home. It was nearing the end of the month. He needed to finish several clients' accounts within the next few days. Aimé ran onto the sand clutching his red football. Beau stood waiting for his mother to pick up his small bag of toys next to the car.

Laura Rose installed herself on a towel, under a palm tree. She knew she was in front of Cassandra and Mark's villa. Beau took his white plastic container down to the waters' edge to bring back some water.

Laura Rose looked along the beach. There were perhaps more than twenty tourists on sun beds, some under sun shades covered with palm leaves. Additionally, there were a few islanders walking along the water's edge or bathing in the sea. There were others from the resort kayaking or paddle boarding across the calm waters of the bay. She knew from JR that things had settled down there since the owners had taken control of the financial side of complex. They were running it on around a third of the budget the previous management company had said they needed. The owners now had a group of American hoteliers that ran the marketing side and looked after all the tourist reservations.

Laura Rose knew however, that there were other holiday complexes on island that had not been as fortunate. Some still stood empty and abandoned. The investors who had paid for their dream homes had lost everything. She

340

had been very relieved that the Condominium Board had never needed to use the evidence on JR's memory stick in court. She would have feared for her husband's safety if it had ever been used. Despite the threats, the Condominium Board's termination of the management company was never contested in court.

'Not enough water my darling,' Laura Rose told Beau when he returned with very little water in his container. 'Mommy will get some for you.'

Laura Rose left her sandals next to her bag. She went back and forth several times to collect sea water. She dampened the sand for her younger son to play with. She kept an eye on Aimé kicking his ball in and out of the waves. And she helped Beau start to make a sand castle. He filled jelly moulds to the brim with sand and then inverted them next to his mother's mound of sand.

'That's really cool,' Laura Rose told her son as the shape of the sand castle started to appear. But Beau's concentration faded very quickly. He soon ran off to join his half-brother to try and play with the ball.

She sat alone watching her sons playing in the surf. Aimé with his pale tan-coloured skin. Beau with a darker brown complexion. She thought herself amongst the very fortunate on this earth. Her life had a silver lining. She had everything she could possibly wish for. She knew that JR doted on her and their sons, even though Aimé wasn't his.

He had told her she was the only woman he had ever wanted to marry. JR had asked to see her after her sister's wedding in Martinique. By then, she had left her job in Doublon d'Or to stay with her mother and Louis for the birth of her baby. When JR had proposed marriage, she had felt very uncertain about accepting. She had always thought of him just as her cousin who she liked, but not loved. But, she had been very pregnant. She was relying on her mother and step-father to look after her until the baby was born. The marriage would solve many of her problems. It also meant she could return to Sainte Marie.

He had told her that he had bought a piece of land there. He was about to start to build a home for them and his mother. However, they could rent something until the house was finished. JR had been empathic that she could return to work if she wished. His mother had said that she would love to look after the baby for her. He had had everything worked out. He had explained that he had work and a good salary. But, he hadn't made it clear that one job was with Damien Janes. So, she had accepted his offer of marriage.

Her thoughts swirled to their simple wedding ceremony in Martinique. Then the celebratory meal at Louis' house with just a few family members. JR had bought her a pretty maternity dress for the occasion and a plain gold ring. He had told her that if she felt things didn't work out she could give him back the ring. After the wedding, JR had left her in Fort de France until the birth of Aimé. Martinique had given her so much. It had educated her. She had learnt French there. The island had trained her as a teacher. The hospital in Martinique had delivered her first son. Her mother had also found happiness in her new husband Louis.

But her heart was in Sainte Marie. It was where she felt she belonged. She knew Martinique was more advanced and more modern, but loved Sainte Marie and its islanders. They saw life so differently than the Martiniquais. She had been very pleased to go back there with her brand new son to join her husband. Within a couple of months she had returned to her teaching job in Doublon d'Or.

Living with JR, her Jordan, had been a little strange initially. He had been very patient with her. They didn't share the same bed at first. But very soon, they were living in harmony and she soon wanted his children. He was a

342

very good man. He ensured Laura Rose had everything she needed. He immediately treated Aimé as his own.

On arriving back in Sainte Marie, JR soon revealed to her that he was working part-time at Fortune Bay and was to become their full-time accountant. Adrian had found a job elsewhere. When he confided his salary to her she had been amazed. She understood why when he explained that he was working illegally with two sets of accounts.

JR had explained how he detested working for Janes. He hated him for abandoning Laura Rose. He despised him for the way he treated the islanders and his clients. He had never let Janes know that they were married. Janes was everything he didn't ever want to be. But he would continue to work for him until he could find a way to discredit the man he was disgusted by. JR eventually unfolded how Janes was also going to pay towards building a home for Aimé and her. A pair he had rejected.

Laura Rose watched her sons running in and out of the sea at Fortune Bay and smiled to herself. She knew, unlike JR, that she did not detest Damien Janes. It was not within her nature. Nor did she despise him. Damien had, in fact, made her life more complete. He had made her see herself differently, as some one more feminine, happier with herself. He had opened up the door to let her see through the looking glass. Had Damien really fooled her into thinking that he cared for her? Or had she deluded herself because at that time, that aspect of her life had been so empty? She really had no ill feeling towards him. He had given her Aimé, her beautiful son with caramel-coloured skin and fine features. Now, Damien was just a part of her past. She had seen him recently in the smart new shopping mall in Anse Argent. He had not seemed quite as tall. His hair had seemed greyer. His face was more lined. Damien had not seen her, or perhaps he had chosen not to see her with her two sons. He was apparently still trying to sell property on the island, but his reputation went before him. JR had told her that his success was limited.

Laura Rose's future looked bright. She had been offered a job with responsibilities at the school. She had accepted. JR now had more work than he could cope with. He was working again at Fortune Bay, this time on a part-time basis for the Condominium Board. He would be going to London soon for their Annual General Meeting to present the yearly accounts. He planned to look up his old friend Lil and her new partner. They were running a tea shop in London.

The school holidays were looming. She would have time at home to welcome her mother from Martinique, who was planning to visit her grandchildren and catch up with her sister. JR's mother had her own apartment on the lower level of their home. Angel was also coming from Miami for a visit with her son Zaza and her husband. From her photos, Angel's son had the same beautiful tanned coloured skin as Aimé, because Shaun, her husband, was of very fair complexion.

Beau chased his elder brother through the waves trying to gain possession of the red ball. As Laura Rose looked further down the beach, towards the headland, for one fleeting moment, she saw a tall, white man throwing a child with a kite into the sea. A tan-coloured horse galloped past him through the breakers. When she looked more carefully, the image had dissolved. There had been thousands of tides since that instant; millions of waves had crashed onto the same coast. All that was left for her to see now were the tourists in kayaks or on paddle boards, her much loved children, and the gentle surf continually breaking onto the shore line at Fortune Bay, the spray from the waves tossing a random pattern into the warm air, before the waters dragged back, pulling the sand seaward.

And the gentle surf continually breaking onto the shore line, the spray from the waves tossing a random pattern into the warm air, before the waters dragged back, pulling the sand seaward.